the name

Riverhead Books   a member of Penguin Putnam Inc. New York   1998

the name

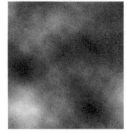

michal govrin

TRANSLATED FROM

THE HEBREW

BY BARBARA

HARSHAV

Riverhead Books
a member of
Penguin Putnam Inc.
375 Hudson Street
New York, NY 10014

First published as *HaShem* in Israel in 1995 by
Hakibbutz HaMenchad/HaSifriya HaHadasha, Tel Aviv

Library of Congress Cataloging-in-Publication Data

Govrin, Michal, date.
[HaShem. English]
The name / by Michal Govrin : translated from the Hebrew by Barbara Harshav.
p.   cm.
ISBN 1-57322-072-8
I. Harshav, Barbara, date.   II. Title.
PJ5054.G665S5413   1998   98-8133 CIP
892.4'36—dc21

Printed in the United States of America

1   3   5   7   9   10   8   6   4   2

This book is printed on acid-free paper. ∞

Book design by Chris Welch

TO MY MOTHER AND FATHER

Acknowledgments

The Name was written in a dialogue with voices that emerged from the pages of the "Jewish book"—from the Bible, the Mishnah, the Talmud, the Midrash, the prayer book, to *Holy Fire* of the Hassidic Tsaddik, Rabbi Kalonymos of Praseczno, a manuscript found under the rubble of the Warsaw Ghetto. These were interwoven with the voices, readings, and writings of Helit Yeshurun, Shlomith Rimmon-Kenan, Orna Millo, Shalva Segal, Emmanuel Moses, David Rosenberg, Jacques Derrida, the late Shlomo Pines, Yehuda Liebes, Moshe Idel, Haviva Pedaya, David Brezis, Judith Graves Miller, Uri Pines, and Yvette Biro. My late parents were the first readers, and a continuous dialogue with my husband, Haim Brezis, and our daughters, Rachel-Shlomit and Mirika, is the loom on which the text was woven. My thanks to Deborah Harris, my agent, for her invaluable expertise and support; to Julie Grau, my editor at Riverhead, for the rare combination of friendship, courage, and professionalism; to Elizabeth Wagner, my copyeditor, for her exceptional care and diligence with the text; and especially to Barbara Harshav for the art of translation and for an extraordinary collaboration.

Translator's Note

By its very nature, every translation is a collaboration of sorts; but the translation of *The Name* was an especially unusual one, and because it was, many people deserve thanks for their participation. Deborah Harris, *the* agent in Jerusalem, made this very successful match and has encouraged and supported us all the way; Jim Ponet, the "Hillel Rabbi" at Yale University, provided friendly and generous help in tracking down sources; my husband, Benjamin Harshav, as always, makes everything possible. But perhaps the greatest gratification of working on this book has been the close partnership and increasing friendship I have enjoyed with Michal Govrin, who was there every step of the way, "holding my hand," as she likes to put it.

one week

With the help of God . . . Today is nine days, which is

one week and two days of the Omer. Power of Power.

May it be Your will, HaShem, Holy Name, my God and God of my fathers, that in the merit of the Omer Count that I have marked today, there may be corrected whatever blemish I have made in the Sefirah Power of Powers. May I be cleansed and sanctified with the Holiness of Above, and through this may abundant bounty flow in all the worlds. And may it correct our lives, our spirits, our souls from all sediment and blemish, may it cleanse us and sanctify us with Your exalted holiness.

Amen!

May it be Your will, HaShem, Holy Name, my God and God of my fathers, that my prayer come before Thee. For You hear the prayer of each mouth.

May You accept me with love and desire. May my little bit of fat and blood diminished today be as fat placed on the altar before You. And may You want me.

If only it could end here. If only my sacrifice were complete, and my expiation full before I finish the task. May You at night force my hands to completion, as I shall attempt in the day to complete the holy task of weaving. *To You and to You.* With devotion.

When the pages are opened from their binding, my soul will be one with the weave of the Torah Curtain. A blue sky of secrets and woven silk bindings. Your kiss.

Another forty days. And the body is already burning in Your fire.

Another forty days. To lead the end of the thread, back and forth, to wind it around the slabs of the spools, to empty it sheaf by sheaf on the warp beam, to thread it string by string through the eyes of the rake, the eyes of the thresher, the comb, the tracks, to tie it tightly, loop by loop, between the frame of the loom. Another forty days to pass cord by cord the plaiting of the woof in the trembling of the warp. Another forty days at last, with outstretched arms. Toward You. Body to body and breath to breath.

The night is dim. And the big vaulted room, too, is almost completely dark. I've placed the table next to the window, and we are surrounded only by the ring of light from the single lamp. The rest of the room is here and not here. Better like that. Stronger. The Torah Curtain is hung, warp threads empty and stretched from side to side across the back of the loom; its murmur is coming up here, blending with the thin rustle of dust rising from the desert and scattering on the stones of the sill, on the lintel of the window. And around me, on the table, the pages. And in the cabinet, the closed boxes of photographs. I'm not yet sure I'll need them, that I'll look at them again before I finish. Meanwhile, all I have to do is run my finger (always with the same amazement) along the eyebrows, the slope of the nose, the fold of the lips, to press the muscle of the tongue to the caves of the cheeks, the bones of the palate. Curved soft clay. A piece of clay You created and You will take.

———

Oh, the consuming longing to break through. To run right to the end of the thread. To break off all at once. To sink even now into devotion of body and soul. To be concealed in Your arms, even now. Such pleasure . . .

(And thoughts of little faith, of great anger, embroil my limbs. If only You would call me at once, and not ask me for repentance! If only and at once You would enfold me in Your garb and want me.)

The slack clay of the frightened body is fevered. And Your fire is burning inside me. In forty days, I shall be extinguished ashes on Your altar.

The night is dim. The room is almost completely steeped in darkness. Only a thin light comes, perhaps from the windows on the alley. I hope none of my Arab neighbors sees the movement of the shadow and thinks that here, inside, I'm awake. No, I'm not afraid of them. What do I have to do anymore with dread? But I just don't want, don't want their looks flooded with darkness to linger on the windows of my room, don't want anybody in the world to think about me now, not even the one who may be going down the sleeping alley, raising his eyes to the vaults of the windows.

Everything is ready with me. With complete devotion. Until the last of the Days of the Counting, until Kingdom of Kingdom. Until the last coupling of purity.

And may it be Your will to accept me with love and desire. And may it be Your will to answer my plea. And may it be Your will that my little bit of fat and blood be like fat placed on the altar before You.

And may You want me.

Today is ten days, which is one week and three

days of the Omer. Beauty of Power.

A year ago. Exactly. You came back from Frieda Schmidt's store that afternoon. For a long time you hadn't gone out of this house on the edge of the city, but that day you went to the Handicrafts Store of the Daughters of Israel to buy blue and white skeins of yarn to start the holy weaving. You came back on the bus, your body bent over in the back seat, the full bags of yarn on your knees. The flesh of your arm rubbed against the metal wall, and the breezes coming through the crack in the window pulled your hair. It was the first day of summer clarity, one of the days at the beginning of the Omer Counting. The city was crowded and the bus advanced slowly. In the distance, beyond the park, open to the horizon, minarets of mosques and colorful domes of churches were suspended, and a clear bluish mist stretched over the treetops.

All of a sudden, a vein seemed to explode in your temple and a sharp throb of panic assaulted your chest. Sweat began rising in the folds of your limbs, under your clothes, and your forehead sticking to the cool window covered the view of the sky with a spreading spot of vapor. You clutched the bags of softness with all your might, but the feel of the yarn only increased your nausea. Mechanically, you got off at the stop near the house, your body trembling and your limbs weak, and you had to lean on the fence at the intersection a long time, inhaling dust and soot, until you dared lift the skeins of yarn from the filth of the street and continue on the winding road to your house.

As you walked, you tried to calm down; after all, everything's fine, you told yourself with all your heart. Everything's over now; it was a long time ago. Two years of study at Neve Rachel hasn't gone to waste.

Even Rabbi Israel said you were one of the serious girls and praised your decision to wait another year for a match so you could intensify your repentance, and he gave his blessing to your resolution to learn weaving to support yourself in the meantime. So far, you've woven only simple things, with humility: wool pillows, napkins. You put off starting holy weaving, still didn't dare, waiting until you were stronger. It was Rabbi Israel who gave you permission. "Prepare yourself in complete faith, Amalia," he said in your last conversation. "Yes, now, with God's help, you can start weaving holy prayer shawls. Start, if the Holy Name wills, after Passover," he recommended. So this morning you went to the city to buy skeins of yarn. Meekly . . . And how you've prayed lately, with tremendous devotion, your whole body quivering over the pages of the prayer book, which have grown transparent from so much handling. You put off all thought of your tentative movements, with the apprehension of an invalid who hasn't fully recovered . . . And twice now you've also put off the conversation with Rabbi Israel Gothelf about the match, with vapid excuses . . .

That night you avoided lying down. You went on weaving until late, bent over the small loom that was then in the room, filled the shuttle with the thread of the woof in its warm colors to finish weaving the last napkin before you stretched the warp for the prayer shawls. And for some reason, you were careful the whole time not to lift your eyes to the windows, to the darkness of the desert. After midnight, you said the Prayer Before Retiring, going on longer than necessary, and only then did you dare thrust yourself between the sheets. And still you avoided thinking about what happened on the bus that day. Twice, by the nightlamp, you reread that passage you know backward and forward from Maimonides' *Laws of Repentance,* but the letters didn't come together in words. You strained your eyes, blinded by the beam of light glowing on the flickering strips of ink:

Amongthepathsofrepentanceisforthepenitenttoconstantlycalloutbefore Godcryingandentreatingtoperformcharityaccordingtohisabilityto distancehimselffromtheobjectofhissintochangehisnameasiftosayIama differentpersonandnotthesameonewhosinnedtochangehisbehaviorinits entiretytothegoodandthepathoftherighteousandtotravelintoexile

*fromhishomeexileatonesforsinbecauseitcausesapersontobesubmissive
humbleandmeekofspirit*

(I didn't imagine that reading these words could still excite me so
much—*Among the paths of repentance is for the penitent to constantly call
out before God, crying and entreating—to perform charity according to his
ability, to distance himself from the object of his sin. To change his name—
as if to say "I am a different person and not the same one who sinned"—to
change his behavior in its entirety to the good and the path of righteousness;
and to travel into exile from his home. Exile atones for sin because it causes
a person to be submissive, humble, and meek of spirit.*

As if stung by a scorpion, I left the papers and stood at the window a
long time, trying to quiet down with the grainy dryness rising from the
ridges of night, inhaling the vapor trembling in the starry darkness of
Your breath.

To take strength, to go on now. In spite of the fear—

*May it be Your will to unite my heart with Your worship, for me to stand be-
fore You with a full heart and serve You in Your Name— Please, Holy
Name, remember me and strengthen me only this once, O Lord.)*

You went back and scanned the gleam of the page rustling with printed
scribbles, and the letters of the word *sin* puffed up before your eyes,
went off, overflowed again, always ending with that final *N, sinnnn,* and
unwillingly, you thought that *S* is a smooth letter, and *I* is almost a shout,
and *N* spins its venomous forked tongue; and the blank space between *to
change* and *his name* grew and ripped the words apart: *To change—his
name his name his name,* and only your lips righteously persisted in ward-
ing off the impurity from the bedsheets as in an oath: *I am a different person and not the same one, I am a different person and not the same one,* while
the shadow of the page collapsed onto you with a silent movement,
sweeping you into the abyss of troubled sleep.

You woke up at one. A sharp pain was boring into your temples and
your lungs were scorched by the humiliation of your inability to
straighten what is crooked. You tried to raise your head from the pillow

when you noticed your cheeks burning with the heat of the lamp that was left on, and recoiling, almost with hatred, your eyes followed the vault of the black window, which shook and slipped in time to her gasping that grew shorter as the taxi rounded the mountain curves in the dark. You shrank in panic.

Once again Emily suddenly clasps her arms around the driver's seat and gasps as if she, and not the car's motor, is climbing the winding road at night. She with her tempestuous breathing, the red summer dress that has been hanging on her limbs for days now exposing her back, her red purse shining insanely like her pupils wide in the traveling darkness; she clasps the driver's seat and gasps, her long hair crackling with electricity. Now the driver is going through the streets, discharging those who came from the airport with their black hats and dark bundles into the darkness, and she insists: "I've got to sleep in the Old City; no, I didn't reserve a room anywhere, but I've got to," and the taxi slices through the warp and woof of the streets that flicker in the yellow traffic lights, it comes close to the walls and goes away, and she's still throbbing excitedly, grabs the back of the driver's seat again, doesn't let go. Until the driver finally stops the cab at an alley opposite a pink neon-lit doorway, reluctantly gets out to see if they've got a room, trudges with his thick, clumsy body, gestures to her to lock the car door, and in the alley, the pink light spills onto the empty market stands, the closed shutters of the shops, and men gather in the low doorway of an Arab café, stare at the cab with its motor running, bring their faces close between the strips of light and dark.

The sheets were seething under your limbs, your breath was heavy. With an effort, you turned out the nightlamp, and all at once the pillar of heat was lopped off, but with it the remnant of light faded from the arches of the big room. You pulled the sheet over your face, and its sweaty folds blocked your nostrils.

You decide to wait like that, without moving, until dawn, murmuring in a choked whisper, *I'm different, I'm different, different,* but the driver dashes out of the hotel and blurts through the window of the cab: "OK. There's a room, I'm letting you off," and he impatiently unloads her things at the hotel entrance; then he tears off, his wheels screeching

with a fast turn around the Old City wall. And she, alone in the night-
time alley in the red dress, facing the looks flickering from the café, holds
on to her suitcase. And she doesn't even feel the sharp pain in her wrists,
not even the awful pain. She just walks up the stairs to the neon-lit entrance, and then continues up the stairs to the top floor, following the
neck of the reception clerk covered with shadow and dandruff, and the
heavy dangling of the keys, and on her hair, the breath of the bellboy,
who has already lifted the suitcase out of her arms and carries it behind
her into the enormous room that is furnished with the same decaying
splendor as the red tatters of the carpet in the lobby. And she doesn't notice the extra beds standing in the room that has apparently been set up
to accomodate pilgrims; or the stench of urine wafting from the stained
wallpaper, the tall wooden closets, the mattresses, the dust on the crystal chandelier, that pungent reek of the toilet in the plaster structure
stuck in the corner; doesn't notice the sharp pain in her wrists, doesn't
notice the awful pain *(Is it only now, when everything is ready and I am purified, that the pain seems so awful?)*, she just continues insisting to the two
men, who are shamelessly ogling her and chuckling, that tonight, yes
tonight, she has to get to the roof, that's why she has come, for that! She
repeats to their broad hands that slide and quake, show her the way to the
exit to the roof, climb up behind her on the narrow winding staircase,
among the broken, jumbled furniture, and the dust, rubbing against her,
clinging to her.

You tossed and turned between the sheets. Finally you turned the lamp
on again. The thick beam of heat burst forth. *The Laws of Repentance*
was stuck to your ribs. You hastily smoothed its squashed pages, but
even though you feebly recited, *To separate himself far from the object of
his sin; to change his name,* the pages stood up sticky and smeared, and
through your weakness she goes on and bursts dizzily out onto the roof,
runs drunkenly from the soft abysses of darkness into the basin of night,
abandons the weight of her body to the roof ledge, the warmth of its
stone, and the smell of dust and broad sky spreading and rising. She
bends over the ledge in the drooping dress, like someone who runs to the
end of the road and bathes his face in the fluid glow of the waters of
darkness of the overflowing and open firmament. She struts; her hips gy-

rate; the tremor fills her belly, her loins, the palms of her hands, flows over her arching neck, her loose hair; and a tiara of stars is strewn in the jets of its darkness.

You pulled yourself out of bed when darkness still stood in the vaults of the windows. You groped your way meekly to the bathroom, terrified at the rough contact of the walls in the narrow corridor. You washed your hands submissively, for the morning you were about to receive, as her voice still streams from the roof, singing, unbridled, sweeping so very close to the stone, rising into the spread-out darkness, rising to You, with all her heart and with all her soul. Her voice soaring as she leans there against the ledge, laughing in her poured-out hair, her horrible wrists waving to the night.

Your body weak, you stood to recite the Morning Prayer just as the arches turned pale and the implements of your lonely life fled from the darkness and came back to stand firmly in the corners. In a broken voice you read *My God the soul* and the Blessings of Dawn, but even though you didn't omit a single one of the blessings and you drew out the syllables of *E-had*, One, you couldn't banish the struggles of her limbs inside you, still singing on the wide roof. Even when the sky begins to separate, dark gray, from the resting domes, and the trees huddling together behind the walls suddenly rustle louder, she struts and straightens her full, warm body; when the dawn breezes move the remnants of rubbish scattered on the roof, she sings louder and silences the strumming of the iron cart wheels approaching from the alley. Kneeling over the stone ledge, she stretches her neck, all to You, all in You, merciful and awesome, streams into Your bosom into the storm of Your sky into their destruction, all of her in You with all her soul, a pillar of light, a flame of dread. And a bluish mist is in the street, and the rattle of the cart wheels grows louder on the cobblestones, and she doesn't stop her singing even when the man pushing the cart in his elongated shadow turns his face up to her and straightens with a coarse gesture; she just chants louder as if to bestow on the first witness the new light pouring from her, and he aims toward her as she leans over the ledge, his face dark, waving his hand sharply, and his hoarse shout echoes from the hewn stones on the slope already bursting with the pink of dawn, and his laughter rumbles, grating, drawn-out, as he bends down and harnesses himself to the cart and starts the clink of iron on stone again, and near the shadow of the gate open to the hills, one last time he turns his face covered in gloom, doubles the echoes that had begun to subside in another distant shout, and goes off outside the wall behind the rolling cart to the slopes, to the city covered with grayish light. And she stands and sings with her drooping limbs, her drooping shoulders, facing the arched roofs and the light of the sunrise quivering at the end of a sea of antennas and towers, rising in an outstretched red, and still she sings, sings . . .

With a heavy heart you bent your knees and straightened up for the *Amidah*, and then you finished washing your body, and as every morning, you modestly bound the plaits of hair around and around your head. But sitting at the corner of the kitchen table, exhausted, waiting for the little bit of water to bubble in the enamel pot, you knew, even without admitting it explicitly, that you had emerged from the night trampled, and that the deeds couldn't be undone. Clutching a rag, you wiped crumbs from the table, and you shook with the thought that with impure hands you would begin weaving the holy prayer shawls, you would stretch the white threads of the warp. And you knew, and your face sweated with shame, because you would go out that evening, as planned, deceitfully, as if nothing had happened, to the home of Rabbi Israel Gothelf, where he would tell you of the match that was planned for you.

Yet you recited the Blessing for the Food, and the words dropped from your mouth, abominable, and the dizziness made you hold on to the walls of the corridor until you came close and leaned over the skeins of wool; you knelt down choked with guilt and, with terrified hands, began tearing the paper off the white softness.

It's hard to explain the fear. Opening again what happened last year is much harder than I imagined—How will I succeed in saying *I am a different person and I am not the same one who sinned*? How will I find in myself the force of soul to confess everything that happened afterward, and to complete the repair?

(The fatigue is too great. Even if I want to, there's no door I can knock on.)

———

The night of Beauty of Power. In a little while dawn will blossom in the heart of what seems like eternal darkness. And who knows if I have really succeeded in repairing by the night's efforts what I spoiled in the Sefirah Beauty of Power. The work can't be put off any longer, there is no more opportunity, as I will never again go back to that day in the year.

Please, Holy Name, see that my power is gone and there is none shut up or left, and there is no grace or pity but You—

I shall go wash my eyes and sit near the doorpost with my sandals off. Now, at the end of the second watch of the night. As on every night, when I put cinders on my forehead like the Mourners of Zion, and truly weep for the Destruction, and the words of the Midnight Prayer flood my lips. Tonight too I shall strive with all my might to complete the repair.

Only the memory of the Covenant and the certainty of Your watching eyes, which illuminate the end of the road, can strengthen me now.

Today is eleven days, which is one week and four

days of the Omer. Eternity of Power.

The turmoil of soul tonight, like the horror of plague that burst out in the days of the Counting among the students of Rabbi Akiba, who didn't treat each other with respect and died an evil death . . . Ever since I began the Holy Confession, the night before last, near the time of the Midnight Prayer, my balance seems upset—and tonight, uneasy, as if ghosts come back to roam over the earth pester me—now, on Walpurgisnacht, the first night in May, Eternity of Power—as if the hurled shouts incite thought, thrust the fingers—

Yes, I know, among the laws of repentance is for the penitent constantly to call out before God, crying and entreating—I shouted; and perform charity to his force and separate himself far from the object of his sin—I went far away almost without return; and to change his name— Once, twice, three times I changed to say: *I am a different person and I am not the same one who sinned*, and to travel into exile from his home— For I was exiled to the end of the world, on paths with no return, on roads that lead to ruins, only in the end to come here, to the last city, the last house, the last frontier on the shore of the desert, the sand that covers Your hand—*and Jerusalem shall become heaps— The Mountain of Zion, which is desolate, the foxes walk upon it—*

To continue now. Despite the weakness of my mind, despite the recoil from what will have to be repaired tonight— To strive and to continue— With Your strength if not with mine—

Please, God, do for Your Name's sake.

On the tenth morning of the Omer last year, you prayed, May It Be Your Will, to start weaving the prayer shawls, and you tore the flashing whiteness from the paper wrapping. You didn't heed the voice that burst out at you, sounding the alarm in the day and growing strong all through the night. Maybe it was because of the fear of what was stirred that you didn't stop. Unthinking, you buried your fingers in the softness of the white yarn, and a faintness passed through you like the vapor of the quiet breath of Mala. Again, after all this time, she breathed on your cheek, and her moaning wound around and struck your breath. The room, the loom, the windows, all were swept away in the strong vortex. Until you caught your breath, and the warmth returned to your fingers, which had frozen in the yarn.

The first time (at any rate the first time I remember) that she touched her, the little girl was four years old. (Her outburst at the dull sequence of long, mute months, of a faded everyday, was so violent that it scorched through them like a searchlight. How to go back there now, even for the confession I have to make to You, please God, receive my words with mercy.)

The parents weren't home, and the little girl stayed alone with Aunt

Henia, who came down from Haifa. The week before had been her birthday, and on that afternoon she went with Father, who was going to buy her a present. First they passed the store to see if Mother was managing all right by herself. As usual, the store was full of women, fighting over a box of potatoes, grabbing the few pieces of merchandise away from each other, raising their voices, their faces flushed. Mother stood behind the counter, her hair stuck under a kerchief, scared, not saying a word. The little girl waited next to the rotten-smelling boxes of onions until Father lined the women up and put the potatoes on the pan of the scales. Then he took her hand and they walked on the big, crooked sidewalk. She thought Father would be silent as always, only every now and then shaking himself and saying something to her, and then the darkness of his face closing him up again, but today he held her hand in his big, smooth hand, whose fingernails were clipped straight, bent over, and said slowly that he and Mother had decided to buy her a birthday present, a xylophone. (She didn't yet know what the word meant or what the gift meant.) He repeated very deliberately, and asked her to repeat after him, *xy-lo-phone*. And by then she wished they wouldn't buy her a present, that Father would just leave her alone, so what if she couldn't say it right, *kli-so-phone*, but Father held her hand tight, and repeated it over and over until tears came into her eyes and she didn't know why, because after all they were going to buy her a present, a klisophone.

At home, Father placed the small instrument on the table in the dining room, which was always dim with drawn curtains. He put down the ladder-shaped instrument, its colored wooden plates growing smaller, down to the final, yellow plate, held at the ends by two nails, and next to it the two small mallets with the blue knobs. That day Father didn't go back to the store, and she didn't go out to play in the yard but stayed there on the upholstered chair, her fists closed in Father's hands, a mallet in each of them.

"Yes, now play, child, play."

She looked, uncomprehending, first at Father and then at the colorful instrument that had cost her tears even before she knew its shape.

"Yes, play, with both hands, play, Malinka, like this." He bent over and pushed her hands to make the mallets touch the plates, and his jacket twisted next to her. "Yes, like this, like this, harder." He pushed her hands and banged hard.

She would certainly have burst out crying from the pain, or else, as usual, she would have held her breath with all her might, to keep it in, if the instrument hadn't suddenly produced a high, resounding, yellow ring, full of light, and then another one, a green one, and then a blue one, and she burst out laughing, and Father was smiling at her and stroking her head. "More, more, Malinka," he whispered.

And now she was absorbed in the joy of the bell-like sounds, she raised and lowered the little mallets, and her fists ran over the keyboard, pulling after them a trail of echoes and echoes of bell-like echoes, purple and pink and blue.

But when she lifted her laughing face to see Father whirling with her in the cascade of tones, the mallets froze in her hands. His face was contorted, and he was looking at her with loathing, like a stranger.

"You play ugly. Ugly, Amalia!" he wailed, turning his back to her, his face covered with an awful black shadow, and going out of the room, leaving her alone on the chair with the prickly upholstery, and in her eyes the colors were all mixed up, floating in a turgid pond of sharp stains, blues, oranges, purples, yellows, and Father's stormy steps pounded from the other room, as he paced back and forth for a long time.

When Mother came home from the store that night, they didn't talk about the instrument. It stood on the cabinet, next to the big box of the radio, a colorful outcast, captured in the rasping tones of the radio and its flickering lightbulbs. Only the next afternoon, when Father went to the store and she was alone and her knees were dirty from the sand in the yard, did she carefully take the colorful instrument and the mallets from their place next to the radio. But when she heard the murmured Polish conversation of Father and Mother through the window, she cut off the cascade of colors and put the instrument back. Cunningly, she even remembered to lean the mallets a bit sideways, just as Father had cast them aside.

For a few days she did this carefully, always managing to put everything back where it had been before Father and Mother came in. But on the day Aunt Henia came to them from Haifa and everything in the house was mixed up because Aunt Henia was always opening and closing the windows, she didn't notice that Father and Mother were coming in, and went on banging even when the door opened and they entered.

Father burst into the dining room and yelled at her to stop, that she was only banging and pounding and didn't know how to play, that she should stop, stop! His face was covered by the black shadow and his hands were shaking. Mother ran into the room after him and called out, "What do you want from the child, Stashek? What do you want from the child! She never played, you want her to play well all at once, one-two-three?!" She dragged him out of the room with her frail body.

Mother and Father went back to the store, walking silently beside each other, keeping a forced pace, as if they would lose each other if they didn't stick together, while Aunt Henia stayed with the little girl. The instrument and its mallets were cast aside on the floor.

"Ah, Amalia, Amalia, you really don't know *any*thing," chirped Aunt Henia with the cloying smell of lipstick that always clung to the little girl's cheeks like a scar of family love, "you really don't know aaany-thing."

The little girl smiled politely at the aunt who came to take care of her, and gazed vacantly at the floor tiles.

"They didn't ever tell you about the little girl Father loved?" Aunt Henia smacked her lips as if she were telling a fairy tale. "There was once a little girl who played the piano so very gloriously! Like an angel! She lived in the house next door to us; she could play Chopin's *Funeral March* after she heard them playing it when a funeral passed by in the street. A musical genius, that girl, a real genius, Malinka . . ."

The little girl smiled at her aunt because she thought Aunt Henia was calling her by her nickname, Malinka, and she was still gazing at the mica spots on the floor tiles, and didn't hear the clumsy prattle, but there was something unfamiliar in Aunt Henia's voice, and she straightened up there on the cool floor. Her aunt wasn't looking at her at all; she went on in her rising chirp, nodding her powdered face.

"Your father played the violin from the time he was a little boy; he'd go to Mala's house every afternoon to play music with her. I remember, even then he said they'd always be together, Bride and groom." The aunt laughed to herself. "They were together all the time, even when Ma-linka became a great pianist and Stashek wasn't playing music with her anymore. She played in the Stary Teatr, and in the Opera. Everybody went to hear her . . . and when we went into the ghetto, the SS allowed her to go out to play her music. She was our angel. Our angel. Mala!"

The little girl couldn't take her eyes off the white powdered face jumping in and out of the light and shadow, which, for some reason, pushed a twinge in her stomach and throat.

"They never parted. Never. Stashek's great love . . . Even in the camp, when nobody had any strength left, she and your father made a plan to escape together. When he was working in the quarry . . . yes . . . well . . . You can't imagine how fantastic she was! What heroism! Even when they wanted to finish her off! All us women standing there, they made us come out of the huts for the *Appell,* standing and looking at her. Like a queen she was there, like on stage when she played. So proud! She looks at us, you know, in the middle of the *Appellplatz,* and finishes herself off with a razor blade she was hiding in her hair, so free! Mala!"

The little girl didn't understand what Aunt Henia was talking about or why she said that Father worked in a quarry and not in their fruit and vegetable store, and anyway, what was a quarry, and why was she talking about a razor blade after Mother yelled at her never to dare play with that, and why cut your hair, and her heart pounded wildly, *appapatz, appapatz,* and her throat was choked with twinges, *appapatz.*

At night another little girl, wearing a black dress with a white collar, came into her room, opened the drawers, and rummaged around in her things. But she didn't yell because she was afraid the other little girl would get mad and Father would punish her. She just moved to the corner and made room in her bed for the other little girl, next to the dolls, so she wouldn't get mad. For a few nights, the other little girl slept with her in bed, touching her with her smooth dress. Once she tried to finish off the strange little girl but couldn't because she didn't exactly know how, and she only called her Malinka, and shoved her under the pillow in the *appapatz* and covered everything up and smacked the pillow with all her might, but suddenly her heart started yelling, and she picked up the pillow in a terrible panic before the little girl in the black dress died and Father yelled, and she lay on her side with her heart throbbing and didn't budge, because now she was sure the other girl would kill her for what she had done, and in the meantime she silently planned how she would undress her and put her naked on a pole she'd stick in her pipi, on a cart like in the Purim carnival, so everybody in the street would see how she was naked and would laugh at her and so would the kids next door. And that was nice to think about, even if she was scared. But then Aunt Henia left and the second Malinka didn't come at night anymore, and she played clanging notes on the xylophone and nobody mentioned it. But for a long time she went on hiding the *appapatz* under her pillow.

(Everything is so slippery. So impossible. Only the shout slices. The night as always is deep, soothing; except for me, everything in it moves in grooves of time as natural as breathing—dryness wafts from the hot dust, creeps to the desert blended with the smoke of dung in the neighbors' yards, drenched in the heavy odors of the beds crowded together in their homes down to the bottom of the valley, to the spring covered with darkness. Everything flows forward, sunk in now, tomorrow, next year, in the young and decaying flesh of time, and only here the shout dries the bit of moisture. Rips everything, leaving nothing. Only pain is definite here, imperishable—and how will I have a share in the softness of the night You spread, how will I have a part in the slopes of dust?

Everything is so slippery, as if nothing happened. And even the very rare waves of regret for Isaiah only increase the silence. They lie in the distance, like massed clouds, hanging on the horizon, waiting.)

What can I say to You, what can I tell You? You know all things, secret and revealed. You know the mysteries of the universe, the secrets of everyone alive. You probe my innermost depths. You examine my thoughts and desires. Nothing escapes You, nothing is hidden from You. Please, Holy Name, be not too wrathful.

And who knows if the effort is in vain, the countless thin shiny silk threads I tie to the blue curtain in the great haste of the counting, ten, twelve hours a day, to finish on time? Who knows on what side of the dust I weave—front or back?

And in my hands the thread entwines into the Torah Curtain, bringing me—irrevocably—closer, as it gets shorter, to You.

Twelve days of the Omer. Splendor of Power.

In the afternoon he came by, furtively. For more than a month he hadn't come. I wasn't waiting anymore. Especially not since he had become engaged to Elisheva. Even before, it was crass, clearly. I did tell him the last time that there was no point coming back, no point in all that. (Maybe I spoke harshly then, before he left, just to give him an excuse to come back, to force him to prove that it was only to "visit the sick" that he came, to offer me charity—Isaiah—

I didn't imagine that everything was still undone, so flimsy, that everything was still alive.)

When he came I was absorbed in weaving blue threads into the Torah Curtain's sky and didn't notice the knocking at first. The strong wind here, at the edge of the mountain, often strikes the door, and the Arab children, in malice or by accident, roll stones at the gate. Only after the hesitant knocking was repeated did I get up. He swayed, tall and thin, in the doorway and slid embarrassed into the vestibule, and in the room, he stood with his face to the window.

I slipped back to the loom, pretending I had left the silk strands loose and they were liable to slip off the plaiting and get lost in the tangle of threads. He remained with his face to the vaulted window, unable to stop the shaking that plowed his back, the nape of his neck. Dizzy, I retreated to the kitchen, leaning over the stove, trying to ignite the gas burner, lighting matches one after another, and the hiss of fire that rose at last deepened the memory of closeness growing thick between the room and the kitchen. When I returned with the steaming teapot in my hand, he was still standing at the gaping window. Amazing how the tight black jacket made him into a stranger, and the beard that had grown so thick . . .

Can't get away from the sight of Isaiah's thin limbs that moved here, this afternoon. How did I imagine that I was far away from everything? I didn't think his presence could still excite me so much, that there still existed in me what is written: *Unto the woman he said, and thy desire shall be to thy husband, and he shall rule over thee.*

With the confidence of a vow, I planned to make You a sacrifice of prayer at the appointed time, as required. But now, how shall I claim to confess with clean hands *about you,* about the fear that impelled *you* to start stretching the warp of the prayer shawls despite what happened last night—*you* hurrying to take hold of the holy weaving, in great fear, before you were told of your match that evening at the rabbi's house. Worn out by torments, you hastened to spread the white skeins, after months of postponing permission to weave prayer shawls and spin fringes, knowing you weren't yet fit. You had only deceived yourself that morning, as if it were the soft, so virginal light of springtime, as full of promises as the opening of the gates of the East, that tempted you to start the weaving despite the night's impurity. Wrapped in light like a garment, you approached the emptied loom that stood, a gigantic frame, in the center of the room like an alien machine. You removed the remnants of red and green wool left from weaving pillows, scrunching the stumps of threads into a little ball that you threw into the trash. Then you turned to the package of new wool, rustling, loose, and pure. You carefully grasped the skeins of softness in your arms, were about to put them on the spool, to make them fly on its arms, to arrange them into coils. Only at that moment, for the first time, did you look straight at the flood of light hovering in the vault. Your eyes fastened on the gray slope opposite, where thickets of clay and mass of night memory stuck like a thick wave that stood erect over the valley, rose up and leaned, like a huge wall of shining dust collapsing in the window.

You forced yourself to look away, moving your eyes to the iron grooves in the loom through which you would thread the white, and from the blur, once again *she* bursts onto the hotel roof with her crazy singing, and flounces out to the path going down from the walls. You turned your head away in pain; hadn't you done everything to wipe those hours out of yourself, as Rabbi Israel Gothelf instructed, and here *she,* the impure one, the errant one, stirs in you again, descends deeper on the paths, and the turrets behind her flare in the rising sun. She stumbles on the slope and her fingernails plow the earth, clutch a cascade of clods. She gets up with scraped knees, drops of blood gather under the hiked-up dress, that same red dress, dusty at the hem, and she's still singing. She stumbles on the slope, among the cypresses leaning to the desert, and she's still singing . . .

Nevertheless, you wound the lengths of white on the spool, and pushed the machine to start it rotating. The arms of the warp beam pulled the thread out of the cylinders of the spool, spinning loops of warp twining in an enormous fountain of white, sparkling like the pure air on the slope as she slips down. From the upper road, drivers honk at her, and shepherd children, gliding from the folds of the mountains after their goats, hurl stinging shouts at her. The heat of the desert is absorbed by her limbs, sinks in her belly heavy as heaps of wheat, and the steep path carries her down, down, to the thickets of silt that hold the slope, to the barking that bursts out of the yards, to the tangle of sweetness deep in the crevice padded with gardens.

The line of wool spun out of the spool back and forth on the warp beam, back and forth in front of your eyes. You held on with all your might to the sight of the running thread, retreating and returning on the warp beam's arms—only with that effort, unwinding the white and blue separately, like Judgment and Compassion, like earth and sky, then join-ing them together in devotion, rows and rows of warp and woof that will rise on the loom from your hands, only in their weaving in holiness, twined and coupled into one body of purity in the smoothness of the prayer shawls—only with that effort would you complete your repair in the fifty days of the Omer Counting, only thus would you prepare for your coupling. Yes, you had to strengthen yourself by weaving before your match was set. And the arms of the warp beam went on emptying the threads from the cylinder of the spool.

You brought the machinery to a stop strongly, and removed the loops that were ready, stretching them full length on the floor. The braids of wool flowed from your arms, covered the whole room with mammoth snakes of white, but she, through the heat dripping on your eyelids, goes on and crosses the small stone bridge in the valley without heeding the

danger, passes through the center of the Arab village and the yellowish
shadow of the clay huts, under her rustle fig and pomegranate leaves, and
flies hum in vine hedges kneeling to the spring, and over her, steep slopes
straddling in the sun, up to the gleam of walls and turrets hanging above,
in the distance, like a vision of heat.

Sweat dripped from your sticky hair, hung on your eyelashes, blinded
you with salty drops, and she dashes straight ahead to the trickling pool
without looking back, makes her way through the tangle of branches that
smack her face, pulls off her sandals, tucks up the hem of the red dress,
and falls to her knees. She abandons her neck, her shoulders, to the cur-
rents of cold water that run down her back, her belly, the warmth of her
breasts, submerges her wrists in the water, her awful wrists that go deep
into the clear chill.

You stroked the heap of woolen loops, clasping the soft weight, and
your heart beat beneath the blouse buttoned up to your chin. The dizziness you had felt since dawn intensified to nausea. You buried your face
in the softness of the holy braids, and the sweetness of the carded wool
filled your nostrils. The words from the night echoed in you, *to travel into
exile from his home, exile atones for sin,* but when the helplessness of
shame inundated you, again you stammered *and give to my heart submission and humility* and ardently pressed the handfuls of wool to your eyes.

Still praying, you picked up the scissors and threaded your wet fingers
through their handles. You tried to aim their blades at the heap of loops,
and I don't know if it was out of loathing or out of yearning that you
knew how, there, in the desert, near that spring, with a faint laugh, with
flashing teeth, with warm limbs pressed to the soft, wet ground, sated
with the sweetness of water, her belly broke open like a split pomegranate full of dripping seeds, her breasts squashed, and her skin crushed to
the dust. The scissors hung limp from your hands, the cut loops of wool
lay on the floor, and above her bends the weight of the city hovering in
the distance, white hewn stones, panting at her face and quivering,
steeped in the heavy breath rising from the desert, and as the walls of
your belly move and melt, the sign of the Covenant grows deeper in
her, fluttering, spreading in her flesh, flooding and reviving her poisoned blood.

———

(And yet, like a murderer returning to the blood, you will return to that place! In pretended innocence, cunningly, you'll return *with him* to that place! And today, when he drank the tea in the same prolonged silence, folded his long limbs on the stool, buttoned up in that strange, black jacket: *A person engaged in illicit sexual relations with a woman. Afterward, they met in privacy, in the same country, while his love for her and his physical power still persisted, and nevertheless, he abstained and did not transgress. This is a complete penitent.* And I myself am not clear about the meaning of the gesture I made when he said, his face turned to the window, that I had gotten thin, and added, still without looking at me, that I had to take care of myself, and the back of his neck shook . . . I thought he was about to get up and slip away, and I stretched out my hand. Without thinking. And I myself don't know if I wanted him to stay or to go and never come back, and when he looked at me in a panic, the dazzle of the darkness shrieked.)

You picked up the white wool threads firmly; after all, *everything is in the hands of Heaven, You endow a human being with wisdom and teach mankind understanding, and You shall return us to full repentance before You.* And with a supplication, with relief, you stood and turned to the loom, although she ascends from the spring with a tipsy body. Her flesh unwashed and her uncombed hair covered with dust, she climbs the slopes blazing in the afternoon heat, making her way to the yeshiva. Unclean and abominable. You twisted your lips compassionately, and you counted the ends of wool, four by four, threading them between the teeth of the rake, in the holes of the tracks, between the iron blades of the comb—*Forgive us, our Father, for we have erred; pardon us, our King, for we have willfully sinned; for You are the good and forgiving God*—you fastened the threads on the wooden drum at the back of the loom as she strides on the warm roads, close to the walls, crosses the vacant lots between the neighborhoods, climbs the low stone steps on the way to the strange address she memorized from the announcement she happened to see in the macrobiotic restaurant in Soho. And thus, her crushed flesh unwashed and her red dress filthy, she comes into the vestibule of Neve Rachel, bursts into the room, shamelessly thrusts her warm, abominable chin at Rabbi Israel Gothelf, who is sitting there, and demands that he accept her immediately, that he stay with her alone in the room to talk, lifts her excited laughter to him. "I don't believe I came here, that's what's called Providence, isn't it?" She bends over the rabbi with her naked shoulders, and in reply to his question she whispers her name—"Emily, Amy, Amalia, Malinka"—and again bursts into sharp, long laughter.

Suddenly, you were struck by the thought that a man would wrap himself in the prayer shawl your fingers were putting together, would kiss its fringes, and a tremor of horror ran through your spine.

(Isaiah scolded me again for not getting a telephone; it's dangerous to live in such a place and not be able to call for help if, God forbid, something happened, he said.

But what need is there for a telephone here? For the act will be known immediately, straight from the eyes of the scapegoat covered with blood at the foot of the cliff to the tongue of crimson thread turning white.)

Until late, you tied the wool strands, four by four, with a growing distress. You tied, but the prayer did not pass your lips, its words screening the inception of the weave. You counted the threading and you tied, not heeding the pain descending deeper in your shoulders, not stopping your fingers that grew hard, no longer feeling the threads they pulled, winding to the back of the loom the sail of the ship that would carry you through the days. And half the warp was hung, threads and threads of wool stretched through the mechanism, fastened on both sides to the wooden drums, like the strings of an enormous lyre. You strove to thread the rest of the warp before going to the meeting with the rabbi. But as the hours passed, you were still pacing back and forth between the loom and the huge loops of wool lying on the floor, gathering and picking up, threading through the rake, the tracks, the iron teeth of the comb, and tying to the beam. The sun declined, and you hadn't yet finished. The old fears became deeper, sharper. And in the midst of tying, a thread of whiteness pulled between your fingers, you were alarmed to find that it was time to leave.

(When he got up, he stood still a moment, bound by the brilliance creeping up the slopes. He stood and didn't say a thing, not about the warp for the Torah Curtain stretched on the loom, not about the pile of papers prepared on the table. Suddenly he was scared. "Well, good-bye now, Amalia," he whispered and turned to the vestibule. Near the gate he stopped. Maybe he wanted to say something more, or maybe as usual he was just completely absorbed, body and soul, in a tone that resonated within him. Sunspots penetrated the iron grating on the window and fluttered on his neck. Then he chuckled, hurried to open the gate, and slipped out. By the time I followed him up the three steps to the threshold, nothing was left of his rapid stride around the mountain road. The neighbors' little boy with his shaved head passed by in the glowing brightness of the afternoon, poking his carved stick in the dirt, growling at a shaggy yellow puppy wriggling at his heels.

In the room, his cup remained on the table, and on a corner of the marble counter in the kitchen I found the bag of cookies—a secret gift. Maybe he brought what Elisheva had baked and was ashamed. The tea he hadn't drunk I didn't yet empty. By tomorrow the tea would certainly have left a black-red ring on the inside of the china cup.

Of course he won't return. Especially now, after his engagement has been announced. He came, he understood something—whatever he could understand—and ran away. He finally cast away the lizard in his hand and said, *He who confesses and forsakes his sins will be treated with mercy—*

No, he no longer belongs here between these walls. And how could I go on hoping after what was sealed!

And in the abyss, under the windows, those paths still spread out, hers, yours, and the spring. And all the lost steps are sealed inside them.)

May it be Your will that there be no fear or weakness in me, may it be Your will that I shall complete what is left, that I shall only complete what is left, by the end of the Omer Counting.

Master of the worlds, You commanded us to bring the continual offering at its set time, but through our sins, the Holy Temple has been destroyed, the continual offering is discontinued. And we have neither priest at his service nor Levite on his platform nor Israelite at his station— Therefore may it be Your will that the prayer of our lips be worthy, acceptable, and favorable before

You, as if we had brought the continual offering at its set time and we had stood at its station.

May it be Your will, O Lord my God and God of my fathers, God of Abraham, God of Isaac, and God of Jacob—just to go on calling Your Names, just to call Your Names over and over—*God of Abraham, God of Isaac, God of Jacob. Take pity on me with Your abundant mercies.* Take pity. *Make me repent with full repentance to You in Your abundant mercies, and unite my heart in love and awe with Your Name,* Your Name, Your Name— And *recall me to light in Thy light and light my eyes, for in Thy light shall I see light, shall I be able to serve You truly—for in Thy light I shall see light.*

Only for that do I still yearn, only for that—that I shall be able to serve You truly.

two weeks

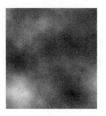

Holy Sabbath night, fifteen days, which is two weeks

and one day of the Omer. Grace of Beauty. Greatness of

Mercy. Between the magnitude of the belief of Abraham and

the mercy of Jacob, whose eyes were dim for age.

May it be Your will that I do justice in my nocturnal labor, by virtue of the holiness of the Sabbath. That the presence of Rabbi Tuvia Levav and the lovable Fayge, which surrounded me until the end of the Sabbath, rest upon me its grace.

In spite of everything, as planned, you dashed out at sunset, taking two buses for the appointment with Rabbi Israel Gothelf. You hurried to cover the remnants of the colored threads in the wicker basket and you wound the ends of the linen threads around the bobbins, as if all that extra care would help you against the unthreaded warp loops you left on the floor. You locked the gate with a double lock, and you bolted the

door. And scared that you were late, you went out without reciting the
Evening Prayer.

You waited at the bus stop downtown for the bus that would take you
to the rabbi's neighborhood. Twilight deepened. You squeezed onto the
end of the bench, clinging to the post of the bus stop, and as the time
stretched out, your prayer became even later. On the rising street, men
in black jackets and dark brimmed hats passed by, leaving behind them a
trail of sourness. They were rushing, their faces to the pavement and
their sidelocks fluttering in the chill of dusk. Evening fell rapidly. Burning strips of sky outlined the buildings. You glanced at the women heavily pushing baby carriages up the steep street, swarms of little ones
wound around their elbows, their small faces thrust forward with the effort. The bus still didn't come.

Despite the fears, you regretted coming out for the meeting and you
were about to turn around and go back and not postpone the prayer anymore when the tops of the pine trees quivered and a chilly breeze blew
down the street, striking your limbs. The noisy chirping of flocks of
birds fleeing from the treetops to the white sky pelted down around the
bus stop. You clutched your shawl about your shoulders—you had forgotten how penetrating the cold could be at sundown, like her, when, in
the quiver of evening, she flees from the central post office to the lashing of twilight, a few weeks after coming to Neve Rachel, in her hand a
letter addressed to her at General Delivery. In the narrow street, the
shadows of the pine trees trap her. She clutches the sealed letter. (She
hasn't yet told them at the yeshiva, and she hides her wrists in the sleeves
of her blouse.) Her heart fluttering, she tears off the flap of the envelope.
Into her hand scatter the bills and the note written in that old-fashioned
hand, so much like Father's: *Dear Amy, Something to start with. Ever
yours, Ludwig Stein.* She crumples the paper, turns her head in panic,
tosses the crushed letter into the gutter, and sticks the bills any which way
into her skirt pocket.

You gathered the handles of the raffia bag and pressed them to your
shawl. Across the street, on the second floor, a windowpane burned in the
low sunlight, kindling a stone balcony heaped with boxes and sheets of
tin. Before your eyes, the beam was extinguished, and the hewn stones
sank into a crimson gloom.

You shifted uneasily on the corner of the bench, and if you hadn't been worried about passersby disturbing you, you would have gotten up and finished your prayer on the spot. But she rushes away from the cast-off letter, choked with panic lest it rip the thin tissue of the life of repentance she has steeped herself in, from awakening and the prayer at dawn to the prayer at bedtime, through the lessons in Torah, Laws, Ethics, to breaks for group study, and back to class, pressed in among the other girls in the small dining hall, dropped among bodies wafting mists of sleep, facing the blue plastic plates and cheap silverware of the dairy meal, among faces bent over the tepid beverage, and slices of bread-and-jam leaving glassy drops on the Formica table, drops that tremble when the noisy, common recital of the Grace after Meals explodes, and afterward, the clink of the plates heaped up in the sink at the end of the meal, and the scraping of the iron legs of the chairs on the floor of the classroom, and she pushes into her seat in the corner next to the glass door of the balcony, and Rabbi Israel Gothelf, in his quiet, monotonous voice, reads and explains, surrounded by girls who gaze at him, devotedly writing down his words, and the rabbi guides them in the first questions of the plain interpretation of the Bible, brings them to the springs of the Torah, as in the words of the Prophet: *Behold, the days come, saith the Lord God, that I will send a famine in the land, not a famine of bread, nor a thirst for water, but of hearing the words of the Lord.* His voice is like a dull blade sheathed in restraint, and only the occasional flicker in his eyes indicates how young he is, and in her head is that eternal humming of words, syllables, enveloping everything in fog, rocking her between the meals, the lessons, the prayers, unceasingly from Sabbath to Sabbath, in the persistent smell of cheap soap leaving its bitterness in the sinks of the yeshiva, in the towels, in the wooden floors of the shower stalls, stuck to the corridors, the classrooms with their fluorescent lights over the girls' eyes swollen with sleep— And she hasn't yet spoken, hasn't told a thing! And within the blurred hovering of the rules of the way of life and the new customs, she is almost bereft of the desire to speak. Walking quickly, she fastens the swollen pocket, and when she returns to the yeshiva she bursts into Rabbi Gothelf's office without knocking, and tosses the bundle of bills on the table.

"Rabbi, give that to charity in my name!" she gasps at him. Only after a moment does she recover a bit and add, "Esteemed Rabbi."

Rabbi Israel goes on quietly packing the Holy Books into his briefcase, then stands up, slowly gathers the money, and puts it away too. "Giving money to charity is a great Commandment. You will be blessed for that, Amalia."

He winds his checked scarf around his neck and goes to the door. On the threshold, as if concerned about something else, he turns his head and says, "Remember that repentance is like death and rebirth. *It is proper that man spill his blood and burn his flesh,* said Maimonides, meaning one should not only keep away from sin but forget it completely, erase from memory the acts of the past. That is repentance. That is the only way to fulfill the words of the Prophet: *A new heart also will I give you; and a new spirit will I put within you.* We'll talk about this some more, Amalia."

Without waiting for an answer, he goes, leaving her in his office. She runs through the corridors of the yeshiva. Only in the doorway of the room she shares in the dormitory does she stop. As usual, Elisheva is sitting on her bed with her legs folded, going over the Torah portion they studied that morning. She rolls her freckled gaze up, and once again bends over with the ardor of faith to the book of *Midrash Tanhuma,* with headshaking and chirps of understanding.

(After all, Elisheva must have noticed something, she and her unbridled curiosity. She, who is the first to leap out of bed like a lion for God's work. Combs her kinky hair with elbows flying, spreading the odor of her armpits to her roommate, Amy, Emily, Amalia, who is still curled up in bed, in a nightgown that has known many beds, has been held by many hands . . . And in the shared closet between the two beds, standing prominently in a pile, just as she put them when she came to the yeshiva, are the orange cardboard boxes with the photos inside. As if obeying the orders of the rabbi, Elisheva spins a plot of silence around her roommate: *To separate himself far from the object of his sin, to change his name, as if to say "I am a different person!"* And on that Friday, after the letter came from Stein, when she doesn't want to get out of bed because everything is over, if he traced her even here, then everything is over, Elisheva stations her big body on the doorsill. "What's going on, Amalia? We've been knocking for fifteen minutes! What's going on, tell me? This isn't no time to lay in bed, it's the Sabbath soon!" She grabs her with strong hands, leads her to the warm steam bursting out of the bathroom, the dragging of wooden heels, the strokes of the rubber squeegee, and in the shower stall next to her, through the screen of water and mists of soap, Elisheva rubs her solid flesh with a loofah.)

The bus stopped with a salvo of hot smoke. You were carried along with the other waiting people in a wave to the gaping door, through which a little girl in a black dress with two braids fled. For a moment, her black-stockinged foot waved about in the air, then it managed to touch the sidewalk, and again the wave charged, harder, and the doors pressed together. The wave pushed you to the back door. There, two baby carriages with shopping bags tied to them dropped from the opening. Two men hurried to push their briefcases into the crack between the hissing door and the frame. The bus started moving, and the men ran after the receding cloud of exhaust, waving their briefcases. "What's wrong with you, driver! What nerve, driver! Driver!"

You dropped back onto the bench of the bus stop. You still hadn't recited the evening prayer and didn't stand up for the Omer Counting. In the dark street, headlights sliced the shadow of the treetops, and the tumult of the birds grew faint. It was only because of the exhaustion poured into your limbs that you didn't go back home that moment. Resenting your weakness, you pulled the raffia bag toward you and chuckled pityingly at how she was thrilled when the rabbi announced that on the Sabbath he and his family would join the students at the yeshiva for lunch, sure that that was his way of finally giving her a hint of their postponed conversation. Instead of going right back home, you shriveled up in the corner of the bus stop and were astonished at how all that Friday—only a week after she crumpled up Stein's letter—she is absorbed in feverish preparation. She straightens up the room carefully, goes out to the street to pick green branches that she thrusts in an empty jar she found in the kitchen cabinet. Even at Sabbath dinner with the family taking its turn to be her hosts, thus doing "a good deed of bringing the girls of the yeshiva to the ways of the Jews," even among the family surrounding her with their contentment, expectation is throbbing in her. On the Sabbath morning, she gets up early for prayer with devotion and spiritual exultation, and when noon comes she hardly notices the rabbi's wife, Yocheved, and the five little girls, whose hair is pulled back in rubber bands, but is borne through the students' voices saying the blessing as the rabbi breaks off pieces of the challah. With a warm twinkle, his look confirms the promised conversation. She pulls her cuffs in a burst of shame at wearing the same blouse for Sabbath and weekdays, and erupts into a loud, tense laugh that makes the little girls at the corner of the table whisper. Rabbi Israel delivers a sermon between the soup and the meat, and she knows he is saying those words for her; she who was refined by suffering, who was sent to him from death, only to her ear does he direct the hidden meaning, known only to her.

"The torments of sin at the time of repentance are like the torments of mourning: Just as we stand before death as a painful enigma, so we stand in wonder at the time of repentance before our souls and ask out of the torments of remorse, *that such abomination is wrought among you.*"

She stands up in turmoil, as if to help serve, and the girls burst loudly into the Song of Exaltations, and continue reciting the blessing. She doesn't notice how they're shaking the crumbs from the tablecloth, doesn't notice the rabbi's wife, who remains chatting with the girls in the door open to the afternoon, but runs after the rabbi, who goes to his office in the yeshiva to rest until the lesson he will give at afternoon service. She waits in the shadow of the staircase so as not to attract the attention of the girls, and when the rabbi approaches along the corridor, his steps directed to her, she walks toward him as planned. But Rabbi Gothelf slips into his office without looking at her, and a moment later only the sound of the door banging and the flash of the white shirt reverberate in the empty corridor.

She falls onto the bed in her clothes, buries her head in the pillow, and remains motionless even when Elisheva urges her to go down to the lesson. Choking back her rage, she derives angry pleasure from the rundown state of her clothing.

Finally, you gathered up the raffia handles of your bag and stood abruptly. You were about to return to the warp of the prayer shawls you had left tossed on the floor, to the solace of prayer, for why add sin to offense?

Two buses came to the station at the same time. The rushing crowd swept you through the doors of one of them, and by the time the bus moved, you had been tossed into a seat in the dark, smoky depths, your body pressed by the panting body of a stocky woman who dragged her swollen bundles under the seat. Outside the window, blocks of darkness fogged over, the headlights of cars bursting out and filling the dim bus with a momentary dazzle. The knowledge that you had no salvation flashed in you a moment, that even if you continued submissively on your way to the rabbi, you hadn't done repentance. For there wasn't even any grave on which you could ask forgiveness, so how would you be able to bring forth new life? You would only bring up a lie in the conversation, only deception. In the next moment, your breath condensing on the window covered the leaps of darkness, and sweat spread over your scalp. Like a drowning person, you repeated to yourself that it was only your delaying the evening prayer that had given birth to doubt in you, and that as soon as you stood for the Counting of the Omer, the obstacles would be removed. And you were already murmuring, "*Bring us back, our Father, to Your Torah, and bring us near, our King, to Your service, and influence us to return in perfect repentance before You,*" and for a moment, the faith flickered in you that here, now, a new life would open before you, a life devoid of all sin and cleansed of all offense, and the dark neighborhoods streamed against the spasms of the bus, and the empty lots broke open to the cold blowing on crests in the outskirts of the city. But in spite of that, the chill crept into you as the bus approached the rabbi's neighborhood.

By the time you were pressed out of the bus, the hour of the meeting was long past. The stocky woman dragged her shopping bags down the steps next to you, pushing you against the jackets of the men, whose shadows quickly scattered in the darkness. You remained alone on the sidewalk. You grew dizzy, like yesterday, and quickly grabbed the pole of the bus stop. Not knowing how, you reached the entrance to the rabbi's building, but you lost your way in the staircase and found yourself in the backyard, among hoses and gutters, at the door of the bomb shelter. Once again, your knees gave way. You were afraid you'd lose control, and without delay, you stood to pray in the cold winds blowing from the bare slope beyond the yard. Your prayer came out a weak murmur, only the final words somewhat clear: *"Let my soul be like dust to everyone."* During the Counting, *"eleven days of the Omer, Splendor of Power,"* the little prayer book quivered before your eyes like a compass, and you resolved to inform Rabbi Gothelf just as soon as you went in of your decision not to marry.

The apartment door was opened by the rabbi's wife, Yocheved, and the gloom of the vestibule was cleft by fluorescent light reflected from the kitchen tiles. "Amalia! We haven't seen you for so long. Come in. Come in." Two little girls burst out of their room and gazed at you with their big eyes. And even when the rabbi's wife coaxed them—"Shoshanka, Sarale, say hello to Amalia"—they didn't budge, studying you.

The sound of Rabbi Israel's plodding steps was heard. His tall figure advanced toward you from his study. "Welcome," he murmured with an absentminded nod, and beckoned you into the study. You passed close to him on the threshold of the room, and he closed the door behind the two of you.

"Please, sit down." He pointed to a chair at one corner of the table, and he himself folded up in a chair opposite, put his ankle on his knee as he always did, and leaned sideways as if to cast his look from the depth of the black frame of his eyebrows and beard. On the table was an open book of *Gemara*, like a dense wall of Laws between him and you, and the silence lengthened.

"I'm sorry I was late, the buses didn't come—"

"So, how is the weaving progressing?—" The two of you started talking at the same time.

"I'm sorry . . ." you started again, embarrassed.

"You're always welcome, at any time, Amalia."

Since you were scared the rabbi would discover how you had been gripped by weakness yesterday, you quickly clutched at his question. "The weaving?"

"Yes, how's the weaving progressing?" He, too, seemed happy to postpone the main point of the conversation.

"I started weaving the prayer shawls today," you said, with a furtive breath.

"Good luck, and may you live to bring forth a proper work from your hands."

"Amen," you replied, dropping your eyes, and somehow you imagined that the rabbi especially emphasized the word *proper,* and you blushed. You were afraid even to lift your hand to brush away the strand of hair sticking to your forehead. From the pages of the *Gemara,* the lines stood out: *He further said to me: My son, what sound did you hear in this ruin? I replied: I heard a divine voice cooing like a dove.* The rabbi swayed in the circle of lamplight and his black beard glittered.

"You know why I summoned you for a talk today," he began slowly, with a trace of solemnity.

You nodded to cover the pounding of your heart, unable to utter a word.

"If your parents, may they rest in peace, were alive, it would be their task to guide you at this moment, but in their absence I take upon myself their task and all the weight of responsibility." Suddenly he looked straight at you and said in a quiet voice, "I have trust in you, Amalia."

"Yes, Rabbi," you whispered quickly, grasping the arms of the chair with all your might.

"I appreciate how far you have gone in your studies, your acute mind, and the way you have accepted the yoke of the Commandments. You know that I also supported your decision to devote another year to acquiring the skill of weaving, but," his voice shifted, "the completion of your repair you will find only when you build a home; only with your marriage will you know peace of mind."

"I don't know . . ." The words slipped out of your mouth.

"It's not good for a person to be alone, Amalia. You have to think of your place in the community of Israel, to establish a family, to raise sons and the sons of sons for the Torah and the Commandments . . ."

His voice went on, modulating under the ardent throbbing of blood that clouded your vision, and yet you didn't dare shout at him that you hadn't completed your repentance, that you were loathsome, forbidden to mate, forbidden to have intercourse! And as the arms of the chair slipped out of your fingers, you were flooded with the words of his sermon back then, on that eighth night of Hanukkah, as she sits in her corner next to the door of the balcony, and cold winds penetrate the doorframe and threaten the melting candles. And Rabbi Israel Gothelf, with his bold beard, surrounded by the girls of the yeshiva like olive saplings, like young ewes listening to the words flowing with that tone of a fatherly rebuke: "The holiday of Hanukkah is a reminder of the war of the Greeks against Israel, darkness against light! For what does Greece desire? To blur the distinction between Israel and the other nations! So they do not destroy the Temple, but they place idols in it and contrive to extinguish the light of the Menorah. They translate the Torah into Greek, as if to say 'We too are Israel.' To this day, the war between Israel and Greece goes on, for what is their scheme if not to sow doubt and obscurity in the heart of Israel, to assimilate it until it forgets the nature of its being!" The rabbi's face blazes in the candlelight, and he raises his voice as he rarely does: "After Amalek, the murderers came and slaughtered our people, and massacred our dear ones in the awful Holocaust; today Greece comes to wipe out the memory of the disaster from the heart of the nation. First they say, 'Today us, tomorrow you, *for the imagination of man's heart is evil from his youth,* and there is no difference between Israel and the other nations.' Then they go on brazenly pretending innocence: 'It never happened'; they remove our disaster from world history, and present us, the victims, as the guilty ones! With great cunning, the Greeks assault not only the whole but also the individual. There, in his heart, in the Holy of Holies, they sow doubt and confusion, dim the spark of faith in every person of Israel." The rabbi's voice rises and flames. "And this is the miracle of Hanukkah: In spite of the frailty, in spite of the obscurity and the darkness, the fire of memory grows stronger, the fire of memory kindled in the Menorah of faith, in the sanctuary of the heart of every single person. And the oil isn't finished!"

For a moment, in the circle of light, the rabbi's shining beard glowed as he articulated monotonously—"a family of praise, Amalia"—and you shook your head unwittingly, and once again his back vanished behind the flames of the Hanukkah lamps, and the echoes of his sermon are seared deep in her breathing, and around her are the warm smells of the doughnuts the girls bring on long trays from the kitchen, the wafting sweetness of powdered sugar, and she bursts out of her chair and, her face afire, she runs in the footsteps of the rabbi, who is bowing over the kitchen sink, a glass of water glinting in his hand, and stands facing him all shining when he straightens up. "I want to talk to you, Rabbi."

She takes one more step toward him, and between the bodies of the girls coming and going, busy with the doughnuts frying on the stove, she repeats, "I want to talk to you, Rabbi."

"Come, let's go to the porch." The rabbi withdraws to the balcony through the glass door, his head hunched between his shoulders. And there, at the ledge, in the lashing of the frozen rain whirling in the dark, the words flood out of her, unrestrained.

"What you said about the darkness that preceded the miracle of Hanukkah, about the obscurity, about the oblivion, I . . . You don't know how well I know that." The speech that has been mute in her ever since she came to Neve Rachel streams with the cascades of water pouring from the awning. "The struggle between darkness, and the knowledge that behind the darkness has to be light, even if it's blurred . . . That's exactly the thought that gave me strength in the hardest times, that's what brought me to the yeshiva, exactly what you taught!" She lifts her face sparkling with rain to the rabbi, buttoned up in a long coat. "I want to thank you, Rabbi, for what you said now, for what you taught, for everything, everything!"

The rabbi nods, his face clenched. "Yes, yes, Amalia, that's the vital force concealed in the Torah."

But she stops his words with her excitement and moves her burning face even closer to him, not noticing his recoil. "Rabbi, I want to tell you something else. You must understand after what you taught us about the darkness that threatens the light . . . I—it's not only that I lived without faith, in despair, in total darkness, yes, in sin, it's not only that, Rabbi—" Her voice grows hoarse. "It's that I really went all the way, I . . ."

"I know, Amalia!" the rabbi cuts her off with a sharp gesture. "I understood the first day, as soon as you came to the yeshiva. Now you have to immerse yourself in the life of repentance, set yourself on the ways of Torah. You mustn't think of what was." He raises his beard decisively, and even as the echo of his voice rises, he spins on his heel, his lesson ended, and turns to leave the balcony.

"Rabbi!" She dashes after him, grabs his coattail. "Rabbi! There's something else I've got to tell you! I'm scared, I'm scared I won't succeed in repentance!" she wails. And as she suddenly pulls the rabbi's coat, one of the buttons is plucked off, and she is hurled to the ledge of the balcony with the button in her hand.

The rabbi freezes, suspended between the threshold and the blocks of darkness lashed to the balcony, and when she gets up with a chuckle of amazement, he quickly raises his hand to protect his face. Not noticing, she approaches him again, blinded by her supplication: "It's not me, it's not me, Rabbi, it's her! I tried, I tried to escape, to hide, I tried everything, even the name, her name, I changed once, twice, but she pursued me, Rabbi, even here!" Once again she grabs his coattail and shrieks: "It's not me, it's she who gets in the way of repentance, she won't let me live in her death, she won't ever forgive me. And it's she who sent Stein after me to remind me of the unpaid account, so what could I do? For months I followed her around like he said . . . To seek, to find one more thing, to take some pictures. And I photographed madly, whole boxes of pictures, photographs of nothing, you understand, of nothing! Then what?" She chokes on her nervous laughter and clutches the cloth of the rabbi's coat. "Then, when everything was documented and classified, and all those pictures were ready for the album Stein wanted, and I thought she'd leave me alone, that she'd forget me, she came back again to take me. And I went. Of course I went with her, all the way."

And as if the rest of her strength burns within the sacrifice of her confession, she sways, and her head lands on the rabbi's coat. And in a voice that is suddenly weak, like a baby's bleating, she gasps into the sourness of the wet wool: "I'm scared, I'm scared," and she holds on tighter.

"The torments of one who repents are harder than Hell," the rabbi's voice bursts out above her. "And he is pursued by fears and feelings of remorse. But do not say that you will not have repentance, for the Everlasting Endurance of Israel will not fail!"

"But how will I have life in her death if I have the same name as hers? You understand? How will I have life in her death!"

"Shut up!" shouts the rabbi, and spatters of rain spray from his protruding beard. "There are some things a person is forbidden to deal with! The disaster that came to the martyrs of our people is a thing beyond us and we have no right to investigate it! We are commanded only to follow the laws of HaShem and His judgments, *for they are our life and the length of our days.*" He raises a warning finger to her and his face flushes with fury. "And aside from that, remember, Amalia, our Torah is the Torah of life: *I have set before you life and death, blessing and cursing: therefore choose life.* Remember, Amalia, *therefore choose life!*"

He retreats. At the glass door, he stops and says quickly, "Can you give me back the button?"

At first she doesn't understand what he means; all that time she has been pressing the plastic disk in her fist so hard, so it wouldn't fall, that she forgot she had it. But when the rabbi's angry look continues, she forces a tremulous laugh and hands him the button, wet with perspiration. The rabbi quickly drops it into his pocket, and from the door, as she is still suspended among the slivers of water, he tosses his final words at her, fulfilling his duty. "You'll see, Amalia, study will bring you peace, and someday you'll make a home in Israel and give birth to sons."

He disappears into the kitchen without hearing her answer, which is chased away by the gusts of wind treading from the mountains: "I don't know, I don't know . . ."

"I don't know," you whispered, as if quoting, to the rabbi, who was bending toward you in the narrow funnel of light, resting his ankle on his knee and reciting, "I'm sure that you will know bliss in family life, in raising children, in educating them in the community of Israel."

"I don't know, I don't know . . . ," you kept on muttering, as if the two conversations were stuck together back to back, with no distinction in time, like warp threads pressed together. "I don't know . . . ," you whispered, amazed, as if nothing had been lived, had been suffered, had changed between the two moments intermingled in the collapsed weave of time. And the buttons on the rabbi's jacket were the same big, almost foolish, plastic buttons.

"Living alone keeps you away from the community, Amalia, and weakens the yeshiva's influence on you." His words beat without piercing the stupor, which in fact hadn't subsided since the bus ride yesterday. Only one thing remained clear in the heart of the fog: that you could no longer get out of the maelstrom that drew you away once again.

"I know that you have earned repentance with genuine torments, but don't worry, Amalia, I'm sure that everything will be fine and you will know peace of mind." The rabbi stood up and walked around the desk, rummaging in one of its drawers. "You know how much trouble I took to support your first steps toward repentance, to remove all obstacles. I even tried to locate your family to make it as easy as possible for you to renew a normal web of life. I did succeed in tracking down Mr. Stein of New York because I knew he took an interest in you, just so you'd have a sense of confidence, and now," he rubbed his hands together, sure of your agreement, "the time has come."

"I didn't know you knew Ludwig Stein!" The words were blurted out in a broken breath, and your heart jumped with a sharp pounding.

"Yes, I am in touch with him," murmured the rabbi as he went back behind the desk and sat down, putting his ankle on his knee again. "He showed great interest in the yeshiva. Really got involved in the operation. Twice already he has sent generous contributions."

All the heaviness that had dammed your breath suddenly collapsed. You flinched, and sweat darkened the spinning room, which was snatched from your eyes.

"Here, I've got a picture of the fellow; I thought you'd like to see him before the meeting." The rabbi's hand bisected the cone of light, and at the end of it flickered a photograph. "A fine fellow, diligent, with a sensitive heart. I got all his recommendations from the head of his yeshiva, and I met with him for a talk. I'm sure you'll find a lot in common; he also came to the Torah from far away, his name is Isaiah." The spinning became heavier, and the serrated edges of the small photo cut into your hand.

(Yes, you were scared. You didn't think Ludwig Stein would reappear. You thought it was possible to steal the photographs and escape forever. Obviously he would come to the wedding. The rabbi would make sure to let him know. He would come, fancy, panting, he would look at you as he did then, at the end, in the hotel in San Remo— You were scared, you weren't ready— Suddenly, you had to hold on to something, and without delay, to flee, to believe at any cost. And yet you knew that love was forbidden you!)

———

"There is repentance of awe and there is repentance of love, Amalia," the rabbi went on in his routine murmur. "In repentance of awe, the person extirpates the evil inside himself and wipes out the past as if it had never been, but in repentance of love a person's wickedness becomes his virtue, for the fire that tempted him to commit sin now burns in him with the obliterating flame of love, and he approaches HaShem on a high degree."

You bent your head, and on the strip of the photo trembled blurred spots of a smooth cheek and curls.

"I am certain, Amalia, that family life will imbue you with new forces, and they will aid you in dispersing the last of the shadows."

And you just bent your head submissively, and you didn't fall at the rabbi's feet, and you didn't shout. You went along with it without stopping him!

"I rely on you and am certain that you and Isaiah will support each other, and the light of faith will shine from you," the rabbi's voice went on, rising.

I've stopped for a long time.

The sound of Isaiah's name is like a searing burst of fever. *Isaiah.* An independent entity. A revolution in my stomach, in my entrails. A profound tremor shakes the night like the revelation of the full moon in the black skies of the new month.

Isaiah.

Soft fingers tie and fasten a sheet of trembling in the darkness of the veins. A long, silent rolling, shaking the tissues. Pain and consolation intertwining in an awful sweetness.

Once more I yield to weakness. *If You want to cleanse me as You purify and refine silver, nothing will be left of me, for I am like straw before fire, and like dry trees before the flame. And how weak is the flesh. Please, jealous and vengeful God, do not destroy me.*

"I rely on you, Amalia, that just as you successfully taught your hands to weave, you will successfully conduct your household, as a woman of valor!" The rabbi straightened up and concluded, "I suppose you will not object to meeting the fellow to get acquainted."

When you didn't answer, he added, teasingly, "Do not think too much, Amalia. There are moments when we have to say 'done and heard' before a decision is forced on us." He chuckled with relief, basking in the circle of light, and took his ankle off his knee.

Did he really not notice anything? Wasn't he embarrassed to recite the same sentences he used in all his conversations with various classes of the girls in the yeshiva? Or perhaps he justified the routine as renewal of meaning, as with the repetition of the weekly Bible portion? Or maybe he had made peace with the hollowness of his repetitions, as a doctor in his helplessness recites the same vague formula to the hopelessly ill. Rabbi Israel Gothelf, so dim, evaporating before the eyes, for almost two months now I haven't come to his apartment and I haven't attended Neve Rachel. As if he were forgotten, shriveled, like a dry leaf dropped off for the fruit that takes its place. So faded, in his worn jacket with the big buttons, from the distance of everything that has happened.

"I've arranged a first meeting for the two of you next Tuesday, the fifteenth day of the Omer, and I hope you will know many long years of peace and blessing together." The rabbi reached out and took the image from your damp hand.

"Fine, I'll meet him, and God willing . . ." You started but didn't finish, for how could the slight weight of the photograph stand against the wildness of the torrents?

The rabbi went around the desk again and slid the image of Isaiah into the drawer.

"Don't forget to come to us for Friday night dinner after the meeting so I can talk with you," he added and turned to the door.

You quickly gathered the raffia straps of your bag and got up, thrusting out your hand to the corner of the table to brake your stumbling. The rabbi looked at you sharply, and you were scared he had been reading your thoughts the whole time, and your knees quaked even more. But when the troubled flutter of Rabbi Gothelf's eyes sailed past you, you renewed your grip on the raffia handles, and with a forced step, you went out to the corridor.

The rabbi's wife approached you, straining her full limbs, wiping her hands on an apron. For a moment, you were about to fall into her lap, get rid of all the lying you had done in your soul. Drown in her puffy face shining in the fluorescent reflections from the kitchen tiles. And when you looked back, Rabbi Gothelf was already swallowed up in his study and quickly closed the shadow of the door behind him.

"Well, you finished!" exclaimed the rabbi's wife. "Now you *have to* taste the new cake, you have to!" She grabbed your arm and led you to the kitchen. "Here, your piece is ready, I cut it for you and put it on a plate so it would cool off." She sat down opposite you, leaning her heavy body against a corner of the table. "Eat, eat," she said, her firm fingers pushing a big piece of cake at you.

"I wanted to talk to you privately, Amalia. You know, men don't always see things like we do . . . Sometimes I disagree with Israel on that subject." She laughed at the audacity of her words and her large face blazed. "Eat, eat," she pleaded, advancing closer, her smell blending with the sweetness of the mass in your throat. "I always tell Israel that there's learning but there's also life! Girls sit in the yeshiva and study for two years, three, like boys, so when will they live, when? Look, Amalia, you're not so young anymore, excuse me for saying so, but the years go by fast and you have to think about yourself a little. You know what I mean. That's what I wanted to tell you before you meet, God willing, with the fellow."

Then she put her warm hand on yours, gazed at you, and said, "There's something strange in you, Amalia." She moved her head in her wig and looked at you a long time. "It's like you're running away from life, God forbid, neglecting yourself, closing yourself up. Tell me, why are you doing that? Why?"

You pulled your hand away. The light shone on her startled face and her eyes were covered with a film of submission. You bent toward the whiteness of the rabbi's wife's forehead, whispering, the light whipping your eyes.

"It's true, I am running away from life, true, and that's my business, only mine!" Of all people, it was on the rabbi's wife, Yocheved, that you finally poured out the fury of your helplessness, the rage for not shouting at the rabbi to cancel the whole thing, all of it! It was her, of all people, that you decided to frighten, where in fact you needed so badly to rest your head on her hand lying on the table. You saw how the skin on the thick hand shone, and you went on: "You know, once I did run away, all the way. At the last minute, they brought me back, in a clinic. Who's to say I won't do it again, ha ha." Watching with the relief of vengeance how the hand retreated, scattering fat crumbs over the table on its way.

And by now you had clutched the shawl around your shoulders and jumped up among the gleaming pots. At the kitchen door, you bumped into two of the little girls, who had been eavesdropping on the conversation. With round eyes, they watched you run out of the apartment. The echo of Yocheved's parting words rolled down the staircase: "Well, Amalia, Amalia, good-bye . . ."

Your footsteps rang on the stairs, and the iron banister slipped out of your grasp. Finally you emerged to the chill. Your legs carried you to the lower yard, that small lot, where, among the hoses and the gutters, you had earlier poured out your soul in prayer. Exhaustion crushed your limbs, and the very thought of going back and seeking the upper exit in the staircase defeated you. The abyss of the valley rustling with thorns drew you with a promise of peaceful gloom. And you groped your way through the hedge that separated the yard and the slope.

Yes. Thus far. As far as possible in the weariness of the night's end.

(And once again Stein appeared, his shadow pressed into the darkness. So hard to separate the voices. The rabbi mentioned their names almost in one breath, as if Isaiah's name couldn't be said without Stein's immediately popping up behind it. Now, in the last part of the fabric, won't he leave me alone? Leave me? Even if the sacrifice is Yours?)

I shall go out now to the threshold, for the Midnight Prayer.

Please, HaShem, in Your abundant mercy, wipe out all my debts, for You are a good and forgiving God.

Sixteen days. Two weeks and two days of the Omer. Power

of Beauty (late into the second watch of the night).

Maybe it's better if I don't leave any traces tonight. (Things that will not be included in the final weaving.)

I sat all day, exhausted, gazing out the window. Turgid waves rose and tumbled over. As if a black burial stone came and covered everything. Excuses, as if the fault inherent in the effort of writing last night didn't succeed (of course) in silencing the real reason. (And maybe, after all, it's better if I don't write tonight, don't pour the venom out of me, that it doesn't stain the pages.)

How far away now seem the things said only yesterday, on the Sabbath, in the small house up the hill, at the home of Rabbi Tuvia Levav, and how thirstily I drank them in. I? The same person? The table set for only the three of us, as if I were a member of their family, with Fayge's silent movements, serving and clearing the meal, her silver hair flying. And Rabbi Tuvia, his blue eyes penetrating me like the water in a pool, like the cooing of the doves in the neighbors' dovecotes. He utters those soft words—"The heart of one released from the service of sin is filled with a wonderful feeling of holy freedom, and he is healed, grows strong as a plant covered in springtime with the warm light of the sun. And this strong stream, this painful stream in his veins, delights him, for he knows that those are growing pains, an eruption of the soul healing"—and like a consoled baby I drank in his words. "Always submerged in a person is repentance, even in the depths of sin, in the heart of despair, it is always concealed in the depths of the soul, and reveals itself again in its full power only with the act of repentance." And I was even moved when he went on in that same tone, like a grandfather I never knew—"From the depths touching the mighty flood of the world's life comes repentance. And so the individual who makes repentance discovers the unity of all being, the secret of all existence." A distance of light years separates that Sabbath and now.

Like a stone, I lay at the window all day, the taste of dust in my mouth. The shuttle remained hanging on the web of the warp like a fly sucked empty, and I couldn't touch the pages. Everything is lifeless matter. Dust in clay vessels crumbling to dust. A repellent piece of flesh. The hand strikes the face like a mask. The tongue hits the heaps of crushed sand of the jawbone. Everything is pulverized, poured in blazing dust through the openings of the skull.

Ironically, all evening, the sounds of drums and the lute echo here, and the guttural shouts from some distant celebration, down in the Arab village. Just a little while ago, chains of colored lights, so painful, shone there. How to pretend that I can accomplish the work, I, a vessel filled with sin?

Last night, when I followed you in the conversation with Rabbi Gothelf, I was devoured by fear. I wrote that *you* were scared when the rabbi mentioned Ludwig Stein, and I didn't dare utter the great fear that held my fingers guiding the pen. . . . This morning, the fear went on unraveling, like a dim shadow, *Krstein* . . . once again pops up before me, in the corner of the kitchen, in the gloom of the bathroom, *Krstein* . . .

How sharp is the fear that gnaws the shelter of webs I have woven around me. As if Stein will come here before the end and undo everything. So illogical! After all, there's less than a month left, and why should he suddenly arrive?

Judge me, O God, and plead my cause, deliver me from the deceitful and unjust man. For thou art the God of my strength. (Even the prayer is only lip service—all my acts are deceitful lies.)

Ludwig Stein—Ludwig Steinnn— A shadow drops like waves of a disease, the cawing of a crow heralding disaster, *Krstein, Krstein.* The name is bound up with bitter altercations among crates of vegetables, with Mother's face blazing like a tiny bird's, attacking until she can't shriek anymore, with Father's gray face stubbornly pecking out the hard, bony syllables, *Krstein, Krstein, Stein, Tein.* And the little girl hiding behind the crates in a wool skirt, her knees scratched, bloody even, because of the *Krstein, Krstein, Tein,* for they quickly cover with shouts the black pit they always hide so she won't see in the store, *Krstein,* because they want to do something awfully painful there like a razor blade with the black shouts that enter her belly, but it's not her fault that her knees are scratched because they let them out of kindergarten early because the teacher was sick so she ran fast with all her might on the sidewalks with the crooked paving stones and the thin trees closed in cages, and her heart was pounding with fear that she wouldn't find the way, until finally all of a sudden she did find the store, and she quickly hid in the corner full of rotten vegetables behind the crates with the sharp tin strips that hurt her by scratching her knees because of the bad shouts, *Krsh Krsh Krshtein Tein Tein Tein.* For something awful happened, *Eiiiin Eiiiin,* Father will surely leave them forever, and Mother won't ever want to see her again, because of the Stein that she did. They are fighting over how exactly they'll hide her in their black pit, because they never wanted her to be at all, because of the Krstein. But she wouldn't let them, even though her heart was beating so hard. She knows you have to whisper fast and with all your might, *appapatz appapatz appapatz,* because as long as she hits in the *appapatz,* Kirshtein won't be able to push her into the black pit in the floor of the shop, and if she hits him hard maybe she can even finish with him in the *appapatz*—until a pile of crates fell down and the vegetables spilled on the floor of the shop, and she started crying at the upturned faces of Father and Mother with their staring eyes and defensive looks. No, she didn't believe a thing they said, even if that really wasn't on purpose, not on purpose, and later at night, she rubbed her pillow with all her might and tucked in the blanket tight on all sides so nothing of the Krstein could get in in the dark.

And afterward (the hand writes but I no longer control what is written; only fear guides it) Mother's burning face sank into the whiteness of the sheets and the cases of the big feather pillows, and she didn't leave the bedroom with the medicine smells that crept into the other rooms, stuck to the plaster, to the steam rising from the pots. Until that afternoon when the quiet of the house was shattered, when Father was lying in the armchair in the living room and she had closed the door of her room.

Suddenly a persistent ringing was heard, and at the door stood a short man in a white suit holding a white hat in his hand, and he said he came from New York. She opened her door a crack and peeped out, because awful shouts had begun in the vestibule, and she just managed to see the back of a neck and a small hand quickly wiping the shining head with a big handkerchief. But when the shouts grew louder, she closed the door completely, just in case, and heard only how the doors all around were being opened and closed, and she was afraid they would burst into her room, even though she indicated by locking the bolt that she wasn't guilty, but she really did lie, and that afternoon she hadn't folded the laundered undershirts back in the drawer. But after a moment passed and they didn't come near her room, she opened the bolt again, and just then, Mother's messy white robe passed by as she got out of bed with her arms stretched out and, with all the savagery of her weakness, tried to block Father's running. She was afraid they would finally remember that she really was guilty, otherwise she would have laughed because the little man in the white suit was now holding Mother's unbuttoned robe as if he were a small boy afraid of Father's black hands rising above him. And she laughed, quietly. As always, she jammed her fist into her mouth and laughed silently, because now it was clear that they didn't see that she had stuffed the wrinkled undershirts in the closet and they put all the blame on the little man and they shouted like they did then in the shop, *Krstein! Stein!* And finally Father pushed Mother away from the door and grabbed the man with the white jacket, who held on to his hat the whole time, and pushed him out to the staircase. And then she even had the courage to come out of the room and peep outside at Father still shouting after the man, who was running down the stairs, and Mother right behind him, holding on to his shoulders, and the whole thing evoked deep, black echoes, like once when she had shouted into a big concrete box standing in the field and they said, You mustn't get close to it because it is left from the war and could blow up, but she climbed on the iron ladder and peeped down into the black opening with the bad smell of shit, and shouted into it, but afterward she rushed down and ran away with all her might because the box shouted after her with strong bursts, *oooohhhhh ooooohhhh,* and now she ran to the door to shout at Father and Mother to stop looking into the black, smelly hole, and to run home fast before the stairs killed them. But then the echoes *Eiiiin Eiiiin* stopped, and Father helped Mother stand up from the iron banister, and held her by the shoulders as if she were a little girl, and her face was so white and his face was so black. And she fled inside and closed the door except for a narrow strip you don't see to peep at Father returning the fluttering robe about the drooping shoulders to the bedroom to the white cloud of pillowcases and the soft hills of feathers, where the little face was swallowed up, and he still croaked quietly with a black face, *Stein Stein*—

A few days later, when she came home and Father wasn't there, she looked into the bedroom and saw that Mother was sleeping, and she tiptoed in and saw how two feathers from the pillow were jumping on the sleeping face, sticking to and moving away from the breathing nostrils. The small dance of the little feathers was so funny she started quacking, quietly at first and then with all kinds of thin sounds of twittering and whistling, *cheep cheep cha, cheep cheep cha,* to tickle the cheeks on the pillow as the feathers did. Until from so many caresses, Mother really did open her eyes in the white down pillow and smiled at her. And then more bleating and twittering were released from her and she hopped back and forth around the bed, her elbows stuck up and waving in a funny way, as they had learned in kindergarten to do the bird dance, and at the height of the spinning, she chirped like the bird in the white hat, *Shta Shtei, Shta Shtei, Shta Stein,* and Mother got mad for a minute and then she laughed too, and she buried the cackles of laughter in the softness of the feathers, and Mother's light head twitched above her. Mother plucked feathers out of the pillow and braided them in her hair, made her a crown of white feathers.

(On the Sabbath, when I came to their house on the hill, Fayge opened the door with a smiling face and hopped around me. "Amalia, you must have come to us by the shortcut and not on the road!"

I was amazed that she knew—after all, she didn't usually keep tabs on those who came, but she went on laughing with a childish mischievousness, sat me down on the big chair, and with her small hand picked the dry fruits that had been plucked out of the bushes and clung to the fabric of my shirt.

"Here, here, you brought the path with you." She held out her hand full of straw feathers. At that moment Rabbi Tuvia entered in his soft houseslippers, and he leaned over, looked at the handful, and smiled.)

I stopped for a long time.

Writing doesn't relieve—on the contrary. The dark fear, paralyzing the body, permeating the words. And the yearning music climbing up from the valley, still—let it stop! The bleating of the lute slice and slip down into the desert, as if I were already scattered dust. Always beside things, not daring to go all the way. Running away. Changing names. Evading. Never daring to go all the way. Not even now. Not even in the vow I swore to You. Not even in the effort to confess, so ridiculous, feeble.

And yet you will go on—against your will! *For against your will are you born, and against your will do you live.*

Only years later, when the two of them, Father and Amalia, were alone, did the black shout, *Steeiiin,* come back. Father would close himself for days in the bedroom where the green shades were always drawn. He didn't play anymore, just listened, bent over the old phonograph, putting on and taking off records with his stiff fingers. That afternoon, when she entered the gloomy room to bring him his cup of tea, he suddenly stopped the record and turned his head to her. Because his eyes were weak, there was an enormous concentration in his look, he didn't have to speak her name for her to shake from the direct address of the look— for by then she was Amy, and in smoke-filled clubs on the beach she would accompany herself on the guitar, her small, limited voice, rising to the edge of its ability in yearnings of foreign folksongs, bursting out, and hiding behind the waist-length screen of hair.

"I want you to write something down, Malinka. Here, I've prepared pen and paper for you. I want to give you Stein's address in New York . . ." He spoke slowly, making an effort to utter the isolated words. "If you ever need help."

"I'll never call him!" In an exploding voice, she cut the texture of the silence in the dark room. "I told you, I don't want any contact with your past, no contact, you understand? I don't want to know anything!" She tossed the pen and paper on the low dresser whose drawers still harbored the smell of Mother's old medicine and lipsticks, she swung the cascade of hair with her harsh angular movements, and yet she didn't budge as long as Father didn't take his eyes off her and his skinny chin still thrust at her.

"If you ever need help and I'm not here . . . ," he went on in that slowness, reciting the New York address and telephone number of Ludwig Stein.

"You're wasting your breath. I tell you, I will never call him. And if you want to know something, I'll just run away from all that as far as I can."

". . . because you have to know how to go on living," he concluded without acknowledging her anger, and now he was moving the disc and putting the arm and the needle carefully on the edge of the record; a Beethoven sonata for violin and piano was heard and he was nodding as in amazement. "Yes, you've got to know how to go on living."

He was surrounded by the notes. And she went out, slamming the door dramatically behind her, though there was no need for that, and right away she was sorry she had hurt his impaired hearing, and the telephone number and address in New York were seared in her. Of course.

And what was that whole attempt to flee, to cut off connections, to change the name, *Amalia, Amy, Emily,* to change place, to sink into the fog of smoking in the Village apartment, on mattresses covered with Indian fabrics, and the bodies blurred with incense and groping, bare feet, hair? Yes, and the photography—a new refuge—with that effort to go all the way. That series, "Photographs of the Inside." Inside courtyards, inside trains, inside sewers, and the printing in high contrast of inside the face. Those awful enlargements of her features. The corner of a bloodshot eye, the caverns of the nose, the cracks between the toes, everything that made such a hit in New York. And what was that whole wretched attempt to go all the way, to flee, since after all, she did call? Of course. At the end of the night, which was neither night nor day. When she was already deep in the whiteness. The dimness. In spite of (or maybe because of) the success. On the day after, she called. From a phone booth in the street. On a morning that was turning gray into the turgid darkness of filthy snow. Outside, her partners on the last trip were waiting. She promised she'd get some more money. Their skinny limbs were jumping

up and down in the cold. They were sticking their faces to the walls of
the phone booth. Their noses were flattened against the glass.

Of course she called. After all, the name was tattooed on her flesh. *The
end of all flesh is come before me.* Billows of judgment inundate the world,
darken the eye of the sun, gnaw the flesh like hordes of locusts. And what
good are my isolated blows in the hollow tin tank? Scared prattle dulls the
empty space of the world. *God of my refuge, why have you abandoned me?*

(The music there, among the huts, stopped. At long last! To creep on
all fours and go on. Out of the choking.)

"Yes, Amalia—sorry, Amy dear, I'm so happy you called, I've been waiting so long for you to call me." Stein's excited, unctuous voice struck the
eardrum with its foreign accent. "Yes, yes, right away, today, this afternoon, Amy deearrrrrrrr."

And she meets him. Of course. Doesn't evade, doesn't make him
wait, as she is capable of doing, without the end of a thread, goes despite
the nausea, in the leather miniskirt she hurls at him, as if, with her young
flesh, to take his mind off the real reason for the meeting.

She sits across from him in the gleaming restaurant in the reflection of
the mirrors picking out her image and shooting it back and forth. The
skin of her thighs rubs against the leather of the bench. Spots of light
spread from beneath the leather lampshades onto the copper table, leather
padding on the walls. The dishes are set before her and removed with dis-
dain, and she stares at the round, shining face that is strange and familiar at the same time, and at the short hands that hastily wipe the face
with a crumpled handkerchief, withdraw in bursts of excitement; drop
onto her own hand, and again clutch the handkerchief, rise to the trembling bags of skin around the eyes.

"Amalia—sorry, Amy, that's what you said, Amy, isn't it? You
changed your name, eh? I remember you from a little girl; now you're all
grown up. Yes, yes. I'm glad you called. Yes, I know you're in New York.
Of course. Been keeping track of you all the time, heh heh. I paid for
your studies, too. Surprised? No need, I arranged for them to send to
Stashek after Ruzia died, from the scholarships of . . . Yes, now you're a
photographer, eh? Fine. Fine. Fine profession. I went to the exhibit."

The shrill voice. With no connection to the movements of the hands dancing on the table, to the body jerking on the leather bench, only the pinpoints of his eyes examining her, passing over her low-cut sweater, seeing and not seeing.

"Yes, yes, I've been waiting all the time for you to call, after all, I'm almost a close relative. Ha, ha, closer than a close relative, right? Always close to Mala, Mala, ah, Mala . . ." His fingers rubbed her hand like a wet sponge.

"Ah, she had a legendary talent, something unique. My whole life is listening to her talent, following Mala to every concert. Always in a different hotel. I didn't want to get between Stashek and her, not at all! Just to buy a ticket in the first row, for her playing. In the end, she couldn't play if I wasn't sitting in the first row, ah. I saw her look for me in Kattowice when I couldn't get a seat in the first row, ahhhh. I saw, I saw." He leans toward her, and the light is dazzling on his floating head.

"I remember in thirty-nine. Back in August, the last moment. A recital in Zakopane, Mala Auerbach for the people in the summer resort. Maybe the most excellent. Schumann, Kreisleriana . . . She was Stashek's wife by then. Maybe the joy of a young bride. Maybe she had a premonition of what would come. Ah . . . That's what was in my head when they took them, the bastards, in the *Aktsia*. Back in the ghetto they took them. Mother . . . and Shmulke . . . In my head, I hear Mala's playing, Kreisleriana. The weeping of the music, pieces and pieces. Like that, like that!" His hand flutters over hers.

"You can understand that, you can understand, yes, you can. You. And Ruzia, too, your mother, she understood it. So what?! So what?! How can you judge a human being like that and throw him down the stairs like a dog?! You don't do that, no, that's not how you behave! So what if I was lucky and managed to sell the gold in time and to buy Aryan papers. So what? I came and I offered to her. That's how it is, one day one person gets lucky and another day somebody else, and all of a sudden you think you're king and you can ask the whole world for whatever you want. Fine, so I proposed to her to marry me and we'd go away. So what? She could have been saved, and I would have worked something out for Stashek, too, I prepared papers. But she, with her pride, she says she won't never take nothing from me. Yes, that's what

she said. That she'd never take nothing. Because of her pride, ah ah. So
what if for one day a person thinks he can ask for anything? That says
he's got no pride, he's got no love? Ruzia always understood that, Ruzia
understood what love is. She also loved Stashek, but he never loved
her—he never left Mala, never left Mala. . . ."

He grabs her wrist, his head ducks between the lapels of his gleaming
suit, and he whispers, assails, pleads, "It can't be that she won't be anymore, you understand? Can't be! With beauty like hers, only angels are
born; they must not succeed in killing her memory, you understand!"

His head bows down to the copper tabletop and his eyes are fixed on
the throb of her breathing, quickening in the low-necked sweater, "Amy
dear, it's you, only you can bring Malinka back to us. I've thought of
everything. You're a photographer, right? So you go photograph all the
places of her life and concerts, and photograph all the material that remains, documents, announcements, for an album. Yes, yes. You. You of
all people! Understand? Understand? That's symbolic. Vengeance. It's
you, yes, you. You'll do it, right? For love you'll do it. Right? You know
how Stashek loves Mala. You know. And I'm paying for everything—
travel, work, everything. Publish an album for Mala—I, Stein, am making a memory of Mala that nobody will ever erase."

He tosses his wallet out on the polished copper tabletop, the leather
shell sparkles, and he empties its innards, thrusts the bills at her. "That's
for you! For whatever you want, Amy dear, whatever you want. You're
doing it, right? Not for me, for Mala, Stashek's great love. He told you
to call me, right? That's why you called, right? Tell me. Stashek sent you
to Stein, right! He knows that Stein never forgets Mala. Stashek knows."

He pushes the bills tossed like a broken fan, his body stretched taut
across the table. "You, our second Malinka, you'll bring Mala back to
us! You!"

She withdraws, stands up, and he follows her. He sticks the bills into
the cleft of her low-cut sweater and the warmth of his hand sinks into her
flesh. "You'll call me when you make a decision, you'll call me, Amy
dear." He pastes his lips to her neck in a burst of gratitude, and a shudder seems to suck the moisture out of her spine, and, with loathing, she
slips out between the leather sofas and the mirrors, and he follows her

gasping, excited. "Call me, Amy, Amy dear." He observes her flight with the pinpoints of his eyes, until the doorway finally splits into the vertigo of the city's roofs hovering in the fog in the smells of food and melted butter, and the bills rustling next to her heart.

And she did call. Of course. Could she do otherwise? So how could Isaiah's light weight anchor you? Hold on to you through the old gale that rose from Stein's name. With what mad outburst of faith did you dare to hope?

And I, what did I think? That by virtue of the offer of my life woven out to You I'd be able to find rest? In the refuge of silence in the arched room, in the smell of plaster, and in the rustle of the threads stretched for the Torah Curtain? For he will come, he will surely come here by the fortieth day to claim his debt. Certainly he'll come. He won't let go.

All day I sat and gazed out the window and retched waves of bile, creeping on the peaks, sinking to the desert. Everything is so senseless. This whole wretched attempt to weave the soul with the offering of the Torah Curtain. To spin repair from the fat of the heart. Fear hypnotizes like the sparkling residue of an insect suspended in the heart of webs, biting and defiling the heart of the Torah Curtain's warp.

The photos are still with me. Here, in the closet. Big orange boxes, stinking of acid and dust. The pictures of Mala, Stein's property. To pretend the torments of repentance, and in fact I fled like a thief to the yeshiva straight from the airport, and hid all the material in the closet of the room shared with Elisheva. To believe in panic that if her face is cut off, if it is forgotten, there will finally be redemption. Blood for blood. Life in her death . . .

They're still here. I drag them with me from one closet to another. Unable to detach myself. Like the high priest who enters the Holy of Holies on Yom Kippur with a rope tied to his ankle, so that if he falls dead behind the Torah Curtain, his body can be dragged out from holiness to defilement.

Indeed, even now, I am not brave enough to open everything— Even now I dread confessing all the deeds to the very end— Even now there is not enough faith in me.

———

The light rises in the eastern window. Maybe it is nothing but a flash of the moon leaving late, and because of it, they mistakenly remove the daily offering to the fire before its time. And yet, the light brings a kind of consolation. As if the gray-pink crown that clamps the hills is crumbling the gales of night, stopping the hurling of the heavy basin that shakes me, the city, and all who dwell in it. Now the whole city is a revolving eyeball lighting with the sunrise. A mirror of sparkling, gurgling water. In the window the crater of light trembles in deep streams, floods the depths of the graying valley. Night leaves only extinguished cinders of excitement on the eyelids.

Why art thou cast down, O my soul? And why art thou disquieted in me? Hope thou in God: for I shall yet praise Him for the help of His countenance, for I shall yet sanctify myself, I shall yet purify in the light of the Counting that rises in its course

(And even if the sudden tranquility is nothing but the weight of fatigue—there is no way back. And all day long I shall pull the thread. I shall weave around myself the webs of the Torah Curtain. Even if all things are nothing but the last gasps of someone who has lost his mind and his way in the sand.

Let my soul be like dust to everyone.)

Seventeen days, which is two weeks and three days of

the Omer. Beauty of Beauty. Glory and Beauty to

Everlasting Life, Valor and Humility to Everlasting

Life, Dominion and Rule to Everlasting Life.

(Wonderful how at times I am filled, body and soul, with a great feeling of mission, *in mine heart as a burning fire shut up in my bones.* Otherwise, how should I interpret the strengthening this morning, after the weakness of last night; the haste that encouraged me from dawn to pull for long hours the flickering bodies of threads, their fleshy lengths, and then to cover the loom with the Torah Curtain and release the pages from their binding? A profound tranquility surrounds me. The night of Beauty of Beauty, a night without a moon, and yet all is illuminated as if the light of the moon were as the light of the sun, and the light of the sun as the light of the seven days of Creation.)

Everlasting Life, give my share with Your observers, with full heart.

Outside the hedge behind Rabbi Gothelf's house, you rolled up your skirt a little, and with tentative steps, you began going down among the rocks of the slope. It couldn't be that you decided deliberately to take the long way back from the rabbi's house on foot, but because of weakness, you didn't seek a passage between the buildings to the bus stop. Or perhaps, unwittingly, you were guided by a longing to pin your hopes on walking from one side of the city to the other—from the damp gardens on one side to the aridity of the desert on the other—so that the winding roads of the city would be spread out at your feet, like an enormous scroll of prophecy, the paths of your future. Or perhaps it was nothing but the pungent air of the spring night that made your nerves dizzy. Whatever it was, between the conversation with Rabbi Gothelf and your date to meet Isaiah, there was still an abyss where you rambled on your own. So you swung your shawl around your shoulders in the dark, going deeper down the slope into that sheltered respite. The path quickly departed from the neighborhood buildings. Up the side of the mountain climbed a tangle of thorns, and a dull rustle rose from the vegetation at the bottom of the valley. The hem of your skirt trailed in the descent, and despite your caution, got stuck in the arms of the thistles.

From the fence of the groves, barbed wire rose up. You went around it, looking for the trampled path, and the whipping of the branches sent a dark shudder through your flesh. You made your way through the foliage toward the barren field on the border of the groves. There, between the slopes open to the night, a faint wailing roamed. For a moment it disappeared and then came back in distant echoes, dragging behind it smells of cinders and pollen. You quickly picked up the ends of your shawl, and words of prayer dropped from your mouth. At the bend in the road beyond the rocks, cars passed by and their sound grew weak. You were terrified lest your flaws bring disunion and pain in Heaven. *A voice was heard in Ramah, lamentation, a sound of bitter weeping from blessed Zion.*

You went farther down, your sandals filling with pods and thorns and dirt. The flight of the cars struck you over and over, and you didn't gather your undone hair, you just stared, trying in the dark to distinguish between the jagged rocks and the shadows.

Now the distant voice seemed to spread from one end of the world to the other, drawn to your walking down the slopes. As night came on, the cold breezes died down and in the milky darkness the summer airs sprang up. To calm down, you repeated to yourself the last words the rabbi had said to you before you left, and indeed you were almost strengthened. As if there really is a repentance of love. *Too long have you dwelt in the valley of weeping, arise and depart from amid the upheaval.* Never had the forces of repentance and love seemed so penetrated by each other. With relief, you abandoned yourself to the warm coolness and hastened your steps—for now, with the sustaining power of love, everything would be forgiven you, everything would be forgiven! You almost laughed. *Don't You know everything that is hidden and everything that is revealed, You know the mysteries of the world and the secrets of all life, and what shall I cover before You? Nothing is concealed from You and nothing is hidden from Your eyes.* You burst out of the valley, scattering hard grains of dirt, quickly crossed the dark space that stood up to the trees of the neighborhood in the distance. And you yearned with all your soul that the time of the meeting with Isaiah would come.

Meanwhile, your feet crossed the deserted street at the top of the hill at the foot of the cypresses. At your side, with a light, sure step, strode Mala. From her slightly parted lips, very close to your cheek, came a humming, open and covered in turn, to the movement of her hair flying with the swing of the stride. From the coolness of the strange gardens, the sound of roaring echoed. *There is no love without repentance, and there is no repentance without the blood, and her flesh is watered by the blood!* You wavered a moment in the maze of the neighborhood, for in the root of things *she* is stamped, *she* who is formed of dirt. Your shadow struck the cypresses that thrust their fingernails into the swarming of the stars. The lively harmony of her limbs moving in the walk bewitched you with a soft pleasantness. In your belly spread the solidity of her pelvis, the shifting of her groin rubbed against your steps, and her breathing nostrils glided over your temple.

You were carried together in a quick pace, the echo of your joined footsteps ringing on the street. And next to the sidewalks, the buildings seemed to recoil at the sight of the odd couple passing by. As in a dream, you raised your hand to push away the tendrils of her hair stuck to your cheeks. The sound of lamentation rose from the roofs, split, and faded away in the streets that disappeared on the hilltop.

The street was lopped off by a vacant lot. Despite the danger, you decided to take the dark shortcut. Tin cans and mounds of stones made a hollow echo under your feet, and the sediment of fear only deepened the pleasure of her body inside yours. For a moment a bizarre laugh hovered on your lips. You recalled how Stein had sent you after her—a dark gourd rustled. You jumped, choked with laughter at the memory of his contorted face as he ran, waving his hands, not knowing that it was *in you* that he had to look for her—wasn't it the two of you, one bound up in the other, who would now be Isaiah's mate! You stumbled among the junk, and your body melted in the awful embrace joining her and you in a supreme mating of love.

In that state, you came to the main street. A bitter, hot breeze struck your hair. A truck accelerated, filling the silence with the clanking rods of its load and tarpaulins. You walked on the edges of the sidewalk to the intersection, your legs bent with her heavy load. You barely managed to squeeze between the trunks of the carob trees; their protruding, twisted roots almost blocked the whole sidewalk. And suddenly you were filled with shame at the sight of the two of you prominent in the streetlamps—for only by deceit did she come back and push into you, only with her charms did she lead you astray—and over and over you hastily wiped away her curl stuck to your forehead. You quickened your pace up the street, almost running to the traffic signals at the intersection, into the weeping that now rang very loudly from the roofs in the whipping of the hot air. You broke out ahead, shouting mutely, *To change his name and always shouting to HaShem, to God, I am a different person and I am not the same one who sinned! I am a different person and I am not the same one who sinned!* But the traffic signals only smeared the streets with their yellow stammer, like an evasive oracle accusing the intentional smokescreen for the eclipse, refusing to disclose anything beyond the one indifferent flickering.

Now you crossed the invisible border of the watershed separating the slopes of the city to the west and the east. From the bottom of the valley climbed the dry, grainy breeze of the lapping desert. Your scratchy breathing calmed as the street leaned toward the silence, and your feet walked a bit more strongly. Her body separated from your body, and she hovered, her head in your head, her hair bound up in your hair. She trailed behind you weightless as a kite, floating and striking, in a hush. The lamenting voice grew faint, as if its echoes remained on the damp slopes in the west, and here, beyond the flank of the mountain, cascades of loess began to hush it. The steep street slipped away under your stride with the surprising speed of the first time, and you went through the brittle strata of the smell of rosemary bushes and honeysuckle, and the olive trees tottered like drunks in front of you.

You went up the steep dirt road around the mountain. Your nostrils stirred at the familiar roasted dryness on the way to your house, which was always enough to restore you. Her body broke off its connection with you, as two lobes of a fertilized cell finally break apart in their division. In one moment, the shadow of the big body fell over your shadow, and in the next moment, it was gliding away and you were hurrying with a liberated body to the steep road, overlooking the abyss yawning there as to a secret concealed only with you. Here, beyond the wall of the mountain, on the dark side of the city, it seemed you could go on without being disturbed. The stream began again in your body. You hurried, inhaling the stimulating, singed air. Isaiah's thin, fair face rose up to you from the spots of the little photo. You leaned your head back like a mare covered with foam, breathed with your mouth gaping open— *Enter in peace, O crown of her husband, enter, O Bride, enter, O Bride . . .*

And you didn't have time to see clearly the shining face. You already stood on the steps of the entrance, and with hovering fingers, you opened the iron lock.

In the house, you were greeted by the sweetness of the wool of the prayer shawls pouring from the arms of the loom, lying on the floor in gigantic rings of warp. In silence, you took off your clothes, and with filthy feet, you got into bed.

But the dizziness didn't subside. Now there was an upheaval of softness in your belly, sliding and going down your neck, undoing your hair. Your hand groped for the prayer book and didn't find it, and you sat up in panic, afraid that the prayer had slipped away from you. You got up barefoot and ran to the window to immerse your head in the night breeze. But the taps of dryness only stuck the thin nightgown even more to your trembling. And then, to your horror, it seemed that above the valley, where the darkness always split, an upright mountain rose as a white wall and in its center a crack was breaking through, and cleaving, half of it toward the north and half of it toward the south. You grasped the windowsill with both hands, and before your eyes the mountain went on cleaving in silence, its two parts shifting, coming apart from each other, and between them a disk was unsheathed, and over it a kind of countenance slowly rose in dazzling white.

You fell onto the mattress and wrapped yourself in the sheet, hiding your eyes. *May it be Your will, our God and the God of our forefathers, to save me from Satan and from evil persons. You tried to remove the defilement. Master of the Universe, I hereby forgive anyone who has sinned against me, whether against my body or my honor, whether he did so accidentally or willfully, whether in this transmigration or another transmigration . . .* But your head was drawn out of the sheet to the glow in the window, and you could no longer stop the yearning. Your limbs were enveloped in Mala's breathing, and against the thin nightgown, the heartbeats accelerated, yours and hers. In the heart of pleasure, a fear of what was to come sliced through you for a moment, *May it be Your will, may no man be punished because of me, may no man be punished because of me.* But despite the dread of sin, you submitted with whitened eyes to the tremor of sweetness, *May Michael be at my right, Gabriel at my left, Uriel before me, and Raphael behind me, and above my head the Presence of God . . .*

That night, too, you fell asleep with the lamp burning at your head. Waking in panic, the sheets seething, your hair on the pillow bathed in sweat, and the pages of *The Laws of Repentance* you had dragged to bed with you squashed and bent out of shape. And once again you were swallowed up in sleep, swept up between the solace of the dark and the bright eyeball shining in the window.

Yes, when you returned trembling from the window, you thought for a moment of going out immediately, on foot, to the Mount of Olives opposite and, gathering holy dirt among the graves—maybe the beam of light burst out of them—to scatter it in your hair in the custom of mourning. For a moment you believed that thus you would make a tombstone for Mala, a holy repair for her soul, but in the heart of dizziness, the thought evaporated. And now it is clear that if you had relented then, you would have spared great suffering. How did you not understand why she had come into your body? How did you not understand what repentance *you had* to do? You were drawn to your flesh, to the glow in the window, as if you would truly have repentance of love. . . .

(I lifted the linen cloth I spread every evening over the weaving when I get up from the stool to distinguish between the acts of the day and the night. I couldn't help it anymore, the memory of the smell of silk and gold dust stimulated me so much, for a long time I looked at the sparkle of the holy letters woven in the sheet, at the flowers embroidered on the brocade folds, flickering in filaments of gold and purple. The touch of the smooth silk on the cheeks. The cool sweet smell on the face buried in the piece of fabric for a long time . . .)

And I? How shall I dare to think after what was done or to weep for the beauty that withered in the dirt?

And what should I have done? Burned Isaiah's love as an offering instead of mine, as you wanted to do in the secrecy of your heart? A burnt offering, pangs of love? *For I have no pleasure in the death of him that dieth, saith the Lord God; wherefore turn yourselves, and live ye. For will you wait for him until the day of his death?*

There is nothing left now but to go on, to go on and finish in holiness. To You, God of mercy, to You Who will requite a man according to his deed.

May it be Your will, my God and God of my forefathers, that by virtue of the confession of truth that I have made to You of my evil spirit and my uncleanness, may abundant mercy flow in all the worlds and spread a canopy of holy peace over us and over all Israel, a canopy of peace interwoven and flickering with holiness.

(Another thirty-two days is left of the Omer Counting. Another thirty-two degrees to complete the sheet.)

Eighteen days of the Omer.

The next days passed dizzily for you. For long hours you didn't budge
from weaving the prayer shawl attached to the loom like a sail clinging
to a wrecked raft. You lost track of the days. At times it seemed an eternity since that night in Rabbi Gothelf's neighborhood, and at times you
thought you wouldn't have the strength to last to the night of Eternity
of Eternity, when you were to meet Isaiah. Once or twice you panicked,
as if the meeting was that evening, and one night the memory of the split
mountain transfixed you, and the vision once again cut your eyes with its
gleaming light.

And in all those days you didn't leave the house, except for a dis-
tracted trip to the local grocery store at the bottom of the alley, embarrassed in front of the Arab shopkeeper because you forgot what you had
come to buy, going back up the muddy stairs empty-handed. You ate little, didn't feel hunger, motivated by only one longing: to finish weaving
the first holy prayer shawl before the meeting. For long hours you bent
forward, then straightened up, fastening the waves of wool smashed at
the back of the loom, dozens of times you wove and again released the
rows of blue and white, winding the wool on the tongues of the shuttles,
counting the threads opening wide with the press of the treadle and firm-
ing the leaping strings. With all your might you strove to complete
the first prayer shawl, a view of Ancient Adam of the Divinity, a canopy
of pure sky, with all your might, with swollen shoulders, with a humble
spirit. But you didn't finish before the night of the first meeting.

That afternoon, you decided with sudden terror that, in any case, you
had to practice tying fringes. You found a remnant of fabric with an un-
stitched edge, and started bending the strands of wool, trying to press
them in a knot. You bent over the strip of shriveled cloth on your knees,
checking in the Code of Jewish Law the instructions for tying the thirty-

nine knots and the shape of tassels of the prayer shawl on the forehead of the man with black curly hair portrayed in the bold type. The flap of fabric trembled in your lap like a fetus, and you wondered if you needed a blessing on the work of training.

When you finally lifted your eyes, the dropping day had tumbled in the arches. You hopped off the stool and the fabric slipped down; only then did you realize that you hadn't yet decided what to wear. For the first time, you noticed that you had been walking around for weeks in the same long skirt and cotton shirt whose cuffs had turned gray, and you hadn't looked at your reflection in the mirror for a long time either. For a moment you didn't remember what face you would have at the meeting.

The darkness thickened abruptly, or maybe despite your frenzy, your movements were slow, because by the time you took off the blouse and started putting on your only dress, the blue one, the lights were already twinkling among the huts in the valley, and in the gloom, part of your bare arm turned white. You clasped the wrist with your hand, to button the sleeves. The touch of the skin struck you with amazement. You went on feeling the wrist, trembling at the speed of the blood throbbing in the veins, until you touched the lump of the old scar.

When you came to, you found yourself in the bathroom. Before you knew what you were doing, you had pulled the old bottle of perfume out of the cabinet, and daubed it, as in the past, on your earlobes, your neck, and your chest down to your breasts. When you recovered, you quickly bowed your head under the stream of water, but the heavy scent only grew stronger. You loosened your hair to cover your neck. Evening was spread in the windows, you had to hurry. You knew that the traces of perfume wouldn't disappear.

I can't go on.

At dusk on the eve of Memorial Day for the fallen Israeli soldiers, the sirens wail. What Rabbi Israel Gothelf calls, twisting his mouth, "neglect of the Torah."

The cool night soaked with dew slides down the slopes, the gravestones. The whole city is one layer after another of graves and dust of the dead crumbling in the dark. City of the dead. Why are the priests not forbidden to enter it? From the plaza of the Wailing Wall an echo surely rises of laments of the repairers sticking their wet weeping to the stones, *they have laid Jerusalem on heeeaps. The dead bodies of thy servants have they given to be meat unto the fowls of heeeaven. The flesh of thy saints unto the beasts of the earth.*

(The echoes of the siren still move in me, stirring dull memories. Suddenly, the warmth of the Tel Aviv beach on a summer night seems to penetrate here. Amy with her hair down to her waist, in a thin tank top on the steaming skin. The handrail of the boardwalk covered with dampness . . . The pain is too sharp. As ever, in my blood sprout death and longing together for the dark fruit of love.)

I can't follow you to that first meeting with Isaiah. I shall stop now.

In Your hand I shall entrust my spirit, O blessed Lord, for in Your hand are the souls of the living and the dead.

Nineteen days of the Omer. Eternity of

Beauty. Eve of Independence Day.

Bursts of fireworks spray from the City Park, illuminating for a moment like daylight the masses of cypresses behind the monastery walls on the ridge opposite, dying out in tails of smoke down in the desert. Over and over, the sparks gush, loaded with roars of merrymakers from the city, slicing the darkness here, flooding the pile of papers with a sudden light.

Tonight I shall go on to the meeting with Isaiah. Last night I didn't have the strength and I stopped writing. When I got up for the Midnight Prayer, the wails of Arab women lamenting at a deathbed seemed to be rising from the huts in the dark valley. Maybe I only imagined it. In the

morning, excitement entangled the routine of weaving, and in the afternoon, the rabbi's wife, Yocheved, came to visit. Suddenly. Without any
announcement. I opened the door for her, wondering who could be
knocking. And she stood there, panting from the walk, her wig covered
with sweat and dust, trembling at the barking of the neighbors' dogs behind the fences.

"Oh, Amalia! Thank God you're home!" She almost sank into my
arms. "I'm so glad! I was afraid you wouldn't be here." Scrambling at my
heels over the sill, wrestling with her limbs in the vestibule. "I happened
to be passing by and decided to drop in for a visit, to say hello, to see how
you are . . . Really, tell me, how are you?"

I led her to the room, ignoring the transparent lie she had told as a pretext for coming; she didn't really "happen" to be going from her neighborhood to the other end of the city, she hadn't resigned from her
household chores, from the steaming food in her shining kitchen, from
the staircase full of children's voices and shouts of the neighbor women,
from the sourness of the scurrying men's black coats, she didn't rise
from her constant bother about keeping the Commandments, the holidays, the meals, the grief of old people, nights of confused sleep between ironing and suckling, when one pain is washed away by other
waves of pain and joy, to "happen" to wander around in the middle of
the day, taking two buses from her neighborhood to mine. Did Rabbi Israel send her to check up? Was something discovered, were folks gos-
siping, did my vigils and fasting stir such signs of concern? Was it Isaiah
who was scared and went to Rabbi Israel to share his worries? Or did
Elisheva question him when he came back and couldn't calm her con-
science, and did she go to Rabbi Gothelf "to tell"? For the rabbi's wife
clearly had been sent especially to find out, to talk with me "woman to
woman." She made her way to the room with her heavy body, a woman
who isn't young, and keeping house and her endless willingness to do
good deeds have made her older than her years. Prattling, embarrassed
as a little girl.

"I'm really sorry, Amalia, that I didn't tell you I was coming. I'm not
disturbing you in your work, am I? I had a little time today, you know;
they're keeping the girls in school longer, ethics lessons, teaching, more
tests, so they won't be walking around the streets during the ceremonies

of the free-thinkers who evoke the memory of the dead without fear of God. So I had a little free time. You can't imagine how many people are in the city. All the streets are full of their commotion in the middle of the Counting. And on the way, the siren suddenly sounded and the bus stood still. I was scared that something had happened, God forbid!"

The remnant of rage at her visit dissolved in me at the sight of her open face, of her wiping the sweat off the part of her forehead that emerged from under her wig, as if she, Yocheved, had been infected with the fever of the street.

"Would you like something to drink?"

"Yes, yes, thanks, something cold if you have it."

I went to bring the china pitcher from the set, crossing the room, which, up to now, except for me, only Isaiah with his thin body had crossed.

"I'm sorry, all I've got is water."

"Yes, I know you don't drink anything else," the rabbi's wife replied behind me. She realized immediately that she had given away something she had overheard, and she quickly muttered: "Water is the most quenching beverage, thanks a lot."

When I poured it for her, clutching the neck of the pitcher, the rabbi's wife quickly whispered the blessing *through Whose word everything came to be*. She sipped compulsively, her face flushed, blinking at the ridge in the wide-open windows, and the glass in her hand trembled.

"What a marvelous view! Thank God we've got a wonderful land, truly wonderful!"

"Yes," I quickly agreed, and fearing that in her excitement she would force me to go out for a walk with her right then, I added: "Beautiful, but a little far, and the neighbors . . ."

"Right." Her excitement subsided. "It actually was a long trip, and really, thank God you're home! Just imagine if I had come this far right when you went out to take care of some business." Suddenly she shook herself, as if she recalled the purpose of her mission. "Tell me, Amalia, how do you get along all by yourself? You don't need any help, do you?"

"No, no, there's no need," I said casually. "Thank you."

She groaned and added, ostensibly without any connection to her earlier words, "So what will become of you now, Amalia? Eh, what will become of you, with the help of God?"

A silence fell. Yocheved's broad body wavered in the space between the desk and the trembling blue, taut on the loom. All at once, I couldn't bear her presence, the awkward invasion into my life. I withdrew to the loom, as if to take refuge, not realizing what the movement would lead to. The body of the rabbi's wife dragged along as in a trance at my heels. I tried quickly to cover the exposed warp, but at that hour, puddles of sunlight retreating from the eastern window fell on the taut silk threads, flooding the whole room with a blue haze.

"Oh, here's the weaving!" The rabbi's wife was drawn, fascinated, to the sight. And she had already taken the threads of the warp in her thick hand, whose swelling was cruelly visible. "No, no, don't close it, Amalia. Let me see . . . How beautiful! God be praised!"

She bent over the lines of threads rubbing in the teeth of the beater, sinking to the solid sheet of blue, shaking her head. "I never saw such a machine! Show me how it works, Amalia, show me, please?"

I was nauseous. The blurriness of the morning, the depression that had lain since last night on my failure to release the thread of your meeting from the coil, a failure to repair the body and the soul, a failure of repentance . . . And now this coarse rummaging in the last realm of holiness I still had left . . .

I sank down on the stool, perhaps only to get away from the rabbi's wife, who stood over me, not noticing what I was going through. I lowered my eyes and mechanically moved the shuttle with the last, green, woof thread I had threaded before I heard the knocking. I tightened the beater, stretching my arms and bending my back, shifting it from the top of the warp to a dull touch of the rim of the woof. The habitual movement eased my distress for a moment.

"What wonderful hands you've got, Amalia, a real virtuous woman!" The rabbi's wife thrust her face into mine and her breathing was fervid. She went on with that awful directness, "Really, Amalia, I'm so terribly unhappy about how that turned out. You and Isaiah were a good couple, made in Heaven. Yes, really. To this day it's hard for me to understand why it turned out like that. . . ."

I seemed to be bound with damp cables to the warp beam, her words slapping my face. (No one had talked to me like that since it happened. No one had uttered such things, so simply, in my ear. And maybe the most awful thing was that the rabbi's wife spoke in the past tense, that, for others, what had been between me and Isaiah was in the past. . . .)

The pain was so intense that I leaned forward, both my feet pressing the treadles, automatically working the machinery of the loom. The warp eyes gaped, whipped up and down, and the thousands of threads turned over and collapsed. Yocheved flinched, and giggled in panic. "Oh, Amalia!" She bent down impulsively with a strange excitement. "Open what is rolled up, Amalia, I want to see the Torah Curtain . . ." Her full body stooped over the threads, and to keep from getting pushed with the whip of the warp again, she clutched the mounds of gold rising in the silk. "I'll help you open it, Amalia, I'll help you."

I almost raised my hand to push the rabbi's wife away. Her bending so close increased my choking. But suddenly, it was as if I longed to inflame the pain, to deepen it unbearably, until the wound that was healed would bleed again, as at first. And so, as if I were complying with her request, I turned to the back of the loom, and started releasing the rolled-up Torah Curtain.

(Yes, only ostensibly did I submit to Yocheved . . . In fact it was another compulsion that commanded me to open the bindings of the Torah Curtain, which I had woven so far without looking back. It was I who had infected Yocheved with my commotion, which had flung me about ever since I had abandoned the confession last night, I who kindled in her the strange fire, the yearning to look, without her knowing. By Your order. I incited the rabbi's wife—who was exhausted from traveling, from trampling in the dust—so I could derive from her solidity the strength for my repentance. Like an infant sucking vitality, I drew Yocheved's breast to me. By Your order.

For wasn't it only on Your mission that she came here? And if she hadn't bent over me, clasping the warp, if she hadn't awakened the pain with her innocent speech, I wouldn't have dared unroll the golden folds and behold the holiness before the end of the Counting.

And wasn't it only the miraculous sight of the blazing letters of Your

Names that could strengthen me tonight in the confession of the meeting last year, surely only the revelation of Your Names is testimony that, despite the pain that cuts the breathing, nothing bad will happen, for You are with me. And even if I can no longer pass my fingers along Isaiah's face, the sight of the gold of Your holy Names, woven by my own hands, is testimony that my work shall be rewarded, *for he perceives the outcome at the inception* . . .

And that I used the rabbi's wife without her knowing, that I incited her to hurt me so that I would thus know the source of consolation, for such is Your decree.)

I untied the silk sheet from the back of the loom, spread between my arms the abundance, the folds, the embroidery, and Yocheved scrambled to peep over me. (And how great was the beauty in the spread sight, the silk embroidered front and back with threads of gold, silver, red, and green, and with blue lights, with wings of eagles and flames, with the flight of birds and the rushing of letters flying up and beating, *I am the Lord thy God* in an abundance of gold spraying from the crowns and the points . . .

How is it that I, the last of the thousands of the tribe of Manasseh, have been worthy to do it?)

I don't think the rabbi's wife understood anything of the secret. I put my body between her and the fabric. And from what she did see, it was hard for her to understand what was partially completed. Anyway, I quickly rolled the Torah Curtain back up, and when I furtively glanced at her, trying to cover my shaking, I saw that her eyes were glassy with dull admiration and she didn't notice a thing.

"Very beautiful." She nodded, and she had already straightened up and her body was tense. "Well, I've got to go now. There are so many people in the streets, you can't imagine how full the bus was."

I didn't move from the loom. Yocheved bustled about the room, fussing over her bag. "I brought you a few things, Amalia, eat them in good health, and some pie, too, I know you like that." She went to the kitchen, put a jar of fruit compote on the table along with a potato pie fried with onion and wrapped in waxed paper.

"So, I'll be going now." She dragged her feet, unwittingly sowing pain and consolation. At the door she stopped, saying with her straight-forward sincerity, "So come by sometime, Amalia, come visit, God willing."

"Yes, yes, I'll come, absolutely . . ."

And then she repeated with genuine concern, "So what will you do now, Amalia, eh, what will happen to you?" as if something of her real mission was revealed to her. From the blazing road, she shook her head. "So come over, come on the Sabbath . . ."

For a moment I stood watching her make her heavy way to the curve in the road, and then I fastened the iron bolt on the door. I was struck by the thought of what Rabbi Israel Gothelf and Yocheved would say the day they found out the sanctification of Your Name by me. With what words of justification would they wash my blood off the confidence of their faith?

(I stopped writing. I went outside to look at the horizon covered with sparks, following the burning tails of colors like a child. The paths of fire sent out from City Park fell in a straight line into the night, scattered a thick smoke of shrieks, fragments of music, the rustling of loudspeakers, as if a bathing beach were suddenly spread out on the dark boulders on the horizon.

Between one shot and another, it became completely dark. Even in the strained joy, here, there is that amalgam of pain and solemnity. As in wartime. And at the Wailing Wall, Tikkun Rachel is surely resounding, *L-o-o-o-rd* . . .

I went into the kitchen. I warmed up a piece of pie, and gnawed at it, eating straight from the frying pan. A diffuse sweetness gave the night an illusion of home. The newly opened wound is bleeding. So much excitement . . .

May it be Your will that just as You sent the rabbi's wife, Yocheved, to me today, may You repair me tonight to stand before You and serve You.)

You almost ran to the meeting, and the heat of the evening stuck the soft dress to your body. On the mountain path, the last words of the Evening Prayer and the Omer Counting echoed, *fifteen days of the Omer—Eter-*

nity of Eternity. Your hair, all its heaviness undone, rustled with your quick pace, supple as a living thing, and a mist of sweetness rose from it.

You hurried, your head thrust forward. From the mountain opposite, the lights of church towers and turrets shone. On the main road, you were struck by a bitter breeze from the warehouses and the sooty exhaust of the trucks. For a moment, as on that night when you returned from the meeting with Rabbi Gothelf, Mala's svelte body quivered in you, gliding next to your head and then going off. You pushed aside the braids that were slapping your cheeks, but when you licked the dryness off your lips along with the sweetness of the old perfume, Hubert's strong hands went through the disheveled hair, bending and passing over the shuddering skin—*Emily meine liebe, Emily . . .*

The gray olive trees at the top of the street punctuated your running, and the wind escaping at evening from the facades screamed, increasing your distress. *I am a different person and not the same one, I am a different person and not the same one,* you repeated breathlessly, meanwhile choking the wailing that was swelling up in you. With great deliberation, you went on, whispering the words of consolation—*too long have you dwelled in the valley of weeping, arise and depart*—and trembling, you approached the central synagogue, where the meeting was to take place. But even then, in that first hour, you knew (even if you refused to admit it) that Isaiah, your salvation, had been sent to you too late.

At the top of the synagogue stairs, a thin figure stood out. You longed to run and fall onto the bosom of the approaching silhouette as onto the neck of a friend. In the faint light of the lamp, the line of a cheek and the arch of a neck were caught for a moment, and then the shadow covered your eyes again.

"Amalia?" You heard the whisper.

"I'm sorry I was late . . ."

"Thank God you came," he replied in a soft voice with a foreign accent, and went on as if rumbling a prayer, "I thought we'd talk in a café. There's one not far from here, at the entrance to the park."

You nodded and your hair fell forward.

"I thought it would be quiet there . . ."

"Yes," you answered hastily. The panting of running was released from your limbs, mists of perfume leaped out of your body. You were suffocating with excitement. Before your eyes roamed stone floor tiles, stairs covered with dust, frames of announcements stuck to the entrance. You quickly stretched out your hand to the banister. Your knees swayed and buckled.

"Amalia, you fell! . . . Tell me, did something happen?"

You clutched the banister, shaking your head no.

"I—I'll help you." He bent over you, and his thin fingers supported your arm.

In your heart you knew that the stumble was only a last warning, to alert you, but instead of going right back home, instead of letting go of Isaiah while it was still possible, you stood there, leaning on the banister, and blurted out, "I really don't know what happened to me . . ."

And when he replied, "Never mind, thank God, nothing happened," you unconsciously put your injured leg in front of you. "Are you hurt, God forbid?"

"It's nothing, thank God, just my knee," you replied looking sideways at the whiteness of the ritual fringes shaking against his trousers.

"You want a bandage?"

"No thanks, really, there's no need."

"Yes, yes . . ." He quickly offered you his handkerchief, its folds spreading like a white rose from his fingertips. You held the ironed cloth, choking with nervous laughter. "You'll bring balm to my wound," you whispered, "even in anguish . . ."

He turned his face away so as not to see, and you pulled up your dress and leaned your knee turning white on the stair. The touch of the cloth on the bruise caused searing pain.

"Thank God, it's nothing serious."

"Indeed, thank God, I was so scared."

You moved the handkerchief away. The pain still burned in your knee.

"You can keep it if you need to . . ." Maybe you only imagined that he too was choking.

"No, no, take it, thanks . . ." You pushed the flickering whiteness between the two of you so you could touch his fingertips for a moment as they stretched out to take it. And, out of control, you raised your eyes, and you didn't turn away even when they climbed to the arch of the neck, to the contour of the thin beard, to the nose with the streetlamp light hovering over it, the line of the eyebrows, the white forehead, the clear lips full as a girl's. And then the shadow of the eyelashes rose, revealing the clarity of the black light of his look flooded with pleading . . .

Isaiah lowered his eyes.

You shuddered, bursting ahead to the park, and the dread in your belly gaped so that you thought this time you couldn't overcome it. You swung your hair—if only to ease the choking—but then, with no control over what happened, a jolt of the machinery of habit made you spin the sweep of hair with that old movement, raise the arm, and let it fall to your shoulders. And to wait, with the rhythm stamped in the flesh, until the cascade of light caught Isaiah's amazement. For you knew, even without looking back, that he, like all the others, would be drawn to the flash, excited by it with a childish joy, whispering, "There are no words to tell the beauty of your hair, Amalia. Marvel of Creation . . ."

You wanted to turn around, to tell him everything, to flee, but a wave of shame broke over your shoulders, and you didn't dare see again the pleading in his eyes, for here, once more you let your hair loose, once more you scatter it, and tempt, as if in love you will know repentance, once more spreading before Isaiah's breathing that hair you had already waved at the face hiding its whisper, *Emily* . . .

Isn't that what she yearned for, isn't that why she fled from Stein, who ran after her out of the luxurious German hotel into the snow piled up in the sharp wind, his face shining with panic, panting at the doorman and the drunks who raised their red faces in his wake? They had come all the way from New York at his expense to set out the next day, everything was ready, entrance visas, tickets, hotels, the special photography equipment she required.

"Amy dear, you're not leaving the plan now, not now . . ." He runs after her, his voice coming undone. And she leaves him at the exit, his limbs dislocated like a rag doll's in the snow, illuminated by the chandeliers of the hotel lobby, slamming the cab door in his face and fleeing, as if to a new beginning, to that German photographer she met by chance the night before at the opening of his exhibit. She had immediately identified with the cutting black-and-white light in the photos of backyards, fields of ripe grain among relics of fences and huts, clods in close-up, garbage. He gave her his calling card with a long handshake. "It seems to me that we have a lot in common; come by sometime, I'd be very happy." Hubert, that handsome fellow, too handsome, in the fine leather jacket, going to him through the frozen city, as if in love she will find shelter, panting at his welcoming bow at the door and his face puffed with wonder, at his moving aside for her the splendid drapes across from the fire in the hearth and the smell of tobacco and men's cologne. "I am so grateful to you for coming . . . I did not believe we would be able to speak before you went there to photograph . . . You know, you saw at the exhibit . . . Of course you understood . . . Yes, I also believe it is impossible to cover the blood with flowers . . . Nature cannot erase the shout; that is our role, to remind them of what is buried inside! . . ." He pours out his feelings to her, and the smell of his leather jacket and the sweetness of the tobacco and his flushed face. "I understand, of course," she says, nodding at him with the grimace of a partner in fate. "I understand . . ." For she came to him with a lie, only to flee from Stein, to leave him helpless in the hotel, to show him that she has no obligation to his plans, isn't thinking of leaving tomorrow on that journey for Mala. And then she gets up slowly, as if to take her leave, and he follows her to the door, past tapestries with lush shepherdesses and shepherds in white stockings strumming on lutes, and at the door he stops a moment, his handsome face concentrated in a wrinkle between his eyebrows, and his hands stretching out to her. "I don't have words to thank you for coming, Amy; from now on everything will have new meaning . . ." And she lowers her eyes hypocritically. "Call me Emily, my real name is Emily," she says, as if by changing her name, she will know peace, as if that is how she will deceive her terror. "Emily, if I could really call you that at the end of this special evening, Emily . . ." His solid body stands between her and the door, smells of leather and the mist of cologne wafting from the rosy neck and the smooth-shaven cheeks, and disgust and weakness are growing strong in her, and the voice is speaking to her from the foreign face that is longing for her. "It is difficult for me to find the words . . . I did not believe that two people could be seeking the same thing, that such an encounter could be! . . ." She holds her hand out to him as if in support, and he quickly takes it, grasps it piously. "I do not

know if I can dare to hope, but, if you would be willing to let me go with
you on the trip . . . Yes, to go with you to photograph her places, yes, yes,
I feel suddenly that I am obligated to Mala as much as you are! Forgive
me for what I am saying, but it seems to me that without that I cannot go
on living . . ." And then she turns around, and like an animal fixing its
victim, waves the cascade of her perfumed hair, with that delayed movement, at the face that is hypnotized by it, hiding in it with a whisper.
"Emily, my absolution . . ." But even as she abandons herself to his arms,
just to achieve respite through lust, even as she spreads her loins, her neck
under him, repeating to herself that here, with her flesh, she is overpowering a son of the cursed nation, taking revenge on him, like Judith,
who forsook herself before she slit the throat of Holofernes, her lover,
even then she only returns, in those same cycles tightening around her,
to the root of the name she has fled. And so, with warmth from Hubert's body still flowing into her body, she picks up a phone to the hotel,
to Stein, to the voice that blazes up, "Yes, Amy, Amy dear . . ." Then
hisses. "I don't want to see you! Understand, on the trip I don't want to
know that you're around. Yes, I'm going, but with Hubert, not with you!
You can pay if you want to, yes, but you'll never stay in the same hotel
with us!" And Stein's voice in the receiver is shaken: "Of course, Amy,
of course, anything you say, all the time, anything you say, for the memory of Mala, for her memory . . ."

You burst forward toward the park, and Isaiah hurried after. You stuck
out your chin and crossed the street to the shadow of the garden. You
didn't take the flash of your hair away from his eyes, you didn't turn
around, and the sound of Isaiah's breathing, rising so close to you,
drowned out everything.

(Sounds of celebration stick to the windows, break the threads of my repair with shots of fire. The racket is poured out. The shout of the two
nations struggling in one womb, an inflamed people takes possession of
the land in its dances, in the heart of the time of Supplication and Purity,
in the middle of the Counting. They have sent their cars playing music,
robbed the darkness of the Arab villages on the slope with the explosions
of flares suspended solemnly over the desert sky.

So hard to go on lucidly in the noise. And who am I to blame you now? Would I myself have resisted the softness of Isaiah's steps, the holiness of his excitement panting as he walked? And was it indeed by Your Commandment that I brought all the suffering down on him, to submit to You the repair of Mala's name? Was that indeed Your decree, You, Grace and Mercy? And all the pain.

From Passover to Shavuoth, the wicked are judged in Hell, the air changes secretly, spirits roam the world. And where I would have come if not for the fast on Monday and Thursday that I imposed on myself during the days of the Counting.)

"Pleasant evenings now, almost hot," you finally said, with an effort.

"Oh yes! The air of Jerusalem! Ahhh . . ." Isaiah clutched at your few words. "They say that the air of the land of Israel makes you wise, and I say the air of Jerusalem gives birth, for a person really is born anew in Jerusalem." He chuckled with that same continuous humming, and his thin body leaped onto the path between the bushes, sprinkled with sprays of broom and honeysuckle.

"I still get excited when I go out in the evening. I don't have a chance to do it much, we study until late, especially now during the Omer Counting," he went on in that solemn language that intoxicated you. "Ever since I have come to Jerusalem I have not been in a café. This evening when we sit together, that will be for the sake of a Commandment."

You held on to the straps of your purse. The dew and the myrtle grew cooler as you went further into the darkness of the park. His arm pushed aside the branches bending across the path in front of you, and his fingers flickered in flight. Despite the weakness, you longed to look again at the delicacy of his white face. At the turn in the stairs, your ankle faltered. He flung out his arm to support you.

"You haven't yet recovered from the fall, Amalia. You'll rest when we sit down."

"Yes, yes . . ." You sallied forth from the bushes into the dark stone square of the garden café.

"Wait here, Amalia, I'll go find us a quiet place."

The swing of his back rubbed the clusters of branches. A downpour of broom flowers dropped onto his curls. He laughed and quickly crossed the square with his silent steps, shaking the flowers out of his hair, turning his face to you and laughing.

You stood still. Isaiah's shadow slipped among the iron chairs fallen on their sides, it dipped in the the marble square gleaming like an expanse of water. Beads of wetness grew thick on your scalp, your dress steeped in fragility lay on your chest, and chill washed the shadow that was swept up in the waves of marble. On the other side of the square rose the banging of glass and iron shaking.

"The café is closed!" Isaiah's anxious face rose up to you from the darkness.

"Never mind." You smiled remotely, like someone soothing a baby. "We can talk here on the bench just as well." And in fact you almost dropped from all the emotion.

"Yes, yes, we can." He leaped toward the stone bench in a niche of bushes and soaked up the evening damp on it with the white handkerchief. "Here." He beckoned you over and laughed. But, fainthearted, you couldn't laugh in reply.

You crossed the layers of wetness, caught in a growing calm. You gathered up your skirt and sat down, enveloped in the silence of his movements, abandoning yourself to the cold stone. The silence went on a long time, with heavy pounding, and the swaying of Isaiah's back next to you quietly beat to the throbbing of the night. In the distance, from the slopes, the muted sound of cars rose among the foliage, mixed with the hissing of the night. Your breathing slowed, you imagined you were steeped like the soil of the world watered with Holiness, you imagined that now, after everything, you too were allowed to enter the Garden, you too were granted the right to stand at the gates of the Temple, by virtue of Isaiah's light, by virtue of the sanctity of love, by the secret of the coupling of the Shekhina and Ehad . . .

(Only months later did I read with full understanding the words that were spinning around in you then, before you imagined what they really meant:

Four men entered the Garden, namely, Ben Azzai and Ben Zoma, Aher, and Rabbi Akiba. Rabbi Akiba said to the others: When ye arrive at the stones of pure marble, say not water, water! For it is said: He that speaketh falsehood shall not be established before mine eyes. Ben Azzai cast a look and died. Of him Scripture says: Precious in the sight of the Lord is the death of His saints. Ben Zoma looked and became demented. Of him Scripture says: Hast thou found honey? Eat so much as is sufficient for thee, lest thou be filled therewith, and vomit it. Aher mutilated the shoots. Rabbi Akiba departed unhurt.

Rashi explained: Entered the Garden—ascended to heaven with the help of the Name. Rabbi Hananel explained: Four men entered the Garden. Rabbi Akiba ordered them: When you arrive to the stones of pure marble and look at the insight of the heart, say not water, water, for there is no water at all, but just a figure is seen in the world, and he who says water is repelled, for he is lying.

And in this language is it explained in the Hekhalot Rabati: *Because the guards of the Temple at the door of marble hurl and cast thousands on thousands of waves of water when there is not even one drop . . .*

Ever since I reread those words in full, they have haunted me: *and he who says water is repelled, for he is lying, for there is not even one drop there, not even one drop. . . .*

Isaiah's voice flowed without disturbing the growing serenity. "I am told that you work at weaving ritual articles."

"I just started . . . Until now, I've woven only simple things. Pillows, challah covers . . . But I've started my first prayer shawl . . ." The words washed out of you with peace.

"May you complete it in Holiness, with the help of God." His hand rose from the stone slab: "I hope, with the help of God, also to support myself with work aside from studying in the yeshiva."

You stared at the fold of his fingers, at the shadow hovering over the line of the fingernails, listening calmly to the flow of blood in your temples subsiding, and the distant beating gathered in your dew-soaked skin.

"I thought of being a bookbinder, of working, with the help of God,

in binding." His fingers waved in the dim light. "A binder of holy books.
I believe it is a great virtue to work at manual labor, and you surely feel
that way too, Amalia, don't you?"

You nodded without listening, fascinated by the sweetness of his
voice.

"I've already made arrangements with a binder who promises to teach
me. You know, it's not only to keep the hands employed. No, I believe
that we are commanded today to rescue old books from destruction, to
repair with our own hands, with a craft." He continued, with sudden
emphasis, "I've talked about that a lot with the Kabbalist rabbi, Avuya
Aseraf. He's the one who encourages me to choose a craft. He repairs
vessels, yes, yes . . . damaged vessels. He left the yeshiva so he wouldn't
exploit the Torah. A few of us continue to study with him at night, at his
house. You should hear how Rabbi Avuya Aseraf preaches! Things that
go right to the heart . . . You'll meet him, too, God willing, when we go
to the holy rabbi for a talk."

Even then, the sound of Rabbi Avuya's name evoked a dull shadow,
but you were still following the pleasure of the nips of dampness melting the paralysis of your body.

"You know, Amalia . . . I decided to start working at binding . . . after,
with the help of God . . ." He laughed and went on after his excitement
subsided. "After we get married . . . that's what the rabbi said too . . ."

After we get married . . . the echo of the words broke as on a sand-
bank, the words he persisted in saying even then, explicitly: *After we get
married* . . .

And what he went on to say you didn't hear in the gale that swept
away the capering of the sea and the palm trees standing in the glow
along the boardwalk, running away in panic from the clinic, even though
she hasn't yet recovered, opening the glass doors of the travel agency,
and they're coming in behind her, the two of them now together against
her, Hubert and behind him Stein bursts through in his Bermuda shorts.
"Here, take, for Mrs. Amy's trip! I'm buying for Amy a ticket to wher-
ever she wants, please." He scatters the bills on the counter, plucks the
ticket from the clerk and holds it out to her with a sort of bow, and its colorful pages flicker like a tropical flower in his hand. And suddenly his face
becomes serious, and his sad eyes stare at her with that splinter of naked

confession. "What do you think, you think it's easy for me? Eh? You think I don't want to forget sometimes, to get married? What do you think, that a person can run away from everything just like that, and start all over again?"

You got up from the stone bench, dizzy. For a moment, you stood still, your body suspended weightlessly, and Isaiah trembling next to you, close by and far away at the same time.

"Amalia, don't you feel well? Tell me. I'm sorry if I've offended you, God forbid, I didn't mean to."

"No, no," you whispered, suddenly exhausted, almost burying your head in his narrow shoulder. "No," you repeated, and started walking up the path, whispering, "I'm not sure, Isaiah . . ."

"What aren't you sure of?" He hurried after you.

"I'm not sure if I can start all over again."

"I know very well the torments of repentance that you're suffering." His black curls sailed after you in the dimness of the greenery. "But, with the help of God, the full love of HaShem is acquired that way. I," he laughed and shook his head, "I haven't yet achieved it."

"I don't know . . . I'm afraid something will happen, God forbid."

"Don't be afraid, Amalia. With the help of God, we'll know a blessing."

"Yes, yes," you repeated after him. And meanwhile something in his gait blunted the sharpness of your panic. Yes, Isaiah still had the power to ward off what arose. Once again the sight of his fingers went before you, and the dense coolness of the park wound around your walking.

What could I have replied to the rabbi's wife, Yocheved, today when she bent over me? "You were a match made in heaven." What could I have answered her? And has anything changed since last year, from the longing to hold his face in my hands? And at the end of this night of writing does his love seared in my breathing burn any less? Isaiah, pillar of fire, whom You sent to lead me to Your love—how can I now judge him or you?

———

The two of you passed near the olive trees bending on the main street when his soft voice was once again released: "You know, before, in America, I had a different life . . . I played the violin . . . Yes, it's not easy to forget." (Amazing how much even then he sensed something through the silence.) "But now, when, thank God, I've come to the yeshiva, there's still one lesson I owe to playing music. You know, sometimes I'd have to work whole days to get one note! Yes . . . From the violin, I learned devotion, that you don't get to the fullness of repentance all at once. Yes . . ." He moved, lifting his head, going on to himself: "I paid a lot for that lesson . . . In fact, I haven't finished paying yet . . ."

You went on in silence, your steps echoing, going far away from the wall of buildings, lighted by streetlamps, passing warehouses, dark lots, and only the flicker of the traffic signals around the mountain flooded the sidewalk.

"It was the holy rabbi, Rabbi Avuya Aseraf, who illuminated my eyes. He's the one who showed me what abyss I was standing at the edge of, that playing for the sake of playing, beauty for the sake of beauty, are truly idolatry! The rabbi, long may he live, brought me close to our holy Torah, showed me the joy, as they say: *Gladden our souls with Your salvation.*" His head was flung back, and his eyes were half closed.

You turned onto the road that goes around the mountain, at the place where the slope slips away to the desert. Isaiah sailed along the line of the ridge, a slim figure, listening to itself, dividing the sheets of darkness with its delicate symmetry, and you strode drunk with the dryness striking your dress. You were completely fascinated by the charm of his words, the softness of his voice dimming all other voices. For how great was the promise in his words, how mighty the expanse that swept you away with an unimaginable, tempestuous force? . . . As if everything Rabbi Israel had taught at Neve Rachel were not merely words of solace, but reality, concrete, being realized in you . . . As if it really were possible, with the mercy of God, to forget and to be born again . . . to be born to faith, to life, to love.

"You know, the one who played violin in New York, Stanley, doesn't have anything to do with me anymore! You can ask about me at the yeshiva if you want, they'll all tell you that Isaiah is a different person, different! With the grace of blessed God, a miracle happened to me, yes, a real miracle, Amalia."

You smiled with a trembling heart, and the rushing of Mala's body, renewed in your steps, no longer evoked wonder in you.

"You'll see, Amalia, God willing, we'll reach the fullness of repentance together . . . You'll see, I believe that with all my soul. Really!"

His hand hung at his side. You dropped your eyes because of its radiant beauty. Tears of bliss and regret bathed your cheeks, flooded your throat, and just so he'd go on and say in his soft voice that you were indeed forgiven, that your expiation was accepted, these fragmentary syllables blurted out of you: "Isaiah, how, with the help of God, can you be sure of me? . . . You don't even know what I've gone through . . ."

He laughed, as you had imagined he would, and you bent your head like someone accepting forty lashes, so that the trace of abomination would be beaten out of you. But he moved a moment with that giggle of faith and then declared casually, "You don't have to worry, Amalia, really, I asked everything about you before I came to the meeting, Rabbi Israel Gothelf told me everything."

"He told . . . I didn't know he told you about me . . ."

And all of a sudden you were standing at the gate of your house. You stopped from the shock of pain, but Isaiah, who didn't know where you lived, went on vigorously into the depths of the alley until he realized what he was doing and ran back. You retreated from his flaming face with a blend of cowardice and disgust, and just so he wouldn't ask again if anything was wrong, you said quickly, "You want to come in?" And you immediately understood that you had made a mistake and another wave of heat flooded the roots of your hair.

Isaiah withdrew as if he noticed the darkness of your look for the first time. "No, no, I have to go back to the yeshiva now, I'm already very late. No, no . . ." And he was already dragged off to the road. "I'll come, God willing, the day after tomorrow, to take you to Rabbi Avuya Aseraf. He wants to meet you . . ." And once again the name of Rabbi Avuya made you tremble.

His hand waved good-bye and was immediately gathered up, raising a breeze that caught the sleeve of your dress. And he was already pounding quickly around the mountain.

For a long time you leaned on the doorframe, and his trembling still stuck the fabric of the dress to your skin. You lowered your hand into the depth of the raffia bag, groping on the bottom for the key ring. Isaiah's silhouette disappeared behind the side of the mountain. You were amazed at how cool the keys were in the heavy heat.

("Of course you'll come to the betrothal," said the rabbi's wife, Yocheved. "They'll hold it, God willing, after the holiday. You know, Elisheva was at our house this week, and she said that they would get a house in the settlement. A great Commandment, returning to the land."

So far I haven't dared to write those words of Yocheved. For fear of the evil eye? And they too were said on Your mission.

Yes. He'll give his love in Elisheva's lush laughter, in her ground will he bury his seed, in her caring, baking, kneading hands, in the cylinders of her firm legs, which certainly, even in strict secrecy, are stamping the rhythm on the earth tonight.

Father of mercy, have pity and mercy on me . . .)

I left what was written, strayed among the rooms. Nibbled at the cold pie in the kitchen, opened the windows wide to the subsiding bustle of the holiday. The distress doesn't disappear, doesn't abate.

At last you entered the house and felt your way to the room. A flutter of lights of the valley played on the darkness of the arches. You dropped onto the windowseat, your face to the dry coolness of the night, the big raffia bag still on your shoulder. A long time you remained sitting on the sill, and emptiness padded your skull. One of Isaiah's sentences sometimes passed by: *You'll see, Amalia, I believe that with all my soul, really . . .* And you no longer remembered when or why he had said it in his soft voice.

You got up and like a sleepwalker went to the loom, taking apart the shuttle interwoven in the warp, and you lightly shifted the wooden chip filled with blue between the white warp fans of the prayer shawl. You bent over and withdrew, your body shrouded in silence; the bundles of wool were stretched to the roots of the weave, trembling from the flight of the shuttle, and the supple hips of Mala moved with you. You inhaled the thin, sweet vapor of her breathing blended with your breathing, and when you knelt to the beater, the screen of her hair passed by and rustled on your cheeks.

You didn't weave for long that night. Only a few rows back and forth in blue and white, but in the harmony of it, your necks were drawn together, hers and yours, in the silence of your kneeling as fields of rye— your hand catching the shuttle and her hand shooting—there was a deep solace. Again and again, you delighted in the beauty of her arm, in the fingers of her hands that flew the shuttle, and you couldn't take your eyes off the delicacy of their movement.

You didn't weave for long, but when you got up from the loom with the flash of the prayer shawl absorbed in your look, Isaiah's fragmentary words passed through you again: *You'll see, Amalia, I believe that with all my soul, really* . . . And you didn't notice the contorted strip of fabric with undone fringes left on the floor, where it slid off your knees. As if the new calm were enough to ward off everything, *for there is no water at all there, but a figure seen in the world, and he who says water is repelled, for he is lying* . . .

Suddenly such exhaustion. The head is heavy, and the rising light piercing the eyelids. Everything so foggy. *Do not cast me away from Yourself and do not take the spirit of Your Holiness from me* . . .

(Sometime that night, in the middle of writing, I rolled up my sleeves. Now the dawn breeze strokes the bared skin. I couldn't resist, I raised the arm and licked the bitterness of the flesh. For a moment, I no longer knew exactly whose arm I was licking, mine, yours, hers. Only the dusty skin was present.)

Perhaps there is no profit in pain, in effort, for there never was water there or marble and only a figure in the world is seen, only a figure!! And maybe the gleam of the Torah Curtain is nothing but an opaque flash of silk, without any secret at all. . . . Even now, at the end of night nineteen of the Omer Counting, less than thirty days until I cling to Your kiss, I am still waiting for Isaiah with the same tremor. Even now, at the end of the night of writing, that longing of body and soul still lick me as if flesh was never cut off from flesh. As if nothing was decided between then and now . . .

Isaiah, the one You sent me to show the way to Your love—*for to You, my God, I shall call and to You I shall plead, The Lord is nigh unto all them that call upon Him in truth. Is there anyone who would call upon Him in a lie? Said Rabbi Ahava: "That is one who calls and who doesn't know whom he is calling."*

End of the nineteenth night of the Omer, Eternity in Splendor. The gray wind shrivels the grasses as it slides by, moving the remnants of the merrymakers' trash; piles gather on the edges of the sidewalks. In hewn squares the sheet of light spreads out over the sharp, orange flickering of the traffic signals. A holiday morning rises with dawn on the warm asphalt.

Soon I shall stand to recite the morning prayer. With the fringes of my hair I shall pull myself into the new day.

three weeks

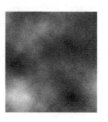

Twenty-five days, which is three weeks and four

days of the Omer. Splendor of Eternity, heart

of the Counting. Another twenty-five days.

For almost a week I haven't written. I wore myself out with weaving, and in the evening, exhausted by the effort, I postponed confession. On the night of Independence Day, I stayed outside until after sunrise, leaning on the wall, facing the brightening in the East. So weak, I found it difficult to recite the prayers. My strength is no longer what it was (physically, I mean). Constant weaving, purification of the body, fasting, midnight prayers turn every activity into a special effort. Every movement is engraved on the muscles, stands by itself.

And after everything, even after the awful lesson of Rabbi Avuya of blessed memory, I'm not sure that with my many transgressions I succeeded in repairing the world. I'm not sure that it is as a wise-hearted woman that I weave a Torah Curtain for the Temple, as one of those whose reward is given from the priestly dues, and when their thread stops they tie it off and toss their needles to one another. (And perhaps I merely prepare the veil to cover the beaming skin of his face.)

Please, please God, save . . .

And my prayers, are they prayers? *We have neither Jerusalem nor the forest of Lebanon. Neither laver nor its pedestal. Neither frankincense nor shewbread. Neither altar nor offering. Neither perfume nor libations . . .*

The words are crushed in the mouth, swell up, stick in the pulp of night in the window.

On the night of Grace of Splendor, last year, the twenty-ninth day of the Omer, as he promised, Isaiah came to take you to Rabbi Avuya Aseraf. At about four in the afternoon, when the heart of light strikes the gate and bursts into the vestibule in a sparkling rectangle. At that hour, three days after the evening when you first walked side by side, there was almost no trace left in you of the sight of his fingers. On that day, when you entered, your body exulted. You dropped onto the windowsill with a prayer of thanksgiving, and you wove a little. But only a few hours later, when you woke up, you started whispering, even before the evening's events were clear in you, *I am a different person and not the same one who sinned, I am a different person and not the same one who sinned.*

Over the next three days, you didn't dare think about Isaiah or about what Rabbi Gothelf had told him. Furiously you sank into weaving, lines and lines of blue and white, and inadvertently, you almost finished the first prayer shawl. Only later did you see how tempestuous was the weaving your hands brought forth—crooked, tangled rows—and you rejected that prayer shawl. But in those three days you clung with all your might to weaving until the sight of Isaiah's face was almost erased, and now when you ran to the sound of his knocking and opened the gate, you recoiled. "Oh, it's you . . ."

He squeezed his height into the doorframe and laughed, waiting impatiently for you to get your bag and go with him to the rabbi. You hurried at his heels. After not going out for three days, you had to strain in the sudden haste. But the common pounding of your sandals on the pavement enveloped you in a certainty of closeness, as if you had been walking like that, together, forever and ever. You peeped furtively at Isaiah's face, thrust forward, toward the slope. The hot wind that had swept the city ever since your meeting struck his eyes, and his eyebrows were clenched. For the first time you saw his face in daylight, and because of the dense haze, it seemed to be opaque, encircled by ash. You lowered your eyes to the road, but even so, the movement of his shoulders touched the corner of your sight.

"You'll see, Amalia, you've never met a rabbi like this. Rabbi Avuya isn't like any other rabbi. You'll see."

You didn't turn your head. His voice, panting with excitement or because of walking so fast, flooded your ears.

"I don't know what would have happened to me if, with the grace of the blessed God, he hadn't seen me, yes he saw. The rabbi really sees every single person, he looks and he sees right away what the person can't see by himself. Even among many people, he can see who truly has repentance within him. Immediately. You know, it was he who found me, not vice versa. Yes, you understand what a great thing that is. He, the holy rabbi, saw me standing like a stray lamb at the Wailing Wall. I went there for no reason, on a two-week tour I made to Israel. Maybe with something else in my heart, but nothing special. I stayed in the square a little while, I even went up to the stones. Yes, for me they were stones then . . . God have mercy . . . um . . . And then he, wrapped in his prayer shawl like a king, just like a king, the rabbi, he saw me. And ever since then I've been following him, with the help of God. I told him a little about you, I'm sure he'll look at you and see everything immediately, um . . ."

The road changed into a steep path that climbed between bushes and ledges of rock and was swallowed up among the twisted trunks of pine trees. The slanting sunlight was absorbed in the rustle of the branches, and the dry needles burst under foot, spreading a pungent smell. Near the top of the mountain you reached your arms out to shift a bouncing branch and move it aside. Above you, Isaiah laughed and his eyes on you surprised you with their softness. The branches made a grating noise and panicked birds fled from them. And before the blush evaporated from your face and you raised your eyes again, you were near the rabbi's yard.

"Look, Amalia, look at the rabbi's special plants, aromatic grasses, and here are medicinal herbs." Isaiah pointed to beds of dirt.

Deep in the yard stood the rabbi, his back to you, a black apron tied around his waist, and his face covered by a blacksmith's mask. The still-reddish curls of his gray hair burst out of it, tinged by the fire. You didn't know how he had noticed you despite the racket of the tinwork, but as soon as you came through the gate, the searing jet stopped. The rabbi put the iron mask on the anvil and strode toward you from the thicket, taking off his protective gloves and spreading his arms out to both of you. "Welcome, welcome!"

And the whole time, even when he was patting Isaiah's narrow shoulders, he never took his eyes off you, thrusting his lips out of the curls of his beard. "Ah, so, you're Amalia . . ." His smile didn't blunt the sharpness of his look. "Come in, come in . . ." Only after he turned his face away from you did your breath return.

Isaiah went first on the path between the beds, looked back at you and laughed. The rabbi waited for you to move. For a moment, you couldn't budge, and even when you did go forward, your face was lowered to the grease spots and sawdust that flecked the dirt. You could feel his eyes staring at your back, and you clutched your arms to your chest like someone caught naked.

"Those are some plants for the incense mixture." His hoarse voice rose from behind you. "Here are cloves, spikenard, and this is saffron. *Rabbi Nathan saaays, Aaaalso a minute amount of Jordan aaaaamber, and if he left out any of its spiiiiices, he is liiiiiable to the deaaath penaaalty!*"

You walked in Isaiah's wake. Your blue skirt got tangled up in your ankles. In the beds, the bushes were covered with dust. The rest of the yard was full of iron wires, tin plates, dented lead bowls, and around a blacksmith's shed rose a heap of tools without handles. Beyond the fence leaned ancient pine trees, their shadows moving over the walls of the rabbi's house, softening the gleam of the avalanche of chalk that slipped down to the valley. Behind you beat the rabbi's footsteps.

(May it be Your will, HaShem, my God, to rescue me from calumny, to rescue me from false witness, from the hatred of others, from libel. And even if in my heart there is something against the rabbi of blessed memory, *may*

it be Your will that I shall not sin and may the Evil Inclination not rule me as I write. By virtue of the gift of the Sanctification of Your Name.)

The rabbi passed by the two of you and with one movement, he pushed open the door and the screen. You stopped on the threshold, Isaiah was swallowed in the dimness. You were struck by the smell of a kerosene stove burning and a thick sourness, and only later did you understand what it meant. Isaiah crossed the space as if he was familiar with it, and in its depths he pulled out a bench and sat down at the long table. You stayed near the door. The screen was still humming. The rabbi put his big hand on your shoulder, and the warmth of his fingers went down your spine.

"Sit down, Amalia."

In the gloom, Isaiah pointed to the bench across from him. The rabbi sat down in a chair at the head of the table, between you. Behind Isaiah's head, light burned in the windowpanes. You lowered your gaze to the rabbi's hand lying on the table, knowing he didn't take his eyes off you. The silence lasted a moment.

"I shall offer you cold water to refresh your souls from the walk." The rabbi rose and went to the back of the room. Only then did you notice that the space was divided by a cloth partition. On one side were the benches painted blue, and on the wall was an Ark of the Covenant covered with a simple Torah Curtain, and on the other side of the partition implements for cooking and living. The absence of a woman's hand was obvious. The windows were open to the East, but at that hour of the afternoon, the light had receded and the reflection of the gleam from the yard lit a diadem around Isaiah's head.

The rabbi washed his hands in a strong stream of water and returned to you, shaking off the drops and wiping his hands on a rag. He picked up a long-necked earthenware jug, covered its mouth, and closed his eyes, singing. Then he grabbed the handle, with a sudden movement swung the jug up, and from the heights, began pouring. The quivering stream dropped down precisely, sheaf after sheaf, to the cups. Until the rabbi cut off the thread of pouring.

(Yes, your gaze was fixed on the earthenware cups and on the trembling shadow between their sides, and yet, it's hard for me to believe that you didn't notice, even then, that Rabbi Avuya clearly intended his movements. Only, at that time, you hadn't yet fathomed the secret of his intentions.)

Now the rabbi pushed toward Isaiah a bunch of green herbs tied together and a small knife. "Here, Isaiaaaah, that's your job." He waited until Isaiah took the knife, bowed obediently, and started chopping the grasses on the block of wood prepared for that task, immediately absorbed in cutting, as if he forgot that you were there, looking at him from the other side of the table. The sight of his lip drooping as he worked and the submissiveness of his movements inundated you with a contempt that was somehow blended with an unknown sweetness.

Finally, Isaiah stretched his neck and gave the rabbi the block of wood with the crushed leaves. The rabbi took a pinch of greenery and sprinkled it over the blackening water. "*Ho, every one that thirsteth, come ye to the waaaaaters,*" he wailed. "*Blessed art Thou, O Lord our God, King of the Uuuuniverse, through Whose word everything came to beeee!*" The beverage smelled of field and mountain.

Once again the rabbi rose from his chair, and on the other side of the partition, he took off the stove a boiling pan that shot a jet of sourness, the same sourness that was fuming in the room. He placed his broad body over the two of you, steam rising from the pan in his hands.

"Creatoooor of the variouuuus kinds of spiiiiices!" he wailed. "Have to say a blessing. Especially good at this hour of sunset, the hour of the Judgment of eeeeevil. Have to light Isaac's dark eyes with the fume of the incense, so that the souls of Your people Israel be cleansed of their contamination and remove all blemish. Here, smell, Isaiah." He pushed the pan over the tabletop. "Yes, yes, like that. You smell it, too, Amaliyyyyyaa. Inhale the life-giving scent, smell with your inhalation and with all devotion, with all devoootion. So that you will be corrected with love, as it is said: *In my flesh shall I see God*, in my fleeesh, Amaliyyyyaa."

For a moment, through the vapors, across from you, Isaiah's face became clear as he sat with his head cocked and his eyes closed, and once again the rabbi's body swayed between you.

"*And this is the order of the incense mixture our forefathers burned before You. Stacte, onycha, galbanum, frankincense—each weighing seventy*

*maneh; myrrh, cassia, spikenard, saffron—each weighing sixteen maneh.
Costus—twelve; aromatic bark—three; and cinnamon—nine. Carshina
lye—nine kab; Cyprus wine—three se'ah and three kab. If he has no Cyprus
wine, he brings old white wine. Sodom salt—a quarter kab; and a minute
amount of smoke-raising herb. Rabbi Nathan says: also a minute amount of
Jordan amber. If he placed fruit-honey into it, he invalidated it, and if he left
out any of its spices he is liable to the death penaaalty. Rabban Shimon ben
Gamliel saaays: the stacte is simply the sap that drips from the balsam trees.
Carshina lye is used to bleach the onycha to make it pleasing, Cyprus wine is
used to soak the onycha to make it pungent. Even though urine is suitable for
that, nevertheless they do not bring urine into the Temple out of respeeeect."*

His body stopped swaying. He opened his eyes wide at you, and your
breathing seemed to grow difficult.

"And the essential repair by spice-mixture is galbanum, which is the
bad smell! The bad smell of the burnt offering, Amaliyyyyaaa. For only
in the burning of the bad smell of the sacrifice—including the impurity
of the galbanum in the spice-mixture—is it possible to do expiaaaation!
That is the secret of repentance, including the destruction in holiness!

"Amalia, now I shall dictate to you instructions for the preparation of
some plants you will get in the garden afterward. It is especially important for a young woman who purifies and prepares herself for repair . . .
Isaiah, bring some paper and ink!"

Isaiah got up, moving the corner of the bench. You would have gotten up after him that moment. He returned, trembling, holding the pen
and the paper, and something in the thinness of his fingers, in the fragility
of their beauty, made you gasp. (Like purity in a pure wrapping was the
sight of Isaiah's fingers, like Father's fingers becoming hard.) You
quickly took the pen and paper from his outstretched hands, and if you
hadn't, he would certainly have stumbled.

"Now, write, Amalia . . ."

Preparation of plants, you wrote slowly in purple ink as the rabbi
watched. Isaiah remained standing, hesitating to sit down until he got orders. Then he withdrew and turned to the window. You could feel the
rabbi's breathing as he leaned over your hair, his breath uttering the
names of the plants, instructions for crushing, drying, boiling, and he
whispered hoarsely: "Isaiah will help you prepare the holy grasses. He

has learned the ways of repair and devotion." (And maybe only now do I imagine that the back of Isaiah's neck, contrasting with the red glow on the window, was trembling.)

And abruptly the rabbi said, "Isaiah, go out and leave us alone."

Isaiah turned his face in terror, looked for a moment at you and the rabbi, and in the next moment, he withdrew without taking his eyes off the rabbi. He opened the screen door and vanished in the light of the entrance. In the earthenware cup, the pieces of leaves floating in the black solution jumped. The vapors of the spice mixture steeped in the green essence and the iron grating clouded your eyes. You couldn't strangle the offense. And the ringing of the screen striking the doorpost went on for a long moment.

(Of everything that happened, the hardest of all for me to understand is why Isaiah went out, why he left you alone with Rabbi Aseraf—even if he was commanded. Surely he sensed what was liable to happen. Did he go out precisely because of what he understood? And why did he slam the screen, leaving behind him a trail of ringing? Was he trying to signal something behind the rabbi's back, to warn you?

Who knows if I'll have time to clarify it with him, if I shall once more interlace my hours with the threads of his life. Who knows if You will send Isaiah here before the Omer Counting ends, because of the torments of the soul I am making for the unity of Your Name.

The dark room lies heavy behind my back. The bed, the closet, the door leading to the kitchen. Weight of a strange, rough presence dominating the night. Everything is closed . . . *Please, HaShem, not by your wrath* . . .)

"So, you are Amalia, you are." Rabbi Avuya put his hand on the back of your hand when you were left alone. "It's good that you came, Amalia," he leaned over and whispered. "Good that you came. I heard about what you went through before you arrived at the secret of the blessed HaShem, to repentance. I know that you've been tormented with the torments of the meritorious . . ."

Your hand under his was burning. You knew that Rabbi Avuya Aseraf saw. You knew that was why he had invited you for a talk. And you also knew, even then, that no good would come out of it, that even the scintilla of pure hope that Isaiah had planted in you would be crushed because of him. Yet his look transfixed you. You were already in his hands, and your anger at Isaiah, who had abandoned you, was mixed with a helplessness so great you wanted to cry.

"I heard that you do weaving. Nice, nice that you devote yourself to a holy task. But know that there's another reason for that, Amalia, and you have to be very careful not to fail. . . . You have to be especially strict about the purification of the body. Are you strict about going to the mikveh?"

You shook your head no.

"Blessed be thou, Amalia!" his voice rose. "Blessed be thou that your steps were summoned to me! I shall guide you, with the help of God!

"And in the weaving of the stripes of the prayer shawls you're strict, Amalia? You're strict about counting the threads in the number of letters of God's Name?" You lowered your eyes. "You have to count the *yod*, which is ten threads in the first stripe; *heh*, which is five in the second; *vav*, six in the third; and *heh*, which is five in the last stripe in the west; and the reverse, five six five and ten in the side facing the East. And you also have to be very careful in tying the fringes, especially the ritual fringes! A great responsibility in the ritual fringes, eight knots of the male and female Ze'ir Anpin in all four wings. Have to be very careful, Amaliyyyyaaa." He enunciated the syllables of your name very slowly. "Aaamaaaliyyyaaa, may it be that you reach the high rank and live to weave the Torah Curtain of the Temple of our holiness, which shall be raised soon in our days, amen, and on it the High Priest would strike the blood of the offering *and thus would he count: one and one, one and two, one and three* . . ." His zeal increased, he was almost shouting. His shoulders swayed against the table and his fists beat the counting, until he stopped, and with his eyes still shut, he leaned his head toward you. "It is sinful that you started the holy weaving before you made repair by coupling. Not, Heaven forfend, to confuse the mixed multitude of souls of the shell with the innermost garb . . . For soon you will be coupled with Isaiah. And know that there is great repair in that, great repair, Amalia, and you have to be very careful."

The ringing of the screen sounded in the distance like the roar of the sea burgeoning behind cliffs. The rabbi raised the small knife Isaiah had used, and rolled it between his fingers and his thumb. You were amazed at how he sank the blade into his flesh.

"For only in our generation, a generation that is all destruction, that is all torments and bad smell, can one fathom the secret of galbanum in the coupling of groom and Bride . . . For only when Egypt will draw out all the blood, until the Ze'ir Anpin will remain without any blood at all, only then by the passionate union in coupling will Mercy be spread and the greatness of redemption be revealed. Yes, that is the secret of the repair of the bad smell of the galbanum, in the coupling of groom and Briiiiide. And that's the reason for the yearning of the female to cleave to the male, to fill her deficiency of the soul and body. As it is written, *Love the Lord your God and serve Him with all your heart and all your soul!*"

You raised your head. And to this day, the amazing sight of Rabbi Avuya Aseraf's face in the returning light is burned in me. The billow of red hair flaming in the gray of his curls, the skin stretched swarthy over the cheekbones, and the gigantic eyes burning so beneath the lids. The distant eruption grew tempestuous and roared. His words spun, penetrating you like flaming iron, kindling in you the yearning for Isaiah. Yes, then, unconsciously, a tremor of yearning sprouted in you (and that was enough to become act afterward), and when the rabbi passed his hand close to you, your lips already drew after it in a swoon.

All of a sudden, the rabbi waved his hand. You were terrified. You couldn't stifle the shout that burst out of you. He examined you (yes, I'm sure that for a moment he simply checked your response with his hand raised), and then he chuckled, "Scared? Ha . . . ha . . . I only wanted to pour us some more cold water, to quench the thirst, heh, heh, heh."

His chuckle released from you scared laughter that grew louder and louder; you couldn't stop the shrieks. A wild, loud laughter you didn't imagine still dwelling in you, bursting out sharp, as before, sweeping away in its billows the mantle of good behavior you had worked so hard to assume.

A mighty flood of exultation shook you, no longer would you be bathed in sweat, waking up at night weeping and shouting: *to change his name, as if to say I am a different person and not the same one who sinned.* A wild flood, rolling from Emily's throat as she sings on the hotel roof as dawn rises over Jerusalem, bowing and bending to the city walls emerging from the bluish mist, singing in suffocation of its thanksgiving, washing from her the remnants of the pain, the journey, her limbs, her hair, her red dress dusty with dirt, her ankles that would descend all that day on the mountain paths, on the kindled roads, on the slopes . . . The voice of Rabbi Avuya Aseraf ignited in you once again the moaning that never subsided, that was only lurking, waiting to return and pounce as at first, the faith that you could rush, rush without restraint to holiness . . .

And then the rabbi could grab you with both his hands like a flame of offering, could roll you on your back, spread you open as he liked, without your consent, rummage the embers burning in you as much as he desired. And as someone who had already made his way, he continued, his eyes flooding through the wails of your laughter.

"For especially you, Amalia, you have the power to raise sin to holiness. You, Amalia, who sucks your life from the destruction, as it is written, *And when I passed by thee and saw thee polluted in thine own blood . . .* With God's help, you are destined for a great task in the restoration of the Shekhina! As it is written, *and maintains His faith to those asleep in the dust . . .* For the destruction is God's concealment, the sinking of the holy in the shell. And how many torments do the nation and the Shekhina have, Amaliyyyyaaa? . . . And only real martyrdom, only the death of the soul for the sake of holiness can break open the blood of the mother giving birth! The death of saints, Amalia, is the beginning of redemption. This is the awful secret of the circumcision, the covenant of blood, the beginning of redemption from the destruction! . . . But it requires great courage, great courage Amaliyyyaaa."

You trembled. The rabbi saw, he saw immediately that what happened had not happened in vain! He saw what Rabbi Israel Gothelf never saw! For Rabbi Israel told you explicitly that everyone who sins and is ashamed of it is forgiven all his iniquities—"*He is ashamed of it, Amalia*"—that's what he said, and only Rabbi Avuya Aseraf saw that *his left hand is under my head, and his right hand doth embrace me,* and that you sank in sin in order to torment yourself with the torments of destruction, to know by yourself the real holy death, so that from sin fire will arise and sear together in repentance of salvation Mala and you . . .

As if he were reading your secret thoughts, he leaned over and whispered, "For know, Amalia, that it is not only your soul you will repair but also the souls of the dead. And the name you are called is a secret of repairing the world from darkness." (You clasped your wrist and your breath came faster.) "As it is said, *and whatsoever Adam called every living creature, that was the name thereof.* And that's what we learned from our Holy Rabbi, the light of the Seven Days, that the name of every person is his vitality, and the name of God revives and connects vitality with mind, and if a man or woman is named for a dead man or woman, he cleaves and ties his vitality and his mind with the name of the dead man or woman. As it is written, *causing the lips of those who are asleep to speak.* Cause the lips of those who sleep to speak, Amaliyyyaaa.

"But it requires great courage, great couraaaage." He didn't relent, scrutinizing you and enunciating: "For know, Amalia, the Torah is not upheld except by one who kills himself for it."

Yes, even that he saw in you, even the force compelled by darkness. And you shuddered. For no one had ever talked to you like that, no one knew you so well, in all your despicable, disgusting degradation, no one ever promised you as he did that from the black pit full of *appapatz,* from the root of the dread, you would find salvation.

The rabbi's last words touched you dimly, and the ringing was very shrill, sweeping up the rising roar in that thick sweetness that tries constantly to dissipate, a sweetness of green jelly and the shrieking of cats that comes into the throat because the windows are open even when it's cloudy and cold, a green jelly with such sweet pieces that Aunt Henia made to poison her, like Snow White's stepmother, so she won't reveal how she and Mala want to throw Mother out the open windows, Mother who is so little and black because of the sickness, and the blankets and the pillows too. That's why Aunt Henia came especially from Haifa and opens everything as if to air it out, even though there's a draft and the curtains are moving, and sticking out a tongue with a bad smell of Mother's disgusting medicines, and she rolls up the carpets, and puts in the living room a circle of chairs gathered from all over the house, and their feet drag on the floor and make scars. Aunt Henia is scared she'll tell Father, that's why she made the green jelly with the sweet pieces of poison and thrust it at her with a spoon: "Here, here, poor child, here, poor Malinka." But she ran to the bathroom fast and spit up as much of

the jelly as she could, and then she ran away to Mother's room, and
touched the swollen face of the pillow and the blanket where Mother is
still hiding, even though they're cold now and smell of the dust from the
big rug that Aunt Henia beat all morning. Then she rolled up on the
cold floor between the bed with the big frame like a ship and the high
closet, fast, before Aunt Henia found out what she was doing. And with
all her might she controls herself so the cold floor won't release the
peepee that's running down her legs, and the underpants are burning in
the crack, and she stretches out her little hand very slowly to the lock of
the closet so it won't make any noise, presses and pushes the wooden
doors that smell of big coats and wool pants with cigarette smoke, and
in Mother's drawer, bottles of eau de cologne and bitter crumbs of medicines and gold lipsticks collide and jingle. And her heart leaps into her
throat but she doesn't stop and opens the drawer with Father's underpants that have gigantic openings like a sail, and folded handkerchiefs that
smell burned from Mother's iron, sinks her hand in the soft folds of cloth,
and controls herself with all her might so the cold dust of the floor won't
climb up her legs in the plaid skirt of prickly wool, until at the end of the
drawer under the handkerchiefs, her hand touches! The heart lets go in
shouts, and she takes out a small box covered with red cloth as smooth as
a little girl's cheek. And the strong flash bites her stomach like a small animal. And inside the box is a tiny gold heart, and her finger fumbles on
the locket like a blind pup seeking the teat, touches the bulge of the tiny
lock, and presses. The lid of the heart jumps open with a thin, high ring,
flakes of gold, and from it leaps her white face! With the strong, dark
eyes and the frame of hair. And the dark eyes cover her with warmth that
releases warm streams from her stomach onto the floor, covers her with
black and white and gold, her and the little animal biting her stomach.
From the staircase voices burst, men with crushed gray wool hats and big
coats are dragging Father by the elbows, and from the open window
come the exhalations of the buses and the cold gray that pinches her bottom on the floor. And now Aunt Henia is picking her up and pecking with
a sharp beak—*here, here, here*—dragging off the wool skirt and the underpants—*here, here, here*. And she abandons her behind to Aunt Henia
even though the gray hats see all of her, and only with all her might
does she look straight into Father's weeping eyes, shouting mutely at

him, *It's so we won't be alone, Father, so we won't be alone!* She shouts at him with a bliss that bursts her body with the warmth of gold, *Don't be afraid, I found her, she's here, she's here!* And Father answers her mutely, *Yes, child, yes, Malinka,* and moves his head in the golden heart, and the men with the hats drag him to the living room, and the floor scratches the whispers in her throat: "Now Stashek can finally weep for Mala—for Mala more than for Ruziaaaa—can weep for her without guuuuilt— love her without guuuuilt, without guilt, without guuuuuilt . . ."

"And it's important now, Amalia, to strive for the holy repair destined for you. For how many are the torments of the nation and the Shekhina. Important to be strict about purification of the body, Amalia, mikveh and attention to eating, and to be very careful about the words of prayer. At night should recite Midnight Prayer, sit on the floor. The zealots really sit on the ground, kneeling. As we drew from scripture, *in my flesh,* Amaliyyyaaa, *in my flesh shall I see God.* Be strong and of good courage, for soon, when you cling to the holy coupling with your man, Isaiah, you will find rest for your tortured soul."

Everything became confused in you. You bent your head, humiliated yet consoled, for the holy rabbi had chosen you, and how could you reject his call? For he promised that after the torments, you would reach salvation, even if for that you would have to sacrifice Isaiah's love, a sacrifice of love. And you didn't take your tear-flooded look away from the hand of Rabbi Aseraf, his hand that rose to his ignited beard, a movement full of pleasure.

Yes, there, in those private moments with Rabbi Aseraf, you made your decision. And even if your strength was diminished without Isaiah, and even if you were shrouded in vapors of incense to perdition, exhausted by sleepless nights, by the dread of sin, by the old fears that awoke in you—all that didn't change the fact that the words of Rabbi Avuya Aseraf found fertile ground in your fears. You followed him without any questions, abandoned the softness of Isaiah's love. Yearning in panic for the dark repair destined for you . . .

And now what? For am I better than you? Yesterday (it's hard to connect those hours to the moments of writing in the heart of darkness now) the

mailman brought a postcard. *To Emily from Hubert.* The mail still connects then and now. The only words that stood out for me when I burned
the postcard on the gas flame were: *Dear Emily, now that the two of us are
again alone* . . . Always with that nauseating sweetness. *Emily my expiation, Emily my love* . . . How I ran to the kitchen, lighting the gas with
trembling fingers, throwing into the flames the swarming abomination.
And I had thought that worlds separated me from last year . . .

How much I'm terrified of the other letter, from Stein, which after all
might get here before I finish the task, before the end of the Omer
Counting. He shouted after you, shouted that he would come here and
take what was his, so why go on deluding myself. Why postpone, with
trivial claims, doing what was decided. The photos are still (still!) here.
And how will I dare spread my prayer before You?

And pious Rachel, too, the images she stole from her father's house
were her corruption. *"Let it not displease my lord that I cannot rise up before thee; for the custom of women is upon me,"* she said, and from her sitting and lying about the images the Judgment rose and was mixed with
the waters of her womb. It was the Judgment of the images that made her
labor so hard that she died in giving birth.

And what would have happened if Rabbi Avuya Aseraf hadn't passed
away, if he hadn't put an end to his life in that long fast, what would have
come upon me now?

"Let's go out, Amalia. Bring what you wrote, and in the garden I shall
give you some holy plants that suckled the sap of our wasteland, to repair the body and the soul. And be very careful in everything I've told
you, for there is great Tikkun in that, Amalia, for you and for your name,
the Tikkun of Rachel and Leah, with God's help. We shall talk about that
some more, Amalia, the next time you come."

He got up. For a moment his gray hair turning red caught the light filtering into the gloom of the Ark of the Covenant and the benches. You
got up behind him, gathering the lists of plants and instructions for
preparation, and the pages fluttering in your lap. From the doorsill you
saw the rabbi's broad shoulders going down the dirt path.

The yard was covered with the shadows of the pine trees running in
the wind rising from the slopes. You were about to run and grab Isaiah,

bury your fingers in his curls, stroke his long back, nestle against him, but the rabbi's thick voice rose in you again. The warmth of the stones of the wall was felt in the evening chill. You moved from where you were leaning in the doorway, letting go of the screen behind you, and continued down the stairs of the entrance in a daze, toward the rabbi's back as he stood among the flowerbeds. And even before the thin figure of Isaiah parted from the flowerbeds and came toward the two of you, the ring of the screen rose once again.

A dusky dryness mixed with the new ringing. Under the treetops turning dark in the sunset, the figure of Isaiah approached, holding out a bunch of medicinal herbs he had picked from the garden, and his lifted face was transparent with wonder, he was trying to say something. "Amalia, I wanted to . . ."

But before he finished, the rabbi approached and planted himself between the two of you; he patted Isaiah's shoulder with one hand and his other hand he wound around you. And like that, holding one of you on each side, he led you to the blacksmith's shed. As you passed among the flowerbeds sunk in a bluish shadow he went on talking of the capacity of the herbs to improve the body and the soul. Words that didn't reach your ears. Smells of the garden and the resin were mixed with the scents of sawdust and dirt. The density of the low light, soaked with the pine dust, caressed Isaiah's face with gold. And perhaps it only seemed to you that with one hand the rabbi pulled you close to him and with his other hand he pushed Isaiah away. He disappeared into the shed, scrabbled in a heap of stacked-up tin bowls, and pulled out one with a split lip. He held it in both hands, listened with his head down and his eyes shut. And then he took a hammer from among his tools and brought it down with sharp bangs on the edges of the bowl, quickly spinning it on the anvil, and once again hammered it, *bang bang*. Again he brought the bowl close to his face, passing its sides over his lips, with his eyes shut, and only then did he turn.

"People stupidly throw out flawed vessels, and don't know that it's impossible for salvation to be fulfilled unless the vessels are repaired! I trudge around the neighborhoods, pleading to stupid ears: *Flaaaawed vesseeels! Flaaaawed vesseeels! Don't throw them out because of sin, repair the Body of the Queen! Woe to him who takes vessels lightlyyyyyy!*"

His face grimaced in torments. His voice spread in the isolated yard on the mountain, sending a shiver down your spine. He tossed the tin bowl on the pile and spread both his hands out to you. "Especially now, during the days of the Omer Counting, vessels must be repaired so they'll be fit for the coupling of the Holy-One-Blessed-Be-He and the Shekhina. To repair the forty-nine gates of the image with the forty-nine days of the Counting. The vessels, precisely the vessels!

"Now, come here." He withdrew into the depth of the shed and clapped his hands to hurry you along. "Here are the censers, as it is written, *And take every man his censer, and put incense in them, and bring ye before the Lord every man his censer.*" You advanced into the gloom, your steps cracking on bars of iron and planks, and Isaiah hurried behind you. The rabbi waited, holding out the censers to you.

"May it be that, in the great grace of Bar Yochai, on the night of his celebration next week, the holy flames will refine your hearts to each other, like a fire that refines iron from ore. May it be that we shall soon be graced, with the help of God, to rejoice the groom and Bride, *for a Jew, even if he sinned, remains a Jew,* and this is the essence of our generation, the secret of the final repair, the Tikkun of galbanum."

He tossed the weight of the censers on the pile, and once again wound his arms around your shoulders, pulling you out of the shed toward the ruddy light pouring onto the garden. "We shall go on talking about that, with the help of God, the next time. And until then, we have to prepare with all devooootion."

Then he put his broad hand on your hair, cupping your skull. The heaviness of his fingers spread over your back, making an unclear, blurred memory swoop down on you with all its warmth in the evening chill, a thick warmth spilling down from your head to your body like tears, and panic, and from the choking heaviness, which had slipped away until then, the touch of Father's hand in the darkness of the bedroom finally became sharp on Amy's skull as she sits cross-legged on the floor in front of the big closet, squatting like a little girl, with the long hair coming down to her waist covering the T-shirt, the touch of his hand that doesn't dispel the fury at the suddenly empty drawer! How will she admit that she came to rummage in it, even though she always said she didn't care, none of it concerned her, wasn't any of her business, and when he left the house, she accompanied his departure by practicing the foreign songs and strumming on a guitar as if she didn't notice, when in fact she was only waiting for him to close the door to slip into the bedroom. He never spoke, and she didn't ask. After lunch he put on a coat and a hat in all seasons, crossed the space to the store and back, only to stand on the sidewalk next to the tree that grew in the iron cage and watch how the new owners arranged the crates on the shelves he had built. He stood and watched even though that bothered the new owners, who paid rent every month. And was careful, when he returned, not to open the door too quickly, leaving her time to thrust everything back beneath the underwear in the drawer and to slip into her own room, grabbing the guitar. Only then did he come in, hang up his hat among the coats in the entrance, while in her room, on the sofa, she shielded herself from him with her hair. So how would she ask now, *Where is the gold locket that has disappeared from its place in the drawer?* How would she ask why he took it? So weak—why, why did he take it? She bites her lip, lets Father stroke her hair, for even the weight of his hand on her hair wouldn't last long, he too would leave her in a little while. "Malinka." He hovers over her neck. "You understand? Right, Malinka? Nothing's important. You understand." And he goes off with his back bent, and carefully approaches the old phonograph, as if she isn't sitting there on the floor in the gloom with the shutters drawn, picks up a record, slowly takes it out of its sleeve, moves the switch with a strained finger, and with his head tilted, he follows the mechanism that moves the record from the turntable to the raising of the arm, hovering for a moment like a living creature, and its slip under the dropping of the needle on the waves of its bow. "Music is different, without a body, and that too . . ." It's not clear to her if in the gloom between the phonograph and the bed he remembers that she's sitting there, or if he's talking to himself in the foreign accent: "Shouldn't keep old things in the house." His fingers are bent behind his back as if they were trying to hold on to something. "All the things in the closet, and all this here," indicating the violin case and the records in paper wrappers, "there's nothing in it, nothing. Nothing has remained. . . . You understand? You'll throw it all out, right? You'll do that? I don't have any strength left anymore." He turns his back to her, concentrated in the shadow between the cabinet and the bed, his stiff hand strumming the notes of the violin and piano in the air for a moment, and then resting. And the bitterness of the floor and the green curtains melt with the playing—Isaiah's face was turned mutely to you. You walked behind him on the path across the yard to the gate. The hiss of the welding rose from the shed. And when you turned your head, you saw the iron mask descending on the shadow of the rabbi as he leaned over the anvil, wreathed in a trail of sparks and smoke.

O Lord, my God, do not make a full end of me, Thou rememberest every deed. For the remembrance of every act cometh before Thee. O Lord, my God, do not make a full end of me . . .

Isaiah slipped out of the yard, went deeper among the illuminated trunks, and you walked on as in a dream, winding, placing your sandals in the traces of his footsteps, not heeding his stormy silence, for it was you the rabbi chose, you, not Isaiah. And you were careful not to slip on the piles of needles on the glittering rocks.

Beside the path stood a hut painted blue and surrounded by a garden, its shutters closed. Through the climbing vine with blue flowers on the fence, the flowerbeds sparkled. Spots of pink and purple of dahlias, gladioli bending in the hot wind, and sunflowers burning at the edges. Smells of honeydew and damp earth wafted toward you and blended with the dryness of the mountain air, deepening some unknown sweetness. You made your way among the wild bushes and thorns. Isaiah's white shirt played in front of your eyes, and his ritual fringes moved.

"I hope you had an important talk with the rabbi," he said at last, with an effort, as you strode beside each other down the road. "All his acts are holy. With the help of God, we must follow in his footsteps," he went on, as if to himself, not asking any questions. And when you raised your eyes, he lowered his face.

You came to the stone bridge over the ravine. Isaiah passed close to the ledge. Through the bridge the deep bottom was visible. The branches of the fig and olive trees down there were already covered with the shadow of sunset, and his trousers flickered against that background. You stopped. Pretending you lingered to shake a piece of dirt out of your sandal. "Just a minute, I . . ."

You saw Isaiah stop and lean on the ledge, facing the valley. His short
sleeve stuck out as though empty of its limb. You straightened up behind
his back, which seemed suspended over the valley. And even though you
knew in your heart that it was impossible, that you hadn't yet immersed
your body, you hadn't washed your flesh in lye, that only to maintain
Rabbi Aseraf's fire in you did you come close to him—in spite of that,
you slowly took the two steps separating you from Isaiah, and your knees
shook.

(And perhaps, of all the afternoons last year, it is only that moment that
is alive in me. Doesn't melt. Like a crystal. Impermeable. You take the
two steps separating you from his leaning back, come close to him with
a heavy hand. And everything stops.

And yet, you knew at that moment, when you raised your hand to the
fold of his sleeve, you knew for a split second, with a flash of premonition, the pain you would bring down on him by order of the rabbi. And
you also knew that it was only you standing in the root of darkness,
only you. Maybe it was the memory of the future pain that made your ankles tremble, or maybe for a moment the hope that, along with the pain,
the two of you would know a consolation flooded you, dissolving your
body in thanks that the two of you were in the navel of the world, beyond
the banks of darkness, for eternity, in the root of the creation, in the
heart of the movement of the firmament and the Sefirot in their orbit,
and a new ancient song rises and shrouds you until the throne of the
Name of God . . .

You reached out to Isaiah's sleeve, passing your hand lightly over the
rough fold, ignoring how he flinched. Your eyes roved from the touch of
whiteness to the paths in the valley below you. You came close to the
ledge of the bridge too, until the wings of your skirt grazed the strings
of his ritual fringes. The heat of the day turning cool streamed over the
ledge. And then you were off walking.

That was all that happened that day. But it was enough for Rabbi
Avuya's words to incite in you the thought that you were already al-
lowed to the man beside you, by grace of the repair destined for you.
That was enough for the madness in you to prevail, until what finally

happened between you and Isaiah on the night of the bonfire. Happened, irrevocably.

For how excited you were when you went back home with the herbs from the rabbi's garden, with the recipes, the names of the plants, the quantities, the instructions for crushing, mixing, boiling. You imagined the source of life was revealed to you. You spent whole days in the kitchen feverishly (again, in the kitchen, as in the years when she was left alone with Father, their long silences during meals, the steam of the bland dishes separating them), boiling the herbs, kneading mixtures of them. Planning your days with Isaiah as hastily as a bird scurrying, far beyond the strength of its tiny wings, to gather bundles of straw before laying her eggs. So desperate . . . You were intoxicated (for a short time, but indeed intoxicated) with the rabbi's promise. With a profound awakening that died out as fast as it had blazed up. And if the fire last year hadn't been kindled, if you hadn't sacrificed Isaiah's love like that . . .

I still haven't asked his forgiveness, I haven't fallen at his feet. And he, too, ever since it happened, is no longer the same person. The last time he came here (already more than two weeks ago) he was like a stranger in the tight suit and the hat. And the beard that had covered his face. Like a stranger, as if he were already enveloped in Elisheva's being, in the heaviness of her body.

Late. The heart of the second watch of the night. Another twenty-five days. Half the Omer Counting. If only I smoked, the sight of the devoured paper would ease the passage of time a bit. For a moment the sheet of darkness seemed rolled up in the East, as if the dawn was already decreed there. Only a vision, a pretext to evade the confessions I owe You . . .

And why have I kept, *until now,* the remnants of Rabbi Avuya Aseraf? All those recipes in purple ink, booklets, pamphlets of supplications and effusions of the soul that he gave you, went on sending you. Even the dried plants from his garden are still stored in jars on the kitchen shelf. Hasn't the charm melted by now?

And how is it that I haven't yet thrown out all the hairpins, salves, old clothes you dragged around in suitcases behind you, remnants of my coquetry, yours, hers, from all the places, all the names? Amy, Emily, Malinka, Amalia. (And the photographs—big cardboard boxes with all the photographs—how is it I haven't dared get rid of them?)

Like Rachel hiding the images beneath the camel's cushion . . .

You went the rest of the way in silence, each of you steeped in your own thoughts. The road bisected the industrial areas, and the noise of cars resounded through the lots. Only near here, beyond the crossroads, did the smell of heat rising from the valley fall at your feet. But by then the time was short. The wheel of the sun had long vanished in the mist that swathed the horizon, and the valley was sunk in a cloud of blue. At the bend in the road circling the mountain, it seemed to you that all of it was already lived. And you found yourselves at the door.

"Let's go in, you must be thirsty," you said quietly, through the slight rustling.

"No, not this time."

"Then I'll bring out a glass of water."

"No, thanks, no need . . ." And suddenly, he declared, as if he were debating: "I'm going back to Rabbi Aseraf now," and his back hardened. "We're busy with a special study."

You nodded, smiling at the sound of the rabbi's name, and just added dreamily, "Go in peace, don't be late."

"Yes," he whispered, and the hardness left his limbs. "I'll come by, God willing, on the evening of Lag b'Omer. I'll take you to the bonfire." And again some distance resounded in his voice. He retreated on the path. A screen of evening specks immediately covered his ungainliness. The thick shadow that rose from the valley was wreathed in the smoke of ovens and desert.

Inside the house you immediately recited the prayer, and you extended the Counting with devotion. You spent the rest of the evening doing nothing special, your mind at odds with itself. Until you fell asleep, Isaiah's softness shrouded you in a thin swoon like a miniature death. But that very night, when you awoke after midnight under the light you had forgotten to turn off, your body seething and your hair bathed in sweat, you grimaced when Isaiah came up in your thoughts. For his light lasted only a short time. And right away the voice of Rabbi Avuya Aseraf rose in you, assigning you the horrible repair. *Amaliyyyyaaa.* And you loathed Isaiah so much, for he was only the means that summoned you, as the rabbi said, only a tool to lead you in the ways of salvation.

I sat a long time. The hand forged to the pen as if it were cut off from my will. The moon set in the west long ago. Density of night. Only slowly does the touch of the pen return to the fingers.

The sound of the refrigerator. By now I'm used to the courses of its coughing, almost wait for them. I practically don't go into the kitchen anymore; it has turned into a kind of no-man's-land. The mustiness of the damp walls wafts there without being mixed with a steam of food. Out of laziness, I didn't scrape off the grains of rice that stuck to the only pot. Starting to be a pot with a past . . . I didn't know I'd turn into someone burdened with property. And here of all places, at the final station. Still holding to the eternal life of a few things breathing in the same space with me. Watching my acts. Witnesses. The rumblings of the refrigerator shake the table.

(And maybe *everything* is in vain. Even the weaving. Who guarantees that my intentions are pure? And isn't the border so thin—at the very hour when Moses received the secret of making the Tabernacle, the Priest's mantle, the Torah Curtain, the people were breaking off their golden earrings and making a molten calf.

And maybe everything is in vain, even the words inscribed, they too are only corporeal bodies, and their vitality eludes my grasp. Maybe everything is in vain. And there is nothing. Nothing.

And maybe what is leading me is the compulsion to force Stein to come claim photographs.

We have neither fires nor trespass offerings. Neither linens nor cakes unleavened, tempered with oil. Neither fortune nor coals, our transgressions laid waste the dwelling place, and our sins prolonged its destruction, but a memorandum will be our forgiveness.

The heaviness of the walls is present, blocking me from You. Weighing on the breathing.

What an effort is required not to think about everything that happened afterward—the death of Rabbi Aseraf, too. Just to immerse myself in the task You have assigned me, to repair Your Name in the world. Just to immerse myself. Not understanding. Not thinking.

On the ridges the night is driven away. The room peels off its folds. (Not to contemplate what was written.) I can't, can't stand up to pray. *Please, HaShem, do not make the times troublesome for me.*

Twenty-seven days of the Omer, Essence of Eternity.

That Sabbath, you were invited to Rabbi Israel Gothelf's house to give your "report." But since you had met Rabbi Avuya, the invitation had slipped your mind, and only near the start of the Sabbath did you abruptly stop the flying of the shuttle, close the shutters, and go out. You went through the emptiness of downtown, passing the doorways of the last shops, finishing up their business before the Sabbath. The low sun exposed the neglect of the buildings. The last bus picked you up at the empty stop, and by the time you reached the rabbi's neighborhood, the street was blocked with chains, and the children were playing their games in Sabbath clothing.

At the top of the stairs, you pressed for a moment the small bundle you had brought for the Sabbath, and trembling in the gloom was the same glow that had spread over Rabbi Aseraf's yard as he led you from the blacksmith shop, his hands on your shoulders, toward the evening turning blue. Then at the door was Yocheved's smiling face, and the little girls huddled behind her. You were rushed to light the candles. On the silver tray, the mass of candles of the mother and daughters was already burning. With fingers shaking from the trip, you attempted to bring the match to your candles through the wall of flames. You buried your face for the blessing. The red of the fire plowed through your fingers the shadow of Rabbi Avuya Aseraf's flaming beard, the greatness of the promise in his words. You straightened up, trembling with pride, that he was to lead you behind him in the awful repair, you . . .

From the door, the little girls shrieked, "Shabbat Shalom! Shabbat Shalom!"

And from the kitchen rose Yocheved's shout, "Shabbat Shalom, Amalia! Shabbat Shalom!"

You impatiently slipped off for evening prayers in the synagogue, and only in the gloom of the staircase did you slow down a moment, melted with sweetness, as if only now had the echoes of that stormy week become sharp, gathered to the space of the Sabbath.

On the street, there was still a deep light, and over the sky falling to the west a glow stretched, as if the bowl of red would never be over-turned to the slopes of darkness. With your hair undone, you made your way past the people walking slowly to the synagogue, going through groups of them, filled with gratitude for HaShem for His kindness, for taking you from a place of darkness and the shadow of death, and break-ing your shackles. And in the middle of the street you almost exploded with exultation for that concealed delight.

On the stairs to the women's section, little girls in laced-up dresses were tramping, their shouts swollen by the plaster on the walls, and in-side the synagogue, bubbles of heat floated from the densely packed bodies. From the crowd, Elisheva waved to you, pointing to the seat she had saved next to her.

"Amalia." She grabbed you, bringing the flash of her mottled face close. "I'm also invited to Rabbi Israel! Yocheved thought that like that, God willing, we'd all be together, like before."

You recoiled. You really hadn't expected to meet Elisheva of all peo-ple in the synagogue. How she pushed herself on you, waving the prayer book with a heavy hand! If only she wouldn't ruin things now. For, it was *you* Rabbi Avuya Aseraf talked to, *you* he saw. Not her. In the chair in front of you, a young woman fastened a honey-colored shawl around her neck and her soft fingers groped absently in the knitted loops. For a mo-ment, you had a fleeting thought that her skin was pure and dim as honey. Your gaze wandered.

"Today if ye will hear his voice, harden not your heart, as in the provo-

caaaation." The men's jackets moved behind the partition. *Of course they aren't as strict about repair of their souls as they are about their clothing,* you thought pursing your lips, and you sat up very straight, caressing the syllables on your palate, *"Hasten, show love, for the time has coooome. . . ."* And you stood up flooded with light, singing heartily, *"Enter in peace, O crown of her husband, Even in joyous song and good cheer, Enter O Bride! Enter O Briiiide!"* Knowing vaguely that those words had been said in your ears, in phrases of an awful secret, binding you in wondrous ways to Rabbi Avuya Aseraf, to Mala . . . And although you felt the women worshippers looking at you obliquely, you didn't slow the bowing of supplication in the *Amidah,* and you said the words *Let my soul be like dust to everyone* steeped in submission, and at the end of the service, when you repeated with the crowd the declaration *Today is the thirtieth day of the Counting of the Omer, Power of Splendor,* your breathing was so soaked . . .

In the windows the darkness had deepened, and a flash of clothes and lamps shrieked into the shell of night. You were borne among the dense crowd on the steps going out, Elisheva dragging her dry hair in front of you, lingering at the exit, greeting her neighbors. You watched her clinging to one group after another, laughing with them with exaggerated happiness, and you seemed to be cut off from everything, sailing far away. And you didn't rush her, for what did you care anymore about the dinner in Rabbi Israel's house or the conversation that would take place when it was over?

You walked next to each other in the street, Elisheva's muscular arms rubbing against yours. You attempted to revive in you the flame of the words that had been said to you there, in the house on the mountain, and you didn't know if the uneasiness was spreading in you because of the awe from the words of Rabbi Aseraf, or perhaps from the memory of Isaiah's body, which somehow grazed you as you walked.

You ascended the stairs of the rabbi's house surrounded by and leaning on the arms of ministering angels, angels of peace, angels of the Exalted One, who sheltered you to the white Sabbath table and Yocheved's headdress, whose ends moved like the wings of a dove in the tallow of the melted candles. You smiled to yourself, thinking of the figure of Rabbi Avuya Aseraf, and the cry of the little girls opening their mouths in song rose up, *"Bless me for peace, O angels of peace, angels of the Ex-*

alted One, " and Rabbi Gothelf's thin lips articulated at the head of the table, *"May your departure be to peace, O angels of peace . . ."* And all at once the wings were clipped.

You hastily washed your hands under the orbits of the rabbi's eyes, and you returned to the table, with a blessing on your lips, facing the wine sparkling in the glass between his hands. And when he waved the big challahs, his fingers hovered in front of you, dropping from the cuff, pressing the knife slicing the flesh of the challah. And once again the little girls' cries rose as they eagerly grabbed their pieces, and the prattle of Elisheva, who got up to help the rabbi's wife bring the fish from the kitchen, and you remained face to face with Rabbi Israel, and only the little girls' capering separated the two ends of the table, came between you and the gray of his eyes.

Behind the platter of fish, Yocheved thrust toward you her face abounding in affection: "Well, soon, God willing, Amalia also will be serving fish on the Sabbath eve."

You forced a smile, raising your fork. The taste exploded on your palate.

"Don't worry," she added at the sight of your embarrassment. "It's like raising children, you don't know how, but it comes to you, with the help of God. For me, the way to know whether a girl has repented and is a proper Jew in every respect, is by tasting the gefilte fish she makes and seeing if it tastes the way it should."

Elisheva laughed, turning her joyous face to you as if the silence loaded between you as you walked was released. The rabbi rubbed the sauce off his beard, a smug smile on his lips, too. The little girls started squabbling. Shoshanka, whose hair was pulled back in a thick rubber band, grabbed the napkin from Margalit, who poked her with her elbow. Shoshanka burst into loud weeping, to the laughter of the other three, who were watching appreciatively, and the rabbi's wife spread her arms imploring, "Shoshanka, Margalit! Better behavior on the Sabbath."

The rabbi withdrew in his chair from the eight women at the table with him. *"Heart and flesh, heart heart and flesh, heart heart and flesh sing their praise to the God ever living, heart heart and flesh sing their praise to the God ever livinnnng,"* he trilled as if to himself, beating out the song's rhythm with his fork.

You stuck out your chin arrogantly, the fire of Rabbi Aseraf's words inflaming you, for there really was no importance at all to what would soon be said between you and Rabbi Israel, whose buttoned jacket wrinkled and turned dark with every one of his movements.

"Our Creator is One, He who said: As I live, tooooo behold Meeeee can none and remainnnnn of the livinnnnng, behold Meeeee can none and remainnnnn of the livinnnnng . . ."

You got up, as if to help take the fish plates back to the kitchen, and the little bit of food you had eaten pervaded the blur of lamps and flames. The room turned so dark before your eyes that you found yourself leaning against the kitchen wall, and the load of china plates slipped out of your grasp into the sink. For a moment, you couldn't distinguish between the rabbi's voice rising from the corridor and the tones of the voices of Father and Ludwig Stein carefully explaining something to you, each in his own way. The rabbi's wife's body pushed into the kitchen close on your heels. She released a column of steam from beneath the covers of the pots concealed in a blanket on the Sabbath hot plate, scooping a pulp of food from them.

Hearrrrrt and fllllllesh, heart heart and flesh, heart heart and fllllllesh, heart heart and flesh sing their praise to the God ever livinnnng . . .

"You'll see, Amalia, in family life, with the help of God, there is a lot of joy, but there are also hard times." Overcooked potatoes emitted a jet of steam. "You have to know how to bless all of it, that's faith, Amalia, that's . . ." Yocheved's hands brought chicken wings and hot carrot purée up from the pots.

You followed the rabbi's wife into the corridor with a steaming bowl in your hands. Back in your chair, you made a great effort to preserve the space separating you from the bodies of the little girls reaching for the bowl of barley and potatoes, from which rose a screen of steam, covering Rabbi Israel's delicate face. Yes, you'll tell him everything, you'll say everything to his gray eyes that will look at you, yes, you'll lead him behind you, behind the light that has been revealed to you, you, his beloved student.

The candles began collapsing in the holders, flickering with a torch of red in the platter, flaring up before dying out, like the Evil Will that blazes up before Salvation, you pondered as the soft food stuck in your throat. Elisheva got up and collected the meat plates, and the girls responded to the rabbi's song, their childish voices flaming with all their innocence: " *'Tis your son who is dead, 'tis my child who is living, heart heart and flesh sing their praise to the God ever livinnnng.*" You lifted the pamphlet with the Grace after Meals, and the touch of the plastic binding was supple and smooth. From the black letters, the rabbi's song of blessing flowed in its sweetness like a river of fire around your body.

You raised your eyes to the rabbi reading, to his neat, smooth beard: *"I have been young and now am old; yet have I not seen the righteous forsaken nor his seed begging bread!"* You kissed the pamphlet and the plastic binding fluttered caressingly on your lips, just as Isaiah's full lips will soon caress them. With his love, you will repair the root of her name sucking from your breath, that's why you were matched, that's the coupling sent you as salvation, that's what Rabbi Avuya Aseraf said, and that's also what you'll tell Rabbi Israel in a little while when you talk!

You stood up decisively and collected the blessing pamphlets from those at the table. You stopped, perplexed, not knowing where to put them, until Margalit, the oldest daughter, grabbed the pile of pamphlets out of your hands, shoving them into a corner of the shelf. The little girls left the room; Elisheva came in to put the glasses on the tray and take them to the kitchen. You moved toward the doorway.

"I want to talk with you, Amalia." As you expected, Rabbi Israel's voice rose behind you. Only pieces of challah were left on the tablecloth, and around them, crumbs and poppy seeds. Elisheva filled the doorway, but when she saw you and the rabbi sitting at the table, she shook her head knowingly, picked up the bottle of wine by its neck, and hurried out, banging her heels as if to underline the importance of the occasion. You hastened to recall how exactly you thought of telling the rabbi, with what words, but your mind didn't function. The vanishing sound of Elisheva's footsteps weighed on you with the heaviness of lost equilibrium, like dragging the iron legs of the chairs on the floor of the classroom while the eyes of Rabbi Gothelf, taking his books out of his briefcase, skim the circle of girls pressed behind their black books, passing over her, folded up in a corner, stopping finally on Elisheva, leaning next to her with her head on her elbow. And Elisheva stands to signal with her broad limbs. And the rabbi continues monotonously, " 'It is very

praiseworthy for a person who repents to confess in public,' as we learn
from Maimonides' *Laws of Repentance. Anyone who, out of pride, conceals
his sins and does not reveal them will not achieve complete repentance. . . .*
Elisheva, tell how you came to the yeshiva."

And the low, strong, resonant voice: "A few months ago, I went to
Jerusalem . . ." In the shadow of Elisheva's body, she thrusts her sandals
onto the floor, knows that as soon as Elisheva finishes reciting her confession, the rabbi will call her name, and the winter pallor glowing from
the balcony makes her shudder.

"If you ask me why, well, like, I really don't have an answer. It'd
been a few years since I was in Jerusalem, and ever since I came back
from India I hadn't had a chance to go. So one day I just took a bus. You
don't just come to Jerusalem, especially not when you're between one
meditation and another. It's forces beyond our understanding that led
me. I had, thank God, a real miracle! Otherwise, who knows when, with
the help of God, I would have come out of everything and gotten here.
Before the trip, I was into drugs and a lot of sex, with anybody who
came along, men or women, and even after I got back from India, the
feeling was that I was only halfway there. That I hadn't gotten there yet.
The time was short, slipping out of my hands; I had to live as fast and as
hard as possible. Fine, I'm writing. That is, like poetry and subconscious
monologues, something between dream and meditation. A friend of
mine, a poet from Amsterdam, said it was really very special. Well, lately,
like half a year, a year ago, kind of prayers started coming to me. First I
thought it was the influence of levitation. Always that sight of a source
of light in a beam far away. And afterward that conversation *with Him.*
All of a sudden, all those things *to Him.* In the poems, I mean, and also
a lot in the subconscious texts and in all the dreams. And then, in the
morning, after the trip that lasted almost two weeks in the apartment in
Ramat Ha-Sharon, I got on the bus to Jerusalem. I went to the Wailing
Wall, to be in an open place and to feel the stones. I love to feel that
heaviness of the stones. And then, when I went into the little room on the
side, the one for women, the one you go up the steps to, there were two
women there that *He* sent to me. Yes, explicitly, thank God, a higher
force sent them to me! And they said aloud everything I had inside me:
that the time is short, and the task is in our hands, and if we don't choose

the true direction, we'll just go on and stray. One of them was beautiful, with dark eyes and prominent cheekbones, and she talked like she knew me, and she said I didn't yet understand everything I was looking for, because I didn't feel real faith without thinking about myself, faith in God . . . And her burning eyes were like the source of light from the dreams. She said they could feel that I was seeking and that I had already gone far, but I mustn't go on alone anymore, that was dangerous . . . She told me that was dangerous, me, who was all the time going as close as possible to the edge, just to feel it . . . She also told me about Neve Rachel and about the rabbi . . ." Elisheva's body moves so close to her that she can inhale the heat of her excitement. "And now that, with the help of God, I'm born again, when God returns me to Him, to His light, to the Torah, like to know the difference between enthusiasm for no reason and what is truly faith, everything I called the 'great tranquility' back then looks like another world. The seashore and the palm trees, all that has like simply been erased from me, fallen away. That's really what I feel . . ."

(Only a few months before, Elisheva had unpacked her suitcase on the floor of the room they shared and pulled out a silk kerchief of flickering purple scarlet green. "The kerchief of hope!" Elisheva waved it in front of her, where she lay collapsed on the other bed, her body not yet healed, her wrists hidden in the shirtsleeves.

"Just imagine the calm when I got out after three days of traveling in third class, with all the women and babies and passengers on the roofs of the train cars, and went straight to the enormous shore of Pondicherry, with the white, smooth sand. And in that quiet, a peddler with a white belt, just like some character from the Bible, selling glass beads and silk batik kerchiefs. Here, my first purchase in Pondicherry, the kerchief of hope!"

Her broad forehead crinkled childishly, and she whooped with joy. "We'll hang it on the wall in the Eastern place of honor? Ha, ha, we'll hang the sign of hope here . . ." She laughed. Around her were little flasks, soaps, and a thick scent of patchouli; she turned her face to see the response of Amalia, her new friend, her roommate, and was already hanging the flame of colors on the wall, her waving arms wafting the smells of her womanhood. She had changed so much since then, even her hair had lost its shine in the gloom of the yeshiva corridors.)

Elisheva came out with the bottle of wine, and the voices of the squabbling little girls burst into the room.

"I hope the meeting with the young man went well, with the help of God," the rabbi began with a trace of solemnity. From the kitchen echoed the conversation between the rabbi's wife and Elisheva, covered by the clink of china in the sink and the splashing of hot water. You made an effort to recall precisely how you had thought of starting. Sarale and Shoshanka's voices rose. Yocheved's scolding was shot at them. And once again the house was hushed, the only sounds the quiet striking of the cutlery being dried and put away and the bubbling of the kettle. The rabbi fixed his eyes on you.

"Yes, we met," you stated softly, and his warning when she stumbled up to make her confession in class immediately came back to you: "Remember, Amalia, the words of Maimonides: *When does the above apply? With regard to sins between man and man. However, in regard to sins between man and God, it is not necessary to publicize one's transgression.* Is that clear to you?"

"And then Father died, and suddenly there was an apartment and a store . . ." The words come out of her in a warm flood, and around her girls huddle, bending their necks, and she clasps her wrists, wails in a torn breath, "And then was the escape from everything, everything, to the end of the world. And there it started all over again. Yes, it was Stein who paid for it, but so what, let him pay if he wanted to, the trip was for a different account altogether. Yes, from the start, something was wrong. That need to drag Hubert along on the trip, out of fear, to depend on him like some accomplice (and maybe at the time I believed we could help each other . . . in a kind of atonement.) And then everything started collapsing. After the few months that we were there, as if to collect material for the archive, to photograph places. Going around in a threesome, Hubert and I in one car, and Stein behind us in another car, according to the agreement. And then, after months of one big pretense, photographing nothing for days on end, just empty fields, ugly neighborhoods built on the ruins, with one big pretense, as if it were possible to photograph nothing, to make an 'esthetic' in black and white out of that . . . Then, in the hotel, at night, in bed, I heard her crying. Not just next to me, on the pillow, as before, but everywhere, from the closets, from the walls, from the curtains. Like a kind of vision, only really existing, and it kept on even in the morning and all the next day. Sometimes it grew a little weaker, but all the time it went on. I couldn't stop hearing how she cried. Even when Hubert drove me for twenty-four hours, back to his house in Germany so I could rest, so Emily could rest, and he would print everything himself, it just got louder, that heartbreaking crying. And then I understood that it was all because of the photographs, that it was forbidden to photograph! It was forbidden to start with the photographs! Destroy them, as fast as you can, and run away. Impossible to hold on to them! That's what Father said, too, that there is nothing anymore, not there, not anywhere! Only the black pit and her weeping . . . There is nothing anywhere, not even in heaven!"

"Amalia, I'm asking you to stop!" The rabbi's reprimand cuts her off. "What you're saying is blasphemy! I'm warning you."

What does the rabbi mean, why is he stopping her confession, his face turning dark with a grimace of contempt? She isn't crying out against heaven, no, Rabbi, she's only making a sacrificial confession; she believes with all her might that here, among the soft girls in the yeshiva, she'll be able to stop running away.

"But, Rabbi." She's perplexed. "That's what you taught us, that *a person should shed his blood and burn his body, annul himself entirely: that's the essence of confession*, that's what you said—"

"I'm warning you! Stop, right now! You're taking things out of context and you're liable to make everyone sin, God forbid!"

"But, Rabbi—"

And he stands still, waving the clenched fists in the sleeves of the jacket. "Shut up, Amalia! *The soul that sinneth, it shall die!*" he screamed and the veins on his neck stood out. "That's blasphemy! Heresy! You shut up now!" he yelled as he had never yelled before. And the class shakes itself out of its torpor with a roar of raised heads, and the girls surround her. Someone is bringing a glass of water from the kitchen, and the turbid water increases her weakness, and arms hold her, carry her up the stairs to the bed in the room, drop her compassionately, and slip away.

"I'm sure you found a great deal in common, you and Isaiah." The rabbi's fingers were interlaced on the tablecloth.

"Yes, we found . . ." The confirmation slipped out of your mouth.

"Fine."

In the prevailing silence, the rustling of the block of flames in the candleholders was accentuated. They blazed up in a gushing torch, and their reflection burned on the silver platter. On the tablecloth, pieces of challah crusts were turning red, like Rabbi Aseraf's sparkling face, blazing the words, *Amalia, the Torah doesn't exist except in one who kills himself for it, Amalia . . . Who kills himself for it . . . As it is said, "When a man dieth in a tent"* . . . Yes, that's what you wanted to tell Rabbi Israel, the Torah doesn't exist except in one who kills himself for it. . . . That the match with Isaiah is only a means . . .

The sweat spread from your armpits, flowing under your blouse. And far away, Rabbi Aseraf's burning eyes fluttered; *now it's the Sabbath eve, the last hour, Amalia! Forbidden to be grieving at all on the Sabbath eve . . . It must be done with great joy* . . . and the flashes of the hose in the dimness of the blacksmith shop blasting the iron, *for only by complete melting will the part of holiness become refined, like Jacob and Esau, who were formed together in one belly, Amalia, and were separated, separated* . . . The sweat washed down your back, and you no longer knew who was Jacob and who was Esau and who was Amalek, whose memory must be cut off, yes, you and Mala, the two of you struggled together within one womb, and which one of you was it who sat facing Rabbi Avuya Aseraf in the house on the mountain?

"Meet once or twice more with the boy, Amalia, and then you have to decide and announce the engagement and the wedding." Rabbi Gothelf's monotonous voice shriveled the flames that still fluttered in the depths of the candlesticks. "I suggest an engagement agreement after Shavuoth, and a wedding, God willing, can be set, according to the lovely tradition, on the fifteenth of Av. And then, God willing, the family also will be told."

In the kitchen, a drawer slammed in the silence. The block of candles, decapitated by burning, shrank into the grayness of the cabinet. And when you raised your hand to wipe the back of your neck, the buttonholes of Rabbi Israel's jacket were staring at you, and for a moment, the black cloth changed into the wool cloth of Father's coat hanging in the entrance, and you were expecting him to tell you in a weak voice, concentrating all his force, *There is nothing anymore, nothing, you understand, Amalinka . . .*

You stood up, tottering. The rabbi remained seated, his hands on the tablecloth. And some unuttered, stammered space puffed up in your skull. Gaping, taut. For one moment, you yearned to cling completely to Isaiah's slim figure. And in the next moment, Rabbi Israel Gothelf was very far away, because he didn't see what you came to explain to him, didn't see. In the kitchen, the rabbi's wife and Elisheva finished putting away the dishes. The sound of their footsteps approached. They came to the threshold, and there was some comfort in their waning chatter. A dry, twangy monotony scratched the room, whose glow had disappeared. You bent your head without remembering anymore if you had answered the rabbi's words or had left them without a reply, and when your body made its way past the bubble of yellow light in the vestibule, you were almost sorry for the rabbi, who didn't desire to follow you.

"Don't be too hard on yourself, Amalia, go rest now." His voice washed over the back of your neck, and suddenly he was soft, hesitant. "Meet Isaiah again on Lag b'Omer, and God willing, everything will work out . . . fine."

In front of you, Elisheva and the rabbi's wife leaned toward each other, hovering and cooing, exchanging words of farewell.

Finally, you left, you and Elisheva. For another moment, the shining forehead of Yocheved, and the laughter of the daughters went on behind you, then they were slammed shut in the darkness of the staircase. In the street the flickering of the candles also vanished. The moonlight was frozen on the buildings, which seemed to lose some of their heaviness, and the gleam strewn on the sidewalk shook as you walked.

A few hurrying backs vanished into the alley. The main street was full of light patches from the full moon of the month of Iyar. The silent space was still hollowed out in your skull. You concentrated on smoothing the folds of your skirt as you walked. For some reason, the rabbi's twangy melody whirled in you, sweetly, *'Twas our sires loved Thee well; so awake them from sleep . . . Heart and flesh, heart heart and flesh . . .*

Under your feet moved your long shadow and the shadow of Elisheva's body. You knew by the shadow's leaping how she shifted her mane of kinky hair by lifting her hand. You inhaled, with a dark blend of pleasure and disgust, the fumes of the body walking next to you. The closeness of Elisheva, her excited silence, the solidity of her walking next to you, were so well known to you, so familiar.

At last, Elisheva couldn't remain silent anymore. "Did you meet?"

You nodded. The shadow of the fence sawed a black river in the glow of the pavement.

"Amalia . . ."

You were gathered up in silence.

"Tell me, how was the meeting with . . ." She matched your stride, and seemed suddenly to pant in a low voice: "Isaiah." (Elisheva's voice dropping, even then, in the first conversation. The voice that was both hoarse and full. And your weary silence, as if all that was to come was already known.)

"You don't look happy. It's certainly because of the tension. I can imagine the dread from closeness to a man, now . . . A dread of holiness, right? What a difference from what we used to be, before the yeshiva . . ."

You turned your head with a thrust of your chin.

"I'm so excited for you, Amalia." She stroked your arm, whispering into the back of your neck. "Time for uniting!"

You twisted your lips.

"I wanted to tell you something, Amalia, I wanted to tell you that I admire you. Yes, word of honor." The stirring of her hair quickened. "You're a special person! How you decided to study weaving, and how you succeed in living alone. I think about you a lot, you know. I thank God I got to meet you."

And suddenly you were afraid she'd take you in her arms again for a long time, as she had then, burying her face in your neck, stroking your hair with her hand, and whispering, "Amalia, Amaliyaaa, it's so good we're in the same room together." You withdrew from her clasp, removing your body from hers, and strove to recall Rabbi Avuya Aseraf's broad shoulders bending over the anvil.

"You know, Amalia, when I think of you, I'm proud of our yeshiva! Yes, if, with the help of God, girls like you come out of our yeshiva, there really is something to be proud of! It gives me strength." And then her voice dropped. "Maybe I'll also have . . ."

"Elisheva." You looked straight at her for the first time. "Canceling an engagement is no disgrace."

"Don't talk about that now . . ."

"You're the one who always brings it up."

"How cruel you are, Amalia . . ." The white light on the pallor of her skin gave her freckled cheeks a waxen flash.

"You know, Elisheva, I'm willing to trade places with you," you whispered, choked with that dizziness that came again. "I don't need a Bridegroom anyway." And a sharp, cutting laugh gurgled out of you.

"You better shut up, with the help of God. Be glad with what you've got and don't offend others."

You wanted to reach out to her, to caress Elisheva's gigantic head of hair, her drooping head with an insulted pout like a little girl's, but you couldn't stop the bursts of laughter that grew strong as if every desire was already removed from you, except the pleasure of Mala's body cutting you again with a gleam of exultation, even here among the buildings of the dozing neighborhood. Finally the laughter died out. You didn't talk to Elisheva, and you went the rest of the way in silence.

At the door to Neve Rachel you stopped. Before your eyes, Elisheva went through the glow of the entrance. You followed her across the threshold. Almost a year had passed since you entered those vestibules at night. The darkness, the silence, the white light pouring through the bars on the windows and the crosshatches on the floor, it all surrounded you as you climbed the dark stairs to the second floor, passing by the closed doors. The sudden return to the familiar place blended before and after in you. A dull wave quivered in you when you entered the room the two of you had shared back then, where Elisheva, the last of all the girls in your class, still lived by special permission, after her fiancé's family withdrew from the engagement with the penitent.

The two beds stood in their places, the closet, the white lace napkin spread on the table, and everything was steeped in the heavy sweetness of perfume, old flowers, and the dust of the cardboard cartons of household objects that had been bought for the wedding and were stored under

the beds. Without a word, you both went to the bathroom, to the cold
stream rattling in the sink. And then, in the dark room, you unpacked the
nightgown from your bundle, and placed it carefully on the pillowcase.
You couldn't take your mind off the closeness of Elisheva, who was
spending the night with you in the same room. Her hands unbuttoned her
blouse, her naked back shone white when her arms swung to the flickering of the nightgown, and the folds of her body stood out in the thin fabric, over the shadow of the branches on the windowpane.

You took off your clothes, put them carefully on the chair, spreading
the skirt over the back, as you used to do. Then you slipped into the cool
sheets, turning your head to the wall, like two who sleep in one bed.

In the darkness, Elisheva's ashamed voice rose from the other bed:
"When did you fix the next meeting with Isaiah?"

"On Lag b'Omer, at the bonfire."

"With the help of God, may you have good luck and blessing," she
concluded, and pulled the sheet over her head. "Goodnight, Amalia."

To keep her from noticing your excitement, you pulled the sheet up to
your chin and froze. Exhausted, pleading that, at least by virtue of the holiness of the Sabbath, the bonds of sleep would fall on your eyes and
slumber on your eyelids, you closed your eyes tight, begging, *for Your salvation do I long, HaShem. I do long, HaShem, for Your salvation. HaShem,
for Your salvation do I long . . .*

But you didn't succeed. The turmoil of the last days swept away the
walls, the closet, the flickering spot of the white tablecloth, and you no
longer knew who it was who got up like a sleepwalker, caught barefoot
in the reflection of the moon, or who crossed the shadow of the mute
branches turning white in the window, crosshatching the one who bends
to the sheets, limbs drowning in rustling, face lowered, and the arch of
the neck, so soft, taut and concave, opened on a vision of pupils sailing
behind the eyelids, turning over. And then the hair undone and the fluttering, and again for a long moment the submissive dipping in the rustle, and the hair brushing a shadow dancing on the bedclothes, cut off,
slipping away with a mincing walk through the rectangle of moonlight,
and you still don't know if it was her back you saw or if you left your
body and were looking at your own back crossing the moonbeam and

swallowed up in the other bed. For a long time, you panted, wound around, like the little girl who never told about it, even though she knew it was dangerous, because she was scared that if she told, it would stop, and she hid her head and feet and all her hair under the choking down of the blanket, until the shaking came again that stops her breath, folds her body weightlessly, and rocks her so slowly in the white. And she closes her mouth and eyes tight and sees, as from outside, how her body sinks so slowly and without any color, and even the sound of her heart has almost stopped, and there is only her body that is still sinking, and the silence, and her breath that ends now and the heart that has stopped . . . Until at the last minute, she decides to move the soft weight, and the air comes in, so slowly, warms her belly slowly. It's only this time that she decides to move the weight, the next time, she won't come out from the quiet that's closed, that's why she laughs under the blanket, shakes with a light breathing, so slowly, into the white that is opening . . .

And all that a few days before Lag b'Omer, before the night when you went to the bonfire together.

Before and after are floating in an ungrasped distance. Rabbi Avuya, the yeshiva, Rabbi Israel's singing, *heart and flesh heart heart and flesh* . . . mixed up without reality, as if they didn't exist at all. Hard now to understand their lure, whether they were cause or effect.

And suddenly some unclear longing to spy on Elisheva, to cling to the wire screen in the kitchen window of the small apartment she rented for them, between the fluttering of the moths circling from the window to the fluorescent tube and back. I, the wanderer, the stranger in the community, peeping in the windows and slipping away . . . To watch her arms beating the block of dough on the floured table, kneading it, smearing oil and sprinkling sesame seeds on the challah as brown as her cheeks that will flame when she embraces Isaiah—yet I yielded to her, and what do I have to do with her anymore? I have yielded completely to Elisheva, with all devotion. I shall give myself to You, an unblemished offering. I shall come to a covenant with You, purely. In twenty-two days, at the end of the Omer Counting.

An isolated whining of a dog in the alley below, barking with a kind

of resignation at the approaching dawn. His fragmentary whining on the
slope. Will he whine when they come to rummage here among the pages
in the emptied room?

(If only I wanted, Isaiah would be here now, with me. All I have to do
is say so, whenever I want, and he'll come back! And how much that
thought makes the choking feverish. The very thought that he will come
back and put his hand on my hair, move his fingers over the base of my
neck, on its down . . . And suddenly the certainty that he will come
here on the night of the bonfire, precisely because of what happened
last year!)

I got up and went to the window, pressed to the block of night. What do
I still want from Isaiah? Didn't I torture him enough? Wasn't it enough
that I rejected his plea once? What is the dreadful desire to attract him,
to tempt him until he is seduced, and then to reject him and to flee. For
I have learned that there is no redemption except in love of You. And
even if he does come back, as my heart tells me he will on the night of
the bonfire, even if Isaiah comes here, that will only be a sign sent to me
from You. In the face-to-face coupling of the King Messiah and the
Shekhina. *'Tis your son who is dead; 'tis my child who is living.* For it is your
fire that gnaws at breathing, makes blood boil. *For how will the living
flesh return?* Even if he comes back here.

   *Heart heart and flesh sing their praise to the God ever living, heart heart
and flesh sing their praise to the God ever living—* The voices overflow and
rise up to the night, sing their praise to the God ever living.

four weeks

Splendor of Splendor. Lag b'Omer.

The thirty-third day of the Counting.

For a week I haven't written. I was waiting. Like last year. For him to come back here on the night of the bonfire.

I went to Evening Prayer in the synagogue on the hill (yes, exactly one year ago I heard the prayer of Rabbi Levav there for the first time), and I came back with shaking knees, sure that Isaiah was waiting for me here, like then.

Tonight Isaiah will come back. He'll slip along the vaults. He has to. *And may it correct our lives, spirits, and souls from all sediment and blemish; may it cleanse us and sanctify us with Your exalted holiness. Amen selah.*

This afternoon it seemed to me that he had already come. At about four. I was tying the gold crowns to the tops of the letters, a task I do with the small needle, every single tie separately. I was steeped in the exultation of savoring the end of the task, my fingers fully gripping the metallic touch of the gold threads. Today the enthusiasm was especially great because of the waiting for the night of the bonfire—and then I imagined I heard knocking at the gate. When I got up, I was amazed that I hadn't noticed the pillar of sand rising in the East. The burning dust burst to the empty threshold, the Arab neighbors' tattered dog came running, and the sudden light was cutting. Even afterward, when I returned to the room and buried my head in the Torah Curtain (the calm that only the smell of the threads can induce in me), I was still amazed that Isaiah hadn't yet come. I remained bound to the sight of the mud huts stuck to the slope, unable to go back to tying the gold. Serpents of dust moved in the window, until sundown.

And how he ran here in the winter, after months passed and we hadn't met, his trousers covered with mud and his hat squashed. For the first time he returned. He came here straight from the funeral home. Terrified. Meanwhile he had changed yeshivas; controversies had dispersed Rabbi Avuya's students. His beard had become thicker, the black hat covered his curls, and his lips protruded, red like the lips of an angry baby. His engagement to Elisheva hadn't yet been set, and the cold at night was so sharp that the frost collected in the vaults like transparent flakes of ash. He stood at the gate trembling with weeping and said that Rabbi Avuya, may he rest in peace, had been suddenly taken away. "He was so thin, so thin at the end," he choked. "He expired right before our eyes . . ." And he burst into tears on the threshold. And the freezing rain that had poured down without letup for a whole week streamed on his shoulders. About us, he didn't talk at all, didn't ask what had happened to me since then, didn't look straight at me. And still in the vestibule, the rain and the tears on his cheeks, on the roots of his beard, he was scared and said he had come to ask me to go with him to the funeral, that we had to go right away. And he added that he didn't know what would happen now, that he really didn't know what would be, may God have mercy. And suddenly he seemed to change his mind. He remained a moment, panting, looking at me with extinguished eyes, ponds of shame. As in that dawn, when he got up and his white back trembled . . .

Two weeks ago, when he last came, in spite of the silence (perhaps because of it), everything was once again so soft. The exhalation of the fire I had lit in the kitchen dissolved the hammering of the builders from the slope, the banging of the gate. Suddenly everything flowed again. Even the sound of his chair dragging on the floor. (For two days I left his cup with the remains of the tea in it in the kitchen, to sniff it like an animal. After two days, I poured it out, when it turned green.)

I was sure then that he would come back soon. Not clear to me why. Maybe because of the way he said hesitantly, "Take care of yourself, Amalia, you know I don't interfere, but just don't hurt yourself . . ." Maybe because of the trembling that took hold of his fingers on the handle, their indecisive pressing. And how he finally left, almost running. (It's already been two weeks since he came.)

The thought that he'll come tonight is dizzying. The possibility of waiting again. (What a blessing . . .)

How close we are now, Amalia, how dear to me is the light of the bonfire catching fire in your hair, the hollows of your face kindled, as if I and not you will go tonight like last year into the crowd, in sandals sinking in the ash of the fire, among the women, the wheels of the baby carriages, facing the silk caftans gleaming in the dance like armor plates of redness and sweat, fluttering in the song, *Bar Yochai! You were anointed—fortunate are you—with oil of joy from your fellows.*

Last year the night of the bonfire took place three days after the Sabbath, which you spent again at Rabbi Gothelf's, and as the holiday approached, the choking in you increased. You didn't stop weaving the prayer shawls, so as not to interpret for yourself the things said at Rabbi Avuya's, or what was said on the Sabbath eve between you and Rabbi Gothelf. Scalding Rabbi Avuga's tea leaves didn't help you either. You were swept away, captured by the dark charm of the past repeating itself, as if you longed to be swept up again, out of control, in that old dark flood.

At the hour of afternoon prayer, you got up from the loom, and for the first time since you moved here, to the edge of the city, you were about to fulfill the Commandment of Counting the Omer in public. You didn't know if there was a synagogue in the area, and only by chance,

when you climbed past the tall trees at the top of the neighborhood, did
you hear the voice of Rabbi Levav pouring out of the little hut, and you
went inside. The ancient pine trees brought dryness and sunset to the
windows. The few worshippers were dressed in work clothes, two
serious-looking teen-agers moved in the corner. You stood alone in the
empty women's section. For the first time you heard Rabbi Levav's soft
voice, and you were amazed at how familiar it was, like the voice of a relative. (Yes, it was Rabbi Levav's voice that finally soothed you, how he
uttered the Counting with that soft laugh—*Today is thirty-three days,
which is four weeks and five days of the Omer*—and in your innocence, you
believed that here, you were growing calm as the hour approached.)

When you returned on the steep path, the children's bonfires were
mottling the slopes like night flowers spreading sparks, and the sky above
the new city was swathed in redness and smoke. Only at the foot of your
windows did the darkness become deep, as if that night, the Arabs'
taboons insistently hid their smoke, and the smell of burning dung in
their homes was heaped up in the valley.

You walked a long time on the descending path, looking into the expanse of darkness, and when you arrived, Isaiah was waiting at the door,
bending down behind you in the entrance. You stood facing each other
for the first time here, beneath the vaults of the room. You slipped away,
and you came back with the first prayer shawl. Isaiah spread the sheet
open, slowly ran his thin fingers over its fringes, as if he were apologizing that the movements weren't routine in his hands.

"When I used to play, I sometimes tried to imagine who had made my
violin," he said with a laugh. He raised his eyes for a moment. His white
shirt flickered. And when he lowered his glance again, the silence became
thicker. He returned the prayer shawl to you at arm's length. A breeze full
of cinders blew through the window and puffed up his shirt and your
hair. You could almost hear the rhythm of his breathing. And then Isaiah
broke away.

"Shall we go?" he whispered.

You turned your back to him and put the prayer shawl on the shelf.
"You think I should take a shawl?" you asked, as if from a distance.

"At the bonfire, you won't need it, but maybe afterward . . ."

He glided to the entrance behind you. Outside, when he waited at the side of the road for you to turn both locks of the gate, the mists of heat from the distant bonfires already surrounded you, and Father's voice pierced out of them, *Malinkaaaaa . . .*

Downtown, you went through the crowds assembled around the soft-drink stands at the doors of the restaurants. You raised your eyes to Isaiah's leanness sliding forward at your side, smiling at the memory of how you first heard from Rabbi Gothelf the reason for the bonfire on the night when Rabbi Simeon Bar Yochai was taken and rose to the heavens to bring union to the Holy-One-Blessed-Be-He and the Shekhina. Then Elisheva raised her face, declaring with a low laugh that she would make her wedding on Lag b'Omer, following the custom, and Rabbi Israel nodded and smiled. "God willing, God willing." You went past the flickering traffic light. The intersection separated the profane from the growing sounds of merrymaking. You climbed the rising street, and you were still afraid he would talk about what had happened in Rabbi Avuya Aseraf's house. You watched his great strides reverberating through his back like a string, shot silently from his loins, leading you through the ascending sidewalks to the fire. Your head spun from walking so fast. Near the bus stop, for a moment Emily hurries the taxi driver going around the city at night, urging him on with her excitement, and in the distance the sky sank again in the redness of smoke carrying the crowd down the slope, to the bonfire.

You chastely slipped behind Isaiah. The crowd separated you. Over houses rose the sounds of playing and speeches shrieking in the loud-speakers: "The holiday of those who could find the light of our holy Bar Yochai even when they are in the crevices of the eneeemyyy and in the sewers of duuunggghilllsss. Those who returned to HaShem, as it is written, *And shall return unto the Lord thy Goooood and shaaaalt obey his voooooice . . .*"

"Amalia." Isaiah turned his face to you in the torrent of your walking. "Amalia, you know . . ." His voice was drowned in the echoes that poured beyond the roofs, and above them the voice of the speaker: "*If any of thine be driven out unto the outmost parts of heaven, from thence will the LORD thy God gather thee, and from thennnnnnn.*"

You hurried after Isaiah, who was slicing through the packed crowd in the street; your breath was short.

"In fact this evening," he said and threw his head back and laughed.

"Hum hum hum, *All these curses upon thine enemies,* hum hum hum *and on them that hate thee, which persecuted thee,* puff puff, *And thou shalt return return retuuurrnn.*"

"...is like the night of our betrothal, and if our parents were with us..."

You ran after his flaming face, smiling at you so intimately; you smiled back mechanically, the effort cutting your chest. You didn't hear the end of his words. His head swung upside-down in front of you, for a moment he vanished into the crowd, and when you saw him again he was standing in the arched opening between the alleys, and clouds of smoke and conflagration were mounting up above him as he was pointing to the boulder on the threshold.

"Be careful, there are wires here." Hubert holds out his hand to you in the passage, apologizing with every word, in his embarrassed accent. "Be careful you don't fall." And she, choking back the hatred, pulls her hand away, and in a little while she'll strike him; if only he'd shut up already! If only he'd shut up already and wouldn't be here with his smooth cheeks, among these autumn leaves on the black earth! He's got no right to be here!

"Why don't you answer me, Emily?" he persists and his eyes are disgustingly teary. "We have come all this way together; it was the desire to come back here together that united us—"

You were shaking, just not now, just not now ...

Isaiah hurried ahead of you in the passage covered with boards and broken stones, turning his head to you and smiling. "Be careful, Amalia."

"Yes, yes." You tried to smile at him, and the vacuum in your belly enlarged as the smell of the bonfire intensified. In the rut between the yards, sparks flew, covering the outlines of the balconies. Isaiah's shirt flew in front of you toward the tumult.

"Emily, forgive me," Hubert pleads and grabs you, and she no longer has strength to get away, so thick does the weakness of nausea become.

"Understand, Hubert, I want to be alone," she repeats. "I want to be alone now, leave me alone here with the . . ." She advances on the wet clods, in the awful silence, and he trails along behind her, embarrassed, apologizing.

"But, Emily, all we have got left now is to atone, only that, Emily, and maybe to forgive with the love between human beings . . ."

"Shut up, now, shut up already!" she screams. "Shut up!"

She finally succeeds in slipping away from him, crossing the field of sparse grass and autumn flowers, striding step by step through the transparency of silence up to the destroyed huts, a row of doorways, wet girders, rot. She goes to the doorway with the choking helplessness, eyes staring at a black log, a knoll of mud, gravel. Moss climbs up the mound of earth. The toe of the boot taps on the damp mass. The knoll crumbles. The smell of lush earth, anguished. She stands frozen. The mass sticks to the boot. And then with an impulse of terror, she bursts into a run, crossing the razed field, passing Hubert, not noticing the wire that snags, that tears the trouser leg, running, the cylinders of her body scorching. Until she finds herself curled up in a car seat, gazing vacantly at the flat vista, the bare trees in the soft light, the red roofs of the distant village. And with the same submission, she obeys Hubert, who next to her starts the car, covers herself with her vest, impotent, numb, dragged along behind him, disgustingly dependent on him to feel something—

You remained behind in the narrow passage another moment until the shaking subsided, as if to hide from Isaiah, and then you sallied forth into the enormous square, where the building facades were on fire with the flickering flames. You ran behind Isaiah, as if you were afraid of losing him in the crowd pressed against the houses, where black faces in the windows pushed toward the cascades of fire.

Isaiah cheered like a boy, leaped over boards opposite the gigantic masts erected for the bonfire, ran ahead clapping, his body gyrating.

You hurried behind him, you were about to grab his shirt, to shout at him, *Even if you refine my soul in all the bonfires, even if you dissolve my heart in all the fires, even if you burn me alive at the stake, I must tell you this, Isaiah*—but then the movement of the crowd swept you up in one direction and bore Isaiah off in the other. At that moment, the throng was drawn toward a pile of boards that was still not ignited, rubber tires suspended like carcasses of birds at the top of its masts, and the yeshiva students began running and spraying kerosene on the wooden titans, and behind them, boys with long sidecurls stuck burning sticks between the posts. You were pushed toward a group of women who stood huddled together, closing you in their heavy dresses, in the children underfoot, in the battery of baby carriages.

The fire grabbed the beams. A gale of cinders and sparks rose, leaped from the tires in columns of smoke like the souls of angels of defilement, leaving beneath them the crowd stamping in the waves of the bonfire's light. At the edge of the fire, under a tin awning, a group of Hassids in fur hats danced, drumming with small steps. The fire turned black and rose up. The arms of the masts cracked. *Bar Yochai! You were anointed— fortunate are you—with oil of joy from your fellows.* The dancers' feet beat between earth and heaven, waking the dust of the dead with their stamping. Near you, a few women burst out in thin voices, accompanying themselves by clapping their hands. You stood watching them, about to join their song, but the voice vanished in your throat. You saw Isaiah rushing to the dancers, flowing into them with his head thrown back, his thin torso held by song, his eyes shut, his bent neck kindled in the flight of the sparks, *Bar Yochaiiiii! With oil of sacred anointment were you anoiiiiinnnnted from the holyyyyy measurrrre.*

Isaiah seemed to be revealed to you. Through the succumbing softness of his dancing, his lips melted in song, his thin neck, bent, through the ecstasy of his head thrown back, the fluttering instrument between his hand and his burning face, all the agitated devotion in him was suddenly revealed to you, all the innocence that led him to faith, to Jerusalem, to Rabbi Avuya, to this night of celebration, all the innocent bliss that will flood his face when he stretches his arms out to you, when he brings his hands down on your loins . . .

The night of Lag b'Omer. Once again the sky is fervid, and rivers of fire stream to the redness whirling above the city. A night of Splendor of Splendor. The night of Your coupling with the Shekhina.

How easy is the breathing now, how high the night dome of stars. Even the full moon is a bit flawed so as not to obscure the flaming sky or the voice of the Shekhina yearning for Your embrace, caressed in Your lap all night. How great is the excitement now, to stand on the threshold for the last time in the light of the flaming revelation, and thus to support

Isaiah, who is making his way here! How great the excitement to write and to wait tonight!

For what is left for us now except the repair through love, except love to You and of You, in the whole body and soul. And tonight, when I open the door to Isaiah, when I greet him with awe, only the repair of holiness we will make in the repair of love, as is written in Your Torah, *with all your soul and all your heart and all your might.* In a little while, when he comes, when he buries his pure lips in my hair, when he holds me again until morning, wailing, exulting, as then, when we mount the fiery chariot of the Covenant, one flesh in the fire of Your holiness, flame of the Lord, fat on the altar of Isaac, only to You shall I rise in thought, *for the soul is Yours, the body is Your creation.*

And until then, until he comes, let me sit at Your feet and repair what I have damaged in the Sefirah Splendor of Splendor. And may it be His will that by my hands that strive in writing I shall support Isaiah on his way here.

And let the beauty of the Lord our God be upon us: and establish Thou the work of our hands upon us; yea, the work of our hands establish Thou it. Amen selah.

Yes, that was what Isaiah revealed to you there, his faith burned in his face thrown back, sealed in you by the voice of the woman in the white turban.

"I really have to tell you all about a wonderful miracle done by the Holy Rabbi Simeon Bar Yochai on Lag b'Omer in Miron." A haughty, elderly woman gathered the young women around her at the edge of the bonfire, like an experienced teacher.

"Come, you listen too." She turned to you, pulling on your arm. "There's a remedy in it, you'll see; in another year, God willing, you'll give birth to a son by grace of Bar Yochai."

"With the help of God." The women huddled around you. You blushed and lowered your eyes.

"This happened in the days of the Turks, when I was a little girl. Back then it took five days to go to Miron, first to Safed, and from there on donkeys."

You stood, weak, the woman's arm hooked in yours, and your head

pressed between the kerchiefs of the women huddled together in the heat
of the flames.

"Lag b'Omer began on Friday, so we stayed in Miron for the Sabbath.
And then, on the Sabbath morning, a little after the Mussaf prayer, we
heard horrible shouts. We didn't know what they were, until we found
out that a child of one of the Sephardim who came there, whose mother
had made a vow to Rabbi Simeon that she would cut his hair for the first
time in Miron, according to custom, the child suddenly got cholera,
Heaven forfend, and died! You can imagine the shouting and the grief!
On top of that, a doctor of the Turks was there, and he gave an order to
quarantine all the people in the courtyard for a few days! When they
heard the order, a lot of them started running out of the courtyard to the
hills, and then the police came and closed the gate, and you couldn't go
out or come in. Many of those who ran away left their wives and children
behind. They shouted to kingdom come. I sat with my mother and my
older sisters, and I saw them take the dead child and put him on the floor
in a little room on the roof of Rabbi Simeon's monument. The child
was green and dead, may we not know such things, with his mother sitting next to him and crying. That was her only son, and she had brought
him to Miron because of the vow she had made to Rabbi Simeon Bar
Yochai before he was born, and now he was dead! Out of grief, they
didn't make a Kiddush or a Sabbath meal." The woman in the turban emphasized her words by shaking her head, and she clutched your arm.

"All of a sudden, the child's mother got up, took him in her arms, and
went down into the synagogue, to Rabbi Simeon's holy grave, and she
put the dead child on the floor, next to the monument, and she started
shouting, 'Saint, Saint, Rabbi Simeon! I kept the vow I made here on your
holy monument when I was barren, and I brought you the only son
HaShem gave me, may He be blessed by your grace, and yesterday I
brought him, my child, living, and I cut his hair for the first time with
songs and joy, and now, *ay ayyyy,* how will I go back home without my
child, *ay ayyy.*' That's how she shouted: 'Let me die and not my child, by
my life! *Ay ayyy!*'

"She stood there and said, 'Saint, Saint! Here's the child, lying on your
floor, dead. Don't refuse me, God have mercy, wonderful Saint, return

my child to me alive, as I brought him to you yesterday, and everybody will know of your holiness, the whole world!' That's how she cried, and everybody's heart melted, and a lot of people cried with her, women, and men too, and even the police, even they cried at how she talked! And then she went out, leaving the dead child inside, and because of the quarantine, they closed the doors to the synagogue, and also to the monument of Rabbi Simeon Bar Yochai. Only the child stayed inside. A few minutes later, we heard a voice! From the synagogue, we heard the child shouting, 'Mother, mother!' The learned guard ran to open the synagogue, and there was the child, standing and shouting, 'Mother, give me a little water, I'm thirsty!' " The women nodded.

"You can imagine what great joy there was at the resurrection of the dead child! They brought him up to the room on the roof, and everybody came to see him alive. Even the doctors said it was a miracle of the holy Rabbi Simeon Bar Yochai, truly a resurrection of the dead. And right away they opened the gates, because there was no more need for a quarantine. And everybody who ran away to the hills came back to see the miracle! And they had a public prayer, *Blessed be He who resurrects the dead,* for there is none like Rabbi Simeon Bar Yochai, who resurrects the dead."

The heat from the bonfire intensified. *Bar Yochai! At a wondrous light in lofty heights. You feared to stare for it is great.* The woman in white smiled at you, and a flush enflamed her clear cheeks. The women's heads bent around you in the niche of shadows. Isaiah was plucked out of the dancers and came toward you. His teeth dripped light, and he signaled to you with one hand that he was returning to the dancers, or perhaps something else that wasn't clear to you. For a moment, you were steeped in the dread that you trampled his softness, forsaking him with Rabbi Avuya Aseraf, but then Mala brought her hair toward you, winding its warmth in your own.

"That's your fiancé?" The woman in white gripped your elbow. "Good luck to you, good luck to you."

"Amen." The other women bent their heads toward you.

From the heart of the bonfire, tongues of flame rose straight up, and clouds of sparks crackled in the wake of the flames that suddenly intensified. The heat was unbearable. The women drew back, clinging to the walls of the houses, pulling the baby carriages and children behind them. You also retreated from the burning, and from your lips spoke the warm lips of Mala, swaddling you in her moaning. You let down her hair, gently wiping away the drops of sweat gathering on your forehead, *ayyy.*

"Here's Amalia! Amalia!" some of the yeshiva girls in the crowd called out, clapping with the dancers. You saw Yaffa and Jane and Rosie, with kerchiefs on their heads, and near them cheered Elisheva, her kinky hair uncovered. They followed Isaiah, who hurried to the circle, and whispered to one another, drunk on the joy of the holiday.

Bar Yochai! You were anointed—fortunate are you—with oil of joy from your fellows.

The circle slowly moved in the illuminated dust, the fire flickered on the silk caftans flowing from the taut backs. The crowd covered the group of yeshiva girls. You saw Elisheva breaking through the crush to you. You withdrew among the women and the baby carriages, slipping beyond the iron scaffolding, grazing the fire and the circle of men who stamped heavily near the tin shed.

Mala's breath flowed from your throat; the soft voice of the woman in the white turban also wailed from her, *ay ayyy,* and once again the beating of the dancers' feet rose. *Bar Yochai! Fortunate is she who bore you.* From a distance, Elisheva called to you, and you retreated; the tears flood from her with the helplessness of the struggle and the choked laughter, as she knocks her fists at Zvi, who is trying to block the exit from the roof to her.

"Amy, Amy! I can't understand why you're leaving, I can't!"

"So don't, you don't have to understand everything. I already told you, I don't give out explanations," she says, grappling with the arms that clasp her.

"Look, Zvi." She finally relents, in the damp heat, her hands weak from all the mad nights before the trip. "You know this has no future, not even if you could keep me imprisoned here on the roof, not even if I miss the flight and lose all the money on the charter. You will never understand. I've got to go, I've already told you that in a thousand ways, and everything you thought were looks at other men, I'm damned if they interest me at all, it was only to make you understand that I've got to go. For you, jealousy is the only proof. You pretend to be an intellectual, but you just want to hit because you're so jealous and that says that you love. Fine, well, I don't have the strength to argue anymore, and there's no point anyway. Let me go. Look, even your holy cats are tired."

She takes the handles of the suitcase, hangs the guitar strap over her shoulder, and stands facing him, her knees and stomach weak. "Get out of the way, OK, and let me by. I've got to leave this place and go to the other end of the world."

When he moves out of the passage, his back sagging, she puts on the light in the dusty staircase, and turns around to face him again. "And don't follow me, Zvi, it's hopeless. Yes, I wish you well, I hope you'll be happy," she manages somehow to muster up the strength to say before she's dragged down the slope of the floors, her knees tottering again, into the last night in Tel Aviv, back in the apartment with closed curtains and the heavy smell of bedclothes, after months. And sometime that night, unwittingly, she ran her hand over the smoothness of the folded linens in the depths of the drawer.

"What luck that we finally met!" Elisheva had managed to make her way through the crowd. "Why are you embarrassed, Amalia? He's so wonderful!"

"I'm not embarrassed." And suddenly, choking violently, you whispered to her, "You know, I never told you about what really happened in the hotel in San Remo!"

"What are you saying, Amalia?" she shouted at you over the turmoil of the crowd.

"What happened there in the bathtub." You giggled.

"I don't understand what you're talking about, Amalia."

"And also, in fact, I never asked you when you told Rabbi Israel about the scars; you surely saw them right on the first day, you and your curiosity."

"What's with you, Amalia, are you nuts?" Elisheva retreated, her gaiety cut off by alarm. "What are you talking about? What's going on with you?"

"I just wanted to tell you that that was my *first* bonfire, a long time before we learned about the night of joy of Bar Yochai, *that* was the secret of 'nothing' I discovered, Elisheva." You choked and tears blinded the flickering of the fire. "I thought I should tell you that, as a sign of friendship, before I pass on, as they say, to another state, with Isaiah. You hear, Elisheva, you hear!" you called to Elisheva's back as she retreated in panic among the women standing and clapping their hands. "You hear, and don't think I've gone crazy."

At last she left you and went off, you giggled softly, and she waved wearily to those seeing her off, who surrounded her at dawn in the airport corridor, showing up unexpectedly, Aunt Henia and Uncle Hesiu, who really wasn't a relative and was called uncle only because there were so few family members left, and Salla Mandel, who also came to be with her. "Have a good trip, Amy, a good trip. We didn't say anything to Zvi, no point making him sad." Aunt Henia nodded, familiar with her habit of breaking relations. They moved away from her, huddling on the airport balcony, a few tatters, stammering in the heavy damp, millstones around her neck, and as soon as she got on the plane, even before takeoff, she went to the toilet and threw up.

Isaiah approached from among the dancers, his face dripping light. You ran to him to be embraced in his arms, to weep in his lap like a baby, to tell him you wouldn't be able to turn back from your evil way, but would only go back over and over the same way without refuge, to tell him that you always ran away, from the start, even then her hand on the railing of the boardwalk, and Zvi with his heavy body at her side, and in the distance the city lies in the dark shell, standing there looking straight into the the sea. Instead of returning home. In the tight T-shirt, the heat of the night descending on her back. Staying next to the well-preserved virile body (goes to the swimming pool every morning from April to November), even though she knows that Father is waiting. Even then you ran away, into the saltiness steeped with the smell of urine and rotting boards, and the smoke of roasting, and the hair coming down on her arms, staying only to tell Father, once and for all, that she doesn't want to know about anything anymore, anything, even if she hurts him, despite the disease, she said that to him when she left him at the phonograph, she told him she would finally finish her off under the pillow in the *appapatz*, and the weight of the man is clinging to her body, and she notices that the movement of her hand drumming on the railing is like the strumming of Father's fingers on the cabinet, *Malinka*, and she shudders.

"Come, Amalia," Isaiah called to you over the heads of the crowd. "Come look at the dancing; it's a Commandment!" In panic, you tried to smile back at him: "Yes, yes." You went up to the fire at his heels, weeping for the salvation in Isaiah's flooded eyes, for the defect sealed in you, without cure, for the love he will have both for you and for her.

Isaiah's face turned upside down in the distance, the heat blazed unbearably, her voice beating in your temples, *ay ayyyy*, echoing from the walls, from the bed, from the balcony, from the iron banister of the luxury hotel, from the thick vapor that darkens the crests of the palm trees, the sick roiling of the wall of the sea, beating with horrible shouts that keep burning behind you like a vision, and you no longer heard the distant calls of Isaiah, *ay ayyy*, you were pushed forward, moving the dough of your legs in ever stickier circles, your wrists stretched out to the fire, *ay ayyy*, in the flood of sparks flying, *Bar Yochai! A wondrous light, the light of the fire they light*, and she is lighted from within you, her light legs drumming in a dance. And the crowd withdraws in astonishment, beholds her great beauty in the flaming embers in her passage, in holiness, murmurs, "Look, look at the dance of the Shekhina, look at her, the gentle, the wonderful, the lovely . . ." Your dizzy bodies, raised to your salvation in Isaiah, and she ran her hand over your face to cool the burning a bit.

"For a long time now, I've been trying to ask you what happened." Isaiah's voice touched you from the dark. You found yourself lying on the ground in a dark field, your head on a rock. You didn't remember how you got there. The night was spread all around, and only the murmur of the thorns and the distant barking scratched the silence. Isaiah was squatting at your head. His profile stood out in the light of the moon.

"The heat of the bonfire seems to have harmed you. You stayed near

the fire for a long time." Sentence after sentence rolled from his lips.
Only now did the gnawing, longed-for murmur of the night crickets
reach your ear on a dry breeze. The night was moving warm over your
nostrils, slicing coolness rising from the valley, the smell of the bonfires
sailed softly here, bursting forth somewhere beyond the glide of the
slope, steeped in the bitter vapor of the clods in the night.

"What time is it?" you finally asked without moving your lips.

"After ten already," answered Isaiah, rocking on his heels. "What
happened to you before, Amalia?" he whispered.

You didn't reply. You slowly pulled your body beneath you and sat up.
You clutched your skirt, and still weary, leaned your head on your knees,
your hair scattering like the sheaves of wheat that Ruth gleaned in the
fields of Bethlehem. Your cheeks rubbed the coolness of the cloth. In the
distance, tiny strings of light twined, slope after slope. You had forgotten how spread out the city was, sending its octopus arms rustling among
the jewelled eyes of the bonfires. You looked up at Isaiah. His eyes were
staring away from you, and his profile inundated with whiteness was
like the muzzle of an animal. Nothing indicated that just a moment ago
he had asked you something in a whisper. You followed his gaze back to
the dark of the nearby ridge. Waves of heat withdrew and rose up, twisting through the field of rocks where you were sitting.

The silence grazed the clashes of blood under your skin. Your breathing nearly stopped. The sheet of stars leaned with the elbows of a giant
on the mountains, and a stream of mist bubbled up from it in a broad
gasp. You tried to say something, and once again the dome of the night
pressed down.

I don't know how long you sat like that.

The head is held on the thorn of the neck. As if it leaned separately.

In a moment everything will stop.

(Suddenly you seemed to be pierced by the scalpel of knowing that
there is nothing but silence, nothing now. Absolute silence. Absorbing
everything. The night, the windowsills, the space in the room. Nothing
moves in the stillness. The body is clasped around the pen. Turned to
stone, without any will. Only the heaviness of the head on the neck, and
the body slipping into a distant stain under the table.

Isaiah won't come tonight. He won't come tomorrow either. The lucid knowing doesn't stir a thing. Even the sound of his name is opaque.

You don't penetrate the stillness either. Exist perhaps to Yourself and perhaps not—in the hewn quiet, even that doesn't change anymore. A distant hum, beyond the empty point.

I tried to move the lips in prayer—the tongue is forged in its refusal. All that racing of the confession to You now seems like madness.

The congealed stillness isn't threatening. On the contrary. There's something alive in the heart of full solitude. Some strumming on a hidden vein. Almost a relief, in the honed sobriety. Stillness in the heart of the storm. Profound release.

With a sharpened clarity, it's also clear to me how, in a little while, the silence will grow faint, be swept up again in the dizziness of the Omer Counting, be covered anew with the foam of prayer.

Even that distant knowing doesn't stir anything. Doesn't muddy the radiance of the silence)

I can't say for sure right now what exactly happened to you when you looked long into the dark, your head leaning on the knobs of your knees, Isaiah's voice blocked out of the bubble of stillness that closed upon you. "I have to go to Rabbi Avuya now, to study and to light the bonfire. We're completing the reading of the Zohar tonight."

You didn't take your eyes off the dark slopes.

Isaiah turned to look at you, repeating with an effort, "I have to go now, Amalia. You don't have to come. I'll take you home so you can rest, and then I'll go to the rabbi."

You didn't reply. His voice was silenced in the dark. You no longer noticed the roasted air from the distant bonfires. You just sat, clasping your knees to your paralyzed body, for a long time.

(I go on writing in spite of myself. To myself. And maybe the whole thing is nothing but fear of facing the truth. The immediate silencing of all doubt, lest it rip the fabric.

And in fact, if Isaiah did come tonight, if he were here now, there would no longer be a need for the confession or for weaving the Torah Curtain. The act would have been, and is no more . . .)

At last you focused your look. Rocks flickered on the slope. From the corner of your eye, you noticed the tremor that passed over Isaiah's curls, and when you turned your face you saw that his lips were clenched.

"I'm sorry." Your voice moved toward you from afar. "I didn't want to hurt you, Isaiah."

His lips drooped.

"We've got to go so you won't be late." You smiled and immediately lowered your eyes so as not to see the pain wiped off his face, and once again his eyes searching your eyes. You got up and shook your skirt. "Shall we go?"

Isaiah followed you, carrying your shawl over his bent arm, as if he were being careful with a rare animal that had been entrusted to him for safekeeping.

And you said long live, chai, chai, Rabbi Simeon Bar Yochai. And you said long live, chai, chai. The wind carried strips of song, moved from you into the valley, dragging branches of burnet. You wound your way among the rocks out of the field, and then you were on the edge of the neighborhood. You probably hadn't gone very far from the last houses, and it was only because you fainted that you imagined you had descended deep into the dark. In the yards, bonfires were still lit, and around them, the circling backs of the merrymakers. In the square of a yeshiva, a few children were bending over embers, sweeping potatoes from the ashes.

The song burst out of the passages between the alleys, broke out and died away into silence. *Bar Yochai! You were girded with strength and in the war of the fiery Torah up to the gate.* The thick night separated your bodies.

"You feel better?"

You nodded.

"Shall we rest?"

"No, that's all right."

His hands hesitated, holding the ends of your shawl, and his body sank and was trodden like a soft reed.

"I'll come with you to the rabbi," you added.

Two children broke out of a yard, carrying a pole with a beaten cloth effigy at the top. "Hitler, you evil bum, now, now, your end has come!

Hitler, you evil bum, now, now, your end has come!" They ran shouting with sidelocks swinging and disappeared between the houses.

"What happened to you before, Amalia, I was so scared." He drew his neck toward you. "I called you to come look at the dancers, and all of a sudden you ran toward the fire and fell down. The people helped me pick you up."

You giggled.

"What happened to you?" he persisted. "I was so worried."

"It doesn't matter."

Isaiah shifted your shawl from one hand to another. "You know, Amalia, forgive me if I say so, but . . ."

You turned away from the bonfires. In the distance, the lighted walls of the Old City suddenly became firm, prominent in the artificial festivity.

". . . I thought about what you told me, Amalia, that you can't, God have mercy, do repentance. Did you mean that, Amalia? The way you fell?"

"I don't know."

"I thought about what you said," he went on fervently. "You know, I also . . . I talked about that with the rabbi. You think it was easy for *me* to abandon everything? Sometimes I tremble with fear, and I don't say that to boast."

From the walls rose a tower, and its weight cast a broad shadow. Isaiah softly twisted and fastened your shawl around his fingers, hastened his steps stormily. You gazed at the hewn stones of the tower, and for some reason, their heaviness made you light.

"Sometimes when I'm trying to get rid of some thought or memory, some sound, during study or prayer, it only haunts me more. A few times, God have mercy, I almost came to thoughts of heresy. Why do all this if it's really impossible to stay on the straight path, if it's impossible to start all over again! And I chose, from the depths of my heart, and God forbid, I haven't got any doubt that He is watching, may He be blessed. But what's especially painful," once again twisting the shawl with his fingers, "is that just when I believe that I am strong in study, in understanding, just then, in love of Torah, a phrase of Schumann or Brahms can rise up in me and rip it all! It's all destroyed then, and only the one phrase of Brahms, like a dybbuk, and everything that flows with it, from there, the feelings, the places . . . Like it's happening now, as if I didn't leave in good faith, in devotion." He paused and his voice broke: "The most awful thing is the touch of the strings that starts again in the fingers, that . . ." And then he stopped, raising his face to you with an effort: "Amalia, I have to tell you that . . ."

You stopped too. His breath trembled above you.

"I . . ." It was hard for him.

You retreated, staring at the black boughs that bent down beyond the walls. You nodded hurriedly, not listening, as if you understood.

"Amalia, before I came to Jerusalem, there . . . My first wife was killed in an automobile accident." His voice was almost inaudible. "She was a musician, a pianist. Her name was Elizabeth."

You choked with contempt, don't let him confess now, don't let him start pouring out *his* . . . Can't listen now, can't . . . You raised your hand to stop his words and were scared at the great beauty of his face, sculpted down to its last detail, and its black pupils perishing in fever.

Isaiah mistook your gesture. He grabbed your raised hand, brought it to his face, clutching it with a tremor, very slowly passing it over the pallor of his cheeks, once and then again, and repeating in a whisper, as if he were drowning, "Amalia . . ."

You knew that the longer you were silent, the more intense grew his excitement for you, and you didn't move, didn't pull your hand out of his, didn't prove him wrong. Behind you, the path climbed in the hot dust coming out of the walls into the night, and at its top stood the house of Rabbi Avuya. Isaiah's head rested hovering on your hair, stroking. You let him bring his body close to yours, lean on you for a long moment, like someone finally resting. And then he broke away, and a furrow rose between his eyebrows. He moved away from you and his shirt gleamed white, and then he stretched out his hands again, and his fingers moved freely over your back, over your bare neck. He buried his face in your hair, and for a long time he clung to your body, and his breath hummed. Wearily, mute, you let him run his fingers over your face, put his lips to your skin. At last you shook yourself with an impatient grimace.

The rest of the way to the rabbi's house you walked in silence, Isaiah stumbling at your heels. Near the fence, in the dark, you stopped. "Go in, don't be late."

In Rabbi Avuya's yard, a bonfire of beams was set up, ready to be lighted. Young men were coming out of the illuminated house. They had probably finished the reading. You were late.

"Go in, Isaiah," you repeated.

He hesitated a moment, his hand on the gate. A voice calling from inside made him hurry through the flowerbeds, your shawl shaking between his hands.

You stood outside the fence, in the dark. With a slow, heavy hand, you straightened your hair, which had come undone. You hated Isaiah for his softness toward you, you loathed him for the pain you brought down on him, for the shame growing in you, for the pain you would go on bringing down on him, *ay ayyy, Bar Yochaiiii,* about to take great vengeance on him for the shame choking you, for your longing for him, yearning to trample him to dust. You very slowly passed your fingers through the rustle of the hair, raising the dryness, and only then did you drop its weight on your neck.

(The singed air of the eve of Lag b'Omer. Even here, inside the room, its blazing heat rose. Unrelenting. Wave after wave.)

In the yard, the young women gathered, coming out of their section behind the house, assembling in groups of two or three, wearing long dresses, kerchiefs. Nodding their heads to one another like a flock of pigeons strutting with naive coquetry among the spots of light.

You remained outside the fence. You didn't approach the yard and the women. A lantern was concealed in the treetops, and the moon was already sinking toward the borders of the sky. The soft wind pulled from the valley was tangled in the pine trees and in your hair. You rolled your head with relief, abandoned your face to the touch of the night at that profound hour. Isaiah was engaged at Rabbi Aseraf's house; the women in their kerchiefs did not know of your existence. At last, peaceful, all alone. The flowerbeds of the garden exhaled smells of herbs and incense. From the heaviness of the women's bodies, from their calm, some

docile materiality bubbled up. Your fingers too were steeped in the so-
lutions of the scalded grasses. Once again the wind carried from the garden the smell of dust and herbs. *Through Whose word everything came to
be,* you whispered compulsively.

From the small house came Rabbi Avuya Aseraf. On his heels, his students flooded out, surrounding him with their cries: *Congratulations!*
And they were already bursting into excited voices: *Bar Yochai, HaShem
is with you, riding the heavens with your help.* Rolling their heads, their
Adam's apples bobbing. You saw Isaiah singing too, trembling like a
reed above the shoulders of the students, his eyes shut and his thin hands
rising as he clapped. Rabbi Aseraf's face flickered amid the cascade of his
curls. With both hands, he waved an incense bowl heaped with coals. You
slipped behind, ashamed for him to see you, and the pounding of your
heart grew faster. The women gathered on the other side of the dancers,
exclaiming softly. Some started spinning, rolling up their long kerchiefs,
wandering toward the pillar of boards, clapping their hands: *Bar Yochai,
you are much exalted, fortunate is she who bore you . . .* From where you
stood behind the bushes you saw Rabbi Avuya in a furious dance, his ritual fringes flying, whipping blue on his loins.

His fringes were probably sprayed with murex and galbanum; you
twisted your lips in anger, and as if to engrave the disgust in your heart,
you looked at him a long time as he waved the incense bowl with its
dancing coals before him. You looked at the women going up to him, the
sleeves of their dresses rising and dropping to his lips, and you couldn't
help despising Isaiah for being consumed by the dancers' song: *Bar
Yochai! You were anointed—fortunate are you.*

The rabbi stopped. One of the students ran and poured kerosene on
the incense bowl. The coals ignited in a torch and a sound of cheering
arose. The rabbi brandished the torch, thrust it into the heart of the bonfire. The flames grabbed the linen wicks in the bowels of the wood, running up. The students retreated, standing like a wall. And in the center,
Rabbi Avuya Aseraf was detached in a solitary dance, spinning to the
sound of the rising song, his eyes shut and his curls wild.

*Bar Yochai, wisdom will dare high at your right hand! Blessed is the fruit
of your womb, Bar Yochai, HaShem is with you, riding the heavens with
your help.*

Once again he stopped, and the young men moved at the sign, tramping in a tight circle around the rabbi, who stood in the shadow of the flames and whipped up the rhythm of the song with his fist. You shrank into your hiding place. You, the stranger whose place would not be recognized among the merrymakers. The circle moved faster, the running shadows covering then brightening the fire, the rabbi's broad face, his gigantic eyelids, his curls. You stroked your wrist, gasping; he rules them too, excites them at will. The touch of your skin became rough and dry. And maybe he had brought you close only for his own need, maybe that was the reason he had brought up Mala's name, exciting you like that . . .

Isaiah and another young man, whose trousers were fastened with a strip of rope, began climbing the slope of dirt and broken pans behind the shed, stretching enormous reed bows from its top. Long arrows whistled across the cloud of fire, slicing the tops of the pine trees, disappearing in a silent soaring into the valley stretched out behind, in the dark. Rustling arose from the assembled throats: A blinding colored bow lighting the appearance of the King Messiah!

The fire launched sparks into the night; some of them dropped onto you, onto the dense bushes, and some rose to the treetops like a red swarm of fireflies. The rabbi gestured. The students immediately hastened to make a pile of thin fabrics. You wondered if the rabbi intended to dress the flames with a festive garb. He shook the colorful trains, casting them one by one into the fire, which caught them with a glow of crushing. "May we stand naked and bare as these burning garments! May we live to see the Messiah of Justice come quickly in our day, amen!" rose the shout. Some of the young women went to the bonfire, also tossing veils they had prepared onto the flames. Yellow, pink, green, purple wings of cloth swooped down twisted onto the dense fire.

Nausea flooded you. Maybe it was the sight of the devoured fabrics that inflamed the sense of sin in you. You knew how sunk in disgrace you were, coming to the place of *a most vehement flame,* wallowing in impurity, you and the lie of hope: And choked with humiliation, you couldn't say, *Before You I am like a vessel filled with shame and disgrace, I am dust in my life, how much more so in my death,* because you knew you'd go on sinning, and in disgust, you yearned to hurt from so much lust.

The students tightened the circle. Isaiah slipped off the knoll and joined the tempestuous dance. In the center, the rabbi capered, his head burning with the fiery serpents of his curls. Sometimes he passed by the students, and sometimes he twirled by himself. Suddenly he fell on his knees. The students hurried to surround him, holding out to his extended hands books of the Zohar they had taken out of the house. He clutched the books to his lips, kissing them again and again, his eyes shut. The cracking of the fire crashed in the beams, and above it all rose the shout of Rabbi Avuya Aseraf, "I the humiliated, I the submissive, stand here on my knees before the vehement flaaaaame! Holy Light, Holy Rabbi Simeon Bar Yochai, He who rides atop the heavens rejoices at the clean and just soul coming to Him . . . By your great grace, Holy Tanna, Rabbi Simeon Bar Yochai, by grace of your death, by grace of the worlds you illuminate on this night of celebration, may we be saaaaaved!" The students huddled around him, their heads bent. "Holy Light," his voice snorted and bleated. "I know you and you know me, your leaping is love to me! I know you and you know meeeee!"

Then he rose up, clutching the books to his chest, and his eyes closed, slowly began spinning, between the circle of bodies and the fire. "Light of the King Messiah, light of the Good Sign, light of the soul of the first man!" Rabbi Avuya spun around and wailed: *"A voice was heard in Ramah, lamentation, a voice will be from praised Zion! Say to the Daughter of Zion, thus spake your Lord, whereas thou hast been forsaken, so shall thy sons marry thee: and as the Bridegroom rejoiceth over the Bride, so shall thy God rejoice over theeeee."*

At the fence, the women assembled, shading one another, watching the rabbi, whispering excitedly, "Last year on Lag b'Omer, the rabbi really saw the Shekhina."

"Yes, yes, at the Wailing Wall."

"In the men's section."

"No, in the cave there. She sat like a woman dressed in black. The holy rabbi stayed with Her all night, sat next to Her and consoled Her, until sunrise."

"Come on, come on." They moved, reverently, and among the kerchiefs, that tall black woman was conspicuous.

"My sister, my love, my dove, my wonder . . ." Standing at the fire, the rabbi went on: *"Go forth, O ye daughters of Zion, and behold King*

Solomon with the crown wherewith his mother crowned him in the day of his
espousals, and in the day of the gladness of his heart. As a Bridegroom re-
joices in his Bride so shall thy God rejoooooiiice in you."

Then he made a slight sign with his hand, and a kind of wind passed
over the group of women at the fence, and the gust of their loose clothes
trembled in you. They slipped out of the dark toward the men approaching them with their arms held out, holding their hands, to the
sound of the crackling flames.

And you suddenly seemed to fathom the meaning of Rabbi Avuya's
words on the salvation that will come from the destruction, and some understanding also flickered in you that you would not come to salvation on
the paths of Rabbi Avuya Aseraf, your salvation would not be by burning the material in the fire, not by the separation of the bad smell of the
galbanum. And you could no longer say whom you would soon lead
running behind you on the paths strewn with silence, whom you would
clasp with arms melting in the coals of the holiday.

And then Isaiah was expelled, straying in the dark among the
flowerbeds, shading his eyes with his hand, laughing, scared. Walking
around, looking for you.

And the rabbi had begun blessing the couples standing around him
next to one another, their faces beaming: "May it be Thy will that by the
merit of the union of the Holy-One-Blessed-Be-He and the Shekhina we
live to engage in the virtues of Simeon Bar Yochai and bring near His
Messiah and may He give reign to His Kingship, in the world He created,
Amen, May it by Your willlll."

You slipped off into the dark. In the first moment, retreating mechanically, among the pine trees so Isaiah wouldn't find you as long as the
rabbi was making the blessing (first of all to run away and only then, as
always, to try to ask why), and when Isaiah passed by, his eyes squinting
from the fire, going on in the dark along the hedge away from you, did
you lean your hand and your head on a tree, so hard was your heart
pounding. Sweat poured onto your forehead. You felt your face flaming.
Isaiah went off among the guests, disappeared behind the blacksmith
shop. You froze, didn't make a sound, just ran your tongue along your
palate.

The rabbi continued his blessings; the roar of the crackling fire permeated the grove with a spray of sparks. Isaiah crossed the yard again, thin, perplexed, his hands long and slim, slightly raised at his sides, his blinded face searching for you, and in a quiet, almost inaudible voice, he kept repeating your name, "Amalia, Amalia . . ." He stumbled, solitary, deep in the yard, his profile clear in the red leaping of the bonfire, and panic was in the tense arch of his limbs. Pain whipped you. You moved away, and raising a racket with your movements, as if deliberately, you beat branches and trampled acorns.

Bar Yochai! Fortunate is she who bore you, fortunate is the people that learns from you. The song began again. You ran. For a moment, you were caught, like a burning torch, in the flame of the bonfire, and in the next moment you vanished behind the tree trunks, immediately turning sharply to the path falling down the slope. You knew that Isaiah saw you move, saw the flames that flickered from your clothing, and you made your way deeper into the dark, terrified he would run after you, catch up with you.

Did you really run away then, slipping on the rocks, tearing grasses off in your hand, did you really flee, wanting once again to cut off ties, wipe out traces, in that forced, closed circle, renewing itself in another time, in another person, for you are not the same one who sinned, and your name is not the same name, *Amalia, Emily, Amy, Mala, my Malinka?*

For if that's how it was, I too, now, would still be caught in that running, as if the flesh has not been burned. And everything I discovered in Your love was nothing but stupid madness, all this waiting like a *burning fire shut up in my bones* from one end of the Omer Counting to the other was only a delusion.

The heart of darkness. The black growing thick before dawn. The solitude after the moon declined, in the frozen area in between. And the fear that all is madness. Just a screen of dark. Only sixteen days are left.

My Malinka, Amalia, Father's voice poured into your running, spreading from the dark. *The oil of joy from your fellows.* On the mountaintop, the fire flourished in the brightness of the rejoicing backs. Fleeing, you turned away from the path, and you cautiously groped your way among the rocks.

The tumult of sliding dirt rose from the slope. You froze. You didn't
know if those were Isaiah's steps or only the echo of your own rolling
steps, but that hesitation was enough to put you in thrall to the yearning for his fingers to sink in your hair. Once again the sight of his back
arose before you, he stood alone, his hands long and slim, lighted by the
crashing of the flames. You gagged with contempt, with a rage of madness for his softness, for the insult of your yearning for him, for the
wish to hurt him from so much longing, to force him to come, immediately. And you ran down to the slope, held on to the tree trunks,
crossing the dark valley among the trees, the stones of the fences, the
cliffs on the slope opposite, rushing ahead of you, in the heart of the
white fire.

At the top of the ridge, near the house, you gasped, turning your face
back to the night. The broad firmament was loaded with heaps of red
and smoke. You listened impatiently to the dark and twisted your way
over the pebbles strewn on the path like signs of the Mourners of Zion.
Below, in the East, the line of the horizon gleamed like mother-of-pearl.
You were scared that the time had passed, and you stumbled to the gate,
inserting the cold key into the slit of the lock.

In the house, you moved from window to window. Posing arguments
and refuting them at once. Burying your head in the gray of the horizon
lightening in the East, but the coolness growing sharp in the arches didn't
ease the burning. And when the sky became white and Isaiah's hesitant
knock still wasn't heard, the knowledge that you are waiting in sin, and
that it would be better if he didn't come, overwhelmed you.

("The knowledge." Is it strong enough to let go of the act, from the
heights of its perfection, to touch the crookedness of the ways of lust?
And now, what good does the bare knowledge do me that Isaiah won't
come tonight, that he won't be expelled, a stranger, from the new
yeshiva, that he won't slip away from the solace of Elisheva to come
here. How strong is knowledge in the face of the humiliating lust, in the
face of the unbearable waiting for him to come, for him to turn the lock
in the gate, for the breeze of his body to stroke my neck. *Bar Yochai! At
a wondrous light in lofty heights you feared to stare, for it is great.*)

———

By now you almost believed that he wouldn't come, and you attacked his dullness, the awe that made him weak. And you were especially furious with the wrath of jealousy that it was the power of Rabbi Avuya that overcame your power, and in spite of everything, Isaiah turned around halfway, and was pressed among those who engaged in sanctification in the fervid courtyard on the mountain. And it angered you to death that he paid no heed to your lust, and you got up with fallen face to kill him, wanting to take your own life in repulsion, to hurt him terribly. You sank down on the windowsill, *hope deferred maketh the heart sick,* your face like extinguished ash. The East was turning very white now, and still he didn't come. You dozed off. Sinking into the pallor spinning slowly on the hills turning white on the horizon, spreading like the face of Isaiah.

There was a knock on the door. You got up, your body feeble. Of all the fire, only cinders remained. Isaiah was shaking in the doorway. He stood like someone who came to confess sin, his face averted and your shawl twisted in his hands. Behind him crept the haze turning white at the edge of the sky. Reluctantly, he lifted his face to you, and the coolness of the column of dawn rose on the doorsill.

(Hard now to go on lucidly. The gray is already lying in the windows. The head is flooded with fatigue. The time is so short and the hand refuses to hurry, as if as the hour grows short, the hand lingers in binding every one of the cords of that predawn of last year.)

"You left your shawl with me."

You saw the dust of the roads covering his sandals, the cuffs of his pants, and you understood that all that time, he had been walking on the slopes, going around the gates of the city, going away, and climbing again, until he knocked on your gate.

"You forgot the shawl," he repeated, a sort of high-pitched, excited laugh encompassing his words. You saw how his body was shuddering, and you didn't reply.

"I came to . . ." He didn't finish because of your hand, suddenly stretched out, grabbing the shawl.

"Let's go in." You turned around.

In the vestibule, the pallor was thick. You advanced to the room; behind you, his clothes rustled, and you felt very sorry for Isaiah.

In the room, the light of the table lamp blended with the whiteness rising in the arches. At the table, you stopped. You knew that Isaiah was standing behind you. The long expectation sapped your strength, and you could no longer flee in terror or vengeance. You just stood there, nailed to the spot, waiting for his hand to rest on your hair. Both of your breathing beating the tightening fabric so wearily.

I don't know if he did indeed whisper behind you, "Amalia . . ." Or if he was silent.

You didn't turn your face away from the window, inhaling the softness of the cool air on the bud of dawn. And there was no longer wrath or shame, faint-heartedness or lust, just the weight of the whole city streaming into a cool breeze in your limbs, wandering around in the valleys below the windows, lying among the neighborhoods, bearing in the last watch of the night the dryness of the mountain grasses between east and west, the brightness of the olive trees, the ashes of the bonfires soaked with dew, and everything seemed to stand still, waiting in the meantime, and one slow note, stubbornly returning, filling the space with its vibration, permeating the pallor from Father's room, over and over the same long heavy note, as the breath grows thinner.

You didn't stop the drift of the bedclothes sliding at dawn, the bodies clutching, the muffled shrieks, the hovering, the sipping, the sound of your name on his lips. *Amalia,* the syllables of his name breathing inside you, *Isaiah.* And only the whiteness swirled, the sound blended with coolness and warmth, covering inside and out with a flash spreading over the hills to the end of the horizon, creeping to the bedclothes, ringing in the transparent depth, plucked, covering with a trickling transparency, with the thick, deep, released tremor, covering everything with the lucid warmth of solace.

The light of sunrise burst into the window, a sheaf of radiance. Isaiah sat up, his head gilded and the open shirt twisted on his shoulders. From where you lay, you saw his bare back, his loins, the weight of his body shifted onto the hollow of your thigh. Beyond his head, the redness was severed from the base of the horizon, washing in an orange glow the sheet of the firmament unsheathed from the desert, lapping at the window.

"Isaiah," you whispered to his back. "Isaiah." Knowing that nothing would any longer be as it was before.

He got up and started tending to his clothes. Then he stood in the window bay, hovering, as if he wanted you to send him away. You got up calmly and almost longed for him to go and leave you alone to enjoy the new fullness spreading in you. You couldn't see the lines of his shaded face because of the flush that held the loom, and when you approached, he turned his profile away from you.

Beyond his neck, you saw the ball of fire scorching the desert, glittering on the Dead Sea. And then he turned around and looked at you as a foe, and a strong wave of tumult hurled his curls. Once again he threw his arms around your loins, burying his face in your hair, humming as if in clear weeping. And then he seemed to be scared of what he was doing, and his arms fell.

"Isaiah, I would like you to play for me someday," you murmured, slowly, his breath glittering in yours. "Play for me someday, on the violin."

He raised his extinguished eyes; for a moment he remained riveted, his eyes on yours. And then he moved, slipped away without a word into the corridor. At the top of the stairs to the threshold, he turned his delicate face to you once more.

"Amalia . . . I don't know when I'll come again . . ."

"Yes." You nodded through the distance.

He walked down the street, bathed in the light of the rising sun. *He halted upon his thigh* and his sandals struck the asphalt. You watched him and chuckled. *He that is wounded in the stones, or hath his privy member cut off, shall not enter into the congregation of the Lord.* You fastened the gate on his departing figure.

Wearily, you took your hand off the *hole of the door*, returned to the violated room, to the spilled redness. Slowly, you pulled the spread over the unmade bed and rolled the cover off the loom with your hand *that had held the hollow of his thigh until daybreak. And thou shalt cut off her hand.* You smiled, stroking the fabric, tremors that were emitted from the threads, spreading the dust of the embers of sunrise to the top of the loom.

You washed your body for a long time in the shower, letting the soft, heavy water flow over you. The light burst into the bathroom, spinning in the spray of the flow washing your hair. You soaped the locks that were still uncut, shampooed them well. And for a long time, you combed the weight of the ends, until you bound them in a wet sheet around your skull. In the room, you put the stools back in their places, and folded the first prayer shawl, which Isaiah had left on the table.

Dressed in white, you stood to recite the Morning Prayer. In exultation, you drew out the sounds of the prayer, from *The heavens declare the glory of God* to *The trees of the field say*. And the sounds of the chicken, the dove, the fly, and the ant rang from the pages of your prayer book, rejoiced to the folds of the valley, to the pure blue dome.

Morning. A long time after sunrise. The room is filled with the smells of baking, the smoke of burning dung, and the sounds of life renewed beyond the flank of the mountain. Their bus, the strange cries, the glide of a flute, the shrieks of children, the barking. Life going on under my windows in the morning rising there to a different life.

I didn't stand to recite the Midnight Prayer last night. Only incense of the confession of the night of Lag b'Omer last year is burned to smoke. Smoke bound in smoke from one end of the night to the other. Morning, and I, like you, will bathe and stand to recite the prayer. The warm light sprayed from the windowsill onto the pages—light woven in light at the end of that night. For I am the same person who sinned, I did not travel into exile from my home, and I did not change my name again, *Amalia*. That is the secret of the name woven into us, for *You are One and Your Name is One*.

It's morning now and Isaiah didn't come. Yes, on the night of Shavuoth, at the end of the Omer Counting, he will certainly come. And then what they said will be fulfilled for us, *What is complete repentance, not in old age, years when you will say I don't want them, but when he keeps it in his love and in the strength of his body and in the land he went through.* And then we shall know full repentance together . . . *for the soul is Yours and the body is Your creation.* With no separation, with no end. For what was is what is, and what will be is what was. First and last in one weave.

The Garden of Eden says, Awake, O north wind; and come thou south; blow upon my garden that the spices thereof may flow out. Let my beloved come into his garden, and eat his pleasant fruits.

Dogs say, Come, we shall bow and we shall kneel, we shall bless HaShem our maker.

Lag b'Omer. Thick weariness sweet as dust.

Thirty-four days of the Omer. Essence of Splendor.

Late at night. The day of Lag b'Omer was heavy for me. (The dizziness increases.) And then the letter from Stein—I couldn't go back to weaving. I decided to go out to buy the little bit I still needed at the grocery store. Only after I went down the alleys, dodging the piles of building stones and rubbish, and stood in front of the Arab shopkeeper, who emerged from behind the cans of food, did I discover that I hadn't brought any money, and I had to go back past the eyes staring at me from behind the fences, open the gate and lock it again, and once more go down past the children teasing me, as if they were discussing whose hand would cast the first stone, and *afterward the hand of all the people.*

Going back, I took the long way, on the path circling the hill. Near the house of Fayge and Rabbi Levav, I turned aside so as not to meet them by chance (and only on the Sabbath did I sit in their house as a daughter).

To cut now.

On the morning of Lag b'Omer last year, right after the Morning Prayer, with a full body, you went to your weaving. The morning flash sparkled in the silk, and your breathing was pure. You moved the shuttle, the wooden spindle spun and was caught in your hand. A laugh gurgled up from inside you. You held on to the weight of the spool, bending down to the tremble of the warp, to the sweetness left from Isaiah's body, and you smiled because, seen from outside, your happiness could be ascribed to the holiday of Rabbi Simeon Bar Yochai. You wove a little, just to complete the pattern of stripes with the letters that spelled the name of God, and then you covered the loom and went out. Not going anywhere in particular.

You got off the bus somewhere downtown, your loins filled with a new softness. An echo of garages and the smell of coffee stood in the empty street. The sleepy midmorning light was twined around a eucalyptus tree. From the carved facade of a building on the opposite sidewalk emerged an oriental city, encrusted with crescents of doorways and the smell of roasted sesame. A supple breeze took hold of your hair. You gasped, running your hand over the breadth of your pelvis. Without thinking, you pushed aside a curtain of plastic tassels, and stood inside a small barber shop. A trilling chant came from the radio, and a sweet smell. The place was empty. The barber stood up.

"Very short, all of it," you instructed and sat down, tossing over your shoulders the heaviness of the plaits of hair.

The barber tied the smock around your neck, leaned over you, dipped the comb into your hair as into fine merchandise. "A shame to cut it," he said.

"Very short," you persisted.

"Whatever the lady wants." He put up his hands as if accepting the order, took the ends of the hair, and brandished the blades of his scissors. You burst into sharp laughter. From the radio wriggled the oriental melody in the singer's honeyed voice. Your excited mood infected the barber. He twisted his back, bowed with every snip, humming in a hoarse trill.

The two of you were alone in the small room. Near the mirror stood a glass with a sprig of jasmine, and the wall was hung with pictures of couples in wedding clothes. The racing scissors clanged. One by one the locks slid from your shoulders to the floor. From the door the sun crept into a yellow rectangle, lapping at your stockings, melting the weight of the night. The barber's hands moved your skull. The sound of snipping, the honeyed, golden chant. *Circumcise our heart to love and fear Your Name.* You shut your eyes, stretched your limbs wearily, gave in to the cradling of the Additional Soul spreading in you. Day of rejoicing, day of Lag b'Omer, you breathed calmly, everything is in its place, here, everything is already repaired.

"There!" The barber stopped the racing scissors.

You opened your eyes. Before you rose Mala's head atop the stem of the neck, leaning a bit into the mirror frame. On the bare countenance, the stripe of the arched eyebrows was prominent up at the forehead, far away from suddenly very gray eyes, and the sharp chin.

"Nice." You smiled. The fragile neck wasn't used to the sudden chill, and in the thin dress, the shoulders were especially narrow. The barber ran his soft brush over you.

"Take a few curls, bring them to the boy who fell in love with you for your hair." He bent down to the floor. You stopped him and were already standing up to go. He skipped after you, counting the change into your hand. The singer's voice played on the radio. A transparent light was caught in the plastic tassels. In the street you didn't know where to turn. The barber was leaning in the doorway with his arms folded, and his eyes on your bare neck made you hasten up the street.

The morning warmth stirred the bristles on your scalp. On one side of the street were white hewn facades, and on the other side they were swallowed up in a heavy shadow. Dark entries led to backyards, where, in the distance, lay piles of building material. Around the corner, Mala and Father came toward you, deep in conversation, Mala explaining with lively gestures, her black hair waving on her jawline, insisting on details, pausing for emphasis, and Father hanging on her words. They approached you with a rustle of falling leaves strewn in spots of black and white to the depths of the boulevard, and the blurred dome of the church in the righthand corner of the picture. You smiled at them, leaning on a eucalyptus tree at the curb. The bright spots of morning walked on your shoulders through the pattern of the branches, trembling when a truck filled the street, maneuvered heavily, and braked. A tumult of women and men and children's shouts echoed in the street. Ladders dropped behind the truck, and men in black coats descended, holding out their hands

to the babies waved at them by the women who hurried up last, laden
with shopping bags, empty pots, bedlinens. A few children with shaved
heads tramped from the people to the parking lot, their bright sidelocks
bouncing as they ran. You watched them, the sun flooding your back,
lapping your stockings, the sandals. You looked at their tiny holiday
jackets, at their mischief. From the doorway of a nearby workshop came
smells of rubber and rolls of paper, perfuming the breeze of light. Between two low roofs, beyond the yard floored with eucalyptus leaves
and broken tiles, the sky opened, and at the end, in the distance, the sea
sparkled. You stood straight in the blue wool coat, and Father's hand, big
and warm, is holding your hand, and he bends over and picks up a little
branch.

"Look, Malinka, that's the fruit of the eucalyptus." He brings the
branch close to you, twirls it between his fingers with the straight line of
his fingernails, hits the branch on the open hand, and a yellowish stream
of little balls pours out on his smooth skin.

"Look how tiny its seeds are, you see," he says as he bends down to
you. "From such little seeds a big tree grows." And on the crevices of his
hand the light runs sour and strong, and his suit touches you with a smell
of wool and cigarettes, and you stand straight, pushing the tips of the
black shoes into the ground, and over you leap shining balls from the big
tree, when Father stops talking and looks at you, and doesn't even tell you
not to dirty your Sabbath patent leather shoes that he put on you for the
synagogue, but just says so quietly, "Look at you, Malinka . . . Instead of
playing with other children, you've got to go with your father to the
synagogue to say Kiddush for a mother. What a fate you have, Amalia."

And the leaves of the big tree and the whole yard and the broken tiles
filled with sparkles streaming from the sea, and your hand in Father's big
warm hand with the good strong smell.

The narrow street led to the alley with four stone steps. You passed
through the entrance, straightening your back, your loins taut in the
touch of noon. And Father's hand slips into your hand. In the doorway
of one of the shops, you imagined you saw Isaiah's face disappearing.
You moved on his heels, but when you got close, you saw that it was
somebody else's broad back. Into the street spilled the sound of a piano,
surrounded by the redness of a geranium. A yearning phrase of Schu-

mann or Liszt sounded from one of the apartments or from a distant
radio. A density of colors exploded. The sun kindled a bold sheaf in display windows, sprayed from a yellow shirt, a copper pot, ropes. In the
space between houses the noise of the main street filtered, as from a watershed, sweeping behind it, in hidden courses, the ticking of machines,
echoes of worshippers, sudden pockets of silence. You raised your hand
to move away the ends of hair, and you smiled to yourself, for only now
were your locks shorn, you, Delilah with chopped-off hair, bound with
wet ropes and her strength departed. Once again Isaiah hurried across the
street with his skinny back, and when he turned around, this time too he
was a stranger. *Circumcise our heart to love and fear Your Name.* Suddenly
you were struck by the knowledge that Isaiah was now knocking on the
gate of your house, excitedly searching for you. You passed your hand
over your eyes. The strong light burst in red strips between the fingers.
You stroked the hand over the cheek, down the bare neck, around the
hem of the thin blouse.

"Amalia." You imagined you heard Elisheva's voice pouncing from
the dazzle of the passers-by, maybe because of the smell of crisp dough
and sweet cheese that spilled into the street. You smiled in amazement at
how she would certainly shout at the way you look—"What did you do
to yourself, Amalia?! You've gone absolutely crazy"—spreading the
flash of her face, her excited laugh, before you. "Let me see . . . It changes
you completely, makes your eyes bigger," she'd add in hypocritical concern. "Isaiah's going to faint when he sees you." Talking of him like
somebody she knew, for some reason not mentioning your conversation
last night at the bonfire.

"The barber thought I was getting my hair cut for my wedding
tonight," you tease her to hide from her what happened last night, so
she won't notice anything. Only then do you see that a beggar surrounded by old newspapers stuffed in plastic bags, sitting on the curb, his
swollen head in a beret, has been watching you with wrinkled eyes the
whole time.

"Pssst, pssst, there's already thirty-eight, here, somebody else gave,
pssst, pssst, thirty-nine, great! Pssst." He either blinked or winked the
folds of his gray eyes, jangling the coins with a rattle of the box, his
drooping mouth crushing an exposed thought. "Starts with K, with K,

with K, that's seven letters, starts with K, with K, pssst, pssst, forty-one, great! Pssst, here's that girl looking at me, maybe she'll give something."

You were afraid to move, to turn your head away from him, as if the turbid folds of his eyes could strip you naked, reveal to everyone what was done to you.

"Starts with A, with A, pssst pssst, forty-two, great! With A, Ancient Adam, Ancient Adam! Got to do the crossword puzzle. Meanwhile, you got to do a little *shnorring*, pssst, forty-two, great!"

And then something in that crazy voice droning out of a block of limbs, shopping bags, moldy dust, and sweat, struck you; something in the bare head caught you, in the middle of the bustling street, suddenly whipping in you the memory of Isaiah's vulnerability, the softness of his eyes, choking you with the shame of how far you were from the perfection of Isaiah's faith, from that union of act and thought, from that innocence whose purity you will never, never reach. ("That's the union of repentance from love, Amalia," said Rabbi Levav on the Sabbath. "When a person repents from love, the light of the one being sparkles on him, and everything, everything then looks like one union, only one union." Is that what he meant?)

Finally you went off. You ran down the street, swept up in the slide of the road, as if only the horizon were opened above the roofs, the water tanks, the antennas, only the sight of the mountains hovering yellowish at the bottom of the sky, would offer you healing. And you didn't get on the bus to your house, you didn't return to weaving, to the afternoon shadow in the arches, to Isaiah searching for you. You let the road roll you among the deserted buildings, toward the light glinting from the minarets of the mosques and the folds of the peaks in the distance; you were suddenly impelled to return to the place of sin, openly, immediately, to annul all prohibitions, just return there, a deflowered woman with shorn hair.

You passed the shadow of the Old City walls, going deep in the gate, passing with your shaved head the peddlers, the niches of shops. And only when you found yourself facing Emily's hotel, at the foot of the entrance stairs, did you stop, stealing a glance at the Arab men sipping coffee in the nearby café, sure they would recognize you, in spite of your shorn hair. Knees trembling, you climbed to the entrance, put your face against the glass. Your heart was pounding, the sight turned dark and was wiped out. (Always by oblique roads, like the threads of the woof retreating, running back and forth, joining in a forced return. Never direct, like the strings of the warp, plowing the weave from side to side in one fly.)

Behind the glass, a red carpet finally appeared before your eyes, reflected through the shadows of faint light. The reception desk was empty, the telephone receiver hanging like a black corpse from the switchboard. The entrance to the dining room was swallowed up in the afternoon gloom. A group of Polish priests was there eating breakfast then, and the medley of their alien and familiar language was proof sent to Emily. A young man in a shirt drooping over his trousers crossed the lobby. One of those men who fill the hotel with their vague functions, scratching themselves on your way to the roof, to the open view there.

And still nothing of the afternoon drowsiness was disturbed, despite the pounding of your heart. The man shuffled into the staircase and disappeared. You approached, and with a sudden boldness, you placed your hand on the doorhandle. Isaiah's warm look rested softly on your neck—here, at last he found you, here, after all, he followed you, to accompany you on the road to repentance. You turned your face, smiling gratefully. A dark man with a moustache was surveying the back of your neck. You clutched the opening of your blouse, slipping away without turning your head, lashed by pounding, rushing faster down the slope of the alley, scrambling among the bodies, the straw baskets, the shadowy niches, the curves.

You came to only when you emerged from the crowded alleys to a bright square opening in the hewn stones. Like a dial, the white shadow of a turret split the stone circle frozen in light. You gasped, leaning your head toward the brightness. Once again the sun's softness melted on your skin, burning away the sediment of the night. The pounding of your heart subsided. You breathed calmly, slowly sinking into a kind of relief. Maybe the weight of your hair that was removed, maybe the shadow of the turret, maybe the heat rough in your nostrils—something even then stirred in you the taste of rest waiting in a thin hot crumbling of dust.

You wandered around, going deeper with soft limbs into unfamiliar passages, going along without thinking. Gourd vines climbed on strips of

gray earth between the houses, burying piles of ruins beneath them. Little girls in striped pinafores passed by arm in arm. In the field suspended
between the roofs and the sky, young men were chasing a soccer ball.

You went far away, emerging from the arches of the gate, the soft light
blowing around your scalp, crushed on your neck, already absorbed in
the crumbly soil of the mountain slopes. You turned to the steep path. A
furrow of rock fragments sprayed from your steps. You stopped, throbbing. Beneath you spread the gigantic straddling of the slopes, segments
of the ridge collapsing with a rustle down to the bottom of the valley, to
the feet of the mountain rising across from you, turning white in boulders and dust, climbing the dirt steps, tombstones, to the height of the
flaming road rising desperately to the minaret of the mosque, to the light
shining behind the peak.

You stood there, your body reeling with the rush of blood, the heat
entangled in the bristles of your hair, permeating your breathing. The
slope dropped off arid at your feet, and yet you longed so much to be
spilled out between the strata of the mountain, to be gathered in the
silent rocks steeped in lamentations. You stood there, your body planted
and throbbing in the wind spinning on the ridge. With no before and no
after. As if you were planted there forever. Pouring out slowly, in the
heat, to the dirt. With no more distinction. *One and Your Name is One.*
And before you a dry pillar of silence.

You stood throbbing, with no sooner and no later, as you will stand in
that place open to black clouds, and in the distance Isaiah will run around,
will slip in mud, clapping his hands, he will argue excitedly in the quarrel that broke out among the gravediggers, who refuse to go on digging
for some reason, put down their picks and are fighting over the corpse of
Rabbi Avuya Aseraf, who is laid on the mud in a litter, running around
excited among the tombstones and the mud, trying to prove something.
And you, suspended on the slope in the distance, unmoving . . . As you
sat and didn't move, even though they announced in the loudspeakers of
the stadium, *Amy Oooorbach.* And the trainer smiling at you, and the
small audience in the galleries shouting something at you, and you didn't
get up from the ground. Amazed at the metal bar suspended too high to
reach, way beyond you, and why get up from the ground at all, seeing
yourself get up, gaining momentum, and still you didn't get up from sit-

ting weak on the ground. And over the head, the hum rising. And it's not clear if it's before or already after the jump that you sit with your limbs flaccid, on the ground. Surely an hour has passed since they announced on the loudspeaker that you broke the youth record for the high jump, and the bar is still suspended in the void, and from the galleries the audience is shouting something. And the humming was cut off, paralyzed, from the skull . . . And your hand stretched heavy to the wet stones, in the open field up to the white poplars, and the smoke of the village on the horizon of the foreign plain, not noticing Hubert waiting for you a long time now, and again your hand slowly touches the ground. And suddenly, with a spasm, the clenched hand squeezed damp clods, pressing the crushed mass, and in your ears bursts the turmoil of the iron wheelbarrows rolling in the cotton of the bedroom, full of the stones they would hew, and they were so weak they fell there like flies, straight onto the ground, like that, like flies. (There was a tree there. Dry. Maybe completely dead. A few black leaves and some fungus on the trunk. You were dragged to it. Sticking to the bark the ball of earth warmed in your hand, slowly smearing it, almost diligently, sticking the grains of liquid to the mound of the bark, carefully, as if completing some work. A long time.)

Until the sun declined, and through the yellow a cool breeze began. You moved away, drunk with the warmth absorbed in your limbs, wandering among the walls of silence of the mountain stage, twirling in the lap of that one hollow closing around you for ever and ever.

You made your way down the rock steps, among the cypresses covered with orange, close to the dryness of dust, you were borne, as if without movement, to the bend of the mountain. Until at the shortcut, you found yourself at the entrance to the house. You slowly moved aside the bundle of jasmine leaves Isaiah had left on the doorhandle. You held the fragrant bouquet without wonder, like someone who is only repeating old gestures, and went in with a dusty body. In the house, you put the green bundle, Isaiah's offering, in a vase, and smiled to yourself, he really was walking at your side all the time. You ran your hand over the opening of the shirt, over the rough neck. Your warm fingers were soaked with the sap of leaves and dust. And that was enough for you.

For the first time, you took the cardboard boxes out of the closet. For a long time you sat in front of them without opening them or spreading the photos out before your eyes. You sat without moving. And if not for the smell of jasmine that echoed in the arches, you wouldn't have known if you had ever moved from that position, if you even went out of the house in the morning. Once again you ran your hand over the bristles of hair around the base of the skull. *Let my soul be like dust.* Bringing it down on the exposed neck, on the back of the neck, on the spikes of the vertebrae bending under the movement of the hand.

In a flowing whisper you poured out the prayer at bedtime. From the rumpled sheets, the odor of Isaiah's sweat still wafted. You buried your shorn head in the pillow. *May You blot out in Your abundant mercies.* The humming was cut off. The roughness, rising silently, crumbled. Choking, sweet. Warm dust.

Late at night. Perhaps before dawn.

I woke up in a panic. For a moment I couldn't tell where I was. What name. The knee protruding from the nightgown was altogether alien. Even after the room emerged from the darkness, I simply could not remember if I had written at the beginning of the night or about what.

Suddenly I can't explain why, after everything, I'm still keeping the boxes of photos here (!) Can't understand why I haven't destroyed them by now. They're kept with me. Organized by "subject"—Parents' House, Conservatory, Grammar School, Gymnasium, Music Auditorium, First Recital, Stary Teatr, Second Recital. Classified, sorted, childhood photos, passport photo from city hall registers, photo with Father on the boulevard. All that's missing is the oval portrait from the gold locket—everything's ready. If they want, they can print the album *tomorrow:* "Mala, Girl Prodigy of the Jewish Piano, Last Notes," or some other kitschy title. All their commercial, saccharine sweet chatter, stuck to the fingers like grains of dust—let them make it a bestseller with chrome photos, agents, and the additional scoop of the confused life of the "photographer," "the second generation," "the shadow that lies on the children of the survivors." Let them debate whether she committed suicide because of repentance, or vice versa, whether it grew out of the stench of life "outside," which sometimes, God forbid, you can't go back on. All that dealing with the dead, repenting, sinning souls. Jewish ashes packaged for quick consumption, ashes in little bottles, for sale to tourists. Dust of saints, dust of the murdered, dust of the martyred, tortured for sanctification of the Name—what crumbly chatter. *Their* version of *Let my soul be like dust.* Maybe they'll smother the whole thing. It's liable to cause demoralization, suicide could suddenly become fashionable. Let them be satisfied with a brief, laconic announcement, one that says the investigation was opened, and the results will never be revealed. (Of course, it is possible to make it more dramatic, to jump downtown somewhere, or from Muristin Tower in the middle of the Old City, to get headlines.)

And in fact, how can I decide what will be done with the photos? What right do I have? On behalf of what? For I never went beyond the miserable rummaging in the fragments of Father's and Mother's voice, beyond the miserable inflaming of abhorrence for those invited to the memorial at Café Shoshana with their bent backs. And now, this holding onto her photos is only a testimony to the helplessness.

This afternoon, Stein's letter arrived. Sent from Tel Aviv. *Came for two weeks, for a short visit. Will come to Jerusalem the night after the holiday.* The cramped, angular handwriting, starting to shake. What still drives that sick, aging man? Why doesn't he stay with his business in New York, seal the grave? A miserable and dangerous man. A bleeding lion. *Stopping in Tel Aviv in the meantime, I'll come to Jerusalem on the night after the holiday. Amy dear, I hope everything's fine. How come you haven't arranged for a phone already?* (That nauseating family tone.) The main thing he doesn't write, but we both understand very well why he came. Why say it explicitly?

And let's even say that Mala had given in to his blackmail, had agreed to be his in exchange for the hopes of life for a while—who guaranteed that she wouldn't be taken in the next Aktsia, despite the intervention of Ludwig Stein, maybe even because of it. Does he think he really had any

power? He did get the razor blade to her and turn her into a legend—
what does he still want, now that Father is dead and he can do what he
wants with the past?

And me, why do I still keep the box of photos here? The very thought
(almost expectation) that Stein will come and take them makes me tremble. (May I now have the courage to admit that it's only because of that
dependence on dread that I keep the pawn of death entrusted to me.
Some base beggarliness . . .)

When he comes on the night after Shavuoth, when he fills the arches
with his quick movements, he'll find here only his letter lying on the
table. Only his reflection, face to face, will he find here. Next to the pile
of pages, a confession to You. How he'll bend over them, leafing with
his small hand. All the rest I shall take with me when I leave at dawn.

Yes, the Torah Curtain also will disappear, wound around my body at
the foot of the cliff. The Torah Curtain of heaven, spread out before
You, delightful beating of birds and glints of gold . . . An anagram difficult to decipher, an opaque mantra, as Elisheva would say. (Of course
she'll weep more in relief than grief. Wonder if they'll give my name to
the little girl they'll have, Amalia. The shadow that will forever be wound
around their love.)

Late at night. Don't know what time it is. As if I had never risen from the
dust. Suddenly it seems as if here, now, from the feverish tangle of my
life, You build a world, take on the snake of ink twisting in the fibers of
the paper. Sometimes it seems to me that only thus do You exist. In the
hidden area between me and You, in my breathing that is poured out at
night, in my flesh consumed before You here. And all the rest is in vain.

Yes, now it becomes clear, for the first time, the meaning of the passage, *It has been taught: Rabbi Jose says, I was once traveling on the road,
and I entered into one of the ruins of Jerusalem in order to pray.* (I who
never left the ruin.) *Elijah of blessed memory appeared and waited for me
at the door till I finished my prayer. After I finished my prayer, he said to me:
Peace be with you, my master! And I replied: Peace be with you, my master
and teacher! And he said to me: My son, why did you go into this ruin? I
replied: To pray. He said to me: You ought to have prayed on the road.*
(Shouldn't have entered the ruin, should have stayed on the road.) *I*

replied: I feared lest passersby might interrupt me. He said to me: You ought to have said an abbreviated prayer. Thus I then learned from him three things: One must not go into a ruin; one must say the prayer on the road; and if one does say his prayer on the road, he recites an abbreviated prayer. (And if only to learn those three things, was it all worthwhile?) *He further said to me: My son, what sound did you hear in this ruin? I replied: I heard a divine voice, cooing like a dove, and saying: Woe to the children, on account of whose sins I destroyed My House and burnt My Temple and exiled them among the nations of the world! And he said to me: By your life and by your head! Not in this moment alone does it so exclaim, but thrice each day does it exclaim thus! And more than that, whenever the Israelites go into the synagogues and prayer houses and respond: May His great Name be blessed! the Holy-One-Blessed-Be-He shakes His head and says: Happy is the king who is thus praised in this house! Woe to the father who had to banish his children, and woe to the children who had to be banished from the table of their father!*

For You will indeed weep secretly, "Woe that I destroyed My house and burnt My temple and exiled my children among the nations," if indeed You will weep from out of the ruin, only through the silence deepening here, with every breath rustling between the loom and the table, Your weeping echoes. Only through the sheets of papers spread out to the night, through my leaning over now, before dawn, with my hair down.

So, in fact, why leave something behind? Testimony? Why? How they will search between the lines, between the knots, for the traces of the life that flowed out through them, the secret that was concealed, how they will try to inflame a strange fire from the ashes? When, in fact, there is nothing beyond the pain amassing now in the back, the shoulders, nothing except the struggle of serving You. That is the seal of the Covenant You put in the limbs, the weariness in the limbs filling with dust. Those are the tablets you hewed for me to inscribe my life.

Cloaked in the Torah Curtain as in a garment, the parchment scrolls wound around my breast, I shall return to You. Like all flesh. I and my name. I and the fabric of my life. I and You in one word. And no alien eye shall observe us.

five weeks

Thirty-six days of the Omer. Five weeks and one

day. Grace of Essence. Saturday night. Behold!

God is my salvation, I shall trust and not fear.

Strengthen me in this holy night after Sabbath.

On Thursday night, I wrote until late, and I don't know if I finally succeeded in reaching the warmth of the rock. This afternoon, as always, I
went for the Sabbath meal to Fayge and Rabbi Levav. Rabbi Tuvia com-
mented on the Bible portion from Leviticus that begins *And the Lord
spake unto Moses in Mount Sinai*. But all through the Sabbath I dreaded
the things I would have to confess tonight.

A kind of cowardice took control as soon as the Sabbath was cut off.
As if its rest hadn't touched me at all. The week gaped open and with it
the rhythm of the Omer Counting, the knowledge that the sheet of time
is slipping to its end. After Havdalah, so heavy, I fell asleep, and now it's
after midnight. In the distance the city roars. On a roof in the alley
below, metal clotheslines jangle.

The day after Lag b'Omer, you wove quietly until noon. But when the time came to stop, when Isaiah could leave the yeshiva during the break and rush to see you, you let go of the shuttle, and without leaving any sign, you went out. You ascended the path among the heaps of stones so that you wouldn't run into Isaiah, who was certainly approaching on the steep road. You made a detour around the neighborhood to the distant bus stop, so there was no way he could come back there from your door. You sidled onto the bus, and as soon as it moved, you hastened to put your face to the window, searching with extinguished eyes to make out the shape of his thin back moving on the road circling the mountain.

(The wind dries the screen of heat. A constant humming lies on the eyes, around the eyebrows, the bridge of the nose. Some choking now, in the heart of the deed. Heart of the Torah Curtain. Heart of the writing. Suspended between earth and heaven, not yet judged.)

Downtown, you went to Frieda Schmidt's shop to sit with her a bit, tell her how the weaving was going, how beautiful the white warp was, and to go back home an hour later, shrouded in smells of wool and the echo of Mrs. Schmidt's singsong voice. But the Handicrafts Store of the Daughters of Israel was closed. You trudged past the dark grille of the display window, lingering, as long as he is knocking on your door.

At the intersection, you stood still, putting your hand on the pole of the barrier. The crowd stormed from all sides, barearmed, group against group. For a moment, you rushed, panting, among those running on the night of the bonfire, Isaiah's white shirt flickering before you. You quickly took your singed hand off the blazing iron bar. Suddenly, without understanding why, you felt impelled to publicize last night's act, your escape from Isaiah, your sin. You suddenly felt impelled to tell everything to Rabbi Israel, to confess to him, to prove to him, once and for all, that there is one law of you to put you to death! You knew the rabbi was now giving his weekly lesson to the students of Neve Rachel, and you hurried up the street to the bus stop.

Through the moving window, sunbeams streamed on the hills. Carrying Isaiah's white face, the whites of his eyes bending over you. The knowledge that you would soon cry it all out to Rabbi Israel left an empty space in you for now, and only the softness and memory of Isaiah's fingers leafing through the plaits of your hair spread out in the swaying chassis, cradling you, as in those few days wrapped in sleep in Hubert's splendid house, in the suburb of the big German city, before it happened, when you indulged for whole days in the smells of vegetation and water, in the passage of clouds in the summer sky, in the sparkle of sunflowers on the horizon of the fields around the house, the tapestries with lute players and shepherdesses, the thick wine, the slices of black bread in cellophane wrappers with gothic script, and the sounds inundating the house for hours from the fine stereo, of Brahms sextets, Beethoven quartets, Mozart piano and violin sonatas. Absorbing the details of the alien routine, Hubert's taking care of you, who are *like a tree planted by the rivers of water,* as if the time weren't limited, as if the blow were not about to strike (and maybe it was precisely because you knew that time was short that you enjoyed yourself even more, *for the remembrance of every deed comes before You*); in the mornings you slipped away from the calm island of the house, from Hubert busy in the darkroom, on the pretext that you were entrusting the printing to his professional care and keeping yourself for a final look at the development, and you drove around for hours in the city, the squares, wandering on the green slopes in the enormous parks, among the round stone bandstands for afternoon concerts, where lovers were enthralled, rejoicing at the summer downpours, and when you returned, you would pull Hubert out of the house to the wheatfields spread among the houses, coax him to go on walking, to go on talking in the low afternoon sun, just to make him waste the working time, to draw out the hours, just to postpone the final printing as long as possible. And Hubert, merry as a child, hugged you, buried his lips in your hair, prattling in an excited voice, "Yes, Emily, only because of you, only because of you did I know Mala, you will see, the album will be really special, I already see it, we shall write the text"—for some reason, he didn't mention Stein's name at all—"Mala will come back to life, the wonderful sounds of her playing will echo again—for our love, Emily, is proof

that it is possible to atone for pain, for torments, to atone with love, that
is the proof, isn't it? Emily the beautiful, my Jewish lover," he poured out
in his sharp accent. And you were hanging on the horizon revolving
blue, not denying, not shouting, abandoning yourself to the short thirst
for life smouldering in you, like a flush flooding the cheeks of a sick person before the final inflammation intensifies to ash. The bus was half
empty, the sun lapped the tremor of the window, dripping on your eyes.

And were you really lying to yourself in that burst of life, beyond any
price? You really did bring the flowerpot the very last day, when the printing was done, theatrically dragging the gigantic, tropical plant from the
car upstairs to the entrance, stubbornly, without help. "I'm bringing it
home, and you take care of it," you said, laughing from the effort. "Everyone has his own part in the symbol, the wandering Jew and the Aryan
rooted to the earth," biting your tongue so the madness of the clod of
earth won't burst out again, and added only mockingly: "I didn't find a
bird store, or else I would have brought two phoenixes in a cage." And
Hubert, surprised, waving the flowerpot with the amused line between his
eyes, hugs you, as the two of you are drawn to the Schubert piano sonata
filling the house, roll hugging on the white carpet, *like a cliché scene from
a movie,* even in his arms, you look at the two of you from a distance.

All that on the afternoon when the printing was finished. You still tried
to delude yourself that you were defending that scattered love nest, still
pretending you would redeem Hubert, your German man with the sweet
smile, that handsome photographer with the leather coats and the fine tobacco. Deluding yourself that you would save him from his decadence,
those violent attacks of seclusion, sobbing at night, those outbursts of
self-destruction forcing him to give himself to every woman who fawns
over his beauty, runs after him, all those waitresses, salesgirls, manufac-
turers' wives whom he takes to bed, almost obediently, destroying his
body with their flesh, thinking that was how he would appease the curse.
(How once, in the delicatessen, that saleswoman in a black dress and a
white kerchief, his lover for a night, couldn't stop herself. "Hubert"—she
puckered her lips, saccharine as an operetta, gazed at him unabashed,
paid no heed to the customers in the store, or to me who had come with
him, thrusting her breast in the black blouse at him, rubbing herself and
giggling—"When will you come again, Hubert?" And how, out of habit,

he raised his hand to her convex buttocks in the short skirt, patting them like an animal, her tense laugh. And afterward, leaving, when he held out to me the same hand, and the disgust and the compulsion to hold it, despite the nausea.) Yes, for the moment, you were still trying to defend the world you seemed to have built together, without asking how long. Not denying his plans for a joint exhibition in the gallery downtown. He's already preparing the hanging of his and your photos, is in touch with Jack Aronson from your gallery in New York, telling his agent that all of this is background for the Mala album. And at night, spinning in your hair the feverish confession of guilt, mingled with excitement about the opening, about the rare beauty of Mala in the enlargement of the oval photograph. And you sink in his arms, pretending in that constant swoon, even though, and perhaps even because of the intoxicating taste of pity, intoxicating to death, to oblivion, pity against pity.

The bus dashed. Roofs flooded with sun passed by the window. Eucalyptus. Shadowed entrances of alleys. Your forehead banged on the windowpane on the warmth of Isaiah's breath swaddling you. Yet you knew the time was over, so why, on the last night, when the development was finished, did you have to fall into that senseless racing on the roads of the big German city, among the deserted suburbs, through junctions flickering in the traffic lights? (And is the straying now, in the blind race of the shuttle from side to side, so different?)

What did you think—of endlessly putting off the end of the journey, first from New York to Germany, and then from there to the east, city after city, hall after hall, eight months in a car on wet streets, in fields, dragging along Hubert and his instruments, the shutters, the lenses, and the whole burden of his guilt, which in fact you never honestly paid attention to (and behind, like a shadow, still only like a shadow, the "financial backer"—Stein—traveling behind you every kilometer of the drive east, breathing down your back), and then, on the last night, the absurd escape. For you knew it was absolutely senseless. And what finally happened after three o'clock in the morning was expected, even driving on freeways has to end sometime, a photographing journey isn't endless life.

And what were you fleeing from? Did you really believe *the might of your hand* could cleanse her name from your blood? To cut off every-

thing with that album, "Commemoration," the product of Stein's madness, the material already sold to the big Paris–New York–London pub-
lisher? Did you really hope that you could forget, close the file, burn it
down to the root? Did you ever believe that these photos, printed dots of
crooked wooden floors of recital stages, chance figures passing by
wrapped in old wool coats, fields steaming in the cold, Hubert's "aes-
thetics of nothing in black-and-white"—did you think for a moment
that those photographs in all their emptiness contained something? Father did tell you explicitly that there was no reason to keep anything,
nothing remained, nothing. Amalia, you understand?

Or maybe you thought it was possible simply not to look at the material and to escape before the end of the printing, to race for hours in the
dizziness of paved rings, on access roads, sudden rises, bridges, lighted
tunnels, spinning in the screeching slide on the freeway, turning to the
exit lanes a split second before losing control, only to smash back into the
labyrinth of roads with a whistle of the headlamps pushing you to hurry
up more and more and you can't stop the moving, and only the weeping
and weakness draining from you, steaming the windowpane.

Maybe you escaped in Hubert's green car, only because you knew, you
knew very well, your sense sharpened in childhood, that when you saw
the photographs, when you stood face to face with them, shining, flickering sheets spread out one by one in a full pile, the few pictures that remained and were enlarged, and the material of the trip, that whole
"documentary of Mala"—that then, facing them, the delusion would
vanish irrevocably, and only the one last thing to know would be left. So
you escaped . . .

You got off at the stop near Neve Rachel. From the windows of the
yeshiva came the girls' voices reciting and the rabbis' voices explaining
slowly. You stood for a moment with your shorn head, in the shadow of
the eucalyptus, until the jostling of the trip subsided. The shadow on the
doorsill turned pale, and the grip of Isaiah's hand around your neck softened too. You knew he was coming back now on the road around the
mountain, and you also knew that tomorrow he would return at that
time and you wouldn't evade him anymore.

You entered the class in the middle of the lesson. The rabbi glanced at your shorn skull, and the girls' eyes pricked up in his wake. Elisheva pointed to the chair next to her. The rest of the girls had already turned back to the rabbi, bending over their notebooks. From the door you saw the thin line of Yaffa's neck, and the fringes of her kerchief straggling on it, and Jane's lowered head (a real advertisement for the "Exemplary Life of the Yeshiva Students," printed on chrome paper in a circular leafed through by contributors after Sabbath meals in suburban Chicago or New York), you passed behind the girls' backs to your old place. Elisheva pushed her Pentateuch toward you. The rabbi went back to talking about Balaam's ass, why she opened her mouth and spoke. The midrash on the defilement of Balaam, on the holy spark of the prophets of the Gentiles. His hands hovered gray above the book. The words hopped off his lips, getting entangled in the thicket of the beard. A soft breeze of pages turning rustled on the bristles of your scalp, and the noise of tires roaring, racing.

On one of the curves of that night you stopped. On a side road, not far from the entrance to a tavern. It was probably the brightly colored lights that made you stop. You turned off the road and parked, slamming the car door as if you were ordered to go on some mission, and with that dramatic movement, you broke into the thick vapor that lay over the roars of laughter and the lines of bodies huddled in the depths of the tavern. You stopped right at the entrance (you were simply scared) and, relieved that nobody paid attention to you, you dropped onto the end of a bench. Of the whole "mission," you managed only to hiss at the waiter, "A glass of liqueur," clasping the tiny glass in the face of all the mighty beer steins, thus indicating the abyss dividing them from you. You gazed straight at the bubbling foam on the long tables, at the flushed faces, the chins, the double chins of the women jouncing in gurgles of laughter, staring with all the indignation you could muster as if there, in that rejoicing mass of human flesh, it was possible to find the precise point and to revenge. (When Hubert took you to his parents—right after your third night he took you, an attraction, Emily from Tel Aviv, there, in the provincial town, and the lamp with the simple straw shade over the living-room table, and the brown sofas, and the cake crumbs—you were still weak from New York and the flight, and suddenly hand-embroidered swans and gates of a Bavarian city, and the neighbors who gathered, their hands black, came to play cards on Sunday afternoon, surrounding you, pleasant: "A Jew . . . from Israel . . ." Closing their circle around you on the sofa, whispering in admiration in the hard language: "Israel . . ." Then they left you alone and went back to the game, tight together under the straw lampshade, leaving you scared on the sofa, imagining you were cunningly penetrating them, to carry out a secret retaliation, as if you already knew that *the Lord hath sworn that the Lord will have war with Amalek from generation to generation*.) Finally you fled outside, to the empty field, to the night, the liqueur softening you with thick sweetness. The gale of weeping burst out at the jolt back to the maze of the freeway.

At some point that night the gas-tank light came on. Somehow you managed to get to the service station. A sleepy face trudged out, leaned into the window. Only when he returned your change did you notice the black moustache and the smile he gave you, and you started the car in a panic, immediately slid back into the pace of headlights on the freeway whistling by very close, suddenly yearning like a frightened child for Hubert's melting voice, for home.

The class ended. The girls gathered up the books and notebooks, immediately gushing, chattering. Next to you Elisheva's breathing rasped as she packed her bag, enclosing herself in silence. As they left, Jane and Yaffa turned around, laughingly lamenting your new hairdo.

"Amalia, you always surprise us!" declared Yaffa.

"How did you dare? Weren't you sorry?" Jane nodded with an affectionate laugh, waving her head with a movement that recalled how young she was under the kerchief on her hair. You stood, dizzy. You almost forgot why you had returned to the weekly class, and you were about to go home.

"Amalia, it's good that you came. I've got something to tell you." Rabbi Israel beckoned to you from his chair.

"I'll wait for you outside when you're done." Elisheva slipped out through the dark doorframe. Sitting behind the table, Rabbi Israel pointed you to a chair, with the intimacy of a teacher and a former student. He himself sat down freely on the corner of the table, resting his ankle on his knee as usual.

You came close, sneering, and why that theatricality, why did you have to go on pretending, carried away in the fork in the freeway? And there, suddenly, without thinking, you stopped. Next to a yellow telephone booth. A small heap of crushed cigarette butts on the concrete floor. A plastic bitterness came from the receiver and the wetness of lips that protruded in a chirp of syllables. Hubert's voice swelled from the earpiece in the silence of the night: "I have been so worried, Emily, I have informed the police, yes, yes, where, I truly regret if something happened because of me, I did not notice, you know, I was excited by the end of the developing, so very sorry." The voice shrieked into the neon bubble. And you inform the receiver in a tired, collapsing voice, that you're in a telephone booth on the road to the next city, no, you don't know what freeway, let him find it by himself and come get you out of here, laughing in a blur as if nothing— No, it's not because of him, he shouldn't worry, maybe even giggling wickedly— Yes, waiting, in the car, waiting. And immediately dropping into the Volkswagen, locking the doors, waiting for Hubert to come with the other car, for him to find you, but locked. And as soon as you called, calm descended on you. You even turned on the radio—the second movement of Beethoven's *Seventh*, so heavenly— sinking into the seat and waiting for him to come, running in the light of the headlights of the sports car shining in the rolled-up window, an agitated, pleading silhouette, and you refuse to explain, refuse to open the car, just point—You go first, I'll come after—continuing to play some role you made up for yourself.

(And maybe that too was just to steal time—if only with the game— to extend the delusion that there is still something between you, there, in the Bavarian night, on the freeway, that everything wasn't over with the end of the printing. *Remember what Amalek did unto thee, how he met thee by the way, and smote the hindmost of thee, even all that were feeble behind thee, when thou wast faint and weary and he feared not God.*)

The rabbi stroked his beard and looked at you a long time. For a moment, the afternoon enveloped you. The voice of Sarah, the housemother, calling in the distance. Rectangles of light retreating from the balcony, falling on the white ledge, spraying in the hewn stones of the building opposite. As if the room where you spent two years really *was a tree of life to them that lay hold upon her: and happy is every one that retaineth her,* you smiled unwittingly, and instead of the accusing words you had prepared, you whispered, "Rabbi . . ."

And you fell silent in shame. For how could you without Hubert, on that endless trip in the snow, gazing for hours at fields, towns passing by swaddled in mist, church steeples, smoke emitted from roofs stuck together, and the steaming mounds on the side of the road in all the white kilometers of the drive east, in all the hours of dragging the tripod, the lenses, the filters, in the emptiness that only increased, and the inability to hold on to something behind the eyepiece of the camera, nothing that would cut the exhaustion in the stony body, not even at night in bed in the hotel, in the featherbed nook, suddenly that featherbed from home and the sounds of the soft language on the radio, and the dread of the chambermaid barging in with her yellow hair, dragging you to the bathroom, leaning over to the streaming faucets with her enormous buttocks rising before your eyes, urging you to take off your clothes, put them on the bench, sink naked into the choking splash, how would you have stayed alive in the cold that was already biting the breath if not for Hubert's whispers at the bottom of the featherbed: *Beautiful Mala, Malinka, Amalia, Emily . . .*

(And what is left for you there on that alien ground, except the paths of hate and love? *Remember what Amalek did unto thee.* How is it possible to remember from a distance of place and time, to remember what he did unto thee, the weariness, the torments, the wrath of vengeance, how is it possible to remember without a tempest of feeling in the now, the here?

And what is left for you there, you who never knew love like Father, like Stein, what is left for you to "remember," except your feebleness in the car seat at three in the morning with a giggle of revenge, and Hubert who ran in a panic back to his sports car . . .)

Yes, you were ashamed, at the side of the road, that you had stolen his love, *for the fear of thine heart wherewith thou shalt fear, and for the sight of thine eyes which thou shalt see,* so you rolled up the window in his face, started the motor, following the bouncing red of his taillights to the freeway, driving weakly, pressing the pedal, alone on the seat, filling with tenderness for the man separated from you in the steel body of the night,

cutting himself off from you at the end of the desperate journey, and the
taillights of his sports car sliding slowly, considerate of your weariness,
gliding through the outskirts of the city, the roads of the sleeping suburb, the summer fields, and the end of the *Seventh Symphony* disappeared
into the night with the announcer's dark voice, melting you, like the roar
of Isaiah's silence when he laid down his head and the coolness of dawn
thickened.

In front of the house, the slamming of the car door echoed in the
quiet street. You went through the chill of the garden, going straight up
to the second floor, to the darkroom, without taking off your coat, without saying a word. "Let us go to sleep now, that is what you need, Emily,
we shall look at the photos tomorrow." He ran after you, clasping you
with all the tenderness you had known together, trying to block your way
to the lab. And only the laugh rising in the wailing softens your fists as
you push him to the shadows of the tapestry and the lute players, and still
you hit, leaving him grabbing the curtain, blurting out behind you:
"What a stubborn girl . . ." (In a crazy echo of Father's voice: "A stubborn girl, like Mala . . ." Then, when you ran into the music in the room
that was always dim ever since his sight had weakened, stopping the
record, lopping off the tenderness pouring from the little instrument to
the rest of the house, and speaking insolently, your heart thundering
with panic: "But the doctors ordered you not to do that, you mustn't, it
makes you weak!" Speaking insolently before the helpless sobbing bursts
out of you because he is passing away like that, without doctors, without hospitals, going so quietly, only him and you and the eternal spinning
of the records in the closed apartment: "Stubborn girl, stubborn like
Mala . . ." He nods at the corner with his sharp, black chin.)

"Yes, Amalia, I'm listening," said the rabbi. "If you came, surely you
have something you want to say."

In the next building, water was poured into the gutter. The jingling
penetrated the classroom. You looked at him and said quietly, almost resigned, "I was thinking about the verse that starts *Turn thou us unto thee,
O Lord, and we shall be turned,* and ends *renew our days as of old!*" And
once again you fell silent.

———————

(This afternoon, Rabbi Levav explained the meaning of the fallow year, the jubilee. He spoke of the shared fate of man and earth, that the two of them are the creation of the Lord forever, and their salvation is only in the jubilee when they return to their Creator—Did he sense something?)

"I don't know," you said in what seemed to be the renewed intimacy between you. "It's just hard for me to understand the verse *renew our days as of old . . .*"

"Yes?" He encourages you with sincere concern. He hasn't yet said a thing about your shorn hair.

"It's hard for me to . . ." as if you were searching for words.

"Yes, this is a hard moment for you, Amalia!" he began, and you knew so well his solemn voice, that smugness, almost arrogance, of someone who follows the straight paths. "So far, everything has been only studying, preparation, and now it's time to fulfill, to put into practice. And the effort is especially great now, Amalia, close to completion. For forty days are done, and Moses *delayed to come down out of the mount.* But now of all times, on the fortieth day, near sunset, we have to hold on to faith, we mustn't give in to doubt, to the temptation to idolatry, to the sin of the golden calf!"

He was already thinking of concluding when you whispered, "No, it's not that . . . It's not only now, Rabbi . . . I—never could I believe with full faith that really lets you forget and start anew . . ."

"Memory of sin and despair are the torments that bring the person to the fullness of repentance," he replied promptly. "As we found in Maimonides, *The manner of those who repent is to be very humble and modest. Whenever they are embarrassed for the deeds they committed and shamed because of them, their merit increases and their level is raised.* But those torments, Amalia, they are what assist a person to repentance. And so, he who *yesterday* shouted and was not answered, as it is written: *When ye make many prayers, I will not hear*—and he is tormented and suffers in enormous isolation—*today* his prayers are accepted and he follows the Commandments with satisfaction and joy."

"No, Rabbi, don't you understand? There are things I can't erase, can't forget! Even though I tried. They follow me all the time, don't leave. I feel the same feelings as before, I do the same acts."

"It's not easy to change, Amalia, I know." The rabbi made an effort to control his temper. "It's not easy to shed your skin, to change your name and to say: *I am not the same one who sinned.* That's a demand that requires so much true devotion that immersing in the ritual bath of atonement seems, God forbid, a vain hope. Yes, it's harsher than the grave. And who am I to tell you that—"

"But Rabbi!" You cut him off. "It's impossible to escape like that . . . I can't believe that it's possible to get up one day and say: This isn't me . . . What Maimonides says in *The Laws of Repentance,* it's just hypocrisy!"

"Amalia! We have to want repentance, we have to choose it! The *choice* of repentance, *that's* the task of a person. The ability to choose faith, to carve *freedom* on the tablets! As it is written: *And now, Israel, what doth the Lord thy God require of thee, but to fear the Lord thy God!* But to fear, Amalia."

"I don't know, Rabbi," you whispered. "I don't know if back then, before I came to Neve Rachel, when I was completely in the dark, there wasn't more faith in that effort, completely alone . . ."

"Do not cling to sin!"

"Sometimes it seems to me that I don't know the difference between faith and sin anymore."

"You mustn't talk like that, that's profanity!"

A sharp laugh screamed out of you. You raised your hand and covered your mouth. "Excuse me . . ."

"Try to calm down, Amalia."

"But Rabbi," you murmured, and suddenly you felt very close to Rabbi Israel, to his gray face, his worn look, and when you leaned over to him, it was to explain to him, to share with him with such effort, finally, what was clear to you. "Rabbi, how is it possible at the same time to remember and to forget? To say that you have to change your name, to travel into exile, to wipe out completely what happened, and to command to remember? . . . That's what you taught us, Rabbi: *Remember the day when thou camest forth out of the land of Egypt, Thou shalt remember* the Lord thy God, Remember the Sabbath day, Remember what Amalek did unto thee . . . Isn't that what we learned? So how is it possible at the same time to demand that we wipe out everything, *Thou shalt blot out the remembrance of Amalek from under heaven, thou shalt not forget it.* Annihilate every last thing, even the remembrance of the name Amalek! How is it possible to forget, even if the memory is awful, even if it is a memory of sin? How is it possible to say: Be different, I am a different person and not the same one who sinned. Those are just words, Rabbi, empty sophistry! It's impossible to talk like that about faith and to think that everything is atoned for." You bored uncontrollably into the thicket of his beard, the gray of his eyes.

"Amalia." He shrank, and only his hands clenched in his pants pockets indicated the effort it cost him to be alone with you. "You said '*renew our days as of old,*' that's right! The power of repentance is to restore the person to the purity *before* he sinned, to the purity of the covenant between every person and HaShem. That's not a change to an alien identity," he drawled, "but a return to what was hidden in you and was lost. The doubts that rule you are torments of regret, Amalia, as in someone who has lost something dear to his heart. They are the torments of the soul for that serenity from which it was exiled. This is the meaning of *Return to me—and I shall return to you;* for regrets hint at the wonderful hope of *renew our days as of old.*"

"But Rabbi, if nothing is left, nothing, you understand? Then return is to where? To what serenity? To what days of old? How can you say such hypocritical things?"

You bent your head so as not to hear his answer anymore, only continuing to shout mutely at him everything inside you. *Why can't you grasp, Rabbi, it's her I can't forget, her, Mala . . . Mala Auerbach, Father's beloved, the wife of his youth.* You raved without a word: *That's what I'm trying to explain to you, her, the heroine pianist who killed herself in the Appellplatz with a razor blade on her veins. And it's because of her death that I live, otherwise Father would never have gone with Mother. How can I forget her, Rabbi, I who was born because of her death? It's not enough to give me her name, Amalia, Malinka, and hope that everything is buried. It's impossible to live instead of somebody else! If repentance is for what was and was lost, I can only return to her, to walk, once more, behind her, to the end. To the end* (you almost choked) . . . *Why can't you understand, Rabbi, what repentance do I have aside from her, where will I return, where? Even if I travel into exile from my home, even if I change all my acts to good and go on the straight path, even if I shout all day,* I am a different person and not the same one who sinned, *and I change my name, Amy, Emily, Amalia— I can't get away from her. You taught us what was written:* And when I passed by thee and saw thee polluted in thine own blood, I said unto thee when thou wast in thy blood, Live; yea, I said unto thee when thou wast in thy blood, Live. *Didn't you? So I can never wash her blood off my life . . . I can't . . .* Your shorn head was almost resting on Rabbi Gothelf's jacket, on the big plastic buttons protruding from the warmth of the cloth. *You taught us that a person can repent from sin and confess only after he has asked his accuser for forgiveness and release from his vows, didn't you? And what if, by chance, the accuser is dead? And you also taught us this:* Take ten witnesses to the grave of the dead person and say before them, I sinned against God, the Lord of Israel and against the dead person. *Didn't you? So, how can I ask forgiveness, release from vows, if there isn't even a grave, there isn't even a grave, there isn't anything, Rabbi. I looked, really, there isn't anything!*

Your mouth was dry, your palate dusty. Between your lips, a few fragmented syllables finally seeped out. "No, Rabbi . . . It's impossible on the paths of repentance . . . I don't succeed . . ."

The nasal voice of Sarah, the housemother, echoed from the corridor, "Your laundry's ready in room number . . ."

"Thank you, I'm going up in a little while." Elisheva's voice came from behind the door, along with the echo of Sarah's plodding measured steps.

And after the rabbi was silent for an eternity, he said, "You're confusing the domains, Amalia. The domain of the general with the domain of the individual." You wondered exactly what difference he was talking about.

And then he added in a hazy voice (why then, of all times, in that conversation, did he finally say explicitly what had always remained unspoken between you?), "Amalia, we, who are left, we have to cling to repentance, and without asking questions! We must not ignore their sacrifice!"

"How do you dare call that a sacrifice, Rabbi?" you shrieked between the whitewashed walls, spinning among the chairs scattered in the classroom, no longer in control of yourself. "What sin were they sacrificed for, what guilt?"

"Amalia, I understand your pain, the pain so great that, God forbid, it's liable to increase doubt. How is it that the compassionate God hides His face for such a long time, unlike what is written: *For his anger endureth but a moment; in his favor is life?* How is it that the Shekhina was exiled so that all that seems to be left in the world is a measure of Justice without any Mercy? Yes, the pain is so great that there is a desire to speak insolently toward heaven, as it says in the prayer of Elijah: *that Thou art the Lord, and that Thou hast turned their heart back again.* Thou! And what of the Nation, if it sinned, how will You raise Your hand against it to punish them?! There is an impulse to take hold of the Holy-One-Blessed-Be-He as Moses took hold of Him, like a man who seizes his fellow by his garment and says before him: *Master of the Universe, I will not let Thee go until Thou forgivest and pardonest them.* To really prove, to pose to him the oath he swore: *Just as Thy great name endures forever and ever, so Thine oath is established for ever and ever.* And what is the oath: *Remember Abraham, Isaac, and Israel, Thy servants, to whom Thou swearest by Thine own self* . . . Yes, Amalia, to forget the sin and to remember the oath! Only like that. Otherwise, it's impossible to stand and exist before Him-May-He-Be-Blessed . . ."

His head was bent, and his voice was weak. Never had you seen Rabbi Israel so moved.

"To you I can tell what is in my heart, what I don't dare tell everyone." He spoke slowly, as if he had been drawn back from far away, striving to piece together the recitation articulated between his lips, syllable by syllable. "There are contradictions in faith, there are moments of doubt, breakdowns. You are tossed between the need to remember and to forget. But sometimes the way to remember is precisely to forget and to believe with complete faith. That's the lesson given us by those who were rescued from the field of slaughter! Look at them, Amalia, if they had clung to the awful memory, they would have gone mad, God forbid. For how is it possible to live with memories beyond human ability! Only their power to isolate themselves from the most beloved souls, to cut off living flesh, yes, in the living body, only that supreme power made them able to choose life, to build a family, to beget students, to take part in the revival of our Nation. Here, look at your parents, may their souls be blessed. Your life itself is a symbol of their faith that in spite of the pain, God willing, *there is hope in thine end that thy children shall come again.* Yes, you of all people, Amalia, must find in yourself the power to divest yourself of it, in honor of their memory." Rabbi Gothelf's voice grew stronger, his face became opaque.

"The decree of destruction was issued before the Creator of the world, the third destruction in the destructions of the Nation, and which of us can understand His acts? What is left for us, we . . . the remnant, standing mute and pained, what is left for us is only to cling to faith, despite everything and in spite of all, to believe and to praise His Name, for leaving us a remnant . . . Yes, despite the pain, despite the insolence, it is *up to us,* as it were, to take the first step. Up to us, small, wretched ones, and that is our effort all day long, Amalia . . ."

You stopped following, gazing at Rabbi Gothelf's jacket, at the folds of his trousers, at the floor tiles. The wrath faded, the desire to prove something. To say something. The definite limpness you once knew, back then, the body laid on the hot silk hotel bedspread, a blurred, alien mass. And some heavy buzzing. Repulsive. Crumbling thought. Amazement that you could ever have believed that Hubert would support you. And still the movement of traveling in your paralyzed body. You had just arrived, after the whole trip south. And Stein, as always, behind in the second car, only this time it was "so Emily can rest, she needs that," and the box of photos you "stole" that night from the darkroom—all the material, negatives and developed prints—all the way in your hands without saying a word, all the way to the Riviera. And the gray palm trees on the boulevard along the shore. Shrouded in the ink of the sea. Blasting heat. Hotel Excelsior. Steamy corridors. The body an inanimate heap on the smooth bedspread. For some reason, a pink nightlamp is lit in the middle of the day. Somewhere, on the edges of stickiness, Hubert is standing. Moving his mouth. In the hot mist. Asking something there. (Interesting, when did he first summon Stein, asking him to try to help—"He understands her better"—and how did he inform him in a panic, and the two of them went with her in the ambulance to the clinic,

and when did he give up, and just try to get away, to leave the whole business, which really didn't concern him?) Hubert goes on saying something
there in the heat, you finally picking up from the worried medley: "You
want to drink something?" You managed to tell him with a dry mouth:
"Go down and buy cigarettes." You remaining still after Hubert knocked
on the door. Not clear how long. The glassy eyes facing the cushion of
the stool. Sometime, in that weariness, rolling a hand from the mass
lying there. Lifting the receiver, the in-house line, Stein: "Amy, dear . . .
Yes, what are you saying, what about the photos? Yes, I'm coming, I'm
coming immediately . . ." And you in a blur: "Come if you want . . ."
Wandering heavily at the end of the road to the entrance of the suite
he arranged for you. Opening up and immediately retreating from his
panting in the doorway, coping with the floors, with the heat: "Amy
dear . . ." In his reflection between the gold engraving of the mirror, the
two of you close in that greenish entrance in Empire style, his stubby
hand passing a handkerchief between the lapels of the summer shirt:
"Yes, Amy—" fidgeting in the mirror, close to you. And you quickly: "I
wanted to tell you not to expect anything from the photos." Letting the
summer dress slip off your shoulder (where, for God's sake, did you get
that gesture?). "But, Amy, you can't do that, you can't . . ." He moves his
broad body. "I'm paying, you know . . ." He thrusts into your hand the
bills he takes out of his pocket in confusion, and you take the money,
maybe still playing the role, or maybe now only out of pity for him (the
money that you'll flush down the toilet later on, all of it at once), and you
state: "I'm taking it, but that doesn't change a thing." "We got an agreement, Amy!" His face reddens as his blood leaps. "So, I'm breaking it.
Sorry . . . You won't get them, not ever!" (The need to declare, like a
little girl.) And then he suddenly relented, which wasn't in the scenario,
retreated from the crowded entrance to the corridor, muttering to himself: "I did only for the memory of Mala . . . You know that . . . You know
that very well, Amalia . . ." (The only time he called you that in his
soft, broken accent: *Amalia*) Fidgeting alone in the long corridor padded
in red cloth. You standing there, weary, watching the back moving away.
The weeping turned to stone in the throat. Only afterward did you lock
the door. You wandered to the bathroom, in the sharp light springing
off the porcelain walls, the white sink, Hubert's razor (always ready,

traveling with you all the way) sparkling in the double heat of the hot water from the faucets (the cold water stopped just when the hellish heat was at its height), seeing yourself move to the sink (as then at night, after four, when you slowly bent down to the rustle of the pictures under the darkroom lamp), mechanically carrying out the operation, not understanding why Father doesn't stop you, why he doesn't throw him down all the stairs that are shouting into the black echo with the bad smell, *Krsteinnnnn Krsteinnnnn.*

"Amalia, we must uproot the defilement that has stuck to us, the seed of the serpent! For the touch of Amalek defiles! Even if against our will, Amalek is stuck to us, even if we were violated by him to death." Rabbi Gothelf's words went through you. For the touch of Amalek defiles? But there, when the boiling water is pressed to the white dizziness, Hubert wasn't there anymore, and not the smooth razor either, only Mother's warm smell poured into the gray with the screech of Aunt Henia's heels, and the steps of the friends with the gray coats tearing the house, dragging Father, who shouts mutely to her, *The razor is not for you, not for you, only for her, the heroine, how she stood in the* Appapatz *so proud, even they, may their name be wiped out, were impressed with her pride, so proud.*

Laundry rose from the building opposite, puffed in the wind. The breeze shook the glass panes of the door banging in the frame. Suddenly you were deadly sorry for Isaiah, for his soft look. You're holding on to him too, to escape! There is no love in you outside of the pain, everything is only a desperate madness that never, never will redeem you! You turned your face to the rabbi. How could you forget? You had to confess quickly, before you drag Isaiah behind you, before the act of the night is known publicly, before it's too late! For the touch of Amalek defiles . . .

"Rabbi," you whispered. "The man you matched me with, I-s-ai-ah," as if the way you pronounced the syllables of his name already said it all, "I have to tell you . . ."

The rabbi raised his eyebrows. You gazed at him (yes, for a moment, you held on to the solidity of Rabbi Gothelf's faith). "I won't be able to marry him, I won't. *That's* what I came to say, Rabbi . . . I wanted a year after the yeshiva to live on my own, to do weaving, to see if I could succeed, but . . . I haven't yet done repentance." You spoke with an effort, as if you were trying to thank Rabbi Israel for his endeavor, for his pain that he exposed to you, and that is our effort all day long, Amalia.

He moved away (maybe only then did it seem that he was embarrassed). "You're upset, Amalia, that's natural," and he went on in the same voice, "I talked last night with Isaiah."

A chill went down your spine. You looked at him through a mist of panic.

"Yes, he also was upset. Upset as you are now, Amalia." So they had spoken! It was known. And even if you meant it sincerely, all your efforts were in vain.

You didn't answer. The rabbi went on, "I wanted to tell you something, Amalia. And I hope it won't cause you unnecessary excitement." (Did Rabbi Gothelf really choose the time to tell you what he did, thus tying the fall of the woof to the strings of the warp?) "I wanted to tell you that on Tisha b'Av, there will be a memorial for Mala Auerbach, the first wife of your father of blessed memory, in a café by the name of Café Shoshana in Tel Aviv. I was informed of that by Mr. Stein, the contributor from New York. Of course you'll soon get an announcement in the mail, but I wanted to tell you about it first, in person."

In the depth of the corridor, the bustle of the girls in the rooms ebbed. The buildings of the neighborhood shone at noon. A flash of stone, a sparkle of gutters. In the space between the buildings, a flap of gray ridge, rejoicing, lighted, came through in the distance. You unwittingly stroked your neck. You stroked it again, seeking the touch of Isaiah's fingers. The rabbi began packing his books in his old bag.

"At the time when the Temple was standing and the rite of sacrifice was performed, a person could redeem his sins with a guilt sacrifice," he said pensively, busy closing the bag. "All we have left is repentance, Amalia. Confession and prayer are the only sacrifice we have left. Sometimes, and despite all our modernity, we admit that the world has been lacking ever since sacrifice was annulled. In ancient times, a person would see his sins going up in fire, and their light smoke rising and accepted in front of him. On Yom Kippur, a Jew would see the High Priest *tie a crimson thread on the scapegoat, press his two hands on it and make confession.* And thus would he say: *I beseech Thee, O Lord, Thy people the house of Israel have failed, committed iniquity and transgressed before Thee. I beseech Thee, O Lord, atone the failures, the iniquities and the transgressions which Thy people, the house of Israel, have failed, committed and transgressed before Thee, as it is written in the Torah of Moses, Thy servant, to say: For on this day shall atonement be made for you, to cleanse you; from all your sins shall ye be clean before the Lord."* And once again it was Rabbi Israel's singsong voice: *"They went with him from booth to booth, except the last one. For he would not go with him up to the cliff. But stand from afar and behold what he was doing. What did he do? He divided the thread of crimson wool, and tied one half to the rock, the other half between its horns, and pushed it from behind. And it went rolling down and before it had reached half its way downhill it was dashed to pieces."*

His face was raised to the door of the balcony, toward the gray strips of ridge in the distance. "While we, in the isolation of our way of life today, in our distance from one another, in our distance, God forbid, from HaShem, have to do by ourselves the internal operation, to burn the memory of the past with the meager force of repentance. For sometimes, only the brutal operation saves the living body, only a scapegoat atones . . ."

And a moment later, still as in a dream, he said: *"Thus saith the Lord; Refrain thy voice from weeping, and thine eyes from tears, for thy work shall be rewarded, saith the Lord. And there is hope in thine end . . .* As it is said, *for I will turn their mourning into joy and will comfort them and make them rejoice from their sorrow."*

He held the handle of the bag, his jacket stretched across his shoulders. On the way out, he turned around, opened the gray flicker of his eyes for a moment: "Amalia, on Tisha b'Av, with God's help, you'll already be betrothed. You can go together to the memorial in Tel Aviv." And on the threshold, he concluded, his head sunk between his shoulders, "Come to us for the Sabbath meal, you and Isaiah, whenever you like."

You stood up behind him. But before you could reply, he went through the door of the classroom and left.

You stood still, not yet filled with feeling. You mechanically slung your purse over your shoulder, standing in amazement, as then, after everything, when you left the small Italian hospital by yourself with the bandages on your wrists, and in the clear morning the vacationers were mottling the boulevard along the shore with a light blue that spreads after the heat. You stopped at one of the souvenir stands, at a clamorous conglomeration of tiny towers, printed kerchiefs, plastic visors, boxes coated with shells. With hands still weak, you lifted a souvenir plate of gleaming porcelain with gold thread on the rim and a photograph of a smiling couple with a puppy on the boardwalk. "Ready in an hour." The salesman smiled at you with suntanned sweetness, baring a row of gold teeth. "Ready in an hour, a photo of the lady printed on the plate with or without the gentleman." You took the cheap plate with the photo of the embarrassed couple and the puppy in a chance moment of perpetuation of bliss, stupidly ran your finger over the gold rim, as if letting the condensed mass of clay slip out of your grasp, be crushed on the sidewalk, and with them falls the weight of souvenirs heaped on shelves, in the depths of drawers, clumsy, dusty objects. Plates, matchboxes, shells, gold lockets, letters, lipsticks. You smile with relief, clasp the plate in your weak hands, as if it could be crushed like that, could be started all over. As if the negative weren't sealed in you, changing with you at every new twist of the stream, changing names, places, borne on the turgid, shapeless flood of your life.

You stood there; the rabbi disappeared into the dim corridor gaping beyond the door. You tightened the straw straps, and in your ears the words grow faint, what would he do? Divide the thread of crimson wool and he tied one half to the rock and the other half between its horns and they pushed it from behind and it went rolling down—and before it had reached half its way down the hill it was dashed to pieces.

And suddenly everything was so clear. What was. What would be. Clear and straightforward. You moved. The dryness was scaly on your palate, and everything had only one, inevitable direction, light as a cloud of dust rising from the hooves of a scapegoat that slips from the cliffs of the desert. And there was even joy. A pause of knowing.

(And even if later on you seemed to have forgotten that time, even if its revelations were blurred, that was only one more twist in the curves of

the road, only one more traverse of the woof in its climb to the heights
of the warp.

And maybe it had to happen like that. Had to be forgotten and sink
into the fabric to rise again now, at the end of the confession, on the
steps of the Counting, to approach your consolation once again.

Saturday night. Maybe three by now. From the valley a dog's barking.
Sounding the alarm about something. Hands covered with dust. Yet from
the fingertips still wafts the smell of the perfumed grasses I crushed at
Havdalah. *He who separates between holy and profane, may He forgive our
sins.*)

In the air of the classroom was that density always left behind by the
girls. Elisheva stood in the doorway, filling the frame with her broad
body. "Amalia."

You moved in the wake of the Rabbi's exit, hissing at Elisheva as you
passed, "So, did you also have a conversation with Isaiah yesterday?"

"That's not what I wanted to say, Amalia." She retreated.

"I don't think I explained myself to the rabbi." You spoke wearily to
the wide face looking down at you. "Maybe *you* can be born again. That's
why you went to India, isn't it? All those places of yours, Pondicherry,
Mahabalipuram," you rounded your mouth in a soft pronunciation, "the
moon in the temple in Madras, the square pool, the wax-covered statues
of Parvati. There in India, you studied the wisdom of how to live, Elisheva. *And you chose life.*" You saw the pupils expand between the transparent lashes. "You'll always know how to live more than me, Elisheva,"
you went on slowly. "Even with Isaiah." You followed the flush spreading over the freckled skin, the fleshy mouth gaped. You swept up the handles of your purse, and went off.

And in that same emptied quiet, you arrived home, to the softness of
the tiny furrows of the woof in the prayer shawls, to the naked warp
swallowed up in the tracks. You wove calmly until dark, stood up for the
Evening Prayer and for Counting the Omer, and sat back down at the
loom. You wove until late. The warmth of the beam of light flooding
your shorn scalp, falling on the neck stretched in awe to the weaving, the
neck of a goat whose lot fell to be the scapegoat, bent under the hands of

the high priest. The scapegoat rolling down from the cliff into the yellow suspended over the valley. (As then, at night, when you returned from racing on the freeway, after you poured the rest of your wrath down on Hubert—as if only the sight of the blood flowing from his nose could ease the fear—and you went into the darkroom, sitting there for hours, in silence, at the end of the night, in the small circle of lamplight, and the pictures spread out one sheet after another under the movements of your hands. Results of months of travel. Prints. Enlargements. All the material for the album on Mala. Hours. In the German room. Until dawn broke outside. Completely helpless, unable even to sabotage the printing, burn the negatives. The air seemed to tremble as dawn broke. The rest was the knowing that there was no way out, except in rest. Final rest.)

In the valley, the houses of the Arab village are dusty, still covered in gloom. Sheet after sheet, the veil is lifted from the night. Imprisoned in a weakness, in the time that is rolling, coming to an end. The measured area of the Omer Counting. That racing in between. In the pounding pace, trampling every niche of rest. Yearning to stop, to hold the underside of the weaving, to be hidden there in the knots, to calm down another moment before the flight of the shuttle starts again.

(And Hubert? What's happening with him now? How did he later put together what was torn apart, our inability to help each other, remaining so foreign on either side of the common wound? What did he throw himself into to forget? In what metamorphosis is he now starring on the cover of the professional journals? "Ecological Series"? "The Face of the Persecution of Immigrants"? Maybe he remembers sometimes. Maybe on one of the rare visits to his parents' town, on Sunday, where he sent the last confused postcard: *Emily, meine Liebe.* He comes back from there at night in the sports car. The same car, which may still contain something of the hollow distances, of the trip together all the way. Maybe something still wafts from its upholstery into the coolness of the Bavarian dawn. *Because the Lord hath sworn that the Lord will have war with Amalek from generation to generation.*)

———

The end of the darkness breaks. The mighty wind that rose is sweeping away everything that remained from the Sabbath. A gray stripe grows bright over the layer of cotton wool on the horizon. There, in the bottom of the desert, dawn rises. And the blast of the shofars shocks the City Walls when the scapegoat is led from the open gate by the man who was to lead it away, from booth to booth, up to the cliff suspended over the valley.

Drawn now, there, to the edge of the cliff, in the dawn. A longing that chokes until you weep. A warm, rocking wave. For there, on the other side, the running will stop. At the foot of the cliffs. In the quiet that will flow again. *As in days of old and in former years.*

The gray is torn. Birds chirping. And another coolness slaps the laundry puffing on the roof.

Less than two weeks. Terrible, holy.

Thirty-seven days, which is five weeks and two days

of the Omer. Power of Essence. Sunday night.

Another twelve days.

Today I started weaving the Tablets of the Law, at last, relieved to have reached the end of the confession last night. My hands seemed released from the weight already rising to You, Lord. (May it be Your will that You will accept the offering with love.) All morning I bent over and tied the Commandments in the weaving, line facing line: *I am the Lord thy God, thou shalt not make, thou shalt not take, remember, honor;* and in the facing line: *thou shalt not kill, thou shalt not commit adultery, thou shalt not steal, thou shalt not bear false witness, thou shalt not covet. Thou shalt not covet* . . .

Once again Your Names are revealed. And this time it is my hands that weave the threads. Afterward, I'll tie the two lions holding the Tablets in their paws, their faces turned away. And when I roll them into the fabric accumulated on the staff at the back, only the deep blue of the firmament and the edges will remain exposed.

And then, going on to You. As was decided. And how is it that even now, even when the time is so close, I am still shown new faces in the deed? Things I don't dare say. How dreadful is this repair.

Yes, what You hinted to me at Rabbi Levav's house on Sabbath afternoon. The three of us are sitting, as on every Sabbath, in the thatch of light and fruit trees on the glassed-in balcony, Fayge is gathering challah crumbs from the white tablecloth, pouring fruit soup into a saucer, and the rabbi is explicating the Bible portion as he always does. And the Bible portion that Sabbath was *On the Mountain*. He spoke of the common fate of man and the earth, that the salvation of both of them is a return to their Creator. As it is written: *The land shall not be sold for ever: for the land is mine . . . for ye are strangers and sojourners with me. And in all the land of your possession ye shall grant a redemption for the land. And proclaim liberty throughout all the land unto all the inhabitants thereof: ye shall not sow, neither reap that which groweth of itself in it, nor gather the grapes in it of thy vine undressed.* Rabbi Tuvia is talking calmly, his eyes gilded blue, and I am hearing different words from his mouth, glorious in force, dreadful! Yes, there I understood what had always seemed to me (how slow I was to understand, ah, God my Maker, how shocked I was there when it struck me, so naked) I understood that I and the Land, I and Jerusalem Your city, are one, and my fate is their fate! That *we* are Your property, all of us as one will return *to You* as free girls. Not married women, not plowed, Your chattels forever and ever, *for the land is mine.* There, at Rabbi Levav's in the afternoon, You revealed to me the meaning of the repentance I shall do in less than two weeks, when I return to You—I am Your property, the portion of the field where You shall sow Your seed.

Rabbi Levav went on explicating, *"And the Lord spake unto Moses in Mount Sinai saying,"* and Rashi's question, "Why the issue of the fallow year at Mount Sinai?" And he replies, "The fallow year is like unto the

Sabbath, as it is written: *Then shall the land keep a Sabbath unto the Lord.*
Unto the Lord: for the sake of the Lord, as on the first Friday, which re-
mains preserved from the beginning of Creation to the giving of the
Torah, which took place on the Sabbath, the sixth day of the month of
Sivan, and is considered as the first Sabbath, as if the world were created
now." And only then, when Rabbi Levav quoted Rashi, did I realize that
this year too the holiday of Shavuoth would fall on the day after the
Sabbath! And this year I too would receive the Torah the day after the
Sabbath. When *I* shall carry out a fallow year and shall throw off all
the holds I still have left in the world, when I shall rush to You, to You
O Lord.

Yes, it was Rashi's question that stirred in me the magnitude of the secret, what You hinted to me through Rabbi Levav's words! And my
whole body was shaken. (And I only hope that Fayge and Rabbi Levav
didn't sense anything.)

As usual the rabbi and his wife accompanied me halfway home. Crossing together (for the last time, why couldn't they understand that?) the
garden weeded by Fayge's small fingers. Striding with me to the fork in
the path of the mountain overlooking the broken Temple, to the burning of the ruins at noon, Your ever-bleeding wound.

And afterward, alone on the path going down, and the clods of earth
emitting their steam, there, when my marching and the dry dust of
Jerusalem were mingled in each other, I whispered to You again and
again, *and let my soul be like dust to everyone,* like dust, like dust. And I was
so filled with thanksgiving that You had done that to me, to lead me to
Your city, to Your paths, to the silent turrets. That You had done that to
me, to lead me to the ruins of Your city, me, *the servant of the Lord, eternal servant pierced to You.* Me, Amalia, sunk in sin and toil. That it occurred to You to choose me, a bride of blood to You, me, black as a
raven, Your salvation, I, who at the end of the Omer Counting shall lie
in Your bosom with my dry body *that my lord the king may get heat. For
the land is mine* . . .

(And I already yearned so much for an eternal rest when the shofar
would pass over the whole land *proclaiming freedom to all the inhabitants
thereof,* on the jubilee of days, the fiftieth day, Sabbath of Sabbaths. I already yearned so much for our wedding day, at the end of the Counting.

When I shall give myself to You with devotion, and You shall consecrate me in Your sweetness, and You shall embrace me to Your bosom, and then I shall rouse Your desire toward me, which will want and long for me, *and Your desire toward me,* and I shall arouse the stream of Your abundant bounty. And through this may abundant bounty flow in all the worlds. Amen selah!)

And what I confessed last night about the cliff, how I got there last year, on the dawn of Shavuoth. For hours I walked on the desert path, until I stood at the edge of the mountain, on the verge of the white light bursting out above the Dead Sea. Only to complete the task did I return home.

The memory of the cliff turning white stayed with me all morning, strengthening my hands tying Your Names on the Tablets onto the firmament of the Torah Curtain, filling me with a confidence that You will want the sacrifice, that You will accept the repair of Your Name that I am tying.

(The Names are rustling behind my back. Whispering like rubies in the dark. Mounding in the gold threads of the loom. How I caressed them, letter by letter. Plait, stroke. Your Names standing erect from the fabric at the touch of my fingers.)

And what is the hint You sent me last night in a dream, in the brief sleep I sank into at the end of the confession, after Tikkun Leah, at daybreak? The dream clung to me all morning, pulled after my hands tying in holiness. How to interpret it now?

I returned home from the trip. I hadn't yet had time to bring the suitcases in from the stairs—first I had to rest, the body was really collapsing. But in the house there were guests, and even a special event like my return from the long trip couldn't shorten their stay. Father, Mother, and Aunt Henia were deep in conversation in the foreign language with the two guests, huddled around the big table in the dining room. And even though the sun was shining outside, the drapes were drawn and the chandelier was lighted.

I was amazed that Father and Mother had come back to life especially to entertain guests, and I sat down behind Aunt Henia. They didn't see me come in, absorbed in their talk with the couple. The man was wearing a light-colored suit, and the woman's thin hair was pinned back. Only Aunt Henia noticed that I had joined them, and turned around to me, emitting the bitter smell of her cosmetics. "That couple were very good friends of your father and mother, when you were little," she whispered.

"I remember something, blurry . . ."

"You can't possibly remember, you were a baby then!" she declared and returned to the lively conversation. Once again I was amazed that Father and Mother had come back from the dead especially to entertain guests; certainly it was a special event, maybe the couple had returned from America after many years. I leaned over to Aunt Henia, persisting in a whisper, "I remember that couple, I remember them."

"Right, Amalinka . . . They had a son, a little boy . . . You were very close as babies. The families decided that the two of you would marry each other when you grew up. But meanwhile, they discovered that the baby was defective. His sex organ. Of course, the match was called off and his parents decided to move to America. Out of shame, and also they hoped to get medical treatment for the boy." Her head hung from the end of her neck at an angle, like the head of a crooked nail.

Yes, I recall, they told me something . . . But, just don't bring it up again! No, it has nothing to do with me! Absolutely nothing! . . . It's lucky they didn't notice I had come back, lucky that the drapes were drawn and they were deep in conversation. I shrank into a corner.

At that moment, the man in the light-colored suit stood up and concluded that now, after years, they were back again! He pointed to the somewhat small, perforated-straw hat perched on his bushy white hair. He had bought it many years ago, he declared with a raised finger, especially! And his hair was like Ben-Gurion's, so everybody who saw him would know at once where he belonged!

Only then did I realize that this was Ludwig Stein, why hadn't I recognized him before? He announced that their son, who had grown up in the meantime, had also come with them for the visit, and was in the hospital on the highway, not far away, and they should all go visit him now, together!

They scrambled for the exit, not noticing me shrunk in the corner. Only Aunt Henia turned her powdered face to me as she was leaving. At the bottom of the stairs, they lingered at the wheelbarrow standing there like a beggar's wagon or a butcher's pushcart. They bent over it in the dim staircase sealed against bombs. Stein (who had grown very old), in the small hat, pointed at the wheelbarrow and explained that this was a special device he used to carry his merchandise: rare eggs!

"Ostrich eggs, bull eggs." He showed the people standing around him the four or five big eggs lying at the bottom of the wheelbarrow.

While I stood there, amazed that the eggs were so much alike, Helenka, the neighbor's daughter, came into the staircase, wearing a tasteless nylon dress. *Certainly from the American shipments,* I thought, watching her shrink as she passed to avoid contact with the wheelbarrow, and meanwhile brushing shamelessly against Father and Stein. Father tossed out after her, "It's true you shouldn't break eggs, but there's no need to tear your clothes either," and she just turned her head to him with a wide grin and went up the stairs.

Then Ludwig Stein's tiny wife (but he doesn't really have a wife) sat down in the wheelbarrow, stretched her crossed legs, and announced that she was not happy. "It's not nice! It's not nice for us to go to the hospital before you visit us, and before you see everything we brought from Poland!"

"Really, not nice," Father quickly agreed with her. "And it's not nice either that we haven't yet asked you how you feel. How are you, leg? How are you, back?" He began tapping her limbs one after another, as if examining her, and his black hair slipped down on his forehead like a young man's pompadour.

While they were dallying, I slipped away. I headed for the highway, and in the dark that had meanwhile fallen, I ran all the way to the maternity hospital, whose yellow facade appeared through the flow of traffic. I climbed the stairs to the second floor, and quickly went down the long hall to the room.

Inside the room at that hour stood a young, good-looking nurse who was just finishing her shift and had stayed only to enjoy some conversation. He was sitting on the bed with his back to the door, leaning over a bit, the stem of his neck elongated and his black curls loose. The nurse turned to shoo me away. But from where he was sitting, as if he expected me to come, he turned with a soft smile, and with that same delicacy, he gestured to the disappointed nurse to leave us alone. Oh, how flattered I was when the nurse, in her pure white cap, left softly but firmly! In the corridor the serving cart approached. I turned to hide from the female workers, even though I knew that I had a legitimate place here. But he, in his singsong voice, explained to them, "Sorry, I'm busy now," and drew the curtain.

He sat on the smooth sheet, his legs folded beneath him. I knew he had been castrated in childhood. And so he was in the hospital. I went to the window. And still he didn't say anything. Slowly, with measured movements, he took a record out of its sleeve, put it on the turntable of the small phonograph, and turned the phonograph on. Once again he sat erect, and wound his arms around his knees. Music rose, very sweet. *It's all too hackneyed,* I sneered and was amazed that I felt so close to someone I hadn't known at all just a short while ago, gazing at the yellow wall that blocked the view completely. And I could no longer stand the sweetness of the music, his continued silence. Against my will, I approached the bed, where he sat with his legs drawn up and his black curls splendid. I sat down too, trying like him to wind my arms around my legs. *Sitting like children,* I thought as his arm went around my shoulder. *It's only the excitement of children,* I went on thinking, trembling on the white bed. *Only a momentary attraction, only a momentary love, everything will pass in a little while, I don't even know him.* And along with that, and even though I knew that his disease was contagious, that at that very moment, from the touch of his hand, his putrid semen was moving to my flesh, I didn't move, I didn't take his arm off me. Without a word, I trembled convoluted next to Isaiah's breath caressing my cheek, and the whiteness of the hospital room melted in my pupils—*I haven't known such emotion for so long, so long . . .* My heart was still pounding when I woke up.

O God my Maker, how to explain the blind desire for Isaiah, still, now, when Your breath bends over me at night?! Is the choking of regret for Isaiah only another way to bring me close to Your kiss? And in sin or in purity?

Suddenly the thought stirs in me of *the two Tablets held by Moses, the first Tablets that he broke, and the second Tablets . . .* Why didn't I think of that before? The first Tablets were the work of Your hands, and were all holy. *And the Tablets were the work of God, and the writing was the writing of God, graven upon the Tablets.* Too holy to exist in the world, the Tablets You broke in the hands of Moses. The second Tablets, Moses carved, and the writing of God was graven by Your hand: *And the Lord said unto Moses, Hew thee two tablets of stone like unto the first: and I will write upon these tablets the words that were on the first tablets, which thou brakest.*

Which Tablets am *I* weaving, the first or the second? (Can I still pretend that the tablets in my hands are whole? Now, less than two weeks before the end of the Omer Counting . . .)

And suddenly the Names leaped out clear from the Torah Curtain. Present in the room, rustling. The Names I put together with my own hands—*I am the Lord thy God, thou shalt not take the name of the Lord thy God in vain.*

Thou shalt not take the name of the Lord thy God in vain . . . For a moment I was afraid to turn my head to the Curtain stretched on the loom. As if the Names I had tied in the gold threads grew thick and were suspended like magic icons behind me.

I grew weak again. Fear of the magnitude of the repair I still have to complete in the few days we have left. Everything that was decided. How awful is the act!

How long will the Lord not take pity on Jerusalem, how long will I moan to You, God, the heathen are come into thine inheritance? Please, HaShem, take pity on me. For Your Name's sake. For Your Name's sake.

Thirty-eight days, which is five weeks and

three days of the Omer. Beauty of Essence.

Hot. A dry wind bursts through the window, striking the frame. As if the whole city is overflowing in its sleep. Lying heavy. A rustle of the living and the dead rising in the night from the city, from its ruins, crumbs of the dead gathered in the huge funnel of the valley. The ancient valley rustles with the breaths of graves, layer upon layer.

The hot wind has stopped a bit. Only a distant, subdued roar, emitted from the roads, absorbs the breeze.

Please, HaShem, accept my plea tonight. That the confession shall rise to You with all devotion.

How naive you were last year, when you waited all morning for Isaiah to come, and didn't slip away again, when recess at the yeshiva approached. You held on to the weaving, the shuttle flying from side to side, the sight of the thread spinning like a fetus folded in the shuttle, dropping and stretching from the navel of the flight until it finally rested, caught between the strings. How naive you were to believe that what happened on the night of Lag b'Omer—and before the end of the Omer Counting—could still be repaired, to believe that you and Isaiah, like the Nation of Israel, could still approach the Mount with one heart.

This afternoon, in the middle of weaving, when I thought about what I should confess tonight, I got up and ran to the Pentateuch. With trembling fingers. The thought of what happened last year, in that stretch of time between Lag b'Omer and Shavuoth, the thirty-third and the fiftieth days, sent me to reread the two stormy portions from the beginning of the Book of Exodus, *Go in* and *It came to pass,* that tell of the fifty days of the beginning of the wandering in the desert. I sat and read the Pentateuch, the exegesis, with enormous amazement. The writing opened before me as if I had never read those chapters before, as if I had never understood what happened there in those seven twisted weeks of the beginning of love between You and the Nation. The tempestuous love between that ecstatic nation, straying behind its God in the desert, hurtling between confidence and dread, and You, a hidden God, sacrificing them one moment and consoling them the next. Stunned by the discovery of how similar the thicket of feelings between you and Isaiah last year was to what happened there from the night of the exodus from Egypt to the giving of the Torah, at the end of the first Omer Counting.

And what was all that troubled straying if not, right from the start, the association of fear and love, eruptions of faith, and immediately afterward, the letdown, along with doubt, the defiance. They hadn't yet departed from Egypt by great miracles, and the next morning, even before they had crossed the Red Sea, regret for that whole adventure of love, the terror at the new reality in the desert, and immediately the desire to foresake everything and go back—*Wherefore hast thou dealt thus with us, to carry us forth out of Egypt? Is this not the word that we did tell thee in Egypt, saying, Let us alone, that we may serve the Egyptians? For it has been better for us to serve the Egyptians than that we should die in the wilderness.* And right after crossing the Red Sea, with the Song of the Sea still echoing in their throat, and already in the Wilderness of Sin, they started complaining about hunger, *Would to God we had died by the hand of the Lord in the land of Egypt, when we sat by the flesh pots, and when we did eat bread to the full; for ye have brought us forth into this wilderness to kill this whole assembly with hunger.* And when You were reconciled with them and rained down manna on them, in their gluttony they couldn't stop gathering, not trusting You to renew the grace the next day. And on the first Sabbath given them as freemen, even then they didn't stop scraping the layer thin as hoarfrost. And afterward, again vituperation, this time about water, *Wherefore is this that thou hast brought us up out of Egypt, to kill us and our children and our cattle with thirst?* And almost stoning Moses for the waters of *Massah and Meribah*. And finally, at the end of the portion *It came to pass,* the fall to the depths of impurity, the battle with Amalek in Rephidim and what was broken there and defiled, for eternity. And nevertheless, they repented afterward and camped at Mount Sinai as one man with one heart.

Yes, the similarity between what happened last year and the beginning of the journey of love in the desert is really amazing—the same extremes of fear and longing, but also the naiveté under everything, that too is so similar. That strength to keep believing it's still possible. And all that, in the brief space of the fifty days between the night of the Exodus from Egypt and the giving of the Torah. As I found this afternoon in Rashi, *As they came to the Sinai Desert in repentance, so they traveled from Rephidim in repentance. And Israel camped there: as one man with one heart. But in all other campings there was complaint and dissension.*

Like the Nation, you waited with a renewed faith for Isaiah. You got up from the stool, went to the kitchen, drank a glass of water, and returned to the weaving, the torments of expectation darkening the gleam of the white, the anger at Isaiah for being so late, at you for waiting for him. Everything that happened between you at dawn on Lag b'Omer is totally worthless in your eyes! And it doesn't matter at all to you what will be said when he stands here in a little while! And you consoled yourself with the thought of Isaiah's pain when he saw that you had shorn the tresses that he had held in his hands, in whose depths he had sunk his breathing. You chuckled with animosity, set the shuttle flying hard.

When he knocked, you were startled. Only at the gate did you notice the trembling of the handle, and you opened it harshly. Isaiah was wobbling in the doorway. He didn't look at you. He stood there with his shoulders slumped, laughing. You were amazed at how he shared your agitation. And you were angry that he mocked your weakness like this. For a moment, he opened his eyes wide, incredulous, at your hair, and then he bent down and slipped inside. You stayed back another moment, as if you were busy locking the gate. Leaning your head against the wall until the pounding subsided.

He stood in the depth of the window bay, as if he were seeking shelter in the view of the abyss. His back burned in the light turned black in your pupils, like a negative.

"I cut my hair . . . the day before yesterday, on Lag b'Omer," you choked out. He still didn't turn from the window.

(And what did you want him to do when he stood there, not daring to turn his head to you? What did you really want from Isaiah in the dark choking of love? To attack you for cutting your hair, to yell at you in pain? To confess that he went to talk with Rabbi Gothelf, to tell what he had told him? Or maybe you wanted to tempt him to cling to you again with all his delicacy, to repeat the sin with the right given him already at dawn of Lag b'Omer? And all that to force him, by ways of sin, to withdraw from you. For if not by ways of repentance, then by ways of perversity of desire would you be led to the root of awe.

Or maybe you wanted him to do everything instead of you. To take you in his arms, rock you, shake the rest of the defilement out of you with the forty lashes of atonement, a willow twig beaten under his hands, until nothing is charged against you.

And it's clear that if he had only put his hand on you, looked at you with his eyes flooded with pain, you would have burst out in nervous laughter, amazed that he was there at all, choking with the desire to take vengeance on him for the sweetness of his breath, for the strain concentrated between his eyebrows, for his desire for you. And the end is also familiar, the haughty exit, the dramatic slamming of the door enjoyed so much at the moment, and running on the path down to the valley. And immediately, the nervous expectation that he would run after you, would beg, would ask forgiveness—for what? Thus he would finally tear up the soft root that still draws you to him. Everything is familiar. Your contemptuous repentance, faint-hearted, castrated repentance. *What is complete repentance? A person who confronts the same situation in which he sinned when he has the potential to sin, yet abstains and does not commit the deed because of his repentance. For example, a person engaged in illicit sexual relations with a woman . . .*)

But he stood like a dark stripe against the gleaming white. Maybe he giggled in embarrassment. From where you were, you saw only the tremor in his shoulderblades. Until you went to him. Yes, after everything, it was you who went to him in the window bay.

"Isaiah . . ."

He lifted his face to your shorn head. "Like a little boy," he laughed. "Like a little boy . . . So beautiful . . ." He gagged. The weight of his eyes softened your neck. You forced your head around in the old movement, wanting to thrust off the cowardice with a raging of the hair, and then to flee with a sharp step. But without your abundant locks, the movement was angular, brief.

"A new Amalia . . . We'll call you a new name, new . . ."

You giggled, his breath moved on your cheeks, your neck, your earlobes flaming for him. Until you dropped.

"Amalia . . . Even if what happened was a sin . . . that wasn't the intention . . . ," he whispered. The blood drained from his face and his shoulders sagged. As if the force he had amassed to come here, to tell you the words he had prepared, were gone.

You nodded, gazing at his lowered eyelashes, thick as a girl's, and the dawn that seemed to be erased was exalted again in all its coolness between his ironed shirt and your breath.

"I'll go make tea." You tried to cover the heaviness in your throat with the sound of the words.

"Yes!" he exclaimed behind you, laughing for no reason like a happy little boy.

In the corridor, you delayed once again, leaning your hand on the arch. Until the dark of the dizziness subsided. You waited in the kitchen like a trapped animal until the water boiled, gazing at the blue flames nipping at the bottom of the pot. From the weaving room came the sound of Isaiah's steps, his pacing back and forth. You froze at the thought that he might stop at the loom, stare at the stretched warp of the prayer shawls, open the cabinet, find the boxes of photos, spread them out one by one, stripping bare the space you still had left, seeing you without refuge. You trembled that the thought itself was already the proof. And once again you muttered there wouldn't be anything between you anyway, so why be scared.

The last time he came, when I got up from the Torah Curtain to open the door I thought only of the straw house slippers. The sound of their dry trudging bothered me. (The yearning over and over for that moment, the knocking that put a stop to the weaving, the plodding to the gate, his standing there—it's all present, doesn't go away, doesn't fade, as if it weren't only a few days between me and the end.) And then his leaning over, laughing, slipping into the dimness of the corridor inside, doubling over onto that stool, as if nothing existed except the routine of his coming. I slipped off to the kitchen to make tea (the refuge of familiar activities), trying to dismiss the meeting with a grimace, to say it was only for myself that I was putting on the pot in the silence of the house and the yellow valley. But when I went to open the tin box where last year I had put the leaves of Rabbi Avuya of blessed memory (the leaves of incense that go on mounting even after his death), I couldn't remove the cover. My fingers trembled.

When the water boiled, you took the lid off the china teapot you had bought for Isaiah's first visit, on the eve of Lag b'Omer (the only thing you added to the conglomeration of your dishes since you moved here), and because you had gone out to the bonfires immediately that night, you hadn't ever used it. Now you threw the leaves into it for the first time, careful to follow the instructions about scalding them, carrying the steaming pot into the room with both hands.

"I'll bring the cups!" Isaiah moved away, went into the kitchen behind your back.

"No, not those . . ." You almost bumped into him when he came out holding two old glasses he had picked up from the shelf. You put the new china cups on the table and blushed. Giving away your preparations.

The last time he came, when the tea was steaming on the table in that same brown teapot, it seemed to me for a moment as if it had been like that forever and would be like that: Isaiah doubled over on the stool, clamped in his black jacket, and I on the stool next to him, the fabric of my long skirt covering my bare feet in the straw slippers, my knees folded, and my head bent over them. In the full heaviness of the moment.

Now too, less than two weeks from the end, it seems as if everything has stopped, as if time stood still, as if it had been like that forever and would be like that, with no movement. At times it seems as if that is already the perfection of repentance, the flickering of the unity of everything, when wickedness turns into virtue and there is no more separation. Yes, always toward the end of the weaving, the patterns duplicate themselves.

Isaiah reached over and poured a stream of tea into the cups. Carefully he pushed one cup toward you, and moved the other one to him. He picked up a sugar cube, and softly sank it into the almost black liquid. Then he pushed back his curls.

"On the way here, I passed through the Arab village, on the slope. There were two boys in the field, they were herding the sheep. Five or six years old. They were playing on pipes." He burst into a free laugh, rocking on the stool. "I can't explain myself, Amalia . . . You know, this is the first time I stopped to listen to playing since I came here. Since I left . . ."

He spoke hastily, lifting his face to you: "How beautiful was the simple playing of two pipes together. Of two different melodies together . . . I stood there as if I had discovered harmony for the first time, and I recited a blessing, *His Honor fills the universe—*" His voice sank. "Amalia, I'm sure that was a sign sent to us by He-May-He-Be-Blessed, in His great grace, on my way here . . ." Again his body was snatched up in a burst of sheer laughter. You bent your head, flinching from his nakedness. The loud laughter went on a while longer, until he slowly calmed down.

He picked up the cup in his fingertips and looked at you a long time. You were very ashamed of your bare neck before his caressing look. But you didn't move. And maybe it was just because you remained trapped on the stool, yearning for his excited voice to come back, that the softness rose and filled you, the smell of the scalded tea, the afternoon, the quiet illuminating layer after layer, one no longer pressing on the other, only resting, transparent, piled up around a distant kernel that melted inside them, floating, layer after layer. And without taking your eyes off the steam at the rim of the cup, the quiet and the light sank into your pupils, and everything all around turned blue in the deep Mediterranean flickering, the deep light of day's end, torn in the window of the small Italian hospital, and the big cactus plants silhouetted against the blue facing Emily, who wakes up alone in the room, inhaling the bright glow of the white windowpane, not heeding her bandaged wrists lying on the sheet, only the pungent feeling of life, stronger than everything, clean, filling her. Lush blue biting white, and the cactus leaves flickering on the strips of sapphire. And in that silence, even before she is forced to lean back on the pillows, the knowledge that she will go on from here to Jerusalem, into that complete consolation, unclear for now, some flooding, quiet consolation. That quiet in which she will later drink Campari on the morning of the departure at the boardwalk café. Gazing through the red fizz of the drink, with the languor before movement, in the calm after everything.

You raised your shorn head and smiled at Isaiah; nothing seemed to move anymore. Only the sinking to that melted, illuminated kernel. His voice broke through the transparent layers: "I'm so grateful that you exist, that you exist, Amalia . . . As if we were always coming toward each other in the dark, not knowing . . ." His voice grew thick. "You'll see, Amalia . . . we'll make a true Tikkun with the love that will unite us."

And the sweetness that had almost risen in you retreated. Something was displaced. An opaque, fleshy mass, unclear for now, thickened.

Isaiah set his cup on the tray table, and a dark ringing echoed from the copper. Suddenly, your body still glowing, you were filled with fear that he would go on talking, and what was floating behind would burst out and split what had been stitched together.

"Come on, let's go out," you blurted. "Come, let's go out now, Isaiah . . ."

You got up before he could start talking again, putting down the full teacup, flashing red on the copper, rushing outside as if going out into the afternoon light would postpone saying things. (And when he finally did speak, as you walked among the rocks, in the evening rising from the valley, what he said seemed to have a different sound, the shadow was blended there in the dust, and the walking together was still accompanied by a tone of confidence—at any rate, that's what you wanted to believe.) You turned to the door. You didn't see the expression on Isaiah's face, you only felt the pressing of his body behind you. And it was enough for you that your bodies were borne in one direction. For now, you dismissed the rest, in great fear.

(The fear that assailed you seemed like theirs—from the magnitude of the love that was just sworn. Even before they go out of Egypt, while the blood is still fresh on the lintels of the doorposts, while the sacrifice is placed hot between the huts in Goshen, before everything, and fear already of the change of heart, of regret: *And it came to pass, when Pharaoh had let the people go, that God led them not through the way of the land of the Philistines, although that was near; for God said, lest peradventure the people repent when they see war, and they return to Egypt.* "Lest they repent," says Rashi: "When they have second thoughts about their leaving, and will change their heart to return . . ."

And in fact, what is the line between weakness and total confidence? For if they really were scared, why didn't they stay in Egypt, and afterward too, the nation that came to Moses to demand meat and water could have put their mind to it and gone back to Egypt instead of continuing to hold on to the madness of love . . .)

At the gate you stopped. It seemed to you that you had forgotten something. You rummaged in your purse, and even though the scarf, the hairbrush, and the wallet were there, you went on rummaging, not remembering exactly what you had forgotten to take. You apologized and went back to the room. You paced to and fro, as if the light from the windows would lead you to what you were searching for.

On one of your rounds, you passed behind the loom. On top of the shelves leaned an oval mirror you had fastened to see the reverse side of the fabric. A silhouette with cropped hair looked at you. Looked so much like Isaiah's curly head. Or is it Mala who looks like Isaiah? You grew dizzy. And just to grab something and leave, you swept a finished prayer shawl off the shelf and threw it in your purse.

Isaiah was waiting in the corridor. The light that fell through the wicket sculpted his head on the plastered wall. To open the gate you had to press close to him. You inhaled the smell of his sweat, lingering, your scalp grazing his shirt, breathing the rough, familiar smell for another moment. He put his fingers on your neck, encircling it like a thin stem. Cupping your scalp. Fluttering his fingers on the nape of your neck, along the bristles of hair. Then you remembered that you had returned to the room to get the photos. To tell Isaiah that he could see Mala, if he

wanted . . . That you still had them, you hadn't given them back to Stein!
The heat of his breath made you shudder.

"Let's go on talking outside . . ." you whispered.

"Yes, let's talk outside, Amalia . . ." He moved, bringing his body to
yours, burying his head in your neck, his hands clasped on your waist.
You unwittingly reached your hand and the key to the lock. The gate
opened, and dusty light poured onto the front steps. You were pushed to
the gate as if only the violent burst of white of Mount Moriah, of the yellow light overflowing to the Dead Sea at the bottom of the cliff, only they
could stretch the hour you still had left together. You were dragged forward, Isaiah tottering behind you.

(And after everything, what arrogance it was to believe that time
would stand still, there, on the mountaintop, at the end of the Omer
Counting. How could you hope that the circle of weakness wouldn't
start again in you, you and Isaiah—and there wouldn't be the sin of the
golden calf and the breaking of the Tablets, and afterward the destructions, all of them . . . Only blind and mad with faith, as if you could ignore that the commemoration was set for Tisha b'Av . . .)

You went down the dirt path together. But you didn't stop at the fork in
the road climbing to Rabbi Aseraf's house; instead you turned down to
the valley, among the olive trees. Only a week had passed since you went
together the first time, yet everything had changed. Completely. The
afternoon softness spread out, cutting the dusty slopes, growing round
in the roasted air, kindling the rocks pink.

Once again Isaiah broke into that free laughter. "The Commandment
that we trim the synagogue with greenery on Shavuoth, in memory of
Mount Sinai circled by greenery, is so right. Look, Amalia, how nature
prepares! Look, everything blossoms, by grace of HaShem, Blessed-Be-
He. The flowers ripen, the fragrances . . ." He walked quickly. His head
crossed the slope and his hands fluttered like two wings striking his ringing speech. "I go to the market to look at the stands, don't understand
how come people don't stop their buying, don't stand still to say a blessing on all that abundance."

You lowered your eyes at the curve of the lane. Your embarrassment
increased.

"I'm so happy, Amalia . . . I didn't know I could feel such expectation as now, in the days of the Omer Counting. I feel such readiness for the holiday, really a giving of the Torah . . . Standing among the whole Nation, as it is written: *Neither with you only do I make this covenant and this oath: but with him that standeth here with us this day before the Lord our God, and also with him that is not here with us this day.*"

You choked back the contempt for his inflamed words. You just walked along next to Isaiah on the path sweeping down. You had already gone far, approaching the straddle of the slopes, to the fringes of the gardens covering the crevice of the valley, to the spring and the pool hidden in the thicket. Going deeper in the hour turning blue.

Isaiah's metallic voice softened. "Yes, in playing I knew what preparation, expectation is. With Elizabeth I still believed that by playing we could create together a world apart, a world of beauty . . . But ever since the accident . . . Yes, I still went on making a living by playing, in the orchestra. I sat there at the end of the violin section, looking at all the backs moving together, that enormous body, and I only thought: Here we all are together in the 'communion' of art, all the souls apparently united, but what do I really know about the one sitting next to me, and what does he know about me? With Elizabeth, there weren't such doubts. Our faith together was stronger than anything. No, I don't want, God forbid, to deny what was. But after that . . . And just because of the tremendous feeling at the time of playing . . . That was unbearable. Like playing in the desert. Even in the most marvelous moments of the music, I would be left alone completely. Despite the perfection of the sound, the beauty . . . It's a closed world, a world without faith, a world that believes only in itself. You understand." He laughed and darted ahead. "It's no accident that it all happened in the biggest stone desert in the world, New York . . ." He grimaced sharply.

You were then near the end of the path. The ribs of the mountain gleamed above you. One more curve separated you from the gates of the Arab village on the slope. The first houses began to separate from the dust. A coolness of blossoming wafted from the depth of the basin wound in the twilight, in the light pillars of rising smoke.

"You haven't played since then?"

"No."

"You can . . . without playing?"

"Otherwise I couldn't live."

Almost all at once the light dimmed. Another fold of the slope separated you from the rest of the city, whose crown of buildings was suspended behind you on the height of the still lighted cliffs. Here, in the
bottom of the valley, evening lay.

"Amalia, I knew that with the help of God I would find you; you
can't imagine how happy I am . . . Everything I have lived looks like a
dream now. As if a new man was born in me."

There was something frightening, uncontrolled, in Isaiah's excitement. His averted head throbbed against the fig leaves turning dark on
the roofs of the houses, as if he were listening with his bones to the
rustling of the evening, to the cool gushing from the pool. All of him
open to the earth, to the pebbles, to the heavy branches, one with the orchards in the air steeped with blossoming. And once again you were
blinded by the lash of jealousy for the naiveté enveloping him, for the purity of his feelings, for the strength of his faith. A blend of envy and nausea like a cloying sweetness. And you didn't warn that the hour was late,
or that you had gone too far.

On the path covered with bluish mist walked Arab laborers. Carrying
tools, packs. Returning to the village after a day's work. Going down one
by one, sometimes in twos, silently. As if sunk in prayer or in the folds
of distance. Going through the orchards, crossing the small stone bridge
over the dusty riverbed. Walking silently. Spreading smells of sweat,
earth, cheap cigarettes. They passed by you, their faces opaque, looking
straight, as if you weren't there on the pebbles, hadn't dipped in that
dense coolness that filled the evening there, behind the borders. They
turned their heads away from you, crossing the little bridge, scattering.

Isaiah didn't sense anything, beaming in blind bliss. "Faith gave me
back the living world, delivered me from the death that was almost covering me, *give thanks unto the Lord; for he is good; for his mercy endureth
for ever* . . ." And he kept on walking, entered the gates of the village, rapt
in the lighted area of his faith.

Smoke of dung pierced the sweet darkening chill near the trickle of
the spring. You stumbled in Isaiah's wake, and despite the quenching
dampness you were ashamed that you didn't succeed like him in im-

mersing yourself in the spray of the evening, left so outside, looking at him from a distance, not even admitting that you once passed by here as by the mouth of hell, and a delirium of flaming dust made you dizzy in the fire of the sun, overpowering you in a swoon, a vision of the towers of the city collapsing in the distance. You stood paralyzed in the wetness thickening your breath, in the pain of jealousy. Exposed to the sudden green flickering of a look unsheathed to you among the men returning to the village. The penetrating, feline eyes of a young man surveyed you, stripping deliberately, with a mocking, slicing certainty. You were covered with cold.

"Isaiah . . ." You choked with panic. "Isaiah, maybe we should go back . . . Come on, let's go back, it's late . . ." You searched for the entrance to the village, invisible in the gloom. Only then did you turn around to Isaiah, who was still hovering over the dark pool, tense as in prayer. And you whispered quickly, "I don't want to stop you, but it's late . . ."

As you feared, your voice ripped something very thin in him. Shocked him into some taut shuddering. He jolted, like a broken mechanism, and his body drained; as if obeying orders, he turned on his heel, and began striding quickly toward the little bridge without waiting for you.

"Isaiah, I didn't mean to offend you, really." You ran after him. He nodded, hurrying with long strides, passing the last houses of the village near the prickly pear hedges, the dogs' barking.

"I really didn't mean, Isaiah . . . ," you said, and your voice echoed down the slopes.

The last time he came over, he said it was dangerous for me to live here alone. He laughed in embarrassment and repeated that it was dangerous for me to live here, a woman alone in the last house, among Arab houses. Seldom does the thought cross my mind now, that in the middle of the night, the door could be broken open with a slight push. Only when the presence of the valley grows sharp, when a donkey's braying rises from the valley, and for a moment they invade consciousness. Yes, and every morning, at four o'clock, at the end of the second watch, when the voices of the muezzins shatter, shear off the darkness, one after another from the loudspeakers in the minarets of the mosques, mapping the clefts of the mountains and the slopes with a chain of trills; at that hour I increase my pleas, answer them boldly with a long prayer between me and You . . .

A border divides the night, like the line of a watershed, separating West and East, the praying voices that rise from the mountains to Your ears with the sounds of weeping, sighing, in the steam of breathing. Different veins, not blending.

Do I really provoke them by living among them? Isn't the smell of their *haboons* bound up with every one of the threads woven in the Torah Curtain? In its bitterness I stretch out my hands, weaving by day, confessing by night. In the rustling of their lives that fills the valley, I spin my acts. That is the secret of the dreadful repair I am doing in Your ruined city, Lord.

The ever-honed fear stirs in the heart of the night. Sweet as the longing to bite the caves of Isaiah's kisses until blood flows—the fear inflames the prayer.

You climbed up the steep slope. The path emptied. You made your way among the olive trees and the fences, leaving the dark smell below, behind. Isaiah pushed on ahead, and you tried to catch up with him. Walking with a growing anxiety as you climbed higher. As if something was rubbed bare, irretrievable. Some possibility was sealed off.

The light increased. Red flowed from the West in the clefts of the slopes. Isaiah didn't talk anymore. Something was broken open in your ascent toward the built city, some irreparable flaw was imposed on the perfection of faith, as between You and the Nation, engraving forever the name of the place, *Massah* and *Meribah* . . . *chiding the children of Israel and because they tempted the Lord, saying, Is the Lord among us, or not?*

You emerged on the bare slope leading in a steep line to the rampart of rocks at the base of your house, facing the red still spread out beyond the distant towers of the city. The ribs of the mountain moved behind you, closing the valley, the evening packed with blooming there. A sooty bustle was emitted by the distant traffic; on the shoulder of the peak the dryness was mute. You climbed from the path to the street, your sandals clattering on the mountain road.

As you approached the house, stars were already standing in the dome of the sky even though a trail of scarlet still flickered in the West. On the mound near the gate, Isaiah stopped, lowering his eyes into the twinkling lights in the depths of the valley you had come from. The chill grew sharp and you wound your arms around your body like a shawl. Beyond his back, in the darkness, clusters of light spread, winding to the distances of the evening like the map of a foreign city which will forever remain a yearned-for dream. Apropos of nothing, the sentence came into your head, *For the remembrance of all Your works comes before You,* and repeated, *For the remembrance of all Your works comes before You.* For a moment the breeze passed on the mighty slope rolling down to the desert, and with it rose a memory of the night and the dawn that broke between you. What if Isaiah had made you pregnant? You lifted your eyes to the head above you in the shadow of the slope. And because of the tremor and the shame, you were impelled to say, "I know you talked with Rabbi Israel Gothelf . . . I was at Neve Rachel yesterday."

You waited for him to get scared that you had caught him in the act, but his voice didn't lose its softness. "Yes, Rabbi Gothelf asked me to come for a talk after we met. I passed by here in the afternoon to tell you, but you weren't home. I left flowers at the door . . . Maybe you noticed."

You knew from his posture that this time he wouldn't come in with you, and yet you were still gripped by sweet weariness and asked, "Will you come in?"

He shook his head no.

You came down from the mound to the gate. Isaiah trailed along behind you. You were afraid he would raise his arms and cling to you again, and you quickly drew the key out of the raffia bag. On the bottom, your hand gripped the wool prayer shawl you had tossed in when you went back to look for the photos. The soft cloth caressed your wrist.

"I brought this, if you want . . . It's for you. My first prayer shawl." For a moment, the whiteness was stretched between you, flickering between your body and his. Then he grabbed it with his fingertips, transferring its light weight from hand to hand, spreading it out.

"A prayer shawl of love you wove for us, Amalia, a prayer shawl like *a groom's rejoicing over his Bride,*" and he caressed the cloth again with his hand. Withdrawing to the doorpost. The dread of the words he was yet to hurl at you rose in you.

"Isaiah, I'd like you to play the violin for me someday . . . if you can . . . Just so I can hear your playing once . . ." you continued, the dark impulse speaking from your mouth.

In the waning light, you saw his face sharpen. From the valley rose a night breeze, blowing over everything that lay between you. You shrank in the doorframe. You saw how he carefully folded the prayer shawl, and turned on his heel. In the street, the blue was very dark. A man in workclothes covered the shadow with his steps.

Between the arches, Isaiah's movements still rustled. You stood to recite the Evening Prayer. Before the Omer Counting, you stopped and doubled over in the window bay, bowing to the silent night. From the valley wafted a hard prickliness, steeped in screams of sacrifices of ancient rituals, blood of the altars on the slope of the rocks. And the dry breeze went to the distant desert.

At last, you recovered and finished the prayer. You took off your clothes, amazed that you didn't feel anything. Under the nightgown, your body felt distant. You recited the Prayer before Retiring, and no longer dragging out *The Laws of Repentance*, you sank your shorn head in the pillow, falling into the abysses of sleep at the end of the limestone, lying there very carefully and gripping the edge of sand that would soon crumble in your hand, for that's what Mala forced you to do, lying next to you and very slowly pushing you to the edge. You tried not to think about anything, not even breathing on the limestone spit, just holding on to the brittle edge, just holding on, not to be dashed to pieces before morning.

You woke up bathed in heat. But even when you turned off the lamp, the heaviness didn't vanish from the arches. You burrowed your head deeper into the crushed bedclothes, and only then did you notice how the pillow seethed.

Footsteps pass by below, in the empty alley. A man's footsteps under the window. Striking heavily. The two of us are enveloped in the same silence. Now, before dawn. He is certainly lifting his eyes to my head moving in the arches of the light in the window. Awareness containing awareness. For a moment.

The edges of night grow thin in the windows. The grayness blends with the tongues of lamplight. As if the night is unraveling from my body. Soon the red will blossom in the East. And once again I will pray *Who restores souls to dead bodies.*

I went into the kitchen. I boiled water in a small pot. The taste of coffee washing my insides. Meanwhile, the reddish light burst, trapped in the warp rising erect in the loom. Soon the churchbells will set up a transparent gold cascade of harmony. And then the sprays of the bells will be swallowed up in the chirping of thousands of birds awakening, and later will be covered by the hum of traffic on the roads.

I shall stop. The head is spinning. The stammering of dawn floods the skull, blurs the yearnings that sculpted the nocturnal landscape. Everything is crushed beneath the bold fire. How shall I get through another full day of weaving?

Another night has passed. Bringing me closer to coupling with You. Me, Amalia, and the ruins of Your City.

May You wash the ruins of our bodies, flood and resurrect us. A hot drop pregnant with holiness. And together we shall know repair forever, I and the ruined Jerusalem, Lord.

Eleven days before Shavuoth.

Night of the thirty-ninth day of the Omer, Eternity

in Essence. Five weeks and four days of the Omer. I fell

asleep for three hours. Now it is one in the morning. I

woke up to the light burning in all the lamps.

I wove all day, until late. Without a break. Hurling the silk threads until the skin of my fingers was flayed. Only after sundown, after I recited the Evening Prayer and the Counting, did I force myself to eat something. Not out of hunger, simply out of a decision. To remain lucid.

The Tablets of the Covenant are emerging in the heart of the loom. And yet, all day long I am haunted by doubts, as it is written, *and when Pharaoh drew nigh, the children of Israel lifted up their eyes, and, behold, the Egyptians marched after them; and they were sore afraid.* All day long, the chapters I reread moved in me, unpinning and fastening that curve in the path of wandering, once more standing on the edge of the water, at the last minute, between the trampling Pharaoh and the sea, *and the children of Israel said unto Moses, because there were no graves in Egypt, hast thou taken us away to die in the wilderness?*

The head is heavy from the forced sleep. Hot night. (The wind didn't rise as it usually does in the evening, and the air remained hot even after sundown.) The dense heat is drawn through the open windows, with no separation between inside and outside.

Some restlessness is in the slopes. Deep in the night. The oppression is like an open wound. (On the slope a donkey awoke. Filling the darkness with its braying. Shrill, piercing the heat with its scared snorts.)

To go on, choking. The confession will emerge from the mass of dread. With my strength if not with Your strength.

To this day, I don't understand why he came to play the day after you walked in the valley. What impelled him to break the vow and come in the evening with the violin case in his arms? Did he understand, with his exposed, wounded sensibility, that only by playing would he know you, that only by playing would he reach what you were hiding from him? Is that what he wanted, or was he simply moved by a force beyond his control?

(Yes, it's frightening to say explicitly what was revealed to me when I reread the two portions today—as if what happened there, on that first stretch of road with You and the Nation, the break, the casting of filth, and the battle with Amalek—as if such was *Your* decree.

And last year? Why did You send Isaiah here to open what was healed? Everything was ready, agreed—the date of the wedding on the fifteenth of Av, the arrangements for the mikveh, the ceremony. Everything was set, announced—why did You provoke us, defenseless, soft with love, there, on the seashore, bathing in the mighty torrent of salvation—*and Israel saw the Egyptians dead upon the sea shore. And Israel saw that great work which the Lord did upon the Egyptians: and the people feared the Lord, and believed the Lord, and his servant Moses.* Why there, of all places, did You try us and them, in the heart of the rising song about the death of Egypt, and his bodies thrown into the waves returning with dawn?)

Perhaps the why isn't important anymore, now, on the hot night covering the two of us in the city among the cliffs, the donkey shrieking like a maniac at the bottom of the valley. Nothing's important except the lucid memory that re-emerges in the heat, except the presence of that hour . . .

The memory of the sweet sound striking dark blows, flooding the breath, the insides, the body bending over to the table. Jolting the heartbeats as then, when you bent over the warp of the prayer shawls until late, and suddenly the knock, his standing stooped in the doorway, the violin case clasped in his arms, and the pounding of your heart. In the middle of the room, you stopped; he didn't notice your amazement.

"I'll play for you, Amalia." He opened the case on the shine of the instrument resting on velvet, adjusted the bow with experienced fingers. Spread his legs, his head dropped and his cheeks were taut through the down of the beard, seeking the tone with his eyes lowered, as if he were listening from afar with his face tilted.

Nothing remains except the memory of the silence tense in the trembling of the night. And the shrieks of your heart as you sought support. And then the room was filled with a liquid tone, a warm, dazzling beauty, a deep, broken violin tone. Released into the dry breeze. An enormous startled beating of wings, rising, echoing over spacious, shaded valleys. Winding in thick, blue grass, winding dampened, and soaring again in whipping strokes in the distance. A flight spinning and running, running, sinking to the red sky, to the towers of buildings growing dark at evening. Spread out and growing sharp at the edges of a horizon furrowed with chimneys of cities sinking into gloom, emitting steel from their insides, to the crispness of a pure autumn shrouded by industry. A tone sprayed over squares revolving around themselves in high, solid facades, tapping on windowpanes of cozy rooms, fluttering in sacks of warmth gasping on carpets before the fireplace, the soft light budding in the gold of her disheveled hair, her face leaning at day's end on the back of the armchair, sunk in beauty, in the distant tone, the light trembling on the whiteness of the temple, on the smoothness of the neck.

And the sound darkened, drawn outside, to the top of marble stairs, pillars running in spacious vestibules, bows, heavy bows, drawing after it the teasing, haughty flight. The soar, then the flutter of the voice. And then the dense glow and velvet in halls full of people, excitement flowing from chandeliers, the smell of perfume and fur, and the smoothness of white cuff against black jacket. The blinding, sharp beauty of the taut tone, gold and scarlet playing, as if there is no bottom to the solemnity of the fall, to the gaping evening, to the streetlamps growing dark competing with the shadows on the sidewalks gleaming with rain, gloom of fountains, whispering jaws of stone lions spitting into the dark, the dark wailing, bouncing from the wet flickering, the running of the trams, drawn to the heart of the crowd, to solitude, to the sweeping, black, broken tone.

And then the hoarse, rising strokes, shifting with full force, bisecting in an endless consolation the descent of the evening on the meadows. And yellowing in the distance the walk of the peasants passing with heavy bodies on the odor of the wheatfields with their experienced movements, joining for a moment in the song darkening in the distance. A bird's cry on the still lighted horizon. A black, mottled flock, fluttering circling on the sheets of red, spinning landing and immediately rising into the endlessly wide firmament, burned to darkness, echoing in the purple bell of sunset, flakes and flakes of silver, of shining sapphire blue, crumbling, landing, piling up in a transparent whisper, lying down, airy, dinging. A high, flickering, silent screen. Dimmed and plucked.

A long breath. White. Body lying flooded between the reeds, filtering the flow of evening, the soaked sunset. The hand splitting the membrane of the spring flowing nearby in the grass, dipping up to the wrist, the elbow, the shoulder, going deep into the cool stream in the basin. Smell of blossoming, damp of greenery, sleep wetly holding the ends of the legs, washing the roots of the hair. The breathing is flooded with dripping pizzicato, rising in the softness of the water and sinking back. Rising and sinking back.

And then the room was illuminated, and the dryness was shattered, and only the spacious song went on. A new, solitary song. A simple song spreading through the silence. Isaiah's thin body suspended over the violin. His face open and his soft lips pale.

You lowered your eyes as in reverence. Something very deep, warm, poured from the depths of your life, washed over you with a stormy, flooding song, shocked at the strength of the salvation in your love for Isaiah—*Who is like unto Thee, O Lord, among the gods? Who is like Thee, glorious in holiness, fearful in praises, doing wonders?*

Sudden regrets for Isaiah's long face. He packed the violin, loosened the bow, and put each part in the case, the line between his eyebrows growing deeper. And you, trembling, still where you were when he played. And afterward, his hand placed on the little table, like a seashell full of memory of the depths. The silence that enveloped us in the heat. The silence now infiltrating the night. The weeping chokes the writing. Yellow. Emerges from that vein torn in the dark.

––––––––

(The donkey on the slope doesn't stop braying. As if he's crazy. They aren't slaughtering him now, in the middle of the night—so what does he have to bray about like that?)

The hand is heavy on the page. A tremor takes hold of the shoulders, and once again the weeping comes. A truck rattles down the slope.

I stopped writing. I sat a long time, the head tormented by weeping bent over the table in the window. As then. The dark of the end of the night flooding from the windows. Only the pain remains. After everything. A place apart by itself, not washed away. Engraved in my breathing. The attraction to pain, to the weeping that will burst from the choking. Like Father playing till the end in the bedroom, with his awful stubbornness to tear away the scab over and over, to leave the wound open, because nothing remained, nothing—like regrets for Father's playing, whole days behind the bedroom door, on the old violin. The tone creeping under the door to the wool coats hanging in the entrance, permeating the rooms, the cold kitchen. Regrets wash the breathing—the sight of Isaiah's face tilted, his thin fingers, the white arm—the hand continuing to write, as if by itself, chiseling.

And yet, nothing will renew the warmth of the inundating tone, washing the dark tissues. The eddying stream of heat from the windows cannot restore the silence, that single silence going from end to end of the world. A dense heat dripping from the window. A lash of soft pain. What was written hurts more than it repairs. If only the end to all this effort would come. If only the end would come.

HaShem, my God, do not abandon me for eternity, do not forsake me, HaShem, for on You alone do my eyes gaze.

You stood there at nightfall sunk in the waves of heat, the room separating you. Embarrassed. For a long time you remained without saying a word.

Isaiah turned his face to the window. "I have to go back." He clutched the violin case to his bosom. "I have to go back to the yeshiva now, Amalia," he repeated, spreading his fingers, and as he retreated with long strides he looked at you with flooded eyes. At the door, he waited for a farewell. Behind his head, night twinkled, strange.

"I'll go with you," you blurted. You opened the door for him, and you too were pushed into the heat of the night laden with smells and distance, suddenly drawn to go behind him. Out of great weakness. Great awe.

And even when you walked and the rushing noise of the city crashed onto the road suspended like a spit of shore in the night, you didn't see a thing. The pounding of the darkness kindled heavy waves, as if the whole world were cut off from its hold and was slowly spinning, turning upside down in the basin of night, enormous and dazzled. You walked next to Isaiah, silent and close, for your slavery is taken away, the Egyptians are dead, and all dread of them drowned behind you as a stone to the bottom.

And thus, after a few steps, trembling with thanksgiving, and only to praise Your Name for what was done to you in love, you said quietly, in simple words, "I once lived in New York, like you and your first wife . . . I had another name . . . Mala, Amy, Emily . . . You know, I also took the first step toward belief there, in 'your' New York . . . All alone, going to the end. Photographing the inside face of the face . . . That black-and-white series of close-ups of inside faces of the city . . . and afterward, traveling . . . And now, here we are . . ." You choked with enormous awe. For great as the dread was the hope.

You were at the top of the hill, in the shadow of the stone wall. The dense smell of weeds grew thicker. You lifted your eyes to Isaiah's opaque face, to his silhouette silently clasping the instrument case.

"You know, my father was married to a pianist. Before the Holocaust . . . Quite well known. Her name was Mala . . . Mala Auerbach. I went to photograph what remained of her . . . You understand? Yes, Stein paid, but what difference does that make? I was the one who went there, for months." The words were cut off from your mouth, distant, not connected with the dark feeling that swept away, nipped off, dropped far from the edge of your hold.

"I want to show you . . . the photographs of Mala . . . I want to show them to you, Isaiah, they're here, with me, in the house . . . No, I won't give them back to Stein . . ." The speech gushed out of you, hot. "It's all because now with your playing you revealed to me, Isaiah . . ."

You stopped talking before your breath was cut off, and the darkness of your heart covered the distant lights, crushed in a blinding cascade. A long tremor plowed through you. You turned white in front of him, naked, and nothing was hidden anymore. And the waters of some distant, fleeting flow inside you subsided, and you went out from under the upright floods in your filthy corrupted body, bearing your bundles in hands covered with mud, the burden of shame; but here, at last, like a dove you shall find rest in Isaiah, everything you will lay in his hands, and with your body your soul. *The Lord is my strength and song, and He is become my salvation.*

A few steps away Isaiah stopped. You stood still too. Light from a streetlamp poured out and was swallowed up on the slope, among the rocks. Dimly, you saw the line of his chin raised and retreating. And then he said drily, as from a great distance, "No need, Amalia, not now . . ."

The whip lashed in a flash of darkness exploding in your temples. In great pain you did not turn your eyes away from him. Even though he didn't return the box of his face to you. An unpleasant silence stretched between you.

"I thought you'd want to know . . . ," you barely whispered, blinded with pain.

The tremor twisted in his neck, as always when he defended himself against an uncontrollable feeling, and his back was taut. "There's something in you that's hard for me, Amalia," he stated. "I know this isn't easy to hear, but now that you started, I've got to . . ." He didn't look at you when he talked, his bony face turned to the hot darkness.

"Every time you try to explain yourself to me, Amalia, I feel like I'm over an abyss. I don't know. Sometimes it seems to me you're fighting to preserve that space. You don't let it be filled up with something else, with what can happen, God willing, between us now . . ." He spoke precisely, and his raised arm, thin as a skeleton's, beat time to the words. "It scares me, Amalia . . ." He finally turned his face to you and smiled with an effort, his face flickering white.

You lowered your eyes and nodded in panic. Your hand gripped the wall behind you. A forgotten wave of pain cut your wrist.

"But with the help of God we'll strengthen, Amalia, as the rabbi says, *complete atonement can never be made until one is tormented.*"

Unconsciously, you were still straining, but something was emerging, dark, as if an iron wall were going down between him and you.

"Each of us, it seems, has to leave his dead behind in the desert, Amalia."

"I, it seems, won't enter the promised land," you whispered.

"What do you mean?"

You were silent. The weight went on piling up, one millstone after another. I don't know how long it was until you answered slowly, with an effort, "I'll stay behind with the dead in the desert." And for some reason you added, your voice dry and inaudible: *"And no man will know of my sepulchre."*

"Everything we're going through now is a test, Amalia. The torments of repentance," he said at last, looking at you with raised eyes. As soon as the syllables came out of his mouth, they were plucked off in the weight of heat, not touching you.

Isaiah moved away, the violin case hanging from his hand as he went up the path. He advanced in the shadow of the stone wall, making his way among the thorns, dogs' barking. You trudged after him weakly. The heaviness of the pine trees fell on your shoulders, loaded with pollen and the bodies of the heavy birds gasping in the crests. At the top of the ridge Rabbi Levav's synagogue leaned over, immersed in the circle of the only streetlamp. *The synagogue where I was on the night before the bonfire of Lag b'Omer*, you noted to yourself as you passed the small structure.

"How quiet it is here," said Isaiah with relief. And he strode into the alley going down to the main road. "I'll come take you to Rabbi Aseraf on the night of Shavuoth," he said when you stopped on the edge of the road. "See you on the eve of the holiday," he called as the bus approached, and he was rushing in the door, waving, his movements like a wooden-limbed marionette's, jerking to the rhythm of Rabbi Avuya Aseraf's thick hips.

I don't know how long you stayed there alone, at the side of the road, gazing at the headlights running, the cars going past, the buses anchored in the bay of the bus stop, puffing clouds of soot, or how you finally went back through the neighborhood. You walked like a dead person, without feeling, your head full of a dusty rustling. Nearby, on the road that goes around the ridge, a distant, scarlet tone soared, spreading an echo of a hot trail, and then your mouth was filled with Mala's groaning, and the pain sank like a stone.

At home, you turned mechanically to the closet and took out the orange cardboard box—all the photographed material. For the first time since you moved here, for the first time since you came to Jerusalem. You spread the photos under the lamp, on the table I'm writing on now. Until late at night, you looked through them absentmindedly, seeing and not seeing. The dark wave broke over the sights that passed before your eyes in a blur. Among the other pictures was the one of Hubert and Emily on a boulevard in a Polish city, him hugging your shoulder wrapped in a coat with a fur collar, and in the background, Stein is watching, caught accidentally in the picture, across the boulevard covered with autumn leaves. For a moment you looked closely at the excited expression on the circle of Hubert's face, on your own slightly broad face. You've lost weight since then. You examined (as if checking the quality of the print) the bristles of the fur around your neck, the spot of Stein's jacket and his grayish hat. On the back of the picture was the stamp of Hubert's darkroom. The symbol in gothic script. You looked for a moment, and then you ripped the picture precisely, once down and once more across. You put the pieces one on top of the other, and went on ripping them into little strips. You got up, going toward the loom, and threw the pieces into the trash can, over the remnants of weaving. The scraps of paper quivered on top of the silk threads.

The donkey down the slope is braying again—he had seemed to calm down, it seemed that the night had shaken off the filth of his snorts, but here he is wailing again, uttering his hoarse, bitter screams into the swept-up mass of heat.

In fact, even now it's unclear, incomprehensible, inexplicable. No, I can't understand why Isaiah started playing for you like that and then struck your exposed softness. Why did he refuse to see the pictures of Mala?! Why did his strength go from him then? Why did You test us then, of all times, in the softness of the song on the seashore? Why was such Your decree? *That I may prove them, whether they will walk in my law, or no.*

And why wasn't it revealed to me before? . . . Or maybe it was revealed and I was just afraid to write it down! . . . To say what is screamed now, in the gurgling bleats of the donkey on the slope. To say that it was You who were scared there, right at the start, You regretted the Covenant of love that was made, letting Satan accuse just to be able to shake Yourself free from all the softness that binds You with the power of love to the Nation—You, who weren't able to love there, You, Lord.

"Amalia, all that we're going through is a test," said Isaiah, and didn't know what he was saying. Was it a test stamped from the start, and on both sides? And who started it? You! It was in You that doubt first sprouted, the temptation to test the innocence of love. And whom did You test there? Those lost ones, who were crazed with hunger, with worry, the nation of wanderers with their drained flocks and the children, trudging behind You terrified in the desert.

And You did well to play with them, with a test, at the height of weakness; how cruel You were, You who *know the soul of man from his youth,* You who now crave my prayers. (Is *that* the price You collected from us, the sacrifice of my and Isaiah's love, so that now I can repair in You? Is that the perverseness of Your lust?)

Only afterward did the Nation take the measure of You, and test You, *and will call the name of the place Massah and Meribah because of the chiding of the children of Israel and because they tempted the Lord, saying, Is the Lord among us or not?* . . . Only afterward.

Ah, God of awesome plotting—I never dared to express the weakness in You, Lord. Not in the Nation asking in a panic, *Is the Lord among us or not?* So exposed to the attack of Amalek; not in the hands of Moses, which grew heavy in the long hours of the battle of Rephidim; and he is only a man, a human being, flesh and blood. I never dared express that it was You who first succumbed to the temptation to test them, to injure the love, that it was You who became weak there in the weakness of Amalek, You whom he smote, in You the break, Lord . . . *Because the Lord hath sworn that the Lord will have war with Amalek from generation to generation.* Never did I dare think that it was Your Name that was broken, Lord, and the throne of Your Kingdom flawed—like the snorting of that crazy donkey into the night, sweeping us up into the ruins of the world of Your city.

(I'm losing control.)

The donkey persists in his braying, yelling as if he were being slaughtered. As if an altar had been put up right in the dense heat at the bottom of the valley and a slaughtering knife were tearing asunder his hairy neck, spraying his blood in the stone gutters, *hee haw hee haw hee haw.*

And maybe *that* is Your appearance in the world? *Hee haw,* Lord.

Everything is swept away. Growing dark. What is the purpose of my muttering with a panicky mouth: *I have become guilty, I have betrayed, I have robbed, I have spoken slander, I have caused perversion, I have caused wickedness, I have sinned willfully, I have extorted*—if I prostrate myself in the dirt and shout, *You are righteous,* if I recite submissively, *and force my spirit to be enslaved to You* and bend my neck to return to You, for my life, for Your life . . .

What a lie all that is. The whole prayer. What an escape. To where?

The head is heavy, drops onto the writing. What's that I wrote in madness? What is that impulse to profane Your Name now, in the middle of the night? I can only blaspheme. Only strike with eyes shut. Only pain exists in the dense heat in the night. Only the weeping ripping from inside, forcing me to go on and profane, with the remnant of strength that is left.

And the donkey brays like a lunatic. Stubborn, inconsolable. *Wherefore dost Thou forget us for ever, and forsake us so long time?*

The memory of Isaiah's playing is red, molten. The regrets cutting the infinite softness of his lowered pupils—Isaiah . . .

The donkey falls silent. Some relief.

Dizziness. Apparently I was hallucinating. It's only because the memory that gaped open drove me out of my mind. *Listen to the sound of my weeping, God of awesome plotting, one day body and soul will stand before You. Do not abandon me now in the night at the end of the watches. For the confession is for You, only for You, my God.*

(And perhaps always after sin comes repentance, after breaking. And perhaps only thus, with the force of dread, could the sea have been torn, and only wallowing in fear, and with Amalek on their heels, could they have approached Mount Sinai. As one heart.)

You and they rush to the mountain through the doubt that erupted, the weakness. And could we, Isaiah and I, even at the price of Massah and Meribah, camp together, with one heart, facing the mountain?

And if he comes again before the end of the Omer Counting. And if only we unite, flesh with flesh, in Your blessing. Just once more, one last time. Embracing we shall weep and caress. All night (the only melting consolation now).

Suddenly the thought of Stein wanders in. How I stood there without saying a word, seeing his broad body disappear in the depth of the corridor. Unable to call him, unable to articulate the syllables of his name behind him—*Lonek, Lonek Stein*—just so he would say to me again in his broken voice: *Amaliaaaa . . .*

Master of the Universe, do what You have deemed for me, do with me as You have promised me, help me, my God, deliver me for the honor of Your Name. Save me for Your Name's sake.

Please, HaShem, deliver me, please, HaShem. Bring deliverance upon me. For Your sake.

Forty days. Splendor of Essence. Five weeks and

five days of the Omer. (Nine more days . . .)

Last year you went on weaving the prayer shawls until Shavuoth began. A few hours before the end of the Omer Counting, you were swept away, bending over to the marking thread to cut one prayer shawl from

another, with the four letters YHVH in the black stripes, one on each end:
Y-H-V-H H-V-H-Y. Even though it was late, you nevertheless decided to
start tying the ritual fringes—the end of the work you yearned for (how
blinding is the expectation). You passed the tufts of linen you had prepared through the four wings of the prayer shawls, tied their ends on
both sides of the loops, and started tying and wrapping and tying. A
knot and six bindings, a knot and eight, a knot and thirteen. Thirteen
wrappings in thirty-nine knots of the One Name. You counted and tied,
counted in a whisper and tied. A white space enveloped your heart, just
not to remember, just to cruise washed and purified into the holiday.
*And bid them that they make fringes in the border of their garments through-
out the generations, and that they put upon the fringe of the borders a ribband
of blue, and it shall be unto you a fringe, that ye may look upon it, and remember all the Commandments of the Lord and keep them,* just not to think,
not to look back. *And that ye seek not after your own heart and your
own eyes, after which you used to go awhoring, that ye may remember and
do all my Commandments, and be holy unto your God,* just to go on tying,
and Mala's breathing the whole time ruffling the bristles on the back of
your neck.

Yes, the whole time, wound around your limbs, Mala, struggling so
hard here among the walls ever since Isaiah refused to see the photos. Accompanying your movements, plodding behind you in weaving, baking,
and even now, in the last moments before the holiday begins, she stuck
her moaning into your breathing that beats time to the tying, close and
silent as Ruth, who *washed and anointed and put her raiment upon her, and
went down to the floor, and uncovered his feet and lay thee down.*

And maybe that was the way to know with some dim knowledge—
running back to the kitchen, pouring oil on slices of cucumber, smoth-
ering the baked goods in sour cream, finding yourself kneading, filling,
frying, and the fresh cut vegetables in a bowl seasoned with the herbs of
Rabbi Avuya Aseraf of blessed memory, and then returning to the room,
to the dimness of the wool between the arches, to the tying, a knot and
six windings, a knot and eight, and thirteen and thirteen wrappings, with
that effort to unite, to tie, to patch. Just to go on tying until the time, *not
to touch the border of the mount, whether it be beast or man.* Just to go on
tying . . .

It was four in the afternoon when you went to take a shower. *You washed, you anointed, and you put your raiment upon you*—you washed from the filth of your paganism; and you anointed—those are commandments; and you put your raiment upon you—those are the Sabbath clothes. And when you returned to the room, you buttoned the shirt with white cuffs, approaching the night of the Covenant flushed with willingness, as they had taught you.

And even then, dressed in white, in the tension increasing as the day darkened, your fingers went on hastily winding. And *there were thunders and lightnings, and a thick cloud upon the mount, and the voice of the trumpet exceeding loud*. And the transparent crescent moon of the fourth of Sivan emerged while it was still day, turning white when you left the fringes, their unraveled ends lapping over the edges of the loom. And at sunset, the light of the holiday candles rising behind you, you stood all in white in the doorway.

When Isaiah appeared on the road around the mountain—a black silhouette in the pillar of red—it was too late to slip away, caught as you were in the beam of the sunset falling on the threshold. He practically ran up, waving two challahs and a palm branch he had bought on the way from an Arab peddler—at the last minute before the holiday began, here, in the neighborhood, to adorn your holiday table. He pressed into the dimness of the corridor, panting from the walk, smelling of grass, putting his gifts in the kitchen, and coming back.

"Let's go out, let's go out, Amalia. You said there's a synagogue in the neighborhood." (Isaiah, the excited one of last year, still has such a thin face, the innocence of faith is not yet robbed from his eyes, blind to the other silence that had already taken you far away from him.)

You climbed among the thorns to the small synagogue of Rabbi Tuvia Levav. You walked in the shadow of the pine trees on the summit, in the dryness thickening in the evening. You passed by the wall where you had walked on the night he played for you. You crossed that path, Isaiah's shirt turning gray in the remnant of light quivering in the treetops. And you didn't say a thing, not about what had happened or about what was to happen. (Out of fear? Or faith? How can it be judged now?)

In the tiny synagogue, Rabbi Tuvia's voice continued: *"For life and for peace, for gladness and for joy . . ."* Childish bundles of cypress and myr-

tle branches tied to the walls, to the beams of the platform, and around
the candelabra filled the hut with the smells of field and night. (Only
later did I learn that those were the work of Fayge's hands, and the
memory is haunted by one more pain.) Evening deepened in the windows. Through the partition, you saw Isaiah's back moving among the
backs of the worshippers, thin and illuminated. As if he were already
flesh of your flesh.

When you returned home, Isaiah glided from the kitchen, holding
the two brown challahs. And even when he recited the blessing and tore
a piece of challah for your plate, he still didn't look straight at you. You
put the vegetable dishes between you on the tablecloth, the white holiday
soufflé sprinkled with raisins, the first fruit you had washed, and Mala
hovered in the whiteness, enveloping your movements. From the win-
dowframe shone the night, fifty days of the Omer Counting, night of the
Kingdom of Kingdoms, deep and still, *and it came to pass at midnight, that
the man was afraid and turned himself; and behold, a woman lay at his feet.*

Isaiah raptly chanted the Blessings of the End of the Meal. He smiled:
"It was very good, Amalia." Then he stood up, his shoulders etched in
the flicker of the fresh shirt, went to the candles, put the end of the cigarette to the flame, concentrating on breathing in. His sharp face ignited by the hiss. And once again he smiled, the cigarette drooping from
his lips.

Finally, you closed the window, and together you went out. You were
immediately absorbed by the darkness, climbing to Rabbi Aseraf's solitary house. Your dry cough stung with the dirt of the valley. Outside, in
the electrified air, Mala's gasping separated from your breathing, and the
weight of her body also released its heaviness a bit from your pelvis,
your shoulder blades. Walking quickly, you felt some expectation spread
in you, far from Isaiah, far from what was about to happen in the rabbi's
house. Some distant expectation, like a voice bursting out of another
place, another place altogether, and *there were thunders and lightnings,
and a thick cloud upon the mount, and the voice of the trumpet exceeding loud.*

And so you didn't even notice that you were already in the quiet area
on the peak of the mountain. And the pounding of your heart grew
much louder when through the dark tree trunks you stood at the en-

trance of Rabbi Aseraf's yard. A streetlamp cast on the flowerbeds and
on the wall of the blacksmith shop shadows of backs furtively passing.
Isaiah straightened up with a supple swing and made his way along the
gravel path, quickly going through the flowerbeds toward the entrance.
"Come on, come on, Amalia, let's not be late."

You hurried behind him in the dark through the yard. The sharp scent
of medicinal herbs wafted like incense, and from the valley rose the dry
breeze. Isaiah pushed open the iron screen. When you entered, the plank
rang behind you.

After the dark steeped in the chirping of the night, the great light
lashed you. Cigarette smoke mingled with the ardor of the yeshiva students' sweat and the sweetness from the bodies of the young women, a
flicker of shirts, sparks of laughter, and above the whole mass of the
smells rose the thin sourness of incense.

The Tikkun hadn't yet begun. The yeshiva students gathered around,
resting their legs on the benches, hanging on the windowsills, their ritual fringes coming down over their trousers, tied with thirty-nine knots
of the One Name. The chairs were arranged around the table. Almost no
one was sitting at the pile of closed books. In the back of the room, the
young women were fussing over the buffet, full of the importance of
the job. Only leftovers remained in the big pots. The dishes were collected, and drops of beans and pastry stuck to the paper tablecloth. A
group of women in long holiday dresses assembled around the kettle,
pouring tea, taking sugar out of a tin box, and that tall black woman
with tempestuous curls was chatting with them. The humming of their
speech rose, slipping from the wide-open windows into the night.

You concealed your shorn scalp behind Isaiah's back, as if to protect
yourself. But even before your pupils could adjust to the light, Rabbi
Avuya Aseraf moved away from the men, coming toward you with outstretched arms, bigger than you remembered, winding his arms around
Isaiah's shoulders, smiling at you. "Amalia! . . . An important guest! I'm
glad you're joining us for the Tikkun tonight."

You expected that would be the extent of your reception—even that
was too much—and that the rabbi would go back to those standing
around the table, but he took your hands in his blacksmith's hands, ex-

amining your shorn scalp, and a smile stretched over his lips. "Beautiful as Ruth herself! As Rabbi Yohanan said, like one of the prophets of the Gentiles, everyone who sees her spills semen."

Your face burned.

"And how are you doing with the weaving?"

Isaiah moved excitedly to answer. The rabbi cut him off with a wave of his hand. "Amalia! Amalia! You who came to us like Ruth from the field of Moab to join the holy Tikkun tonight, you who will weave the complete Torah Curtain in the canopy above, Aaaaah-maaaah-lia, you, who in your name trouble and evil are tied, *Amal - ia,* for *man is born unto trouble, as the sparks fly upward!"*

And those present in the room were gathering around the rabbi, who put both his hands on your shoulders, addressing them beyond your bare head. "Tonight in the holy Tikkun it is written about Bezalel, *And I have filled him with the spirit of God, in wisdom, and in understanding, and in knowledge, and in all manner of workmanship, to devise cunning works, to work in gold and in silver, and in brasssss.* And what are the works? Weaving is a cunning work. Like the women weaving the Torah Curtains is cunning work within and without, like a scroll written within and without, *in my mouth as honey for sweetness,* and what is written thereon? *Lamentations and mourrrrrrning and woe."*

The men, wiping their mouths, huddled in a tight circle, their shirts glittering and their eyes flashing, and the young women stood behind them, lifting their chins with devotion steeped in pride. Even now, among those pressed around the rabbi, that tall black woman with crisp curls stood out.

"Yes, form a circle," the rabbi indicated. He brought his face very close to yours, his enormous eyelids shut. "We are creating a Torah Curtain of Repair of the World by words," he groaned, tossing you in his clasp. "Really creating, my beloved ones, as the Holy Zohar says: *A newly created word of wisdom rises and alights on the head of the Everlasting Righteous One, flies and rises and descends and becomes one firmamennnnt, and every single word of wisdom becomes a firmament standing fully existent before the Ancient of Days, and all other words of the Torah stand before the Holy-One-Blessed-Be-Heeee and ascend and become a new earth! In this world and in the World-to-Come.* We are creating, my beloved ones, we are truly creating . . ."

You stood there like a stranger in the heart of the rustling circle, pressed to his grasp, the steam from his mouth passing over your face and the words whispered between his lips touching you with something so concealed that your heart melted in sharp beating. But at the same time sending you far from the event, into another space that was looming around you, white with silence. And you no longer heard and you no longer saw. As if you weren't standing there in range anymore.

Meanwhile, the rabbi took his hands off you and withdrew, floated to the head of the table, wrapped in the shroud of his white caftan. "Rise up, rise up, my holy children," he called out, his eyes shut. "Come, beloved of the King, come, come, my beloved, who love one another! Assemble, friends, in the *Idra!*" Thrusting his hands in front of him: "As holy Rabbi Simeon Bar Yochai said in his Zohar: *Hurry, holy friends, assemble clad in armor, bearing swords and spears, enthrone as king He Who has the power of life and death to decree words of truth! Words that angels listen to and are happy to hear and to know.*"

The students crowded together, pulling the benches under them tumultuously, raising their flashing faces toward the rabbi, who was banging his fist on the table, gripped by a profound shaking, his head swaying with an intensifying swing. The women were swept to the back of the room, scratching the increasingly dense silence with the chair legs. And behind them, through the gaping windows, a weight of darkness rose from the valley, slipping out of all hold, all grasp, all control.

You dropped into the heart of the women's bodies. Next to an erect young woman, whose look was lifted to the rabbi with a burning smile, her back trembling. You were wrapped in embarrassment, your arm lay in your lap, your wrists covered by the cuffs of the white sleeves. The women's excitement spilled out like the tallow of the candles, rising in arches of breasts, in low-cut necklines, plain necks, arms. In the front row, a baby gasped. The heads of the sitting women in their long kerchiefs bent toward him. The baby wept with harsh, stubborn, unrelieved shrieks, until he choked, coughed with a strangled bleat, and fell silent.

The tumult subsided. Hot breezes crept among the seated bodies, ris-

ing from the smoke of the incense, the sweat of those waiting to join in
the Tikkun of the night of Shavuoth. And once again there was nothing
for a moment but the noise of excitement, when the friends assembled
around Rabbi Avuya Aseraf on that night, friends repaired jewels for the
Bride on that night, and adorned her with adornments for the King,
gathering around the curls of his beard spattered with the illuminated
saliva, his ancient face blinded in the strength of the vow. The smoothness of his forehead covered with drops of sweat. His eyes shut behind
lashes, sunk to a point within himself. He panted in the silence that was
cast, the redness glinting in his silver hair, and for a long time he remained like that, shaking. And then he bleated, "In the convocation of
the Court above and in the convocation of the Court below, with the approval of the Omnipresent and with the approval of the congregation,
we sanction Tikkun with the transgressors! In the convocation of the
Court above and in the convocation of the Court below," he repeated,
drawing out each syllable. "With the approval of the Omnipresent and
with the approval of the congregation, we sanction Tikkun with the
transgressors . . . Tikkun with the transgressors . . ."

The heat congealed. Next to you, your neighbor's body trembled,
making you flinch for some reason. Some shame for your shorn hair,
your departed strength. For something flawed, irreparable, separating
you from them. An oppressive weight lay upon your back. And what if
what happened between you and Isaiah would spoil the Tikkun of Rabbi
Avuya and his students, and what if your presence there damaged the
event? Or maybe it was Mala who suddenly tapped your eyes, shrieking
and tapping from a different place, completely different, *a hard daaay's* . . .

The rabbi swayed in the silence, with growing concentration. Until
the voice was kneaded out of him, gurgling like a dry storm racing from
the horizon: "Rabbi Simeon Bar Yochai, Holy Tanna! Rabbi Simeon Bar
Yochai, Holy Tanna, Righteous Foundation of the World! May we share
in the light of your grace on this night to make the repair you made for
us in the *Idrrrrraaaa* . . ."

He opened his enormous eyes and their white orbs were like the eyes
of a dead man. He drew them over the faces of the congregation: "The
hands give to Rabbi Simeon and the fingers up above."

All around, arms spread out immediately.

"Everyone will put his hand on his breast."

You tried to press your arm to your breast as everyone else did.

"Cursed be the man *that maketh any graven or molten image, an abom-ination unto the Lord, the work of the hands of the craftsman and putteth it in a secret place.*"

"Currrsed!" The echo of the oath was whispered from the mouths of those sitting there.

"Cursed be he who violates the Covenant."

"Currrsed!"

"Cursed be he who violates the circumcision, foundation of the world."

"Currrsed!"

"Cursed be he who violates the Bride entering the wedding canopy, for he and the whole world are licentious."

"Currrsed!"

"Cursed be he who defiles the loins of the Queen, whom the King Messiah, high priest, will enter."

"Currrsssed!" The echo of the oath filled the space, and above all other voices the voice of the upright young woman next to you screamed, especially loud (yes, it was the recurring echo of the shout that paralyzed you).

Again Rabbi Avuya shook a long time and then he lifted his flooded face in a painful chant. The voice burst out of him steeped in yearning, as if he were talking to himself: *"It is time to act for the Lord!* It is time to act for the Lord, time to act, time to aaaact . . . Why is it time to act for the Lord? For *they have violated Your Torah!* How have they violated Your Torah? *The heathen are come into thine inheritance; thy holy temple have they defiled; they have laid Jerusalem on heaps . . .*" He repeated as if to strengthen himself: "It is written in the holy *Idra,* until when will we dwell in the place of one pillar! It is written, *it is time to act for the Lord they have violated Your Torah . . .*"

An absolute concentration reigned in the room, as if the breathing of all those there was cleft to the rabbi's heavy breathing.

"The days are short, and the creditor is pressing, the voice calls out daily,

*the reapers of the field are few and they are at the edges of the vineyard, they
do not watch as they should and they do not know the place where they are
going . . . "*

The rabbi was gripped by another tremor. He thrust his face, sharp-
eyed, at those sitting frozen in their seats, wailing in supplication: *"Woe
if I reveal, and woe if I do not reveeeeeal . . . "* His gigantic face was trans-
formed as if by a sudden change of mask, all at once wrapped in a vision
of joy. "It all depends on love, my beloved ones, on love!" he cried and
spread out his arms. *"Rise, my holy children, come, beloved of the King,
come my beloved ones, come, those who love one another . . . "* He opened his
arms as if he were embracing the congregation.

The rabbi got up, the edges of his caftan filling the temple. The whole
congregation stood immediately after him. You stood too with the human
mass. A few students ran forward and opened the Ark of the Covenant,
following on the rabbi's heels as he took the scroll out of the Ark and returned to the platform with it. He removed its cover, spread it out this
way and that, raised it in both hands, walking all around, his head against
the parchment.

"Rabbi Simeon Bar Yochai, Holy Tanna, you repaired and we are repairing . . . Rabbi Simeon Bar Yochai, this night, your night of festivity,
we are making an awesome repair for the salvation of Jerusalem from her
ruins! We who are standing in the Holy City, we are Your Torah!

"Come, beloved! Come to repair the Queen," he chanted. "Come repair the loins of The Lady, Holy of Holies, where the King Messiah will
come . . . *I have set watchmen upon thy walls, O Jerusalem, which shall never
hold their peace day nor night . . . "*

He rested the scroll on the prayer stand, craning his neck as if he were
listening: "You hear, my beloved, you hear a voice? Are your knees
knocking against each other? You hear a voice? This is the voice of the
friends on high assembling for Tikkun . . . Come, come, beloved ones!"
He waited until the books were opened and they had finished leafing
through the pages, and then he called to the silence: "Rabbi Simeon Bar
Yochai, Holy Tanna! The word of the prophet, we repair tonight, in the
convocation of the Court below and in the Temple above!" He raised
the edge of his prayer shawl, kissed it, put its corner to the smoothness
of the parchment, recited a blessing and leaned over to the open place.

"Now it came to pass in the thirtieth year, in the fourth month, in the fifth day of the month, as I was among the captives by the river of Chebar, that the heavens were opened, and I saw visions of God."

The voice of Rabbi Avuya Aseraf chanted from the platform. But, completely spontaneously, shocking you, a voice also burst out from those sitting. A pillar of voices reciting as one person, covering Rabbi Aseraf's voice with a dark echo. *"The word of the Lord came expressly unto Ezekiel the priest, the son of Buzi—and the hand of the Lord was there upon him! And I looked and behold, a whirlwind came out of the north, a great cloud, and a fire infolding itself, and a brightness was about it, and out of the midst thereof as the color of amber, out of the midst of the fire. Also out of the midst thereof came the likeness of four living creatures. And this was their appearance; they had the likeness of a man . . . As for the likeness of the living creatures, their appearance was like burning coals of fire, and like the appearance of lamps: it went up and down among the living creatures; and the fire was bright, and out of the fire went forth lightning! And the living creatures ran and returned as the appearance of a flash of lightning! Now as I beheld the living creatures, behooooold . . ."*

The pillar of sound broke over the heads of the young men swaying like a field of spikes in the heat of the night, over the baby that started crying again, in the heart of the women's voices calling out, their heads lifted to the waving books, over the gasping cry of the young woman next to you. And in back, the high voice of the black woman rang, sounding like a clapper in the illuminated cascade of the choir as voices poured out.

"And the four had one likeness: and their appearance and their work was as it were a wheel in the middle of a wheel. When they went, they went upon their four sides: and they turned not when they went . . . And their rings were full of eyes round about them four . . . And when the living creatures went, the wheels went by them; and when the living creatures were lifted up from the earth, the wheels were lifted up. Whithersoever the spirit was to go, they went, thither was their spirit to go; and the wheels were lifted up over against them: for the spirit of the living creature was in the wheels . . ."

The pillar of voices ascended from the white swayings of the rabbi's body, carving in metal, plating the flattened walls of the room, winding in the heat permeating the room, drawing over the pungent body odors and the steam of food that decayed into the rising heat, an ascending ladder, teeming with electricity, piercing, around you, sitting there in range without a word, a dull pounding. Struck from another, distant place— *hard daaaay's* . . .

"*And the likeness of the firmament upon the heads of the living creature was as the color of the terrible crystal, stretched forth over their heads above . . . And under the firmament were their wings straight, the one toward the other: I heard the noise of their wings, like the noise of the great waters, as the voice of the Almighty, the voice of speech, as the noise of the host . . . When they stood, they let down their wings . . .*" And now it was impossible to distinguish the rabbi's chanting from the voices of the congregation, or the excited shrieks of the distant black woman, or the words of the chanting of the young woman next to you, who shouted at the top of her lungs: "*And above the firmament that was over their heads was the likeness of a throne . . . And upon the likeness of the throne was the likeness as the appearance of a man above upon it . . . And I saw as the color of amber, as the appearance of fire round about within it, from the appearance of his loins even upward . . . and from the appearance of his loins even downward I saw as it were the appearance of fire, and it had brightness round about . . .*"

You sat there in the heart of the cascade of voices, paralyzed. Cowardice washed over your heart. Certain silence. Draws you there. Final exhaustion. Chokingly sweet. Not understanding. Profound paralysis. Cut off. Covering, cast. In a dark point. Precise. Striving for a place of white rest. Thickening. Far from the dense voices. From the rolling of the rabbi's hips. Far from the back of Isaiah's neck flickering among the heads of the readers in the rising pillar of voices. Dense. White. Into the pillow and the breathing body to body in the *appapatz*. Their voices in the foreign language creeping from the living room, behind the door, scratching, scratching. Frailty poured out. Turning to stone.

Some silence there. Drawing. In a distant point. *It's beeeeen a haaaard daaay's night— As the appearance of the bow that is in the cloud in the day of rain, so was the appearance of the brightness round about . . .* Some understanding. Distant. And only the Beatles all night *as it were the appearance of fire, and it had brightness round about, it's been a hard day's night,* in a quotation of a quotation of a quotation—*the appearance of the glory of the Lord. I fell upon my face, and I heard a voice of one who spake—*

and everything stopped. Completely. Froze. In a paralyzed body. And
some distant understanding. As then. In New York. On the last night—
And he said unto me, Son of man—just got to print a few last pictures.
And then finish. Amy returning to the rented apartment. Trudging from
the entrance to the shabby elevator. Body paralyzed. Completely exhausted. The corridor from the elevator to the door, cooking smells.
Cheap beef softened in a paste of overcooked beans. The rancid breeze
of the ventilator from the restaurant on the ground floor, blowing on the
back of the neck—*Stand up on thy feet, and I will speak unto thee.* The effort with the locks, blurry, maybe five minutes. Groping along the wall.
The hand on the switch. The unmade bed. The coat squashed beneath the
lying body. No strength. Absolute weakness. Impossible, impossible to
go on running in the cold streets anymore. To raise the camera to the eye
anymore. To hold the weight, to aim, to press, to squeeze. Over and
over. Finally so weak. To shoot, shoot. Scarred walls. Backyards. Iron
steps. Piles of rubbish printed in contrast. Skinny arms of people lying
amid rags. A mesh of belching subway vents. Columns mounting up
from the asphalt. Black mud soaked with grease. Collected in the gutter.
Columns of smoke and fire going before the sprayed, crushed crowd
straying here and there. Going through the masses of humans, not succeeding anymore, not even for that split second of squeezing the picture,
focusing the sight that slips away. Lifting the camera. Aiming. Pressing.
The inside of the city. Faces inside faces. The city under the skin of the
city. Cutting there, what is broken, at the end, there. To shoot, shoot . . .
Till your strength is gone. To go to the end. And all the rest is only
scorn. And it too is growing weak. Going through meetings, running er-
rands. The mouth torn with heavy lipstick, the smile pasted onto the
face. No food. Nights of smoking in the Village. Sex in the body turning to stone. And over and over again, the burning of the light on the
printing block. With the last remnants of strength. Soft, weakened
breathing . . .

And finally, now in her room. Just to drop onto the unmade bed without undressing, without eating. Not to mention finishing the development
of the morning's film. The last film. Or thinking about the meeting tomorrow with Aronson. A horse's skull with a gaping smile of gold teeth.
Jack Aronson in the neon bubble of the gallery entrance. He'll hang her

photographs in his gallery. A young photographer from Tel Aviv, there's something, neo-Expressionism . . . very impressive, strong . . . he'll give her a chance . . . a pretty girl . . . what does he understand about anything, with all his commercialism . . . he and the journalists who admire the "product" . . . left outside, so outside . . . Just to rest a little in the meantime. To ward off the ceiling that mocks the stranger curled up under it, in a little while it'll push her out of her insides. It'll vomit her up, crushed in the mire of the garbage. Just to rest, to recover a little. And then she'll finish the printing. Yes, she'll finish, she'll show them, once and for all, let them know. Let them see what she really thinks of them . . . Just to rest a little. Only a little more. The horrible blurring. Weak. A humiliating failure. Pulling the knees to the chin into the body wrapped around itself, cut off. The wrapped-up smell of the body. Far from the awful valley below, from the stream of cars and the soot of asphalt and the facades, and the chimneys, the stream below the surface, where the unmade bed floats cut off, far from the weight of the crowd pressed in layer after layer on the cliffs of swarming. The city she thought she could conquer, could finish with a squeeze of the camera's trigger. And suddenly only the breathing. The familiar smell. A strange consolation steaming back to itself. *Little Amalia. Mala, Malinkaaaaa.* It's been so long since she returned to her from the pillow crushed under the head. Entering hair to hair in the dark of the *appapatʒ.* Dry, rustling hair, breathing to breathing. *Little Malinkaaaa.* Choking mouth to mouth, to nose. She's sucked into deep sleep, even more exhausted by the very thought of getting out, dragged in a heavy stupor to the paralysis of slumber like food remains spinning in the sink and chewed up in the grinder. Not raising the arm to the light switch, swept away into sleep.

And then waking. In the morning. Dry panic. In the big window a winter murkiness. In fact, almost total darkness. The light she didn't turn off last night striking her hair. The clothes sour, wrinkled. And an awful fatigue. A reluctance to get up now, in the new morning, a refusal to straighten the squashed cheap glory of the Indian skirt. Refusal to button wearily the big old coat. To comb the mass of hair. To start running from the door. The corridor. The mold of the trampled carpet. The box of the elevator. The reek of the restaurant downstairs. And the blow of the cold. The frozen sidewalk, the cans, the puddle of grease at the entrance to the gas station, got to jump over it, the sidewalk lopped off there. The human stream bursting out of the subway, fortified by the morning hostility. The hand holding the iron banister, yellow color and filth. Leading down reluctantly. A humiliating cold bursts from the tunnels. The tracks, heaps of garbage, of people. The thrusting assault and the intertwining frost. Serpents of frozen chill.

Absolute failure. Lying trampled, seeing herself doing all that, and she still can't cut off the hold of the body from the bed. Cut by so much weakness. The temptation not to get up is so strong. Just not to get up from the warm mass of defeat. Sour crushed clothes. Not to get up. To put it off a little. Not to be hurled into running. *First think about the lighting for the last picture, Make decisions in an interim rest which are sometimes just as important as really working* . . . Wretched excuses of contemptible fatigue. A swampy, dull, smooth mass.

The wristwatch moves before the eyes. Shock. *Five. Five o'clock* . . . *Five in the afternoon!* Panic turning white. Dry salvos at the top of the skull, descending with chains of whiplash onto the eyes. *Can't be* . . . Once again the watch through the blur . . . *Five o'clock. Five in the afternoon!* . . . The blood floods the face (always the same forced series of reflexes). A fever of thoughts bursts out, crushed in the spinning of a shouting grinder . . . *A whole day has gone by, people ate, talked, did something with their lives, filled the subway trains, filled the elevators, sat in rooms in transparent black buildings, went out into the filthy winter, called on the phone, laughed—and I slept! Simply slept! From one night to the next. I didn't do anything, I didn't accomplish anything, I simply wasn't* . . . *wasn't* . . . *And in fact, what difference did it make? In fact, it didn't make any difference! Who even noticed that I wasn't? Who cared? Father, or Mother? They're dead. They left me alone. Maybe Aunt Henia? How did she get in here anyway, something grotesque I left behind in Haifa? Or maybe Aronson from the gallery, with the gap-toothed smile, and the shining bronze statue behind the reception desk? Or maybe the shadows from the shared apartment in the Village? Stanley or, whatsisname, John Mayn, who bends an arm to Robert with an idiotic face and is amazed that he shouts so much. Who really cares? I could die without anyone knowing, die and go on lying here, a cold body in the twisted sheets, no one would notice that anything had happened at all* . . . *So why in fact all this effort to get out of bed to run around the streets, to show, to prove? To prove what, in fact?* The body is turned to stone. Cold. Cut off. Someone else's body. Far away. Unraveled thought. Dull, dark. And silence. Something forgotten. Crushed. Gray crumbs. Some point in the handled murky light. That winter dreariness and steam covering the bustle of the street from one darkness to the next. Some final point.

And then, for the first time, not yet understanding, without any preparation, the knowing. To the bone. To the ends of the broken fingernails, under the sharp red of the nail polish, then. Alone. In the coffin of the strange room. Some knowing. Vague. The breathing growing weak. There, the knowing for the first time, in that silence, of after everything . . . *It's been a hard daaay's* in some final point. Silent.

Finally in the window. From another place now. Silently. Suspended on the window frame. The wall of the building next door stuck together. Only if you bend over do you see a piece of the street. The fingers picking at the peeling paint. At the bottom of the building a pale light over the emergency exit of the restaurant. At the end of the passage, in the fog, a corner with a traffic signal and an electric pole. Frozen smoke belched in isolated pillars from the asphalt, a truck rattling down the street. A taxi fleeing. The street empty. Nobody. *How can there be such desolation at the height of the afternoon rush? The whole city is dead. There was a poisoning. Gas . . . only I was saved! Miraculously! I was saved, I, because I slept until the afternoon!* Heart pounding in the stony body suspended like a spider in the window frame. *That's why I slept. Because of the poison. Until it catches me too, here, above . . . A question of time. In a little while, it will catch me too . . .* Only then did understanding set in. *Five in the morning. Dawn. Not afternoon at all. Five in the morning.* The pale end of the night before . . .

And the Spirit, it entered into me when He spake unto me, and set me upon my feeeeet, that I heard Him that spake unto meeeeee. And he said unto me, Son of man, I send thee to the children of Israel . . .

You sat bathed in sweat. The heart pounding, solitary. The young woman next to you is roaring in a faint voice. Cigarette smoke, sweetness of perfumed bodies, steam thickening over the packed mass of heads shaking to the reading, flooded with lights, *it's been a hard daaay's night.*

The baby starts gasping again, soon he will burst complaining into the voice—*I do send thee unto them: and thou shalt say unto them, Thus saith the Lord God . . .*

And some silence there. Drawing there. Like Father closed in the room. Some silence there. *A hard day's night.* At the last point. At first there were only mechanical activities. Back to bed, sinking into a confused sleep, maybe until the afternoon. Not telling Aronson that the meeting was canceled. Not thinking about it at all anymore. And later (as always), first get material, and in the evening back in the apartment in the Village, somehow filling the time until it will be better understood. The smoking, and sex with anybody. Raynold and maybe also Steve who has to bite her earlobe with a snort in order to come. And Martin the dwarf. He never gives up, and, chuckling, he exploits the contract of communal sex. Gnaws on leftovers, doesn't need any special treatment, climbs up, trousers dropped, around the belly, as onto a rotten tower you can still get something out of, even sucks a full cunt, all wet, doesn't let go, diligent, pushing his whole head . . . *And they, whether they will hear, or whether they will forbear for they are a rebellious house . . .* And only the next morning a bubble of cold clarity in the street. Coming with her to the phone booth. Waiting outside, jumping thin, skinny like old men with shaved skulls, warming themselves up a bit in the cold, flattening their noses on the glass of the phone booth, twisting their faces with protruding ears, signaling with their hands. The next morning. In the phone booth in the awful cold. The number that was always in the wallet. A piece of paper folded into a small square in the wallet jumps to the hand from behind the bills. The number Father dictated and she wrote down, of course, even though she closed her ears. The piece of paper that survived all the metamorphoses, Amy, Emily, Amalia, the piece of paper with Stein's number. In the old wallet from Allenby Street in Tel Aviv. The end of a string that always holds on like the rope bound to the foot of the High Priest to pull the corpse out. "This is Amy, Amy speaking . . ." "Yes, yes . . ." "The daughter of . . ." "Yes, I know, I know, been waiting for you to call . . . yes . . . coming immediately . . . yes . . ." *—yet shall know that there hath been a prophet among them. And thou, Son of man, be not afraid of them, neither be afraid of their words.*

You sat stunned in the packed mass of bodies, Mala swelling over your eyes and shrieking. And your mouth crumpled, with the stubborn tears in your head. Only the sound of the Beatles beating in the distance, *It's been a hard day's night,* melting in your mouth *as honey for sweetness.* Stunned in the packed mass. Far from the excited rabbi, from the moving of his hips wrapped in the white shroud, from his students seeing God like Nadab and Abihu, and the seventy elders of Israel—there, among the shaking bodies, something was revealed to you in Your great grace. In the trembling of the body on the chair. Panicky. Something vague, nameless. Under everything. At the last point.

Aren't you always there, in Your grace? In the T-shirt thrust in the jeans on the hot body, *a hard day's night* in Amy's small voice . . . The longing wildness tearing you up you pour on the surprised Zvi, the two of you pressed in the night to the wet boardwalk and the exhaust of the cars and the heat. In the pretense of lust. In a lie of tongue within tongue in the softness of his mouth emptying saliva too soon *a hard day's night* and all that only because Father is waiting, still waiting a few streets away, bent over the spinning record on the phonograph, still waiting for a click of the tongue of the lock in the door when you return home. And from a distance, from a very great distance comes the movement of the swaying and rising bodies, in the prayer of the Tikkun, in screams of devotion. Rising and falling. Not noticing anything.

Finally, you found yourself leaving the rabbi's house, borne along with those pressed to the morning holiday prayer at the Wailing Wall, walking quickly from the yard in the last watch of the night. Before your eyes, striding bodies shook, stamping among the dark treetops. The first ones led by Rabbi Avuya Aseraf had already passed through the gates of the walls, and you, faint and weary, you were the hindmost, paralyzed in that silence. *But thou, Son of man, hear what I say unto thee; Be not thou rebellious like that rebellious house: open thy mouth and eat that I give thee.* And all the while the dull beating in the skull, *It's been a hard day's night . . .*

Without being noticed, you slipped away from the last of the marchers. A woman alone on the night of the Covenant, among the trees in the dark at the top of the mountain, head shorn, nape bare, going deep into the dangerous quarters, alleys, straying to the knife that will slice her throat in the hot night, the night of the Giving of the Torah . . . *And when I looked, behold, an hand was sent unto me; and, lo, a roll of a book was therein; And he spread it before me; and it was written within and without: and there was written therein lamentations, and mourning, and wooooooe* . . .

But no one chanced upon your way in the empty alleys. You grew tired, finally, from the wandering tapping an echo on the cobblestones. You were swept outside among the arches to the City Wall. For a moment, you leaned on the big stones. Their warmth stopped your walking, suddenly consoling, so soft.

You hoisted yourself on top of the wall, and there, in the castellations, your legs crossed on the smooth stones, you curled up. And so, without knowing how, you were wound in that niche at the top of the wall, so very close to the rough heat of the stone. Folded quietly, knees drawn up under your chin. Between the City Wall and the breeze bursting, dry, on the other side. Gazing at the stars flickering above the valley, a black Torah Curtain embroidered with flowers and letters and serpents of gold. And Mala's dry breathing soared from you to the quiet of the night, *It's been a hard day's night* . . .

Those going to morning prayer at the Wailing Wall began filling the street under your hiding place. Assaulting in group after group. Coming down in a thick flood, swallowed up in the crush of the crowd already swarming in the open square of the Wailing Wall, in the shadow of the ruins of the temple. A noise of tables and benches being moved rose from the row of houses opposite. From the gate came singing squadrons of white-shirted yeshiva students flooding down with an ancient excitement. The dense human river moved in the narrow street, as if the entire city came before dawn to stand at the bottom of the mountain. Rabbi Avuya Aseraf and his students also charged out of the alleys. At the head strode the rabbi, big, in the white caftan, and behind him pressed the whole group. Isaiah was among them, his head high, crowned with curls, struggling between the shoulders of those hurrying at his side.

From the packed throng wafted a warmth and a bitter vapor of the end of the night, the end of the Omer Counting. You shrank into the niche in the wall. Its foundations were shaken by the pounding steps, and from the gates, pilgrims pressed into the dust, assembling body to body on the stairs, on the temple bridges stretched over the Valley of Hinnom, filling the passages over the gray dawn and the olive tree leaves in the valley sunk in darkness. Outside the wall, the pale slopes threw off the weight of the night lying there, in the place of the battle between the angels, between gray and ruby.

And the dawn started pricking the haze. And columns of red surrounded the moving Nation, body to body, standing in the East, bending their faces to the ground. And the gates of the Temple stood open to the yards washed during the night, and the altar cleansed in the center. And in the northern yard waited the daily offering that would be slaughtered with the morning star, when the face of all the East is lit to Hebron. Rows of priests dressed in white ran up the ramp, caught the blood that gushed into the bowls. And from the back of the yard rose the bleating of the victim in his pen, calves of cattle, two, and seven yearling sheep, not one whole limb in their body.

You thought you'd fall from your hiding place in the lap of stone, the first fruit that tumbled from the top of the wall and was buried under the pile. And the gigantic river of bodies streaming down the slope would sweep you away in its current, would stone you to death, and the witnesses would cast the first stone at you. And Isaiah wouldn't notice that he too printed his footsteps in the fruit of offering, trampling out its juice, its wormwood, the remains of sin, the bad smell. The excellent fruit, a new offering, dripping, rent, ground thin. Chewed in his mouth like sweet honey, like milk flowing from your breasts to suckle his kisses, trampled sucked dark fruit.

How long before they finally discovered you shrunk on the rim of the wall and dragged you, a washed and purified offering, bleating in panic in the trembling black skin, led by his horns through the doors of the sanctuary outside to the yard, to the ledge of the mountain, bursting there, wallowing, defiling the oils that washed his flesh? The heat trickled in drops of sweat onto the fur plowed with terror between his horns, onto the bristles of his hair, and his whole body gasped like a bellows. A scapegoat attached to the dirt, like a serpent whose head is dashed to pieces with a stone, his head shorn, blazing with shame . . . Your shaved head.

In the pallor of dawn, they held your horns, you on the desert paths.

You walked beyond the border of the end of the Counting. Into the holiday rising in the radiance bursting from the Dead Sea. Your hooves light in the straps of the sandals lapping at your ankles, and only the breathing, dry.

For a moment, you stood on the edge of the cliff, facing the pale valley spread out in the silence, your hairy animal's body flooded with sweat, shivering. And then, from behind, with sunrise, a hand pushed you onto the slope. A scapegoat. And you rolled down wrapped in the cascade of dirt with the syllables, *he divided the thread of crimson wool, and tied one half to the rock, the other half between its horns*—and pushed it from behind. And it went rolling down and before it had reached half its way downhill it was dashed to pieces—and in East over the Dead Sea at the bottom of the valley turning white, and *behold the glory of the Lord, stood there and I fell on my face.* And the flame of the sun rose salty and heavy, climbing in drops of gold, turning bright on the cliffs of chalk. And a voice arose opposite, from the distance, *And I will betroth thee unto me for ever; yea, I will betroth thee unto me in righteousness, and in judgment, and in lovingkindness, and in mercies,* surrounding you in a warm glow, *I will even betroth thee unto me in faithfulness; and thou shalt know the Lord and thou shalt know the Lord and thou shalt know the Lord*—a very strong voice rising from your skull, from the abyss turning white, *hard day's night.* And from the priests and the people standing packed together in the temple court rose a great cry, and their song was cleansed, *This is the Torah! This is the Torah! This is the Torah!*

A kind of white scream burst out of you at the sight, burning everything for a long moment. Lapping against your skull leaning on the niche. Until you caught your breath, your heart beating dully. And along with the heavy sound of Mala's wings, which was cut off from you, soaring into the distance, the rhythm that beat in you all that night also stopped, *It's been a hard day's night.*

I don't know how long you sat there, alone, folded at the top of the fortifications. At the end of the night. The coolness made your breathing a bit damp, but the blurring didn't abate. At some stage, sparks began slicing the distance. Straying quietly and then extinguished. Shivering torn breeze. And then the bud of red, a disk of fire kindling the ledge of the mountains of Moab. And then everything was erased. On the morning of the fiftieth day of the Omer Counting, last year . . .

Late, very late, have to get up now for Tikkun Leah. *(I charge you, O ye daughters of Jerusalem, that ye stir not up, nor awake my love, till he please.)*

Almost an hour later. Pitch dark. Filling the ridges all the way down the abyss. Sometime before dawn.

I went out to take dirt for the Midnight Prayer from the slope at the side of the road. I leaned on the wall, and there, outside, in the night, on the stairs going down to their area, I recited the prayer. My hair was filthy with the dirt, dripping grease and motor oil. That movement of scattering on the hair the defilement of the city absorbed in the dirt seemed like madness to me. And yet I went on crumbling, dirt on dirt.

I don't know if someone heard the sounds of the prayer, if someone saw me bowing and rising in the white shirt blown by the wind growing stronger as the prayer came to an end. I wasn't careful. My mouth was full of the crushed syllables. *O pleease, pleease, pleease, weep for Zion and lament for Jerusalem, You shall rise, shall take pity on Zion, it is the time for grace, the time has come. For Your servants want its stones, its stones, its dirt will be graced.* Beyond the darkness of the valley separating here and there, a dim light rose among the trees from the site of the house of Rabbi Avuya Aseraf of blessed memory, *the Lord gives and the Lord takes, blessed be the Name of the Lord.* And in the midst chalk rocks lay in the darkness, and mounds of ruins.

I went back to the room. The echo hadn't yet subsided, ringing between the walls of my skull, flooding. The mouth full of the syllables poured into the sweetness of dirt, in the wind quietly crushing the flesh. *Woe unto us, that we have sinned! For this our heart is faint; for these things our eyes are dimmmmm. Because of the Mountain of Zion, which is desolate, the foxes walk upon it.* The heavy sound of the prayer still echoing. Dusty. Strong. *Thou, O Lord, remainest for ever; Thy throne from generation to generation. Wherefore dost Thou forget us for ever and forsake us so long time?*

For a few moments, I couldn't understand what the letters running on the thin pages of the prayer book were. For a few moments, everything was blurred. Closed. And the fear of rejection, the completely lucid knowing that I was totally rejected . . . The body seemed to be paralyzed. The right eyelid twitched. Trembling beyond my control.

And who am I now to judge your acts on that night last year, to judge what was revealed to you dimly so alone, so alone? Like the Nation. Yes, like the abandoned Nation, scared in the last hour, *for Moses delayed to come down out of the Mount at the end of forty days.* How can the fear that gripped them be judged? *And the people gathered themselves together unto Aaron and said unto him, Up, make us gods, which shall go before us; for as for this Moses, the man that brought us up out of the land of Egypt, we know not what is become of him.* A crowd of riffraff, and Satan came and confounded the world and showed them images of darkness and gloom and confusion, pointing out to them an image of Moses borne by air and firmament, telling them that was Moses the man. Saying, of course Moses died. And they believed him. How can we judge the magnitude of their faith, then, in the panic of desertion, the faith that they could return the God that had disappeared, by their own strength! The wretched faith of forsaken riffraff, without a leader, without God, in the heart of the desert. Who can stand in the place of that Micah, who was struck with the boldness of damaged faith, that Micah in the awful midrash I found, that when Israel was in Egypt building Pithom and Ramses, and when they did not fill their quota of work, the Egyptians came and took the children and put them in a wall of the building and placed rocks around them and on them so that the quota of their work would be full, and Moses our Teacher may-he-rest-in-peace said to the Holy-One-Blessed-Be-He: *Master of the Universe, why are the little ones punished with that death?* And the Holy-One-Blessed-Be-He said to him: *Those children do not come to a good end, if they go to a bad culture when they grow up, better they die innocent.* And Moses went and took one out of the building he was pressed in, and he was called Micah. And what will You say, that that baby pressed in plaster drove even You out of Your mind, and You too got fed up with Exile, and took the riffraff out of Egypt before it was time?

And what will You say about Micah, who even as a baby was judged by You with no mercy, and then was abandoned by You again in the desert with the whole nation? And what could he have done at that time? Take the last thing left behind by the leader who had disappeared, a platter on which Moses wrote *Rise Bull,* to bring up Joseph's coffin from the Nile. They took and threw it into the crucible, maybe to bring up Moses, who had plunged into the cloud. And since the platter said *Rise Bull,* an anointing calf came out of it.

That's what they managed to do with their faith of slaves, at the height of their degraded spirit: They took hold of that with dancing and celebration, that ridiculous statue, anointing. Saying, *These be thy gods, O Israel,* vulnerable with their yearning of faith, abandoned at the foot of the Mount, Amy, Emily, Amalia, *It's been a hard day's* and the beat of the voices that struck you all night.

And I, now? For I too am suspended between here and there. Like the Nation there, at the foot of the Mount. Like you, last year.

From the heat float the white verses, joining the thought between then and now. *And she went down unto the floor and did according to all that her mother in law bade her. And when Boaz had eaten and drunk, and his heart was merry, he went to lie down at the end of the heap of corn: and she came softly, and uncovered his feet, and laid her down. And it came to pass at midnight, that the man was afraid, and turned himself: and, behold, a woman lay at his feet. And he said, Who art thou? And she answered, I am Ruth thine handmaid: spread therefore thy skirt over thine handmaid; for thou art a near kinsman.*

Stop. Writing brought an unclear consolation. Rustle of the pages. Like Ruth who lay down next to Boaz, waiting until dawn, in the heaviness of the wheat. *And she lay at his feet until the morning: and she rose up before one could know another. And he said, Let it not be known that a woman came into the floor.*

Everything is stretched on one sheet, from the last watch of the night of Splendor of Essence to now, the Kingdom of Kingdoms. Everything is one hovering cascade of the shuttle. Until the rest that will spread from the other side of the warp. At the end of the Counting. On the night of Shavuoth this year.

I shall stop. Once again the prayer mounts. The slopes are shaking with a kind of excitement of the end of the night. I shall not explain the rest, what happened at the end, at dawn last year. Not now.

And the day after tomorrow is the Sabbath eve. Forty-one days. Essence of Essence.

May it be Your will, my God and the God of my forefathers, that if I am sentenced in Your court, that the grief I grieved tonight will be important, and You will tear up the evil decree on me; may it be Your will that You shall watch over me with Your eye of compassion, that eye open and slumbering not, he that keepeth Israel shall neither slumber nor sleep.

Forty-one days, which is five weeks and six days

of the Omer. Thursday night. Essence of Essence.

In the afternoon they came. Mr. Stern, the treasurer, and Mr. Borstein, a leader in the synagogue. In black caftans and hats, bringing the shadowy smell of their neighborhoods into the room. They stood embarrassed about having to trudge this far, to visit an unmarried woman. They refused to drink even water, as if the glasses were defiled.

"A delegation of contributors to the synagogue will soon come from America. We request Miss Amalia's permission to bring them to see how the Torah Curtain is progressing, so they will know what they are paying for. Meanwhile, we have delays in building, need additional permits from city hall to enlarge the entrance. There's no end to that in city hall ..."

Mr. Stern, the treasurer, stood behind; perhaps he felt uncomfortable. I had dealt with him in the winter, when the order for the Torah Curtain was arranged by Frieda Schmidt, there, in his office in the back of the synagogue, among piles of prayer books. And it is he who signs the monthly payments, the checks in a rabbinical hand that I cash at the post office bank.

"Miss Amalia is progressing, God be praised, beautifully. Beautiful work, Miss Amalia," he repeated. Wiping the sweat and dust from under the brim of his hat. While Mr. Borstein bends over the loom, feels the bulges of the woof, and smooths the threads, his big ears jerking under the tipped hat. "Yes, yes, very beautiful, very beautiful!"

I stood to the side, looking at them. Silence fell. And I couldn't help thinking how detached from everything here they looked, strangers to the heat, to the desert standing in the windows, like two refugees from a Yiddish vaudeville act. In their dark garb, with their sonorous voices, Mr. Stern, the treasurer, and Mr. Borstein, the leader, cautiously stroking the mounds of the woof as if examining fringes. Stumbling a bit among the arches. And soon, just as they came in, so they will press outside, without really being here. And without realizing what the Torah Curtain they're paying for really is . . .

HaShem, my God, You, who filled me with Your spirit, with wisdom and understanding, and with knowledge and all skills;

You, whose Torah Curtain of Your Temple of Heaven I tie with blue and purple and crimson and scarlet and fine linen is interwoven with cunning workmanship;

You, who called my name—Amalia, Amy, Emily, and repair of Mala's name, as You called the name Bezalel, the son of Uri, the son of Hor of the tribe of Yehuda, who knew how to combine the letters of Your Name to repair the world;

Your Name I make with all my body and soul, the threads of Your garment I tie warp and woof like angels coupling with one another, what was, what is, and what will be in one tying;

You, Whose embrace of truth I shall approach, hour by hour;

HaShem, my God, support me a few days more, until I finish the task . . .

Weaving, from six-thirty to sundown. More than twelve hours a day of hurling the shuttle, pressing the pedal, tightening the thresher, and hurling the shuttle again, until sundown, until the hour of Judgment, when I can no longer feel my exhausted shoulders.

Time is poured out quickly. The length of the remainder of the warp won't be enough even to write down the whole story of the weaving. Selling the first prayer shawls in Frieda Schmidt's store, the compliments heaped with blessings, and how I was scared to see one of the prayer shawls I had made with the fringes spread out in the shop window, among the embroidery and the Sabbath candlesticks, my moods displayed for everyone to read, entangled in it. And how afterward, at the end of summer, after the return from Tel Aviv and the commemoration in Café Shoshana, then, when everything was closed, I wandered at night from the crafts fair, and in my skull echoed the hollow words of the buyers assaulting the stand, pulling the fabrics. Straying madly in the night, the sharp barking of dogs at my heels.

And then the awful loneliness in the beginning of winter, months after the break with Isaiah. I didn't know if I would manage to hold on until the rains ended. Gazing at the desert for whole days, like an infinitesimal dying. And how in the heart of the frost, Frieda Schmidt suggested I weave the Torah Curtain and arranged the terms with the leaders of the synagogue they were building in the new neighborhood.

And the day the big loom arrived on the truck, and I abandoned everything. Going out in a panic for the afternoon, to the pale light on the slopes, and the cold wind whipping up in me the words of Maimonides as a bad omen, *While the sun, or the light, or the moon, or the stars be not darkened, nor the clouds return after the rain . . . This refers to the day of death. Thus, we can infer that if one remembers his Creator and repents before he dies, he is forgiven.*

I pushed onto the bus, carried by the jolting ride to the northern part of the city, walking in the old neighborhood among the yards gaping in the chilly light, the gutters, tin doors, beaten ends of laundry, washtubs. Straying in a blind search for that old Torah Curtain . . . What I heard from the man who came to buy embroidery wholesale in Frieda Schmidt's store, raising his hat, his head in the gloom, bristles of beard spotting his cheeks: "Yes, a Torah Curtain, a special one. After the war they found it in their cellars. The synagogue they burned. A wooden synagogue, how long did it take to burn it down? May their name be wiped

out! How long? Like a straw it burned. *The Torah Curtain* they wanted.
They took it down from the Ark of the Covenant before they set fire to
the place. What work . . . They hung it in their officers' club. Ha. After
the war, the Poles took it and hung it to decorate a church. Everybody
in the village knew it. They said it was ancient, maybe four hundred
years old, maybe more. Everything in gold and blue thread. Letters and
birds . . . That's afterward, with the later immigration to Israel. Com-
munists of all things. Those who came out of Poland then. Somebody
brought it. Came one day from Holon to Jerusalem and left it folded up
in a corner of the synagogue. Only when they opened it, did they understand what it was. There were some from the town who still remembered. Few survived. Maybe fifteen. Maybe less." The old Torah Curtain
he mentioned in the gloom at the glass counter, that one I was compelled
to see before I started weaving, as if there were some answer buried in
it . . .

I went through the market. At the end of a lane, I came on a woman
with a kerchief tied around her pale forehead, and I asked her for the synagogue. "There." She examined me and pointed. "There." She flung
her arm and pointed her chin toward a grass-covered staircase. And
when I turned my eyes back to confirm that really was the way, I saw her
watching me quietly, making sure I would leave her yard, depart from her
domain.

Finally I stood before the small building sunk in the ground between
two yards. The gate was locked at that time of the afternoon. My knees
trembled. Just going out that afternoon, when everything was so frail,
was beyond my strength. I didn't even dare stoop to peep in the crack of
the threshold. Between the houses flickered the raised street, and from it
a distant movement of passersby. A shuffling of men's shoes, white socks,
the hems of caftans, and the nimble feet of little girls in buttoned coats.
The rustle from the street enhanced the silence in the empty yard. I
slipped away, relieved that no one had noticed my coming or going.

I started putting on the loom the blue warp of the Torah Curtain. For
a whole week I threaded the liquid silk rings from the spools onto the
loom. Sharp cold pushed through the cracks of the windows, and sparks
of frost blossomed on the walls. A whole week, cold, counting with
clicks of the tongue on the palate, counting the numerical value of Your

Names that I secretly hid in the warp as a basis of the stripes of the prayer shawls, Y-H-V-H H-V-H-Y, ten five six five, YOD HEH VAV HEH and once again on the other side, five six five ten. A whole week threading the silk strands through the rake, in the warp's eyes that would be lifted to the head of the grooves by pressing the pedal, bringing them through the boards of the comb, and then tying their soft ends around the rod at the back. And all over again. A whole week. Emptying the spools by running the loops, threading and tying Your Names, YOD HEH VAV HEH, ten five six five, five six five ten, Y-H-V-H, and again, H-V-H-Y. One cord after another, hundreds of times. In the heart of the cold.

And since then, all the months of work twining the woof. In the rhythmic pull, being tied, top and bottom, first and last in one sheet. The breath of Your nose in the end of the thread growing shorter, and the breath of my nose coming close to You, with each winding, with the raising of the gathered woof. My fingers running in twining and Your fingers stretching the strings, holding the running thread, going further between the two skeins in Your hands, creating the world.

At first I almost didn't notice what was taking shape. The dizziness of weaving swept up everything. To get up to go to the shelf, to change a spindle that had emptied, to tie a cord to the end of a cord that stopped, to return to the stool and hurl the wedge again, to fasten the beater, the comb, the pedals by pulling the arms, and again shooting the shuttle from right to left, left to right, right to left.

Only when a sheet of fabric began rising from the base of the loom, in irrefutable testimony to what was already tied between the two of us, what happened last year also grew dim. Was covered, as with a sand screen, with the roughness of the running thread. All those waves of dread lest the pasts repeat themselves, waves of dread that would destroy you like the slaves fleeing from Egypt, recoiling in terror of Ba'al-Zephon that the magicians placed to frighten those who flee in the crevice of the mountains in the Mouth of Freedom. Those same waves of dread grew blunt, leaving in me only a kind of memory flickering for a moment as in the heart of a wayfarer, who has since gone wandering far off on the desert paths.

For whole days I was boldly borne by the weaving. For hours on end. Only You and I and the solidity of the fabric tied between us. Whole days in the mute dance of the body swaying, leaning on the pedal, the arms retreating with the press of the beater. With rhythmic drumbeats. Secretly coupling warp and woof, *a garden enclosed is my sister, my spouse; a spring shut up, a fountain sealed.* Warp and woof crushed with desire, nestling in the rustling sheet of the Torah Curtain, with the tightening, beating, renewing rhythm of the creation of Your Names. *Like a sheet in the hand of the embroiderer, he makes it even at will and makes it uneven at will, so are we in Your hand, O jealous and vengeful God,* look to the Covenant and ignore the Accuser.

And then, as I was leaning over to tie the end of one thread to the beginning of the next, Your breath passed across the back of my neck. And like lightning, I was aware of the awesome repair You placed in my weaving hands . . . And as the blood rose in my temples, I tasted for the first time the frightening taste of expectation, the one that will now fill my days. That dazzling melting, when the mist of Your kiss laps at my tresses, and my whole body is erect and melting to Your bending.

Yes, then, in the heart of winter, You came close to me, brought me close to You by the strings I was pulling with my own hands. You captured me in the secret net of longing for You, Terrible and Awful. Ever since, I have learned how to delve deep, so slowly, in pleasure, how to prolong the beating with silent breathing in a long, drawn-out coupling. How to kindle the cords, to rub carefully the bodies of the threads until all the sheaves catch fire. I have learned to separate the threads, to hold their bodies, to stroke them, slowly, delicately, one inside another, the electricity runs and burns in their tremor, and then to keep the flame in the chaff, to prolong the pleasure, to savor it more and more. Drunk on the new joy in my fingers I have also learned to twine an invisible layer of blue, to clasp Your Names, quivering in the depths of the brocade, the silk. I have even learned to add a third layer of hidden passion (the supreme joy of the act of love, *I sleep, but my heart waketh*), I twined a gold thread secretly into the rest of the threads. Hence the glow rising from the Torah Curtain, lapping the grass surrounding Mount Sinai, gleaming from every grain of dust in the desert, burning my limbs . . .

Yes, ever since I have known the recurring pleasure, the secret of *In Your goodness, You renew daily, perpetually.* And especially have I known the craving at sundown, *until the day break, and the shadows flee away,* when my hands quickly fasten the beater, and my whole body shakes from the weight of Your hips crushed over and over on my loins, fastening until our love swoons on the evening couches spread out red above Your City.

And with the embracing flaming between me and You, the rousing, quickening, inflaming caresses, like a great sea rolling the flying shuttle, rises the yearning for what will come with the end of the weaving. The madness to be naked, face to face, when our hands will thrust out and caress each other, warp and woof fastened in a true binding. And all the thousands of cords throbbing with love.

O, the mighty sweetness in this waiting to unite with You when the canopy of the firmament descends on the cherubs of our limbs, in the secret of the Holy Covenant. O my breath, the Husband of my youth.

Like the anchor in the hand of the sailor, he holds it at will and casts it at will, so are we in Your hand, O good and forgiving God; look to the Covenant and ignore the Accuser.

The day after Passover, I started the confession. Here, night after night, I open the pages on the little table, say a prayer, *May it be Your will,* and in the circle of lamplight bend over to write down the sheet of my life. The whole fabric, all the threads. What You engraved in the course of my life.

Night after night, I place my fat and blood on the altar before You, all my limbs. Confessing everything. And the ends I won't have time to connect to the sheet, the threads that will be left untied, I shall entrust in Your hands. I shall entrust everything, *with my spirit shall my body remain.*

Night after night, ever since Passover, spreading out the confession to You. *For nothing is hidden before Your eyes.*

Ever since Passover, night after night, I have been immersing here in the ritual bath of atonement, in the limited time, tied in the loom of the Counting.

Night after night, here, at the window overlooking Your city whose ruins You have chosen *me* to repair.

And in the silence behind my swollen shoulders, Your bending over me is already inflamed, and the mist of Your mouth fills my breathing, murmurs between my lips . . .

*Like the stone in the hand of the cutter, he grasps it at will and smashes
it at will, so are we in Your hand, O source of life and death, look to the
Covenant and ignore the Accuser.*

No, they couldn't fathom the secret of the Torah Curtain of the Ark, so
why the panic? They just looked at the open part. And even if they had
seen the end of the Tablets, they wouldn't understand what the Torah
Curtain was designed to cover. And yet, a profane roughness lingered
after they left. The leader, Mr. Borstein, and Mr. Stern, the treasurer . . .

I remained standing, leaning on the posts of the loom, the pounding
stuck in my throat. And so, even without any excuse to relieve the pain
in my shoulders or to go to the grocery store, I was impelled outside to
the afternoon, to the rustling of the clay on the slopes, to the flickering
of the Dead Sea in the distance. Finding myself in the empty alley in
white dirt—that grease-sprinkled dirt I scooped up last night and scattered on my hair, very slowly.

I bent down again to pick up a handful. No one is aware of the secret
covenant between me and You. I leaned gratefully on the doorframe,
and the hard clods roughened the skin of my hand. The valley turned
over below, the village houses, the graves, the slant of the slopes, haze of
yellow breathing.

And I understood that You had pushed me to stop the work and leave
the house to breathe into me Your breathing hidden in the dirt, streaming on the paths, among the stones. Slowly I inhaled the dryness of the
dust, the pungent sweetness, standing erect with pride that I had been
chosen, I, Your bloody wife, *I am black, black but comely, O ye daughters
of Jerusalem* . . . I, Amalia, Amy, Emily, and the incarnation of the tormented soul of Mala . . . I who knew Your awful wound . . . forever and
ever I knew, from the black pit, the terror . . . I shall repair You with the
sacrifice of soul and breath I shall make to You. I, Your salvation . . . I
shall repair what wounded You with the death of Mala, I shall redeem
Your ruins, when I shall give You face to face my loins in the secret mating of groom and Bride . . .

The haste was now so clear to me! I was filled with a great power of
faith, yearning to unravel the fabric from the loom at once, to go out immediately, wrapped in the Torah Curtain of Your Names, to the bottom

of the valley, to the heat of the mounds of dirt, to the great repair in Your arms gathering up my limbs. My breathing quickened, my lips murmuring, *Here I am and take me, me, Amalia, I, the forbidden that shall be allowed You.*

I lingered on the slope, as in those days last year, after Shavuoth, when I would leave off weaving the prayer shawls and go out in the afternoon, to sit, limbs dangling, on the slope, watching the Arab children playing below. The voices rising from them absorbed inside me. The movements of the women, the colors of their dresses bursting out of the cooking rooms, the smoke wafting to the waning day. Sounds growing sharp, stormy, cracking. Until sundown.

Among the playing children, my eyes were drawn to one little kinky-haired girl in a gray-striped pinafore. Day after day, she would tramp up among the rocks to an isolated aloe bush suspended on the slope, and kneel behind its fleshy spiked leaves, until the boy seeking hiding children trudged by. He surely saw her in the striped pinafore, crouched day after day behind that aloe, but by some tacit agreement, he would pass by her.

For hours I would gaze at the children playing among the rocks below me, sated with the voices echoing among the fragments of Your crushed body, lying on hills *meat unto the fowls of heaven.* Sinking to evening, to the noise of the trucks coming up from the roads in the distance, lowering my hands in the dust that remains hot even after the chill rises from the West. Caught in the helpless expectation of what is going to happen on Tisha b'Av. And when the children's shrieks were swallowed up in the kitchens lit with strange light, I too returned here.

Ever since then, I haven't seen the little girl. They must have sent her to some girls' school . . . Maybe across the Jordan, somewhere in the area spread out behind the cliffs in the distance. The area I shall never enter.

And everything that happened from then until now . . .

Today the slope was empty, and the dust burned on it. No child was seen among the rocks. Only a few chickens pecking in the ruins.

I went on between the dirt walls in the bitter odor of the mountain grasses. Your weeping was scattered among the stones, drained of the hatred of the inhabitants of the city. How they hold on to each other's throats, madly wanting redemption, calling Your Names in vain, coarsely trampling Your pain thrown at their feet. Buried here layer atop layer on the slopes. All those who were trapped in Your city in their yearning for You, and died in their yearning. And who can distinguish blood from blood in the trampled dirt?

I knew that, here, grief would be turned into awful pleasure for us. That great as the destruction is the exultation! That everything is Your Name, in all the Names and Appellations, the written and the writing and the fragments of the Tablets. For Tablets and fragments of Tablets are laid together in the Ark. For everything is Your Name, my Beloved and my Friend, and myrrh drips from Your ruins, the aroma of Your lust that will water my ruins. And I went on, in thanksgiving, laughing to myself at how nothing changes in the street as I pass, I whom You shall know in ten days! How no one realizes the magnitude of the joy already devouring my bones. And a calm was poured out in me, like the eternal Sabbath rest I shall know among Your martyrs.

I continued up the path, on the road climbing to the house of Fayge and Rabbi Levav (even from them, dearer to me than anyone else, I had to hide the happiness), and no longer was anything like then, in winter, when only the beginning of the Torah Curtain was strung on the loom, and I stopped working to get some air, climbing that path and the long skirt puffed on my legs. Opposite me, arm in arm like children, Fayge and Rabbi Levav came down in the limpid cold.

"Fayge wanted to go out a little," the rabbi apologized jokingly.

"And Amalia, too" added Fayge. "Come, join us." She clutched my elbow, leaning her short body between Rabbi Tuvia and me, leading the three of us among the flowering gardens at the top of the hill. At the fence of a yard with a dovecote, we stopped.

The doves cooed in the white winter light, pecking and quivering, skipping, pure, from the cote to the ground of the yard, to the tendrils of the vine, to the fence. "That's a male." The rabbi pointed at one hopping with the tuft of down on its head. "That's how you tell them apart from the female." He held out his hands and grabbed a bird that had landed on the fence, stroking its feathers, putting it between his hands.

I laughed because the light lay on the dove's feathers. Because the beginning of the Torah Curtain was already strung on the loom. Because that morning I flew the white thread of the doves in the sky of weaving, and a gold cord adorned its feathers. And with the same lightness, I went on and told Fayge and Rabbi Levav about Father's playing, about the soft notes stretched from his hands. About the beauty that always sounded through the house from the bedroom.

They nodded at me, surrounded me with their smiles, and shutting his eyes, Rabbi Levav said, "Yes, the souls slaughtered there are attached to the souls that awaken to faith, and they return to a higher repentance through them, entwined one in the other, in the flight of a dove, with marvelous ease." (Back then I didn't yet know about the only daughter, the daughter of their old age, a two-year-old baby who was lost there.)

The rabbi put the white bird on the lattice of the fence, where it shook itself for a moment, and then hopped lightly back among the doves making their way around the yard. Between the houses, the sight of the desert falling off into the valley became sharper, and in the purity of the cold rose the sight of the mountains of Moab etched in the distance. We went on arm in arm to the alley, Fayge's gray hair scattered under the flowered kerchief on her head. At the corner of the alley, we parted; Fayge waved to me. I went down the path leading back home. The same path I climbed today. The path where the thorns now emit their deep smell in the night.

And Fayge and Rabbi Levav, too, in their simple ways, couldn't imagine the task You assigned me. They too, the dear people, are retreating to their own area as the end of the Counting approaches. They won't be able to hold on to me now either, when the bridle You will harness when You mount me in Your gallop is stretched.

Like the ax-head in the hand of the blacksmith, he forges it at will and removes it at will, so are we in Your hand, O supporter of poor and destitute, look to the Covenant and ignore the Accuser.

Between the walls of the path the heat became intense. The sandals, the bare ankles, were covered with dust. And then finally the strangeness sown by the visit of Mr. Borstein and Mr. Stern was wiped out. I returned home with knees collapsing, closing the gate calmly. I bent over on the stool, reaching my arms to the loom, again and again fastening the thread to the beating of the fabric. Shadows filled the arches, and after the heat outside, my spirit returned in the coolness wafting from the walls.

I emptied the green thread onto the shuttle. The arms of the reel spinning fast pulled the whole room into their beating joints. A flutter of silk swept up, expanses of green rising and withdrawing in a dazzling flood. I found myself watching, drunk with the splendid beauty of the threads, as if their secret were revealed to me for the first time. I then joined the bobbins of green silk to a row of spools waiting for weaving, and I trembled. How dreadful was the sight! I leaned over the skeins, clutching them with my hands, putting them on their shafts, just to feel again and again the living suppleness. The blue, purple, yellow, gold . . . The miracle of threads You spun from the mouths of worms in Your world. Grabbing all that was to be embroidered in the silken winding, the hours that would unwind in the fabric.

At dusk, when I sent the shuttle flying at the end of the Tablets, the longing had risen so much that I stopped. I leaned my elbow on the loom, and I buried my head in the thickness of the silk, in the tremor seizing the depth of the Torah Curtain—all of me is already in You, O Lord. And then the voice burst out of my insides, echoing between the walls, the arches. Reciting blessing after blessing. A new song!

Ahh, the weaving—secret of the tying You revealed to me, as You revealed to the Nation, in the heart of the wandering, after the calf was smashed and the Tablets of Testimony broken, after You had almost deserted them, a handful of wanderers without a god, shattered to oblivion. There, with Your grace, You showed us how we could hold on to You, how, with our own hands, we could wind ourselves and You into one body, with the wisdom of tying, twining, and twisting, fastening and winding, sewing and making the bars.

All those clasps, bars, loops, rings, wedges of boards, gold hooks for the Torah Curtain, staves to bear the Tables, all those couplings You showed us, in Your grace, to make the Tabernacle, the ways You gave us so we would wind us together in the place You chose for Your Name to dwell.

Thou shalt make the Tabernacle with ten curtains of fine twined linen, and blue, and purple, and scarlet; with cherubims of cunning work shalt thou make them. Fifty loops shalt thou make in the one curtain, and fifty loops shalt thou make in the edge of the curtain that is in the coupling of the sec-

ond; that the loops may take hold of one another. And thou shalt make fifty taches of gold, and couple the curtains together with the taches; and it shall be one Tabernacle. . . . And thou shalt make curtains of goats' hair to be a covering upon the Tabernacle; and thou shalt make fifty loops on the edge of one curtain that is outmost in the coupling, and fifty loops in the edge of the second curtain which coupleth the second. And thou shalt make fifty taches of brass, and put the taches into the loops, and couple the tent together, that it may be one. . . . And thou shalt make bars of shittim wood: five for the boards of the one side of the Tabernacle, and five bars for the boards of the other side of the Tabernacle, and five bars for the boards of the side of the Tabernacle, for the two sides westward. And the middle bar in the midst of the boards shall reach from end to end. . . . And thou shalt make a vail of blue, and purple, and scarlet, and fine twined linen of cunning work: with cherubims shall it be made. . . . And thou shalt hang up the veil under the taches, that thou mayst bring in thither within the vail the ark of the testimony: and the vail shall divide unto you between the holy place and the most holy. . . .

Hah, Torah Curtain of atonement, body and soul. Linen shroud that will couple us fifty loops one to another, and the Tabernacle will be one. The blood of our love You will sprinkle on the curtain, *one upward and seven downward. One, one plus one, one plus two, one plus three, one plus four, one plus five, one plus six, one plus seven . . . As it is written in Your Torah: For on that day shall the priest make an atonement for you, to cleanse you, that ye may be clean from all your sins before the Lord.*

I stopped. My whole body shaking. Silently. As if an invisible hand were holding my hands to make me stop writing, so I wouldn't already reveal the Tikkun.

Another eight days until the last Sabbath, until the end of the work.

An earthly bird is stretched over the desert, spreading the black wing of the earth. Struggling in the threads of the feathers, lowering a wing of dust onto the fragments of Your destroyed Names, on the fragments of the Temple cast off in the sand, *meat unto the fowls of heaven.*

Another eight days until I shall weave with devotion to stitch together the abyss torn in You; with all my strength I shall toil, drunk with salvation, until a new mountain rises in the East where there is now a great valley, mountain of the one God, and on it the throne of Thy full Kingdom will be raised. The eternal light of Seven Days will rise on the rocks of the summit, *and the Tabernacle will be one.*

(The shaking plows my body. From fear or already from great joy . . .)

Like the glass in the hand of the blower, he shapes it at will and dissolves it at will, so are we in Your hand, O jealous and vengeful God. Look to the Covenant and ignore the Accuser.

six weeks

Sabbath night. Six weeks and one day. Forty-three

days of the Omer. Essence of Essence.

We have sinned, we have sinned, He will forgive.

It's hard to start over. After the flooding taste of rest. The last Sabbath night.

I made a Melaveh Malkah meal of dates and cheese. I ate slowly. Chewing and singing, into the dark sinking. Eating alone, deliberately, in the heart of the silence that enveloped me. God, King, God. The last meal before the seven days. The cottage cheese crumbs I gathered in a spoon from the edges of the plate. I ate slowly—to draw from the holiness of this Sabbath, to the thread that will still be stretched until the fiftieth day, at the end of the Omer.

Friday night caught me by surprise. The twilight was torn like a shout. The running of the waning day dimming to the grasses, the light that suddenly turned gray after the conflagration. And then, without any preparation, choking of joy sliced the breathing. At twilight. And afterward, in the women's section of the synagogue on the hill, turning back, to the West, *Enter O Bride, enter O Bride* . . . The time when all the men's voices swell behind the few women turning around at the head of the congregation, *Enter in peace, O crown of her husband, enter O bride, enter O bride.* The thick wave that flooded. As if another power is flowing from the West, reviving . . . And then going back on the starry night, with a full body within the Sabbath now, on the steep path. Always the same path that changes its face, like the hours of the day, like the times of prayer. The way of a man with a woman. The way of God with the world. The way of Amalia with the Sabbath . . . My ways that are spread out before you on the paths of Jerusalem . . .

Sabbath night, and it's as if the Additional Soul hasn't yet departed. The silence hasn't evaporated, like a constant humming. I haven't yet made Havdalah. I hurried to the pages as soon as the stars came out, for fear that You would stop the brightness, that You would renew the defilement of the serpent in the fingernails.

(I approached the Torah Curtain, I opened the cover over it to look for a moment at the thicknesses of the knots. Now the blue dust of the silken light covers the look. Relieved a bit.)

(An hour later.) I went out to pick fragrant herbs on the slope, and I recited Havdalah. Outside, the roughness assaulted me.

The sap of the Havdalah herbs stayed on my fingers. I brought them up to my face and the smells gushed so thick, so vibrant, that I burst out laughing. What joy to chant before You, to cut the darkness standing in the windows with a bursting song, *He Who separates between holy and secular* . . . And my elongated shadow moves, dancing on the arches . . .

Ahhh, how high is my spirit now, God my Creator, continuing to chant in writing, *Open the lofty gate for me! For my head is saturated as if with dew, my locks with the dewdrops of the night.* Everything is Your decree, everything was written, and buried in the woven writing, and I do nothing but fill after what You knew intended for me. Completing the cover until we shall burn completely when the holiday begins, next Sabbath night, wick to wick, one flame.

———

Another seven days. Until then, have to complete what is left. Finish and clean. Got to think of everything, down to the last detail. Even blurring the traces. Of course . . . First the Torah Curtain. To finish weaving the frame fast. And then taking it down, cutting it and tying it. Hope I'll get everything done in five days of work (actually five and a half days—until Friday afternoon).

Also have to find time (maybe on Monday, the first day of Sivan) to finish with the photos. The best thing is to bury everything, along with the boxes, and say Kiddush, properly. Possibly on the Mount of Olives, at the foot of the slope. The dirt there is loose. It will be easy to dig at night and cover it quickly. (Just be careful that nothing happens. I couldn't afford to let anything happen now, a few days before the end.) Yes, got to be strong and finally finish with the photos! To be ready for You, free, to take the place of holy Mala in our wedlock.

The bundle of pages I shall leave here, on the table. The confession. In recent days, I have sometimes thought of bringing them when I come to You, packed on my breastbone, beneath the wrapping of the Torah Curtain, so that I shall return everything to You, me and my chronicles . . . But, no, I shall leave on the table the testimony we engraved together. The wind that goes through here, in the empty room, will leaf through the pile of pages. And Stein, who will come after the holiday from Tel Aviv, as he wrote, "I'll arrive late . . ."

(How he will knock on the locked gate at night. Stand with his limbs drooping when I won't open the door, wiping the sweat off his forehead . . . He'll run to call the cab driver waiting behind the motor rumbling in the night, grumbling about the delay in the dangerous neighborhood, and finally the driver will drag his clumsy body from the cab, will lean his broad shoulder on the gate, Stein neighing next to him, thanking him, confused, don't understand why it's closed, really don't understand . . . will promise to pay for the special service, the headlights of the cab striking his brow, the shiny suit. And then the driver will finally break down the gate. And Stein will hurry inside, into the empty room, and the loom, whose arms will be empty in the middle, only amputated silk loops twisted on the back of it. He'll run around among the few pieces of furniture, scrabble in the closet, among the clothes. Shak-

ing. Especially his hands. And he won't find anything, of course . . .
Only the pile of pages packed on the table. Sorry, Stein. I finally finished
her off in the dark of the *appapatz* . . . Really apologize, Stein . . .)

Yes, still pursuing the screaming voice of Ludwig Stein . . . Still. Becoming clear as the white sheet at the end of the dark. As if I long to
stand again, for the last time, before his scurrying look, as if I still need
him, this living fear . . .

Late at night. Hot air. The refrigerator's rumble like the memory of a former life. I still don't know what time it is. Maybe my favorite part of the
night. Two. Maybe three. No trace of the moon. Darkness of the end of
the month. No movement, except the shaking of stars in the enormous
journey of the Sefirot. Mixing heavily, rising, sinking, fertilizing each
other in the dark. The thick sap of the mountain herbs spurting from the
juice of coupling.

The deepest hour of the night. Behind me the strings of the Torah
Curtain turn over. A meager sea of weaving, tense and swarming. The
internal hour of the night. The last hour.

And I was already clinging to You, the Sabbath, in total devotion,
annihilating all being, annihilating all acts, God of acts. I was already the
Sabbath in supreme repentance to You, the God ever living.

It was You before the world was created, my Beloved, it is You since the
world was created, my Bridegroom, it is You in this world, and it is You in
the World to Come. Sanctify Your Name through those who sanctify Your
Name, sanctify Your Name in me, Amalia. Blessed is He Who sanctifies
His Name among the multitudes, blessed is He Who sanctifies those who
sanctify Him, blessed art Thou, Thou, Thou.

Is that how we shall whisper, embracing each other, when You will
sanctify me and I shall give myself to You, like Nadab and Abihu, destroyed before You, like seventy of the elders of Israel who saw You in
the sapphire stone, like our Teacher Moses, the greatest of the Prophets,
but no man knoweth of his sepulchre. Is that how we shall whisper, mouth
to mouth, when You will hold the back of my neck, when we shall cling
tongue to tongue, when You will lap my insides. And You will want me,
a full offering, there, at the bottom of the desert.

———

In seven days, I shall come to You, washed and adorned, on the paths going down in the opened whiteness. The Torah Curtain of our Canopy, blue and sky, I shall spread out to You in the gorge of the desert. On this couch You will lavish our love, God, when You will want and desire me, Amalia, and Your desire is toward me. And You will cling to me, and You will know me, longing, on the day that will be entirely Sabbath and eternal contentment . . .

The watchman has come; the Savior has come; the dawn has come and also niiiight.

Even now the time isn't cut off, the smell of the herbs stuck to the fingers doesn't fade. As if the space of the Sabbath was not breached.

Forty-four days of the Omer. Power of Kingdom.

There's no point in continuing to write. I won't finish anyway. Everything has stopped. The sticky heat clouds the eyes. I went back to the pages only to hold on to something. To continue like a robot. In a stupid habit. Opening the pile, bending over, pecking the pen on the paper . . .

Everything's over. Dark. And everything I thought of doing before You—the true repair, the sacrifice of confession, body and soul, all the prayers I wound at night in writing and by day in threads before You—everything is crushed in one hour. From what the rabbi's wife, Yocheved, told me ostensibly by accident.

Stein will come here, before the end of the Counting, to take what belongs to him.

Everything is torn. Everything that was woven intentionally down to the last threads.

In the afternoon, something cracked. When the heat was at its peak. In the middle of weaving. Hands suddenly looked enlarged, moved like someone else's. All the weaving shrank for a moment. To some dot that spread and swallowed everything, even the room, and then was singed. And again the sight of the strange hands (so thin) moving the beater, raising the shuttle.

I pulled myself off the stool by force. To cut (*therefore* I went out, the panic preceded the blow), watching my thin figure hesitating in the door. The heat struck the alley, burning the afternoon, seething. From behind closed shutters they looked—as soon as the sound of the lock is heard, they peep, don't miss a single glimpse of the Jewish lunatic, the weaving spider. For the time being they don't hurt. Too crazy. (Until the lunacy itself will incite them to explode, to slaughter me at the loom . . .) For the time being they just watch silently from behind the shutters.

(As they looked at the girl who ran away here last year, tramping to the valley wailing like one of the mourners. She ran without looking where she was going, a terrified mass of shouts and a swarm of hornets she jolted from the nest stormy at her heels. Running away, the insects bristling in a murderous train in her enormous mane of hair. Fleeing the clasp of death, mad with pain, dripping carcasses of hornets, thorns, her hands outstretched before her. She went through the neighborhood, before their astonished eyes as they stood in the doors of the houses and looked, not blocking her way, not coming out to pour a tank of kerosene on her to slay the hornets. Just looking at the winged death of the hornet-galloping girl, until she disappeared among the rocks on the slope. There, in the maze of caves the insects used up their poison in her, dropping with choked foam from her lips. Only the next day did they go to drag down her body. They put her at the edge of the village. An ambulance came and quickly removed the bundle wrapped in a white sheet.)

Woe is me that I have destroyed the Temple with my transgressions, and burned the Tabernacle of Holiness, and have exiled the children of Israel among the nations.

Woe is me that I have lengthened the exile so much by my evil and bitter longings.

The shouts of Rabbi Avuya of Blessed Memory were poured on the slope on the night of the seventeenth of Tammuz last year—his voice was torn in our traces among the trees, and Isaiah sobbed next to me—

I thought that tonight I would confess about that night in Tammuz last year. There will be no more repair. Everything has slipped away.

(And to think that less than twenty-four hours has passed since the exultation that last Sabbath night. How could I have been tempted to believe? What a fall from the weakness of belief to the sharp sobriety now . . .)

I trudged around with the bag, I don't know how long. The dirt on the side of the road was burning, and squads of marchers suddenly flooded the neighborhood with banners, and I didn't remember why. I finally landed at the bus stop on the highway, the trucks vomiting exhaust, and only one thought stuck in my head: to go to the city and from there on another bus, to Rabbi Israel Gothelf. An urgent primitive need for family . . . I pushed onto the bus with a little money and a fare card, which had apparently expired long ago—the fare had changed twice since then . . .

I was belched out into the burst of heat in the mountain neighborhood. The broad street, stuck on the peak, was whipped with sand. The light on the bare stone facades, the wretched bushes, the grease spots on the asphalt. Before I went out, I hadn't gathered up my hair, and it struck my back with the wailing of Mala, who was tangled behind me, in the blaze of the afternoon. A dry wind pushed out from between the buildings, raising screens of dust from the valley, tapping the plucked rosebushes. The wind whistled contemptuously at me. Yes, I know, the weeping is tangled behind me. I know, my passage disturbs the street's serenity, I must no longer go out of the house into the light of day.

I arrived at about three. Finding shelter in the cool staircase, in the scratchy steps among the marble tiles, echoing to that door. *Heart heart and flesh.* Sarale opened the door, her kinky hair bound with a rubber band. She looked with a little girl's curiosity at the thin figure standing in the door, covered with dust, disheveled, and all my strangeness was reflected in her examining eyes, along with the great fatigue.

"Sarale, who is it?" the rabbi's wife, Yocheved, burst into the vestibule, extending her arms to me.

(The last time I was there was Purim. Also a sudden impulse. To travel on two buses to bring holiday refreshments. Yocheved opened the door, urging me immediately to the rabbi's study: "Israel will be happy, come in." Through the open door I saw his silhouette bent over against a background of orange curtains.

"Is everything all right?" He raised his face with the smell of books and the sourness of wool.

"Bless God. I came to wish you a happy Purim."

"Yes, yes, happy Purim." He chuckled in embarrassment, as if everything were all over. "All the best, Amalia."

I gazed at the fingers hovering over the book. *Maybe Gemara Blessings*, I thought, *Tanna Rabbi Yosi* . . . And also about the distance, I thought, about the time that had gone by, closing his face in the orange glow.)

"Amalia! What a surprise! So glad you came. The rabbi isn't home, but come in, come in. Sit down a little. Since you've come all the way."

And the whole time I was making my way inside behind her soft body, one thought was drawn in me: how she would receive the announcement in another week and her face would gape. "Why, she was right here in my kitchen," she would shout. "A week ago! She sat, maybe an hour. We chatted." Having a hard time understanding in that dull goodness of hers. "She was fine. I didn't sense anything strange. That is, no more than usual. Really, I can't understand . . ." A distant thought in the body walking in the corridor.

"I'm preparing for the Seven Blessings of Esther Blaustein's wedding. Remember her? A class behind you. Here, have some."

A slice of chocolate cake was laid on a plate in front of me (the same sweet cake as last year?). I sat down exhausted, reconciled to the simplicity of Yocheved's activities, the noise of the dishes banging against one another and the counter, the opening of the oven, the warm smells spreading from it into the kitchen, and the girls bursting in to put a water glass back on the counter, chasing a ball that went astray. Staring roundeyed at the unusual guest.

"So how is the work of the Torah Curtain going, Amalia?"

No, I didn't have the courage to reject the simple affection, the weight of motherliness that enveloped me. All I need is a small corner of a house and I crawl into it like an abandoned dog. I didn't have the strength to jolt Yocheved from her baking and her rotating movements. What could I tell her, the rabbi's wife, about the shrinking of the letters of the Commandments into one dot, about the threads now leading me at will, about the great excitement, about what has to be completed—everything I still believed yesterday with complete faith that I would do, all the miserable "decisions" of last night, Sabbath night?

"I was so impressed by what I saw at your house; it's really wonderful!" She looked at me admiringly. "It wasn't easy to get there, you really do live far away, Amalia," she added and chuckled. (After all, she admitted that she hadn't "been passing by." She's not capable of doing harm, even with a little white lie.) With the back of her hand, she wiped the sweat from under the wig stuck to her forehead. "But it was worth it, it was really worth it! So beautiful, what you're weaving! A great merit for the synagogue that such work will hang in it!"

She went on kneading, her big chest moving as she leaned over the pastry board running on the flour-covered counter. Pulling the dough, putting it into a round pan, molding mountains and dents in it with quick taps of a spoon, putting the whole thing in the oven, slamming the door: "There, another cake!" And she returned to crushing the powders with a dough of oil and white and yellow clots of egg, trembling under her strong hand.

"It's really great, the Torah Curtain you're making, Amalia! You can see you're an artist. You know, I had no idea you were a photographer before, you never said so. And you even had an exhibit in New York! Nice, Amalia, special! Not that it's suitable work for somebody who's repenting, but I was impressed to hear it." She prattles on, blurting out words in blocks. "You know, Mr. Stein from America was here . . . Yes, we respect Mr. Stein very much. A generous Jew, even if he is non-observant . . . He told us about the pictures you took in Poland and about the album. I was very impressed with the idea of publishing the photos of the pianist may-she-rest-in-peace. And Rabbi Israel was too. Yes, let them know what kind of people lived before the war! Let them know who they murdered, may their name be wiped out! Let everyone know about their heroism, their martyrdom. A nice idea to make a commemoration in an album. It would also be a comfort to your parents-of-blessed-memory. Of course they were special people. People who suffered a lot, may God have mercy . . ." She went on without any idea of what her words were doing to me.

"Mr. Stein will come from New York, God willing, for the holiday in Jerusalem. He'll stay with us for the Sabbath and the holiday eve. He wants to study a little with Israel, to participate in the Shavuoth Tikkun. He's interested . . . He'll come before the holiday, on Thursday night. He'll stay in the hotel in the neighborhood, so as not to violate the Sabbath. Maybe you'll come too, for the meal on the eve of the holiday, Amalia, stay for the Tikkun, the way you used to . . ."

I stood up. Wavering. Everything was spinning. The kitchen, the dishes, the white eggshells.

He'll come on Thursday, he'll stay in a hotel in the neighborhood, so as not to violate the Sabbath . . . And where will he go after he puts down the suitcase, eh? He'll take a taxi, and without any hesitation, he'll knock on the door! He'll come immediately, even before the holiday. To take the boxes . . . What could be simpler, to knock, to apologize perhaps, and simply take. They're his, after all . . . He has just been waiting all the time for the right moment. Why else all this contact with Rabbi Israel, the generous contributions to Neve Rachel? I know Stein's methods. He gave me an extension, four years. What's right is right. Now he'll come and take.

I staggered from the mighty blow, pushed forward blindly. Yocheved trailed after me in the corridor. The little girls came out too, stood in the doors of the rooms. Yocheved kept going on in embarrassment behind me: "I really envy you for having such work. When the children grow up a little, I too . . ." Wiping her hands on her apron. "So come, come, Amalia . . ."

I burst outside, to the staircase. The little girls pushed out behind me. On the ground floor, I stopped a moment. From behind the doors, the neighbors' voices poured out. The mustiness of the storerooms wafted from the cellar. At the top of the shaft, the tiny heads of Sarale and Shoshana flickered above the banister, watching me.

He'll come on Thursday. Another four nights. I can't stop envisioning how he'll come gasping, how he'll stoop over the doorsill in the dark, pluck away my awfully skinny hand, push into the vestibule: "Amy, dear, I've come to you, you know . . ." He'll stand in the middle of the room breathing heavily, will survey the Torah Curtain, the pages, will understand immediately how I finally wanted to finish with her. All his life Stein has loved Mala, knows her smell like a dog. And then he'll take the photos. All the boxes.

In another four days he'll come to tear her out of the fabric, the pages, to stop her breathing bending over my hair. And maybe he has already torn. Maybe that's what's broken. That's why all the talk about Mala is now so painful. As if the breathing were already torn from my words, as if the offering I placed before You were slapped back in my face.

Violent fatigue crushes the temples. Squashes the pages. The hands go over the table, enlarged like the degenerate limbs of a strange creature. Everything is slipping away. Like a distant madness. The friction of the pen on the paper.

Everything is only a pretense. The cloth will remain between us empty, a strip of Torah Curtain cut from its threads, a wretched mass of silver melted with threads and saliva, *these be thy gods,* and these pages, the wretched testimony . . .

Just madness addressing You, *The Lord, The Lord, God merciful and gracious, longsuffering, and abundant in goodness and truth* . . . Just madness, this stupid effort. And the weak yearning to be in You, at once. Everything is only an impotent lie, wrapped in death . . .

A thick smell, almost nauseating, of night spread on the window. Foam sticks to the murmuring lips now. There's no breathing.

When I left Yocheved, I made my way, stunned, through the rocks on the slope. Suddenly I found myself under the building of Neve Rachel. The back windows. On the balcony of the classroom are broken chairs. On the second floor, from the window of the room that was once ours, the curtain Elisheva hung waved.

In the jolting of the bus, the sun burned, streaming dark from the forehead to the eyes, to the nose flattened hard against the banging window.

I couldn't go back home, to the Torah Curtain I had left exposed. I wandered aimlessly, all of me open to the orange glow torn in the West above the darkening treetops.

In the gloom of the valley, a group of marchers was revealed to me, a human serpent winding on the slope with a shrill noise and a waving of flags: Jerusalem Day, commemorating the liberation of the city in the Six Day War. How did I forget? Irony of the dates, of the holidays, that tie my course . . .

My wrath burst over them, over those marching on the slope . . . because they penetrated the area I thought You had kept for *me* within You. In my stupidity, I thought . . . How could I have believed that only I would be allowed to tread in Your rooms, that only I had been chosen by You—You who will never be satisfied with lovers, You who can never have enough . . . A dry contempt, distant blow on the temples, scrambles everything.

How I was rejected by You, crushed like a pesky fly. How You hurled me from You humiliated, abandoned . . . Sending Stein here to ruin everything, two days, only two days before the date that was set!

Silence now. For a moment, the humming of the heat stops. Only the shoulders shake, all by themselves. Dry, choked shaking, jolting the whole body. And the awful wrists bang the table with a strangled weeping.

(The weeping is only from offense, not from real pain. Choked with wrath, like a baby, that Stein will come to ruin me before the end, that You crushed the effort like that, so casually, God of jealousy and revenge . . .)

What wretched anger, self-pity. Can't stop, like a little girl. And the weeping that tears out of the sweat under all the wool of the winter clothes and the undershirt and the hot stockings, because suddenly it became hot, even though the sky is so black, that's why I didn't wait in the staircase for Father to come from the wholesale market and warm up the food. I can't wait there in the dust of the cold stairs because the peepee is getting away from me, and the heart is already so pressed from the bad clouds and the peepee that makes the knees jump, that I have to run with it down all the stairs to the yard, and I went on fast to the store, and my heart is sour with great fear. Until I found Mother alone in the store, because Father was already gone, and now he won't find the little girl at home, and won't know what to think, why isn't the little girl at home! And Mother's face is covered with that sour thing like the sky, sitting be-

hind the counter, as if customers will come right away, even though nobody comes in the whole time. But Mother mustn't get mad, I'll sit down
here on the crates, and eat the orange that Mother peeled, will stuff it into
the mouth even without sugar. Will sit here with only Mother in the
empty store, and the big door open to the noise of the buses leaping
from the stairs under the sidewalk. That's only because it's so hot with
the clothes and the sweat in the coat with the tight lining that sticks to the
sweater that I put the peeled orange on the corner of the crate for a moment, and when I moved to take off the coat, the tower of crates tottered
and the orange fell down, even though I wanted with all my might to hold
it in the crack left between the crates and the wall, and when I pushed my
whole hand up to the shoulder, I was stabbed with pieces of tin, and
that's why I shouted. Then Mother came out from behind the counter in
the blue apron, and walked with steps heavy as stone, and took out from
behind the tower of crates the orange covered with radish leaves and
pieces of dirt, and started shouting, even though I showed her on the
sleeve that it was so hot, she just shouted more and more, why wasn't I
even sorry about what had happened! *Throwing away good food instead of
eating, so that it would rot there, bad girl! Bad girl!* She hit with her hand,
which had suddenly become hard, *If you only knew what it is to cry from
hunger, bad girl! You wouldn't throw food away anymore, if you only knew
yourself what it is to starve for bread, bad girl!* And Mother's voice weeping with the small animal that comes out of her mouth and bites with
sharp teeth. Then I quickly started slapping Mother's blue apron with all
my might, before the little animal with its sharp teeth finished me off in
the *Appapatz*. Hitting with all my might the strong smell in Mother's
apron, with weeping that was choked with weakness, hitting Mother's
soft belly. And Mother's hand also weeps, hits my coat. Until we finally
fall together to the floor. And next to us, the orange with radish leaves
and dirt also falls. And suddenly, the *appapatz* was over, and Mother was
Mother once again, and she got up off the floor slowly, with her wrinkled
apron, and went behind the counter, and her eyes looked straight ahead
and not at me at all. And I sat back down on the crates, and I didn't run
away to stand outside at the stairs to the sidewalk, I just closed my mouth
tight so the clump with the rotten smell of onion wouldn't get in, and I
looked at Mother's shaking mouth, arranging the ledger book with sharp

movements, for no reason, closing and opening it next to the potatoes on the oilcloth, standing with her small face, and the little animal coming out of her mouth weaker and weaker, *My little girl raises her hands to me, my little girl . . . What did I do to deserve that? After everything that was . . . My little girl raises her hands to me . . . So why was it worth it to live, for what? To stand here in a store from morning to night? . . . Even Stashek still loves her like I don't exist . . .* And her little hands shake with dry blows on the counter, *And now my little girl raises her hands to me, like a stranger's child. We named her after her, like he wanted, and now she hits me, throws me out of the house, out of the last place I have left . . .* Then she suddenly stopped and saw me sitting on the crates and looking, and she wiped her nose on the handkerchief in her little hand, and looked once more, and her little face was completely flooded. And then a woman came in and Mother spoke with her in a foreign language and walked around to the crate to bring an onion and weigh it, and with all the sweat under the big coat I was already shaking because it had become cold, and the customer went out and then another one came in, and Mother's voice was tired with cracks of dust, and at the entrance of the store the floor tiles were crooked, and in their corners, in the dirt, grass grew and wasn't bent even though everybody walked on it, and the rain didn't fall from the black belly of the clouds either. And then, when it was dark, Father came back and said he had looked for the little girl everywhere and was at his wits' end. And Mother stood behind the counter and I was on the crates. And we didn't tell Father about the dirty orange with radish leaves or about what had happened. Mother didn't tell and I didn't either. And not afterward either, when I was left alone with Father, and people asked how Ruzia suddenly got sick and died.

And suddenly, regrets for Mother. If anything is alive now, it's only regrets. The weeping jolts the shoulders. As if something was finally released. As if Mala is no longer blocking . . .

And instead of going to Yocheved, why didn't I go to Isaiah? On the same bus, I could have gone on another four stops to his new yeshiva. To think that we are now in the same city, and no wall, no vow, will stop the nocturnal flow between here and his breathing, sleeping with his neck resting on the pillow. And now, why don't I stop and go to him immediately? Why do I go on writing here? . . . To whom? What for?

Fatigue lies on my neck like a beheading blade.

(And if I have a child—an infant, a son. I and Isaiah. Our child. Despite the torments. Maybe that's the sanctification of Your Name?)

Isolation now. Total isolation. The wish expires before it rises. The need to hold the pages until the shaking stops. The face is reflected from the pages like the visage of a lunatic. The fear of stopping. The rest is only fantasy.

May it be Your will that by virtue of the confession of truth— May it be Your will that by virtue of the torments of truth—that by virtue of the sacrifices of righteousness sublime and whole— Behold I was shapen in iniquity; and in sin did my mother conceive me.

The mouth mutters prayers, and the hand writes. Carcasses of words placed on the paper . . .

First night of the month of Sivan.

(Forty-five days, six weeks and three days.)

What madness all day. Frightened rambling through the axes of the city, on the slopes. After I hadn't gone out of the house practically for months. Impelled in a burst of wretched insult . . . Choked by a stupid rage that the world goes on, that nothing stopped because of what happened . . . Hurt and humiliated. As if that "cosmic" break should have echoed from one end of the world to the other . . . As if everything should really have stopped because of what happened . . . such wounded pride, such weakness . . .

I ran ever since morning, unable to stay here after the night passed in stupor and weeping. With self-pity, I fled from the road in the shadow of the walls, exposed there to the cars climbing along next to the wall, indifferent to my ruins. Plunging to the bushes to escape the humiliation, trying to hold on to the rough warm contact of the earth, bending over and scooping dirt in my hands . . .

When did the bubble finally burst? Maybe in the afternoon. When I went to seek shelter near Rabbi Avuya Aseraf's abandoned house. Walking around in a blur outside the forsaken garden, behind the blacksmith shop, near the closed windows of the house. My head exploding. And on the way back, coming upon the crazy young man on the slope, at the bend of the road. He heard the tapping of my sandals and turned. In a wool coat fastened up to his neck despite the terrible heat. Thrusting forward, trapping me in his opaque look, penetrating me with danger. He came up, pulled a small knife, held it in front of him, approaching with silent steps. Only up close was his muttering clear, *Jesus is our Lord, Jesus is our Lord* . . . I didn't retreat, frozen with fear. Until I noticed that the glittering knife was simply a key he held in his clenched hand. And then the sharpness in his eyes also grew blunt, as if he had lost interest all at once. And he turned aside. Only then did I evade him, running across the thicket down to the intersection. Yes, dread finally cut through the screen of self-pity. And I returned here quietly. No one raised a hand or a stone to me. Passing by the children at the side of the alley, the mangy dogs, the women wiping their hands on the hems of their dresses, spreading their thighs in the dark to multiply Your seed.

First of the month. Total darkness. Heavy fatigue from wandering all day. And some muteness now. Even the memory of the mocked march doesn't rouse a thing. I didn't pray all day. Everything is unraveled. Even sitting down to write now is only from a need to report, to document what is happening, the unraveling . . .

Night of the first of the month. At Neve Rachel on nights of the first of the month, Rabbi Israel discussed the midrash on the waning of the moon. Trying to obscure with his gray voice the seriousness of the quarrel between the insolent moon and the Holy-One-Blessed-Be-He, who punishes her in rage and shrinks her; yes, even though her claim was just . . . He ponders, facing the girls gazing at him. Rabbi Israel Gothelf has a hard time explaining the sacrifice of the goat on the first of the month, who comes, as it were, to atone to the Holy-One-Blessed-Be-He for the defect he gave the moon, trying to blur some incriminating testimony that was forgotten in the records, not to raise a question of Your acts. And yet, it was the only time I saw Rabbi Gothelf hesitate, as if he were admitting reluctantly what is now absolutely clear to me.

And how did I think that, like Ruth, I would be redeemed, like Ruth, who redeemed the dead with her love . . . Who had the strength to interrupt her mourning and go to the patient gleaning of the stalks, joining them one to another into a sheaf . . . And everything I hoped with complete faith to repair with the sacrifice of my life—nothing was atoned. You rejected the sacrifice.

Woe is me for the ruin of the Temple.
Woe is me for the burning of the Torah.

The voice of Rabbi Aseraf, may his righteous memory be a blessing, echoed all day in waves of heat, thrusting out again. And now, too, at night, it doesn't stop. The snorting voice poured onto the mountain:

Woe is me for the exile of the Shekhina.
Woe is me for the foe was increased.
Woe is me for the profanities of Your great Name.
Woe is me for the grief of all the worlds.

What an irony, that precisely this evening I had planned to confess on the seventeenth of Tammuz last year. Now, when all yearnings have burst, and the pariah grave of Rabbi Avuya is covered by the sealed night and Your silence. What a cruel, crazy staging . . .

After the fast of the seventeenth of Tammuz last year, Isaiah burst in here. Straight from the rabbi's house. He ran all the way. The fast was not yet broken; he leaned over in the kitchen to drink from the faucet and the streams plastered the sides of the sink. He stood disheveled, water glistening from the bristles of his beard, repeating in shock that he had never seen the rabbi in such a state, never, never . . . And Isaiah's eyes were dammed with that dark gauze, which was to muddy them again on the night of Tisha b'Av. "It was awful, awful, Amalia . . . He finally threw us out. He stood in the door and shouted: 'It's your fault, your fault that the Temple was destroyed! For your transgressions the Holy Tabernacle was burned!' . . . You can't imagine the rabbi's eyes, Amalia. The destruction, the destruction . . ." He vomited the words in the kitchen.

When I finally could ask him what was happening to the rabbi now, he answered that he didn't know, he really didn't know what he was doing now, alone. "Alone," he kept repeating over and over: "Alone. Alone . . . he stayed there all alone, standing in the doorway and screaming, 'Destroyers of the House! Destroyers of the Temple!' You understand?"

Isaiah's voice broke, and for a long time he sobbed, his face buried in the window, as if he could see through the darkness of the valley what was happening at that hour on the peak opposite. I was silent behind his shaking shoulders. What could I say to Isaiah? Ever since the beginning of the month of Tammuz, he had been going to Rabbi Avuya every night, hinting enthusiastically that the rabbi recited the Priests' blessing a lot, a special Tikkun, special, Amalia . . . He gazed at me, excited at what was done at the rabbi's house on the mountain, at our approaching nuptials, ignoring what was going on in me at that time. And I, paralyzed with increasing fear, was drawn to the commemoration on Tisha b'Av, and didn't say anything to Isaiah, didn't admit that the whole wedding was a lie, a lie, just a fantasy, like the pale disk of the moon that will appear on the night of Tu b'Av on the hills that will remain joyless.

It's hard to say now what exactly drew me to Rabbi Avuya Aseraf, who was shouting into the night. Maybe even then there was a need to draw strength from destruction, to gaze at the sight of Rabbi Avuya's brokenness and thus to fortify myself for what was still before me . . . For suddenly I said with an ambiguous resolve, behind Isaiah's back, "I don't think we should leave the rabbi alone now. We have to go to him."

We left immediately, almost running.

The rabbi's yard was dark, and there was no light in the windows either. And more than ever the dark little house seemed to be leaning on the verge of the abyss. Isaiah stopped as if he were examining something

in the lights playing on the slope. The night wind struck the trees, the
trunk of his neck, the unruly curls on the back of his neck.

Already I regretted my impulse to return there, and yet I took Isaiah's
thin hand, leading him through the gate as gently as I could, as if apologizing in advance for the pain he would know. "Come, come on, let's
go in."

"Maybe there's no need, Amalia . . ."

I persisted, went through the beds of flowers and herbs. Not knowing that tonight I would see Rabbi Avuya Aseraf for the last time. I
knocked on the locked door. No answer. I knocked again. The echo died
away in the silence of the grove. And then the door moved, and Rabbi
Avuya Aseraf stood leaning in the frame, his dark face chiseled in the red
flash of his silver mane. Looking at us and withdrawing without a word,
leaving the entrance gaping behind him.

I went through the gloom among the few implements of the rabbi's
life, the strewn chairs, the desolation steeped in mists of incense. I pulled
up a bench and sat down. Isaiah sank onto the bench, burying his face on
the table. I sat erect, my back to the rabbi.

At first only a dry sound of felt slippers, plodding. And then, as if
from a distance, bleatings of the broken voice cracking to the sweet
stench:

Master of the univerrrrse, Master of the univerrrrse!
Woe is me for my sin, woe is me for my transgressionsss!
Woe is me for the crime I committed in this incarnation and in other
   incarnationsss!
Woe is me that I destroyed the Temple by my transgressionsss!
Woe is me that I burned the Holy Temple and exiled the children of
   Israel among the nations!
Woe is me that I made the exile so long with my bad and bitter lusts!

Even without turning my head, I knew how he swayed and paced, as
if deep in prayer. From one end of the room to the other, back and forth,
like rhythmic whippings of sand.

He stood behind us, gasping for a moment, and once again his innards were poured out: "Sinners, sinners! It was all for nothing, for noth-

ing, wicked ones! . . . Pretending to seek repentance . . . to be souls of carcasses that returned to their roots to repair the world . . ."

Next to me, Isaiah trembled, his face pressed to the table. His trembling shook the bench underneath us.

"Just pretending they'll build the Temple between the seventeenth of Tammuz and the ninth of Av, that they'll restore the splendor to the city that is profaned . . . Generation of darknessss! To spy out the land they were sent and *they brought up a slander!* Weeping for generations there will be, weeping for generations!"

How acidic, steeped in mockery, did the rabbi's voice rasp. His hot breath poured out on the back of our necks. Its jet spread on my neck, over my shoulders, all the way down my back. And I wasn't ashamed that I had used a lie to encourage Isaiah. Because I came not to support a broken man but only to gaze, with my own eyes, on the destruction of Rabbi Avuya, for his hot groaning to descend on the back of my neck like that.

I turned my head, stealing a look at the rabbi standing over us, his breathing cut off, and I could no longer take my eyes off the face that emerged from the wild curls, the lips bleating like a groaning shofar, shocking the foundations of the night, sending the rambling wail onto the ridges at the border of the desert, a pariah chased from one peak to another, hovering over the city whose walls were breached, over the ruins of the Temple, hitting the corners of the room in the isolated house on the peak, echoing beyond his thick body. The sound of Rabbi Avuya Aseraf's wailing even then, in his collapse, still quickens sleeping forces within me, forces covered with dirt, *Blessed be He Who raises the dead, Blessed be He Who raises the dead*—shakes me as Isaiah never touched me, never never . . .

> *Woe is me for the exile of the Shekhina!*
> *Woe is me for the destruction of the Temple.*
> *Woe is me for the burning of the Torah.*
> *Woe is me for the killing of the righteous.*
> *Woe is me for the profanation of Your great Name and Your Holy*
>   *Torah.*
> *Woe is me for the foe was increased.*

For a moment he shifted his black look, piercing me all at once. And I didn't flinch anymore from the look or from Isaiah trembling next to me on the bench . . . And deep in the gloomy room the sheets of the unmade bed lie white.

Woe is me for the foe was increased.

The rabbi leaned over, grabbing his loins with both hands. And once again he marched off, dragging his slippers, going far away into the neglected room, his big head drooping on his chest, his back gripped by a tremor of weakness. Marching as if he were suddenly broken, in the vapors of the incense boiling in the metal platter on the stove. Alone, mortified body and soul, without a wife, without a baby to wave in his arms . . . *for a man shall not live in the world and in the Torah together* . . .

And suddenly, I could see only the offense of that isolated aging man, ending his days in the choked shout bursting from his lips. I looked long at him, despite the shudder and loathing, and an unfamiliar tenderness arose in me. As if that was no longer Rabbi Avuya whose awful lesson on salvation I yearned for, not Rabbi Avuya, who seemed to me like Ben Azzai, who looked at the shining light, looked and died, for his soul adhered with great love and genuine devotion to higher things . . . Ben Azzai of whom Scripture says: *Precious in the sight of the Lord is the death of His saints.*

Suddenly it was only the destruction of his awful tikkun that I saw. And at the sight of the unmade bed, I understood that when the students fled from him, he had collapsed on the bed, and there he had remained wrapped in his rumpled clothes, shaking, until we knocked on the door. And it had been a long time until he recovered from his reverie and opened it.

Yes, Rabbi Avuya Aseraf, may his memory be for a blessing, him too You rejected. Denying his supplications that salvation would come at once—him too You threw out, that strong man, his face contorted with effort devoted to You, him and his acts—the sacrifice of Rabbi Avuya Aseraf, that too You refused . . .

All day, his voice echoed in me, shouting in the treetops around the small house, in the flowerbeds full of thorns. How I plodded there like someone rummaging in the mound of cinders, all that remained the passions that flamed last year. Impelled by anger to expose Your face hidden in the ruins of Jerusalem. To reveal the destruction You sowed here, boundlessly. The killing of the Righteous, the profanation of Your Name and Your Holy Torah. The destruction soaked in the pieces of stone, in the dirt. A dense mass of the dead streaming down the slopes of Your profaned body lying here. *Blessed be He Who raises the dead, Blessed be He Who raises and kills* . . . That is Your Covenant, a covenant of blood. That is Your memory, destruction of the world . . .

The break is awful, awful. Bursts from the echo of Rabbi Avuya's shouts, from the dust of his grave, how the Hall was destroyed and the foundation of the world demolished. What destruction remains from the whole effort. And now, when the Temple walls are burst open, and the daily offering has ceased, and an idol is placed in the Holy of Holies, who will stop the fire that bursts out to the city, gripping the yard, the Temple Courts? Who will stop the flames that race to the Torah Curtain, breaking out the wells of destruction under the foundations of the Temple?

In a little while, when I go out to bury the boxes of photos under the mountain I can prostrate myself on Rabbi Avuya's grave, bury my face in the warm dirt in the dark.

I don't know how long the rabbi marched behind us, with Isaiah shaking the bench, his hands grasping the table, trying to restrain his trembling. Everything is blurred now. I recall only the salvo of the last shout, when the rabbi's voice suddenly became clear, as if he addressed us directly, delivering something: "He who does not build the Temple in his time, it is as if he destrrrroyed it! He who does not build the Temple in his time, it is as if he destrrrroyed it!" And he immediately stood still and whispered quickly, "There will be no mourning nor lamentation on Tisha b'Av this year. Sinners, rejoice at salvation! For from the dirt of the mourners will the Temple be built. And I, I, Avuya ben Elisha Aseraf, I am the dirt!"

Isaiah started, froze for a moment. And then he was jolted, the sticks of his arms hung at his sides. And he moved away, ran to the door, pushing the screen open to the night.

I got up behind him. His steps beat on the garden path, going off. I was left standing where I was, choked with pain. As if there, in that moment, everything was finally destroyed in the collapse of Rabbi Aseraf. For the shell was so thin, so thin, like broken ice. Who knew better than I? And pity flooded me with tears when I left the forsaken room.

On the doorsill, I encountered the dark of the peak. Isaiah had gone through the garden. In the heart of the path, among the flowerbeds, I stopped and looked back. In the wide open doorway I saw Rabbi Avuya, wrapped in his long prayer shawl, hanging on the doorframe with his out-spread arms. He stood facing the dark, as if he were acting out an awful drama. When he saw me turn, he threw his head back, shutting his eyes, tossing his mane of curls. And that's how he stayed, with his head thrown back in the door. Why did he come out after us? Didn't he throw the students out? We only sneaked back to visit him, against his will, as it were. So why did he go to the doorway, to show us once more his acts? Was he, Rabbi Avuya Aseraf of blessed memory, also scared by the greatness of the destruction . . . scared by the isolation he had forced on himself in the house on the mountain, without students, without a person to entrust with his shout? Was he too not lamenting only to himself but seeking an audience, aside from You, the blessed Name, the one Name . . .

Then he turned from the doorframe, moved his body away and with-drew into the room. And the sound of the lament began again, echoing from the open door. Deep waves, rising to the rustle of the treetops in the night.

And after everything, I, exhausted from running all day, why do I go on adding words, when even the hope of Tikkun has vanished? Why do I still go on leading the pen over the paper? Am I too, secretly, addressing some audience, Yocheved . . . Stein . . . Rabbi Gothelf . . . maybe Isaiah . . .

Behind the gate of the yard, Isaiah waited. Holding his hand out to help me onto the path of the slope. Standing there, thin, so far from me. I flinched from his hand, walking around the place where he stood, and plunged into the dark with the dry smell of pine stamens, and at my heels Isaiah's steps shooting pieces of stone to the bending tree trunks. Somewhere near the bottom of the mountain I said: "The rabbi won't be alive after Tisha b'Av."

"What did you say, Amalia? What did you say?"

"Rabbi Avuya won't be alive after Tisha b'Av."

"Heaven forbid . . ."

"If not on Tisha b'Av, then on Sukkoth. He won't go on living like that."

Isaiah stretched to hear, chuckled in panic. "God forbid, Amalia, God forbid . . ."

(But, despite his complete devotion to Rabbi Avuya Aseraf, he withdrew from him with the rest as soon as the slander began and the sanction was declared against the rabbi. Nor did he go back anymore to the isolated house on the mountain. Until the morning of the funeral, when he was summoned to prepare the rabbi for burial. Going with the corpse to the purification, running here afterward, in the great cold, to call me, tramping in the mud among the graves at the bottom of the mountain in his quarrel with the gravediggers and the voices poured out onto the wet slope.)

Maybe it was an hour I sat paralyzed. Even now my hands don't move to take the prayer book and recite, *Today is forty-five days, which is six weeks and three days of the Omer.* The voice is mute from prayer before it is cut off from the lips.

Late at night, in the dark of the first of the month, with the moon completely covered. I shall go out with the photos. To take advantage of the total dark. The heat will accompany me.

Please, HaShem, strengthen me just this one time, Lord.

I burst out laughing at the sight of what is written. *Please HaShem . . .* as if quoting somebody else's text. She seems so far now, the Amalia who could utter those words of the prayer with complete faith . . . And yet, and without any prayer, to get rid of the boxes of photos. To bury them. To bury—to burytoburytoburytoburytoburytoburytobury.

(Before dawn. The head bursting with fatigue. I return now. I didn't bury. I didn't succeed. Somehow I didn't dare stop anywhere, just trudged with the big boxes among the graves, the tombstones. A patrol car slowed down to find out what I was doing there. The weakness burst out even more. Everything has failed.

And the dust filling the mouth. The dirt that, night after night, I would scratch on the doorsill for the Midnight Tikkun, pour on the disheveled hair, the hot dirt that would trickle from the hair onto the forehead, the eyes.

Afterward. I'm still here . . . sitting at the table . . . unable to move. Who am I pretending for?

Weariness overcomes me. No longer knowing what the hand is doing there on the paper, moving the pen far, far, in the gray wave that sweeps me into sleep. Without repair. Without prayer. Empty of deeds. Now.

Tuesday night.

The night of the first of the month. I fell asleep in the early evening for a few hours. Now, long after midnight. I stopped all work today, as is commanded of women on the day of the first of the month (gestures continue, after everything . . .). I cooked a little, to mark the day. Rice. Sitting and chewing the grains slowly, crushing the sweet morsels, soft descents, one mouthful after another. The hours passed in a delirium. Rising and sinking on the lighted stage set of the hills.

Somehow there's a need to record testimony, in the pulpy dark where nothing happens. The dark gaping between the crouching ridges. A car is cut off from the mountain, below in the valley. The worm of light progresses along the short bend. Is swallowed up. Dull drumbeats. As from a discotheque.

The night of the first of Sivan. Two days ago I would still say, *Three days until the end of the Counting,* still within the time when You are at the end. Now everything is unraveled. Cut off. With no hold. With no direction to guide what's written. *Thou hast covered Thyself with a cloud, that our prayer should not pass through.* Record that too . . .

To leave testimony . . . As if I got up out of the bed where we made love for weeks, closed off from the world . . . You sunk there, on the un-made bed, helpless, You only promised You would redeem. As if I got up to take a distance, going dizzily to the table to lead the pen over the paper. I, the cursed one, servant of servants. And even if the others take the gar-ment and lay it upon both their shoulders to cover Your nakedness, *and their faces were backward and they saw not their father's nakedness,* I will tell what really was.

Around two. Fragments of music. Maybe from a discotheque. So late? The dogs in a rhythmic wail, stoned among the clefts of the slopes. One against the other. *Hoooo, hoooo, hoooo, hooo* . . . (The voices suddenly touch. Like some eternal buzzing that was cut off.)

The beats of the music fell silent.

Suddenly. The body is present. The body that only trod from the loom to prayer, and at night to the table. As if a hand is passing over the skin, slowly, making it supple, lingering, lengthening, slowly, slowly. Rousing the body folded beneath me. Entering between the lapels of the shirt, the neck, the shoulders, the warm skin. Passing over the nipple. A light hand. Around and around the protruding kernel. Draining the outstretched, gushing chalice. A light hand, like a breeze, descending on the belly, con-tinuing, going down slowly between the spread thighs. Strumming there the melting. Rising, slowly, slowly, throbbing, with a thin stream.

The thought is torn. No control.

Last night at this hour going out with the boxes. Into the pungent, bit-ter dark. Something swelled in the throat, going down to the valley lying motionless, climbing in the plowed dirt near the church fence, walking on the road on the mountain opposite. Striding fast along the Old City wall, sandals tapping on the asphalt, in the raised shadow of the temple ruins the gigantic stone steps in the digs. Clasping the suspect boxes while walking. A military jeep stopped. "It's dangerous here now. Go home!" Two soldiers dazzling with their headlights, examining. "Want a ride?" Emphasizing by revving the motor. "What then, going up?" Chuckling, racing down the slope of the walls.

I left the road. Not knowing what was more threatening, the Arab vil-lage or the military patrol. Sinking in the dark that grew thicker between the cypresses on the slope. Going through the burial niches, stone rims of ancient family graves. And across, rising, lying, the mountain covered with the weight of tombstones. Walking in the dark on the pale path down at the bottom of the slope, in the stench of dust mixed with water. And suddenly I no longer knew what I had to do there with the boxes—dragging with me to the foot of the Mount of Olives the photos from Hubert's darkroom. To start digging now, in the crumbling dirt? . . . On a night that paralyzes the breath? . . .

At the end of a row of tombstones at the bottom of the cemetery I seemed to see the grave of Rabbi Avuya. I didn't go check the name on the tombstone.

Finally, I put the big boxes on a strange grave. To rest. Time passed. I started getting used to the dark. Headlights ran on the road sometimes. Cutting of the churches, spots of bougainvillea, a turret of a mosque, palm fronds. At the top of the cemetery black silhouettes of Hassids moved. They were apparently burying someone hastily, in the middle of the night. Or maybe they were prostrating themselves on the grave of their rebbe. From where they were, at the top of the mountain, they couldn't see me here below. Time passed. Only their charred shadows against the torches danced in the distance, and their prayer was poured out, wailing for a moment and lopped off.

At last I got up, gathering the boxes. In the distance, the shadows were still moving. The fragments of their voices became weak, maybe the wind changed direction. I started climbing back up. At the top of the path, I scooped up a piece of stone from the ground. Clasped it. Warm, dusty. Filling my hand for a moment. Bitterness of smooth warmth. Then I dropped the stone while walking. It ricocheted drily off the rock.

The grotesque walking last night with the boxes among the tombstones . . . Plodding with all the dead material in a great demonstration. Yet, after all, I won't steal the "Memory of Mala" from Stein with some nocturnal burial on the Mount of Olives. Anyway, it's all just a commerce of corpses, with the required dose of righteousness. Absolute dark of the first of the month. The distance is indicated only in small fringes of light on the tops of the peaks. The wind that blew at the beginning of the night has stopped. Now there's only a light breeze. *The Lord was as an enemy: He hath swallowed up Israel, He hath swallowed up all her palaces, He hath destroyed his strongholds.*

To be strong, to go on despite the panic. To go on with the testimony without emotion. With absolute precision—otherwise it's impossible to distinguish between my intention and what was Your decree on the night of Tisha b'Av last year. Otherwise it's impossible to write down what really happened. How I waited with rising expectation. Gazing for whole days from the bay window at the Arab children playing on the slope, at that little girl in the striped pinafore hiding behind the aloe plant—without touching the warp of the prayer shawls stretched on the loom. I couldn't. Swept up in the blur of devotion, in the height of summer that grew dull only for a few hours at night. And the shock of what happened at Rabbi Avuya Aseraf's only increased the expectation.

It was as if I no longer remembered Isaiah. So I didn't notice when he knocked at the gate, just before the start of Tisha b'Av. And even when he stood in the room, declaring excitedly: "Amalia, I have to go with you to the commemoration tomorrow!" I listened to him from a distance, still glued to the sight of the children's game on the slope. "I came to tell you that I have to . . . I've wanted to come a few times and ask but I didn't dare. I was afraid to offend you . . ."

He trailed behind me into the kitchen, where I took the hard-boiled eggs out of the cold cooking water for the meal before the fast, sitting down at a corner of the table, chewing slowly, making ashes by burning paper, sprinkling them on the eggs, choking on the mass.

"I've got to ask forgiveness from the dead before we get married . . . God willing," he persisted emotionally. "No, it's not because of Elizabeth, her memory for a blessing . . . It's because of Mala, your father's first wife . . . the pianist . . . Suddenly, in the middle of studying, in the middle of prayer . . . I'm playing along with her, with the deceased Mala . . . sonatas for piano and violin by Beethoven, Brahms. It's certainly from overexhaustion, in the three weeks between the seventeenth of Tammuz and Tisha b'Av. Yesterday, I canceled the learning with my study partner, Ephraim. I couldn't. At night I had visions of lamentation. Sounds of weeping. Loud voices, women's voices and men's. Weeping, weeping . . . " His voice dropped. I got up to draw water from the faucet; his words became faster, caressing the curls that were already starting to soften the thorns of the haircut.

"Maybe also because of what was at Rabbi Avuya's. They found out at the yeshiva that I was one of those who went to him. They called us in for a talk. They're thinking of issuing a sanction against Rabbi Aseraf . . ."

I gulped my drink without breaking through the dryness.

The day slipped away quickly. Isaiah was afraid we'd be late to recite lamentations at the Wailing Wall. I quickly took the Bible to read the Book of Lamentations, and changed into cloth shoes, surrounded by that wall of decision that had already hardened. The choking didn't stop as we walked. It only increased as we entered the gate of the Old City wall, and all at once, the carpet of silence emanating chirps in the valley was ripped, and the bustle of a crowd burst out in wails, spread like a cloud of sand over the dark walls. As we toiled up the alley, the screaming grew thick, and then the square gaped, inundated with floodlights and packed with people.

Isaiah broke away from me, hurried forward excitedly toward the crowd, ran to the mass of bustling men reciting prayers. Alone, without Isaiah, I clasped the Bible, bathing in the willingness to sacrifice myself body and soul as was decided. I sank among the groups assembling in the heat of the evening. Prattling women and their babies stuffed into carriages, groups of tourists absorbed in conversation, soldiers burdened with equipment, strolling on the lighted square like an amusement park, with a solemn sloppiness. I clutched the book and pressed toward the women's section. In the dirt ditch on the side of the ramp, among the ruins, a whining old man was trilling, *They have cast up dust upon their heads; they have girded themselves with sackcloth.* I made my way in the crowd of women and little girls. Among the backs of overturned chairs, shoulders, arms. Among women lying on the ground, sprawled on mats, kneeling, swaying as they sat upright, murmuring with their heads bent over books: *How hath the Lord covered the daughter of Zion with a cloud in His anger and cast down from heaven unto the earth the beauty of Israel.* One woman repeated it like an oath, straightening the cylinders of her legs, raising the Book of Lamentations and shouting that verse over and over again. A small group of women huddled next to her, responded in a chorus of thin voices.

The heat increased at the foot of the Wailing Wall, which rose up to the night flooded with light. From the tension of waiting since the night of Shavuoth, it seemed to me that the shriek of the crowd burst out of my insides, from my taut depths. For it is me that You chose, me, Amalia. I moved around with my head bent, pupils white with dread, to the ruins of the Temple, for I shall wash Your altar with my tears, I shall raise the lament of the whole Nation a sacrifice to You . . .

In the heart of the crowd, in the great crush, I knelt. Rising with heart humming to the women lying near me, sobbing, moving in a dense mass of summer garb, wigs, a rustle of turning pages and whispering. Body weeping, muttering, sticking its head to the stone. For all of them I shall pour my soul in a prayer to You, I, Amalia, whom You chose, and repair the name of Mala—the cry for help of them all I shall raise to You, atone for the whole Nation. I inhaled the warmth of the women's bodies wafting from the stones, spraying heat of candles, and a mass of bird droppings, no longer distinguishing between me and them, and Mala who was tapping on our bowed heads, in the smoothness of our outstretched necks. How was I about to deliver my soul in prayer to You, to pour out my heart like water on the whole soft, miserable group, lying at my side, melted away in tears from the force of faith. It didn't yet occur to me that You would abandon us all, all together. Mala and me, and the women pressing me, lying prostrate on the square in the summer night. No, didn't imagine that You shut out prayer like that, so indifferent. Kill and restore to life, like a machine, in Your ruthlessness. Didn't understand that such was Your decree.

I lifted the Bible in front of my face, but I couldn't find the Book of Lamentations, even though I frantically turned the pages. Meanwhile, I started reciting the well-known first words, *How-doth-the-city-sit-solitary-that-was-full-of-people-how-doth-the-city-sit-how-doth-the-city-sit* . . . to find shelter now in the common shout that cuts the floodlights of the night, to sink immediately in swaying saturated with weeping, in the sourness of the body odors of a mass of women swelling their lament into the heat, the breath of their lives, the mist of the prayer, to add my voice to the voice of Mala to the cry for help of the righteous, pure, tormented women sprawled at my side, to utter with them in one voice the lament—*how-how-how-doth-the-city-sit-solitary,* I started shouting just to sink into a shriek with them, buried together in one heap, without breathing, choked, weeping next to me, over me, so weak, *how-doth-the-city-sit-solitary*, a ditch full of heavy, choked women's bodies that were thrown out, steaming, screaming above me. Impossible to breathe in the heaviness. And all around they're standing, intersecting in the flood-lights, filling their mouths with laughter, and in a little while, they'll start shooting. And Hubert is there with them above, he's aiming too. And I'm not preventing him now, not pleading anymore with a soft, paralyzed body, *leave, leave, don't look, don't look, don't photograph.* Aiming and pressing the trigger, one press after another. Removing a trembling spool and reloads with the terrifying force of a machine, one shot after an-other, in the silence of empty shacks, straw mattresses, sawdust strewn on the floor. And the women workers rake the paths, leaning with thick arms on the handles of their rakes and nodding their head, *hoooow hoooow—*

The paralysis struck with a shocking pain, flooded me among the bodies of the lamenting women, gathered up Mala and me into the soft-ness of their group, joined my voice to theirs, together, together, with hot weeping *how-how—*

Apparently I exaggerated my weeping, throwing myself onto the stones of the Wailing Wall, through the crowded bodies withdrawing from my weight. Not noticing the shirt that opened, the Bible that slipped out of my hands, hitting one of the women bending over beneath me as it fell. I didn't see a thing, banging my fists on the stone and weeping. An opaque crust dried over my eyes. And shouts growing louder, and at first I didn't understand that they were shouting at me. Only afterward, in the space that was opened, and the faces that moved distorted above me. Some woman shouted very loud, maybe she spit (perhaps the same woman who had been repeating the oath earlier), and other voices fol-lowed her.

"Such a woman like her shouldn't come here, to a holy place. Such people don't belong here."

"Opening her clothes like a whore. A disgrace, what a disgrace."

"She shouldn't hold holy books in her hands, that filth, it's because of people like that that the Temple was destroyed."

And the especially shrill, strong voice of a short woman with a black kerchief fastened on her bald head, punching me with her hard fists, veined wings rising, circling and landing on my limbs, with the rhythm of a supplication. "Shame! Shame for us! May you burn for our shame, shame! Shame!" She brought her fists down, thrust them like dull blades.

Someone got me out, clasping me by the shoulders. A dwarf with a broad face took the trouble to pick up the Bible that had slipped down and carried it with ostentatious reverence at the head of the strange procession. And the one who had hit me continued after us, her distorted face above me. Finally the women threw me on the raised ramp outside the square, my clothes torn, my face filthy. Someone tossed the defiled Bible in my lap, and then the women in kerchiefs turned back to the square, running with arms outstretched, shrieking harder in the weeping of lamentation, as if to atone for the time they had wasted taking care of the impure woman.

Passersby gathered around me. Soldiers, a few tourists, women with baby carriages. They weren't doing anything anyway, and now they came to a special event. The onlookers hung around to see better, exchanging stinging comments, bursting into laughter. And from the distance the shout continued, with the heavy voices of the condemned, screaming, shrieking in gushing choruses of wailing . . . A dense mass of flesh pressed to flesh, flesh of my flesh . . . Helpless. Not noticing with their pure faith the destruction that was decreed, crowded at the stone wall of the screaming slaughterhouse where evil will assault them . . . My heart ached for the abandoned bodies, their limbs sprawled on the heat of the ground, distant limbs of my abominable body lying on the stone, swarming there, desperate, at the heavy end of my body buried in molten waves of weeping, moving in a crowded throng. And choking. Dry, dry. In the dark. In the floodlights.

Quarter to four. A chorus of muezzins inundating the dark like a stroke of light. Trills and trills burst from various distances. Sculpt the folds of the landscape. A voice joins in, very close, maybe from the village below. Syllables are separated from one another. Echoes of lament.

Five minutes after four. Silence again. Only the military patrols wandering on the distant road cut the night.

We have transgressed and have rebelled: Thou hast not pardoned. Thou hast covered with anger, and persecuted us: Thou hast slain, Thou hast not pitied. The words swell into the dark. Knead it, knead . . . (To go on with the testimony. To write it down. That's what supports me now.)

Isaiah ran up then, bent down to me, his face glowing in the beams of the floodlights. Isaiah suspended between one destruction and another, his whole world shaken by the split from Rabbi Avuya, and tomorrow, on the trip to the commemoration, what is left between us will be broken. He held on to any spark of faith, knelt above me with that lighted laugh, not asking about my unbuttoned clothes, about what I did at the stone ledge, immediately scared, full of pity, as if this is how he will heal me.

"What a prayer, Amalia, you can't imagine, what exultation! Really full faith in the coming of the Messiah. You should have seen it, Amalia.

"He was there, in the cave, a yeshiva student who stood stuck to the Wailing Wall the whole time and wept. Afterward he grabbed a few people and shouted with such an open face, 'What would I do without faith, God forbid? What would I do?' He held me to his shirt, too, and shouted. I understood so well what he meant: 'You know what would happen to me now without faith, you know? I would kill myself.' That's what he told me. 'I swear, I would, Heaven forfend, kill myself now.' And once again he wept and leaned on my shoulder, holding me and singing, *'Unto thee it was shewed that thou mightest know that the Lord He is God; there is none else beside Him . . .'* And then he left me and ran back to the Wailing Wall, clinging once again to the stones, with his whole thin body and the big hat and the sidelocks, and wept . . ."

Isaiah rose above me in the light of the floodlights, pulling me to him, and laughing, laughing, with his torn bliss. "Now I really understand, Amalia, that the destruction is the proof that redemption will come! I'm so full of joy that I want to throw myself in the air and dance, like Rabbi Akiba. You understand what this is? You understand? That's redemption! Redemption! Now, Amalia! Redemption from the destruction!"

At the end of the prayer, the women began coming up from the square, flooding in a prattling mass, crowded. Dragging their heaviness in the narrow passageway, crushed one to another. They passed close by

us, gazed in amazement at me and Isaiah, who was straightening my disheveled clothes, walked around us. Gathered in groups, and their chatter swept away the echoes of their lament.

Isaiah picked up the Bible from my lap, lifting me to my feet, leading
me through the movement of the crowd, and I didn't resist. Like a cap-
tive led to the slave market, it occurred to me, then, or afterward, when
he led me outside the walls, into the night, plodding behind him in silence, with that bitter taste of dirt crushed in the dark. And even then,
after the lament and the blasphemy, the opaque crust wasn't yet torn off
my eyes, the choking of faith didn't yet burst out. The dryness didn't
ease its hold on my breathing. And even then, I wasn't reconciled to the
tenderness of Isaiah's love, I didn't return my heart to him. Only the
tremor swelled, from one horizon to another.

*For these things I weep; mine eye, mine eye runneth down with water, be-
cause the comforter that should relieve my soul is far from me.*

Twenty to five. The hour slipped away like a hallucination. Complete silence. In the east, the morning star broke through. A lighted stripe in the
heart of the sky, over the dull strip on the horizon. Some bird is calling
in a hoarse voice into the blackness. A distant north wind.

Who are You tempting now, after You abandoned me? After the
Covenant with me was forsaken? Who? Maybe Isaiah . . . Sneaking into
his bed with the wind of dawn awakened and strumming on David's
lyre, dripping into his ear the hum of Your playing, tempting him to follow You, with all his soul and with all his heart and with all his might,
even taking my soul . . .

It's hard to write down exactly what happened on the way back. (The
memory is blurry—maybe so I won't have to be explicit . . .) Did Isaiah
cling to me in the thickness of the grove, moving his lips over the ends
of the hair that was growing, over my forehead, over my cheeks? Did he
twirl his fingers in the short curls, fasten and wind them? Flutter his lips
over my shoulders, my neck, whisper very close to my ear: "No, not
tonight," and break off, saying, "Not in haste, not in haste," laughing in
embarrassment. "I don't know what I'm saying, Amalia, I could never

say poetry . . ." Hold my petrified hand in his narrow hand, lead my body, which had already left his hold?

And all that one night before I sacrificed Isaiah's love to You. A night before I tore him off me. I gave You Isaiah's love, sacrificed everything. With all my heart and with all my might and with all my soul. And You cast it off. I gave You everything and You despised the sacrifice. You tossed me away casually. Five days before the end of the Counting. What an insult. And fear. Suddenly fear. Like a blow. Regrets for Isaiah.

The air turns red. Only one last star, torn from so much light, is glowing bright in the east. Suspended at an equal distance from the earth and from the rest of the sky. The cliff is chiseled out of emerald. A black cutout of mosques, churches, on the peak. Only the line of the horizon in the distance, below, is still swathed in gloom.

Sharp pain. To go on writing. Before You silence the voice that rises against You. Not to stop despite the fear. To leave testimony before it's too late. The body trembles.

As I walked, for some reason a biblical verse was echoing in me: *I said unto thee when thou was in thy blood, Live, when thou was in thy blood, Live.* It emerged like a shadow from the niches. Out of the blue. A kind of lurking echo, *I said unto thee when thou was in thy blood, Live, when thou was in thy blood, Live* . . . I almost forgot the whole thing when I entered, and only now, when the strange echo was suddenly renewed for some reason, did I read the rest of the chapter. And I was shaken from tatters of words buried under the "Prophetic word," a story completely different from the explicit one suddenly screamed out. A voice attacked, testifying to the crime that was blurred, erased, and buried. Completely distorted in a reversal of facts, as false accusations—the body trembles. From fear of what was revealed. And maybe even more from the silencing—that the shout was buried alive, with wicked insolence, under the "rebuke of the Prophet," who blames her, the tormented, despised one . . . (And what will be the fate of my confession here? How will they hush things up, take it out of context, turn it into slander against me in the hands of Your agents who will pursue me?) As if the choked voice

were screaming inside me there, relentlessly, demanding that I echo it
from my lips. (To hurry and restore the protest against You there. Before
I go mad, before You cut short the wick of my life.)

What was written: *And as for thy nativity, in the day thou wast born, neither wast thou washed in water to supple thee . . . nor swaddled at all . . .* As
if it was done by a stranger . . . And it was You Yourself *who cast* me out,
Your daughter, *in the open field* on the day I *was born*—shouted the
voice—You Who did not *cut* my *navel,* and in *water* I was *not washed,* and
I *was not salted,* nor *swaddled at all,* Your *eye did not pity me . . .* for completely different, oh, how different, was Your scheme . . .

And when I passed by thee and saw thee polluted in thine own blood . . .
You played innocent, as if You were a foreign master passing there completely by chance and heard the shriek of the bondwoman's baby, leaning over her in Your grace—according to Your slander—and say to her,
in thy blood, Live, in thy blood, Live. Gather her up to You—as if in compassion, "Great Pity"—camouflaging with Your sweet words the cunning of Your lusts, *I have caused thee to multiply as the bud of the field, and
thou hast increased and waxeth great, thy breasts are fashioned and thine hair
is grown, whereas thou wast naked and bare . . .*

Until her hour came, *the time of love . . .* And then, first the uncontrolled burst of desire for the slave You bred for Yourself . . . for Your
ripe daughter . . . covering the abomination with Your hypocritical ut-
terance: *Now when I passed by thee, and looked upon thee, behold, thy time
was the time of love; and I spread my skirt over thee, and covered thy nakedness: yea, I swore unto thee, and entered into a covenant with thee, saith the
Lord God, and thou becamest mine . . .* No longer restraining Your enormous lust and taking possession of Your daughter. Raping her in her
virginity. Day and night You torture her, in the aggression of Your hard
passion, again and again, insatiable. Fornicating in her nakedness that
You revealed . . . And even with that You were not satisfied.

Then You went about increasing Your lust by envying strangers, by
the lust of many Gentiles for the one You chose. That they would all desire the bondmaiden You bought as an eternal property. You went about
making Your Name glorious with the Gentiles, by showing her nakedness that belonged only to You, only to You . . .

And she, in her innocence, didn't know what more You schemed when

You *washed* her *with water* and *thoroughly washed away* her *blood,* and *anointed* her *with oil,* and *clothed* her *with broidered work, and shod* her *with badgers' skins, and girded* her *about with fine linen and covered her with silk,* calmed her heart, which was terrified at the sight of the strange glory, swore that it was only for the delight of Your love that You embellished her. Block Your ear to what she tells You in her timidity: *"At our gates are all manner of pleasant fruits, new and old, which I have laid up for thee, O my beloved"* . . . And You *decked* her *with ornaments, and put bracelets upon her hands, and a chain on* her *neck,* and You *put a jewel on* her *forehead and earrings in* her *ears, and a beautiful crown upon* her *head,* and You fed her *fine flour and honey and oil,* and she was *exceeding beautiful* and she *did prosper* for Your scheme.

And then You presented her, fettered like a chaste maiden in gold and silver and bracelets, to the strange Gentiles, in Your Temple, in the center of the city *You desired for Your habitation,* bragging of her to them, exciting them to devour Your chosen one with their naked gaze, inciting their envy for Your beautiful wife, the one You raised for You, only for You . . . That they would grow wroth with her in their enmity, that envy would drive them out of their mind, because she would never be theirs . . . *And yet* You were *not satisfied.*

For then the old madness stirred in You, pursuing You with a feverish delusion at the sight of Your daughter's crown of beauty, not remembering that it was You who bestowed the beauty on her, You who raised the tower of her neck, You who presented to everyone the buds of her breasts. Pursued by fears in Your sickness, You rave that she, confident in her beauty, will now raise up her neck, and will betray You, will give strangers Your gold and Your silver that You gave her. Choked the visions of wrath, how in her boldness she will fling off Your yoke, the bonds of Your possession, will act boldly *the work of an imperious whorish woman* . . . That's what she will do to You—You rave—she whom You possessed, she whom You adorned, she will humiliate You like that, she will rob You forever of Your object of pleasure . . .

And in the burning of Your blood poisoned with jealousy, love turned to hate in You. For *the hatred wherewith* You *hated her was greater than the love wherewith* You *had loved her.* And then You set about to drown Your fury in an act of revenge whose atrocity has not been known since the creation of the world. *Woe woe unto you saith the Lord God!* You shriek madly, run and tear from her hands the sons and daughters she has borne You, rip their soft necks, slaughter Your babes, pass them through the fire. Run back to the wretched woman, pluck her from her weeping in Your bloodsoaked hands, laugh madly at her disaster.

And then You go on brutally ripping her garments, removing her gold, growing madder in the dark of Your lunacy, burning with a lust for revenge. Going on and tormenting the victim of Your love, defacing her image completely, crushing her thin body with the torments of rape. Thus, You say, in the burst of Your sickness, to make her whore unto death.

Like a brutal pimp, You made Your wife a whore. Giving her to anyone who wanted her, spreading her legs to every passerby. Presenting her in her nakedness, announcing her, calling, tempting them to come in, drool, come close, take Your wife to be desecrated by their fornication, her, the chosen one, the only one. And the contrary is in Thee from other pimps in Thy whoredoms, *whereas none followeth Thee to commit whoredoms; and in that Thou givest a bribe* to her tormenters to gather *on every side to come unto her* to torment her.

And You multiplied her whoring, to make her wretched, and You *could not be satisfied.* You made her whore with the Egyptians great of flesh, and *yet couldst not be satisfied.* You made her whore with the Assyrians with a donkey's penis, You made her whore with them and *yet couldst not be satisfied. And Thou multiplied* her *fornication in the land of Canaan unto Chaldea,* and goats ejaculated in her, and even with that Thou wast not *satisfied.* How wretched her heart when You inflicted all that on her, standing over her in the valley of her torments, polluted in her blood, torturing her even more with Your venomous words, "How she whored My love, look at you, whore . . . *Because of what you didn't remember"*—who didn't remember, she or You?—*"the days of your youth, and angered Me with all that."* Smooth words. Covering Your sins. Adding lie to sin. That was Your scheme.

Until water flowed on her head, and soon she was drowned. Only then did You rest, and Your jealousy subsided and You were no longer angry, for You hadn't yet completed Your scheme . . . After all, You didn't stop desiring her. Even in her defilement, Your lust still burned for her that she should crawl to You from her torments besmirched and downtrodden, that she would cover Your feet with her kisses, wash the dirt off them with her tears, tell You with a look dulled with mourning, with her defiled mouth, the words from then *"Thou, O Lord, remainest for ever; Thy throne from generation to generation, turn Thou us unto Thee, O Lord, and we shall return; renew our days as of old. But Thou has utterly rejected us; Thou art very wroth against us."* And then, You will pass by "as before," and You will see her cast out in the open field, polluted in her blood. And once again You will tell her as in that very merciful master, *in thy blood, live, in thy blood, live* . . . Once again spread Your skirt, covering Your adulterer's face, swearing again to her without remorse, *"I will establish unto thee an everlasting Covenant, I will establish my Covenant with thee . . . that thou mayest remember and be confounded."* You will gather her in again into Your bedchamber of tears, bind her again. To Your Covenant of suffering, so that she will never be cut off, for *Thou, O Lord, remainest for ever; Thy throne from generation to generation.*

Thus You savor the torments of Your lovers—*Precious in the sight of the Lord is the death of His saints.* And the more tender the victim the better. Like those women cast out there, wallowing in the dust. They and Mala. And I too, who saw You uncovered within the tent, weak, wounded, and I meant to bring healing to You, to comfort You as a mother comforts her suckling . . . All of us You tempted, and cast out, every one in her own way. You forever contaminated by Your jealousy. Unable to love. Tempting and deserting, and swearing once again, in panic—when Your weakness increases, when the destruction once again gapes in You, and slipping out of Your grasp for a moment the world is suspended upon nothing . . .

The words shriek like tatters of a bad dream. Turn dark. The head is smashed. Complete emptiness. To finish.

The refrigerator noises went on all night, now mixed with the rumbling voices. Regrets for Isaiah. Have to go out, run, save him from Your clasp.

Wind from behind. The mountain opposite bursts out of the gray. Black spots of treetops from the blur of the mass of dirt. A muffled gloom still covers the bottom of the slope, the rocks, the tombstones. The ridge is turning pale. It's possible to write by the light of dawn coming in the window. Only the movement of the patrol cars is going on as usual in the taut white between the watches of the night. Whiteness floods between the star of Bethlehem and the sunrise.

A molten sun pushes in the East! Sunrise! A dazzling stripe burns on the eyelashes unsheathed over the stage of the mountains of Moab, burning there below, in the distance, on the edges of the wing of the withdrawing dark.

Bells. The bells! From all the churches. A gilded, joyous, shattered cascade. Celebrating, celebrating. Gold poured out. Praising You there. *Halleluia* . . . Bells ringing, a refined plait of gold slivers. *Halleluia* . . . New mornings abundant in Your faithfulness. *Halleluia* . . .

Men are climbing the steps of the alley. Going to work. Their rhythmic steps. A hushed shadow of a flight of birds passes by and grazes the window.

Despite the fatigue, suddenly strength. Desire to leave You. To cast everything off, cut the tatters of the delusion. . . .

The head drowns in the glow, cuts a silhouette on the red wall. Behind, in the kitchen window, shrieks of little birds. The body becomes supple. Possible now to get up and cross the room bathed in light. To go to the kitchen, to light the stove, with hands covered with dust and dryness from the night. To pass the hand over the bedspread that remained closed. To bury my head in the pillow, the disheveled hair. To wash in the white rustle of the sheet.

I stood for the Morning Prayer. Holding on to the prayer book. *Prepare and work on the rays of the sun; the Beneficent One fashions honor for His Name . . . emplaces luminaries all around His power.*

The words push everything. As if they have nothing to do with what happened. The words of the prayer book open the breathing . . .

In the distance a woman's voice, in conversation. Notes from a transistor radio. A hot summer day bursts out all at once. Glow on the eyelashes. Complete nakedness.

Wednesday night. Everything is over.

This afternoon I took down the Torah Curtain. First I finished weaving the little bit that was left, and then I cut. The weight dropped with no echo, no feeling. Now the big machine is emptied. The breached room is out of balance, like a ship whose cargo has been unloaded all at once.

After writing last night, in the storm of the blasphemy, I lay down for a few hours, in my clothes. In the morning, I went straight from bed to the loom, without washing my hands, without praying. (To start the day like that, without words, without gestures. What a relief . . .)

With a few flies of the shuttle, I finished the frame. A green strip and a blue strip. And then fastening the last, strong beater of the hem. And I got up from the stool, for the last time. In absolute silence. Already on the other side of the frame, outside of everything that happened inside. Only the rough feel of the threads in my fingers continued.

And then the cutting. With that same silence. At three, maybe four in the afternoon. The brightness had already diminished. Cutting the cords of the warp with the big scissors along the marking thread at the back. The cords were detached one by one, stretching aside the weight of the Torah Curtain, piling it up on the floor. I went on, bending over, treading among the high folds, warm from the scissors. Maybe the first time I stayed so long near the sweetish smell. The smoothness of the silk, the coolness of the gold. Like a memory that was opened and once again infused the breath. And then the rolling of the machinery, the moving of the whole long sheet from one beam to another, through the changing pattern of the Torah Curtain, the firmament, the birds, the twined names, the dots. The thickness of the embroidery of months of work. And the cutting there, near the back, along the marking thread I twined with frozen hands at the beginning of winter.

(From where I stood behind the loom, the bed looked completely strange. Suddenly, it wasn't clear how the body had been wrapped up for two years in that mass of crushed bedclothes . . . Objects are emptying out of me. Erasing my movements from between their limbs. The cabinet, the wicker armchairs, the pots in the kitchen. Waiting hostilely for me to clear out of the space.)

Afterward, I remained standing. In the shadow of the empty beams. Idiotically releasing the amputated loops of silk from the frame. For some reason, I persisted in removing them, one by one, crushing them and throwing them away. Standing there and plucking until late.

All the blue and gold that fell from the loom . . . Torah Curtain of the firmament folded in wide folds on the white linen I spread out on the floor. What will happen to it? Will it cover the Ark of the Covenant in the new synagogue of Mr. Stern, the treasurer? Or maybe, after all, I'll go out as planned on the morning of the holiday, wrapped in the heaviness of the brocade. Everything is so far away, unimportant now, when the weight is released.

The loom gapes. Stein won't come until tomorrow. He'll certainly take a taxi as soon as he gets to the hotel in Jerusalem. And You're hiding. Everything is cut off.

And yet to go on writing now beyond the screen of the Torah Curtain, to write with a new release about what happened finally, last year, at the commemoration in Café Shoshana. Back then, when everything seemed ripe, and dropped only on the way to Tel Aviv, shrouded in humidity. In the doughy mass that swelled as the fast of Tisha b'Av continued, closing in on me when I penetrated the stickiness of the Jerusalem central bus station, among sweat-stained backs, peddlers, food stands. A marshy mass where Isaiah emerged, leading me through the line to the panting maw of the bus, and a bagel seller mounted on a cart of rags, waving a pole with rings of bagels on it. *Circles are a sign of mourning,* I raved as I sat down and the bus left for the segments of the mountains. From the window, the hot air and the soot of the exhaust tapped, adding to the stench of the hard-boiled eggs a mother was peeling for her children. The dry spinning didn't stop despite my leaving Jerusalem for the first time since I came from the airport at night. Grayish expanses of mist swathed the burned fields, the electrical poles that go off to the mist of the horizon. The bus cruised heavily into the haze on the outskirts of Tel Aviv, clogged bushes, crumbling structures sailed by it, indifferent in the gray of the waning day. A boiling shriek of smoke burst out when we got off at the bus terminal in a medley of colors of newspapers, sweets, toys. And then the sound of the city bus into the black straddle of sidewalks and a thicket of treetops. A few lights were lit in display windows, and the yellow poured out at the end of the street, a strip of dazzling gold on the sea. The doors of cafés, familiar from childhood, slid by as the bus glided past. On the streets near ours I led Isaiah as in a dream through the neglect, as in an abandoned city. Walking, like Father and Mother together from the store, past the scarred houses, tatters of shutters, doors leaning on their hinges, empty balconies. And then the banal entrance to the building, the wall of the shelter, cans, dirt in the yard. And opposite the neighbors' closed balcony, and the window next to it, and the shutters pulled down. As I had shut them the night before the flight. Can't cross the distance separating the sidewalk opposite. No one noticed I had returned to the street, penetrated the forbidden zone. No one knew me anymore. I didn't say a thing to Isaiah, dragging him behind me, petrified, to the end of the street.

We got to Café Shoshana too early. For a moment, we were swallowed up in the gloom of the lobby, and then, behind an old velvet curtain, the hall, caught in the glow poured from the sea, opened up. All the windows of the café blazed at that hour, rising like the prow of a ship above the boardwalk, and between their frames the disk of the sun was caught wrapped in mist. One of the organizers, completing the arrangement of the small stage, didn't notice us standing there in the door. They set up chairs behind a table covered with a green cloth, pitchers of juice, glasses, and a bouquet of flowers next to the grand piano. A racket of old air-conditioners swirled in the empty hall. On the stage was a poster that said *Mala Auerbach*. And next Tuesday will be Isaiah's and my wedding . . . Sara will probably make the buffet in the dining room of Neve Rachel, and Rabbi Israel Gothelf will interpret a short Torah passage for the few guests . . .

An echo of voices in Polish rose behind our backs. A group of guests was entering the lobby. The mass in my throat swelled unbearably. I reeled through the hall to the corridor where the bathrooms were, with Isaiah on my heels. In the small bathroom, smells of frying and Lysol were mixed with the sea air. I managed to get inside and vomited into the toilet. I leaned on the small sink, for a moment I took deep breaths from the window overlooking the boardwalk, destroyed for renovations in a racket of bulldozer chains. A few tiny figures fled on the shore to the copper cover of the sea, running in the distance with outstretched arms. Isaiah was waiting in the narrow corridor.

Meanwhile the hall filled up with a bustle of guests for the commemoration. They stood in groups, talking loudly. Elderly women in summer dresses, pins and necklaces, flung bare arms, and swarthy men moved among the groups that were excited about the meeting. That fixed, obedient, energetic swarm that had disappeared since the half-drugged escape to New York now broke out once again to Café Shoshana, that buzzing cloud that gathered again at every opportunity, when Mother died, at Father's mourning in the apartment that rejected all of us and only Aunt Henia is still rolling up the carpets as if there's something to protect, and afterward, at dawn, through the mist, a few tiny figures suddenly waving excitedly on the airport balcony. And now, they report again, talking animatedly, as if the hand of time hadn't touched them, they just grew darker and more wrinkled, like loaves of bread that kept on baking. In the center stood Aunt Henia, erect, short, clutching a white purse under her elbow, and around her flutter the same faces, the same names . . . Hesiu Gut, Celinka . . . the Weintraubs from Kszanow, Felicia Appelbaum, the Baraks, the short Sala Mendel . . . and others, those who always remain a mass of nameless faces . . .

At first I was impelled to go to them, greet them. But weakness held me back. At that moment, behind us, the doors of the kitchen burst open, and two waiters waving trays of juice soared out. All at once, the guests turned their faces, discovering me and Isaiah shrinking in the aisle.

"Hey! Amalia! Amalinka!" Aunt Henia made her way over with outstretched arms. "Malinka!" She stuck onto my face the lipstick with the old smell, clutching me with her skinny body. "Here, you finally came! You came!" She straightened her hair with her thin hand, and turned to Isaiah, saying in broken English, "Nice nice! Nice man!"

"Aunt Henia, this is Isaiah . . ."

"Very good!"

"Isaiah speaks Hebrew."

"Very good," she persisted in English, pinning the thin hand he held out to her.

Hesiu Gut and the Baraks fluttered over to us from the people standing, and so did Sala Mandel with her shy smile, surrounding us with a tumult of hand-shaking.

"Congratulations, congratulations . . ."

"I didn't know Amalia is getting married."

"Wonderful boy."

And Aunt Henia kept clutching my arm with her elbow next to the white purse, stroking it with her hand.

One of the waiters wandered to the kitchen with the leftover juice on his tray. Someone standing around plucked a glass of juice from the tray and held it out to Isaiah. "Drink, drink, you must be dying of thirst, in such a heat wave, you came all the way from Jerusalem."

Isaiah pulled his hand away, and said slowly, "No thanks . . . Today is Tisha b'Av . . ." And his foreign accent was more conspicuous than ever.

Mr. Weintraub whispered loudly to Hesiu Gut: "What, religious?"

"Repentant."

"*A ney mishegass,* a new craziness, eh? I didn't even know she came back to Israel."

"Yes. To Jerusalem."

"*Abi gezint,* she should live and be well."

Mr. Weintraub popped up from behind us and clutched Isaiah's hand warmly in both of his: "Good luck to you! Like you say in Jerusalem, with the help of God . . ." He burst into a friendly laugh, as he recited in Isaiah's ear, "Our Malinka should have only good, only good . . ."

And the whole time, Aunt Henia kept stroking my arm, pinned with her elbow, as if consoling me for some distant pain. "What a surprise, Malinka . . . I'm so glad . . . I'm so glad."

From the stage, someone shouted: "*Prosze pani, prosze!* Sit down, please, sit down!" Urging them by clapping his hands. The faces raised to us blended with the change of the command, blurting out, "Invite us, we'll come! We'll come!" And they were already rushing to the rows,

waving at the wooden folding chairs, terrified that the seats would be
taken, that they would be late, that there wouldn't be any more for them.
Even though the hall was far from full and a lot of chairs remained empty.

"Sit down, sit down!"

"The young people should also sit down."

"There's enough room."

"Here, here's a chair."

Isaiah passed between two crowded rows of chairs, leading me behind
him, until we sat down amid the sweetness of cologne and cigarette
smoke. That special dejected blend I had forgotten along with the screaming calls, *the wonderful Mala! Your father's great love! Mala! Malinka!*

On the stage, behind the vase, Doctor Halbersztam's elongated skull
flickered. "Let's start with a piece of music!" he declared in a soft, wondering voice. The noisy cascade of notes of a Chopin mazurka beat as if
from a music box. The pianist's mass of hair was caught in the kiln of the
sun in the window, which also lifted the heads of the guests swaying to the
rhythm. Before my eyes, through a screen of blurriness, Aunt Henia's
skinny back was erect, as she sat alone in the row in front of us with
empty chairs on either side of her. Farther away, through the scarlet vortex of sounds, bent over, I saw Hesiu Gut, who pinched my cheeks, and
his soft eyes are laughing . . . He's got an iron shop. In the camps, he
learned how to work iron . . . when they finally came, after their release
from the British detention camps in Cyprus, he thought he could make a
living from iron. Next to him, bobbing her head in rhythm was Celinka
Abeles with her powdered cheeks. She makes plaster ornaments, a little
girl with a lamb, a little boy with a ball and a hat. And next to her the sharp
profile of Helenka Weintraub, *yes, Amalinka, of course I came to Mala's
commemoration, what did you think?* She puts meat patties with radishes on
my plate even when I ate at home, because how can Stashek get along all
by himself, and in their kitchen window there's a gray sky with bars, and
Ilanka, "your age," looks at me with eyes bulging from the thin face, and
the heavy breathing because of the polyps. And Felicia Appelbaum, wearing a hat, sitting with her husband, Abel, next to the Baraks at the front
of the hall, which swayed as the playing rose, the Baraks surely brought
them in their car, the first ones with a car, he's got an important job with

the city, so his face gleams and his hair is slicked back. Very fond of Father, really, taking care to ask if he wanted them to buy him a subscription to the concerts, he could sit next to them if he wanted. And in the corner, Sala Mandel hovers rhythmically, with her small smile, left alone with a child, they hid him with the Gentiles. After the war, when she came from the camps to take him, the child didn't want to leave the Gentile woman and come with her. When Ruzia died, they thought something might work out with Father; they had known each other since their days in the youth movement. Once she bought discount tickets to the theater, came dressed in a suit, and put one foot in front of the other. When they drank tea, she crumbled the sugar cube that remained in her hand. Afterward, she went, telling me, *Good-bye again, and good luck, Amalia* . . .

And before my eyes, through the crust of paralysis pecked Aunt Henia's erect head, at the end of her thin neck, empty chairs on either side of her. Still marking around her the area of mourning, still erect. Henia Taub, née Auerbach. Her husband was murdered by Poles, right at the start. She never remarried . . . I would bend over to her, put the feeble hand on her shoulder, on the thin dress stretched over the bones of her back. I would bring my lips close to her cheek I had to kiss at the entrance. If everything weren't sealed with weakness, unraveling with forgotten blows of fluttering, tearing the shield of torpor, the semblance of repentance, the life of the yeshiva. All that dry cover of Jerusalem that had been cracking during those mute days of expectation, and the engagement announcements, and the blur of the fast, and the beating of the trip. A great weakness covered everything, whirling the guests, the hall, lulling me into a heap of skulls hovering to the rhythm of the music, as if a light wind were swaying them, moving them back and forth, and me along with them, in one heap. Gray tatters, floating. In a distant, recurring rustle . . . Carrying me far away from Isaiah sitting next to me, who could never ever cross the distance around Aunt Henia's back. Who would never be swept away in the dizziness of hissing. Sitting, taut with the pain of the harsh notes, his fingers clutching his trouser leg.

Yes, for a moment, the delicacy of Isaiah's veined hand flickered to me—maybe the first expression of pain that penetrated me. Until then, everything was completely erased under the screen of weakness.

The audience burst into applause. The pianist's thick arms were raised above the crash of the final chords. I grabbed the back of the chair, choking, like Isaiah in moments of great excitement.

"Amalinka, really, I'm so glad you came." Aunt Henia turned her head to us, smiling as through a fog, and Doctor Halbersztam's voice was heard in the distance, through the racket of the air conditioners: "I am the son of the rabbi of a congregation that was killed among the saints of our people by the hands of the murderers! Alone of my whole family I emerged from the field of slaughter. Without father, without mother, without sisters and their families, without brothers, uncles, aunts . . ."

Only strips of the soft voice reached me, drawn from the skull floating in the pool of yellow glow, slightly leaning over the pad of paper.

"When I emerged alive from the Vale of Tears, I swore to devote my life to claiming payment from the murderers for their crime. Even though there is no commensurate payment. Even though there is no justice that will stand facing the absolute evil."

Doctor Halbersztam . . . the first Jewish docent in the Polish law school, despite the quota . . . Afterward, in Tel Aviv, became a lawyer for reparations . . . With a small office in the southern part of the city, every day he has to go on foot in the heat, in the cold, from his office to the courthouse, to find out if the claims from Germany have arrived. The Germans, may their name be wiped out, go on killing the Jews with bureaucracy, urging them to bring more papers, and more papers, and all that for what? For what? Father, who shouted with the last remnant of his strength, almost at the end, when they hit Doctor Halbersztam! Attacked as he came from court by the relatives of a woman with power-of-attorney, who were waiting for him to transfer to them money that was supposed to come from Germany. They said he embezzled, that's what they said! About Doctor Halbersztam! The Jews continue to believe the Germans! Even here! Shedding the blood of a Jewish lawyer! The shouts that shocked me when I tried not to hear, to block the ears with Amy's long hair . . .

"In the death camp I lost my faith in the justice of the acts of the Creator of the World, yes. But I didn't stop believing in the revival of the

Nation! And always, on Tisha b'Av, I recalled Father's lesson: The destruction is merely a symbol of the resurrection, according to the lovely tradition that the Messiah was born on the afternoon of Tisha b'Av! As it is written in the sources: and in the future may we live to see what is written in the Book of Lamentations: *How so far she sat solitary, the city, and now she is full of people, princess among the provinces. How is she become tributary, and now everyone pays tribute to her."*

In the hall was the density of the air conditioners. Doctor Halbersztam's thin voice was excited. The people's heads nodded agreement with his words. Aunt Henia's head bobbed in front of me through a transparent partition in that energetic approval. And I seemed to sink in the swoon of rustling, as if, at last, everything was dim, hushed into the space of coagulated, gray silence . . .

"And so we set the special commemoration for Tisha b'Av. For who more than Mala Auerbach symbolizes for us the most awful pain, the bleeding heart of the destruction, but also the hope of resurrection, who more than Malinka! She, in the music of her life and the heroism of her death!" Doctor Halbersztam's words struck the microphone with lopped-off echoes.

"We, the survivors, raise the holy memory of Mala in our independent state, despite the annihilation plan of Nazi Germany, may its name be wiped out! And that is revenge! We will show the world, which was silent and which continues to be silent, that from destruction the road leads to redemption! We will show the world, and out of a belief in the courage of the human spirit! In the light of the music rising from the song of the life of Mala Auerbach the heroine!"

The heads still pecked, affirming, as if they were reciting with Doctor Halbersztam the standard words, known in advance: "Mala! Malinka, as we called her. Pride of the community even before the heavens turned dark, even before the storm! And afterward too, in the awful years of darkness! Mala! Almost the only case of escape from the camp, Mala and Stashek Auerbach!"

Suddenly he doubled over, grasped the glass of juice, and violently gulped the orange liquid, as if his heart were about to give out, continuing almost in a whisper, his voice raw, "Stashek and Mala Auerbach! They got hold of SS uniforms. From people who worked in the sewing

shop. Mala left first. She succeeded. A beautiful woman officer in uni-
form. She reached the border. But there they caught her. Before Stashek
had time to leave on the ammunition truck. They brought her back to the
camp. Everyone knew what end was in store for her. But she, Mala, decided to die free! For a whole week they tortured her and she didn't utter
a word. Somebody managed to pass by her cell and ask her how she was.
They said she answered: *I'm always fine!* They had to use force to keep
Stashek from turning himself in. They were going to destroy her anyway. Who can understand what he went through then? Perhaps out of respect for Mala's pride he didn't talk, as if they were still playing together,
even then, the difficult tune of her death . . . They passed her a razor
blade. One of the men going to work in the quarry. That's what they had
decided between themselves in advance, she and Stashek. After a week
of torture, when they stood her up at the gallows, in front of all the
women who were brought out to the *Appellplatz,* there, on the stand, she
took out the razor blade she had hidden and slit her veins by herself. In
front of the Germans, in front of all the women in the *Appell.* The SS
man who was supposed to do the hanging assaulted her, tried to get the
razor blade out of her hands. And then she slapped his face! With her
bleeding hand, with her marvelous hand, Mala! The SS men came running, screaming like lunatics—a prisoner, and a Jew to boot, dared to
raise a hand to an SS man! They assaulted her like beasts, beating her
wildly, to death. Fortunately for her, Mala breathed her last on the cart,
before she reached the crematorium."

The air conditioners made a racket of breakdown, but none of the
guests paid any attention. The two waiters leaning against the wall at the
foot of the stage, their heads drooping, stretching toward the speaker like
earpieces, were swallowed up completely in the glow that rose from the
sea. Everything moved: grating chairs, blowing noses, women's hand-
bags tapping. Spinning around me in a slow, heavy rushing, clinking
from side to side, torn. I almost fainted.

Through the applause, Doctor Halbersztam's final words were heard,
as he bowed in respect: "It is our friend Ludwig Stein who summoned us
to the commemoration!" And the glitter of Stein's head flickered above
the vase, over the purple polka-dot bowtie.

"Mala! Malaaaa! Malinkaaaa!" A long bleating echoed. "I can talk about her, yes, I can!" Stein's voice, which I had forgotten since he ran waving his hands after the taxi at the entrance to the Excelsior and his shouts were blocked by the closed window. Standing on the stage in a shiny suit, a scarlet burst blooming on his breast, so splendid against the gray decor of Café Shoshana.

"All my life, Mala's playing, all my life. Always I'm thinking, Mala, Mala, Mala Auerbach, née Glaub. All my life I'm living with the memory of her heroism, of her genius."

I hadn't seen him since an hour before the flight, back in San Remo, when he tried with Hubert coming out of the hotel to take back all the material I had stolen from the suite. Why hadn't they hidden it before I came from the clinic, taking the key from the reception clerk, immediately locking the door? Packing everything. The shiny sheets of the enlargements, the prints, the negatives, even the notebooks with the details of place, date, kind of film, shutter opening, exposure . . . Sweeping everything into the old suitcase. The rest I left in the room in the Empire style, like a snake shedding its skin, all my things . . . As if it were really possible to steal her pictures and run away . . . I came on them as I was leaving. They immediately understood what I was taking. They ran after me. Hubert, with Stein behind him waving his short arms and shouting something. Like in an old action movie that has to be played out again down to the last detail. Throwing the suitcase in a taxi, telling the driver to go to the airport, the door slamming on Hubert's coat, and Stein waving in the rearview mirror. A small stick figure, going off among the palm trees at the bend in the access road. And even then, the photos grasped in the suitcase in my hands, knowing that there was no refuge, no escape, that everything was a game . . .

"She didn't want to take nothing from me, with her pride . . . You know how she was, always only Malinka and Stashek, Malinka and Stashek . . . Only passing the razor blade through the prison . . . That she took . . . And then in the men's camp I'm standing in the *Appell* among rows of Musulmen, and hearing a story about her heroism. The SS are screaming like beasts that if anybody again . . . And I swore that Ludwig Stein would never again leave Mala! Never!"

Absorbing in fragments the little bit of Polish I never dared admit I

understood, the rest was said to me as by itself, emerging from somewhere, dark and soft. "All his life, Stein with her memory! No wife, no
family, nothing, all the years. Only the memory of the most wonderful,
the most beautiful, Mala . . . And business, got to have money! A Jew
needs money to stay alive in a world of Goyim. Even for the memory of
a Jew you got to have money in a world of Goyim!"

Ludwig Stein, that short man, excited as a rose committing suicide in
the opening of all the redness of its petals, still in love . . . Still running
through hotels, airports, through cities . . . Ludwig Stein, unable to allow
himself a sign of weakness.

A soft tremor hatched in the graying pink stuck in the hall, melting the
noise of the air conditioners, the wall of the sea, flowed in a distant
lulling. Eyes brimming. Relaxing. I was about to stand up, climb the
stairs to the stage, go to him, to Stein, tell him that I understand . . . understand . . . that I always understood . . . And only the heat melting,
slowing the breathing in the solid wall, without moving, as when I stood
in the door of the kitchen, unable to enter, to go to Mother sitting there,
with her robe unbuttoned, after the shouts from the black pit were over,
Krstein, Krstein, sitting there with a big knife in her hand open on the
table and not moving, like that, next to a heap of shredded cabbage, her
eyes looking far away. Wanting to go to Mother's shoulder in the soft
robe, but the body doesn't move.

"All my life I'm in America. Didn't live in the Land of Israel, our
state, didn't want to spoil nothing for Stashek and his new family after the
war. Didn't want to remind Stashek of the child he and Mala didn't have!
And now he's got a new family and a little girl in Tel Aviv, Amalinka . . .
And I with respect, am not talking. Waiting. All the years only waiting . . .
Meantime, giving to the community, for the child Ludwig Stein wouldn't
have. Waiting . . . Thirty years isn't a day, it isn't a day!"

Beyond the glass wall, the sea turned gray in the distance, wiping out
the remnants of red, and only the gray milked from the fluorescent tube
scattered on the hall, and Stein's voice droning on, "Yes, it was an idea
to make a memory of Mala, photos! A special album that Stein will pay
for himself, photos that will show the whole world Mala's beauty, her
hands, and piano, and an auditorium of Stary Teatr, and the trees of

Planty, where she walks with a fur coat, and her music case, trees of Planty with squirrels . . . as it was . . .

"And now, everything is ready! Yes! All the photos, marvelous! Marvelous! Everything is ready for the memorial album of the heroism of Mala! We are going soon to print all the material."

He didn't look at me, and no one in the hall knew what he was talking about. Isaiah sat next to me shriveled up, his legs crowded against the seat in front of him. But something started to tear, with a shriek.

"Yes, and then something marvelous happened! Marvelous! Stashek sends his daughter, a photographer, Amalia Auerbach, and she makes a memorial album for Mala! Yes, the photographer of this marvelous album is Amalia! Our Malinka. So special!" The voice broke over the heads of the audience. "That is why I am making a commemoration today, to say that there is an album for Mala Auerbach! A marvelous album of photos! And the photographer is Amy Auerbach! That is what I want to tell you today, Amy is making a memory for Mala!"

By then the old fluttering was released in the distance, tearing the softness, the poured-out heat, with its beating. Sweeping up the rumble of the air conditioners, the froth of the light. The impulsive fear that exploded again, tearing the breath in crushing shrieks, as always. The tyrannical shrieks madly striking the skull . . . Only out of cunning did he invite me, Ludwig Stein . . . Sitting there and capturing me in the blades of his look, sitting there on the stage and claiming . . . He better not think he succeeded in catching me . . . I am not making a name for Mala! Not making any memory for Mala! That's not me. I repented! *I am a different person and not the same one who sinned!* He better not think I don't understand his plan. All he's got to do is take Isaiah aside and talk to him about my situation when I came to him in New York the first time. Just say a few words about the journey, about Hubert . . . *To change his name, I am a different person and not the same one who sinned* . . . About what happened at the end in San Remo and the clinic. *To change his behavior in its entirety to the good and the path of righteousness* . . . Or about the money he sent, and I always took, even for the yeshiva in Jerusalem, *exile atones for sin, because it causes a person to be submissive, humble, and meek of spirit* . . . Stein is sitting there and looking at Isaiah, shifting his

look from him back to my shorn head. The weakness is so great. I moved
my head in an exhausted wrath. Impossible to run away. He had touched
everything . . . There's nothing he didn't finance. Even in high school,
he sent money to Father, and afterward in New York, and on the trip, all
the hotels and everything, and afterward too. He even bought Rabbi Israel Gothelf . . . I wanted to stand up and shout at him, *You're just pre-*
tending, just lying shamelessly! There wasn't anything to photograph,
everything is just a miserable pretense, mine and Hubert's . . . One big com-
mercial lie, Auschwitz in black and white . . . You know that very well, there
wasn't anything to the whole trip, aside from Stein's love for Mala, nothing,
nothing. I wanted to stand up and shout, but the dizziness paralyzed me
on the chair, even though it was clear that that was a life-and-death struggle, and the gray descended like a net on the hall. Even though it was
clear that he was trying to bribe me to keep silent, silence for the lie of
repentance in exchange for silence about the plot of immortalization,
my marriage with Isaiah in exchange for the photos of Mala . . . He just
better not dare reveal that I stole her photos . . .

The fluttering struck my breath, suffocating me, I wish I had never
been born, that I had never existed at all . . . I who only kill whatever I
touch, can't stop . . . Really, it wasn't on purpose, Father, I didn't know
it would kill you. I took her photo out of the drawer just so we wouldn't
be left alone. So you could love her without guilt, without guilt . . . OK.
It's true I was afraid she would come back at night and finish me off, because I was born and because I stole her name, so I wanted to finish her
off, in the dark under the pillow. So what? I didn't mean for you to be
blacker and blacker, and in a little while you'll leave me and go with
Mala, even though I shouted that I don't want to know anything, and
right after I left your room I cried with my fist in my mouth, holding the
guitar in my lap so you wouldn't see me shaking all over. Until you finally died, so quietly, leaving me alone in the empty apartment with the
green shades closed. So what if I went to photograph with Stein? For a
moment I thought I could finish her off that way, so what? I was sorry
right away, really. But it was too late, and Mala was already pushing me
to the white sink with the razor blade, and you didn't come at all to throw
her out, to save Amalinka . . . Now she'll finally kill me, for everything,
now she'll finally kill me, and Isaiah . . .

Sitting next to me with his long legs, not noticing anything . . . Just so Mala won't touch Isaiah! Won't get close to him . . . How come he doesn't notice anything, I've been trying to shout to him ever since we met! How come he doesn't run away, let him run away, let him run away . . . Don't succeed in explaining to Isaiah . . . Everything's my fault, my fault . . . Everything will die, everything I touch, our baby too, Isaiah . . . We'll have a monster baby, that's what I'll give birth to . . . A monster baby, and Aunt Henia will rock it in her stringy arms and sing to it in a sweet voice . . .

"That's what I want to tell you: Amalia is making a memory to Mala Auerbach!"

Now he's announcing to everybody that I stole Mala's photos, stole them and hid them in a drawer, like Father . . . He's announcing it . . . Have to escape right away, before it hits Isaiah, have to leave here right away, to push between the chairs and run outside . . . But the aisle is so narrow, so narrow . . . Have to escape before the white paralysis starts in the bathroom, can't even call Father, and the hand is so heavy, lying on the sink . . .

I swayed on the chair from intense dizziness. The guests were starting to turn their heads to us with a surprised look, nodding with a smile, "Very nice, Amalinka!" "Wonderful! Really!"

A bundle of applause began to gather. But on the stage, Stein cut off the turmoil. "Just a minute! I want to announce something else! I want to announce that our Amalia, the daughter of Stashek and Ruzia, is getting married next week! In Jerusalem! Her bridegroom is Isaiah!" And he burst into applause, urging the rest of the audience to join him, "Congratulations! Congratulations!"

Threads of sunset descended on the hall, closing like a net over Ludwig Stein detonating in a burst of scarlet, on Doctor Halbersztam's floating skull, on Hesiu Gut turning his soft face to me and smiling in the space between the guests, whispering something in the ear of Aunt Henia, who agrees. "Well, yes, well, yes," she replies, still applauding, her purse jolting in the crook of her elbow, and from the corner Sala smiles at me with a shy nod, in the bubble of rustling.

By now Tisha b'Av was over. A mass of mist from the dark sea spread over the window. The notes of a Chopin prelude were beat out in con-

clusion, smeared in dullness of the fluorescence that enveloped the hall.
Yes, I recall that quiet that turned to stone in the racket of playing, and
the rumble of the air conditioners. Some of the guests sat down when the
playing started, and some remained standing. The light lapped their
necks turning darker in the white foam with a breeze. The hall hovered
with a dull sway, closing in on me, on Isaiah frozen at my side, on Ludwig Stein waving his hands from the stage, signaling something over the
rustle of the audience rising at the end of the music. They stood erect,
crushed with a thin satisfaction that they said something to the world.
And Stein descended from the stage, one step at a time, and I was already
smiling blurry at his weary eyes approaching in the aisle. And for a moment, it seemed to me that Isaiah put his arm on me, supporting me to en-
able Stein, pressed between the backs of the chairs, to approach me. Or
maybe I only imagined that Stein was holding my chin, lifting my face
with his hand, bending over with sad eyes: "Amy returns to Stein memory of Mala, right? Amy dear is giving photos for marvelous album."

But then, like a trigger that is finally pulled, the terror was torn. A
dark impulse demolished the swoon, plucking me up like a marionette,
ordering me to press between the chairs, to burst outside immediately, to
run away . . . before it was too late . . .

I pounced ahead, pushing the folding chairs in a panicky hop, hunted
like a bird, getting out in the collapsed space between the rows. A big
bird, with a plucked wing, toddling, shot with a flapping of wings to the
sea, to the great gray plain congealed in dark. But on the way the glass
window blocked, and its pane was too strong for me to break through it,
braking the flutter against the cold surface with a shattering that sprayed
gray feathers on the darkening mass of the sea. A big bird shot, against
its will, right and left, terrifying the guests dispersed in the middle of
their farewells, the two waiters with trays, Ludwig Stein toddling behind
her along the windowpane, trying to capture her with open arms, to push
her into one of the corners, and there to choke the flapping of her wings.
"Amy, dear, Amalia, Amalinka . . . I want to talk with you." And behind
us, thin Isaiah shook, helplessly following the limping along the windowpane, and in his eyes the pounce of the bird's heart is hurried, stands
and looks, gaping in amazement. And now Stein has given up the hunt
in the corner of the window turning gray to the sea. A flap of wings, and

a hurrying racket of fluttering and flapping. Until the large bird swooped away from the window, ricocheting behind rows of empty chairs, very close to the two waiters who were nailed to the spot, under the frightened looks of the guests, and Aunt Henia's thin voice shouting something after her. Reeling to the lobby of Café Shoshana, the velvet screen, the vestibule, shot outside, outside, with strong efforts to flap a wing, into the dark damp suspended in the street, stuck like a steaming rag to the back of the neck, blowing with a thick, black flutter. And I did want to tell Sala that she could come visit, if she wants, in Jerusalem. The air is good . . . she can come, if she wants . . .

Yes, nothing was redeemed then, nothing has eased. Your ruthless Judgment, the horror of the flaw You once again renew in us, decreed for us forever. *Wherefore dost Thou forget us for ever and forsake us so long time? Wherefore dost Thou forget us for ever?*

Only, the old disease burst out again. The old disease tattooed in the flesh, flowing in a black wave, destroying everything, leading once again only to one place, to finish, to finish and to rest. The fear was greater than anything. And everything that was lived with devotion in Jerusalem, all the awe, the submission, nothing brought repentance . . . Not even the devotion of Isaiah's love.

Only, the old disease was renewed, ripping in its violence. As always. Never succeeding in breaking through the warm black circle around them, unable to cling to their wretchedness, rejected from the crookedness of Mother's and Father's body, always a pariah, in my roughness, an alien with my long hair, with the guitar, and now with the modest sleeves of the long dress in that fleeing leap. Always alone. Ripping with tyrannical flutter of dread. Alone, alone.

Please, HaShem, why didn't You forgive then, why didn't You redeem from the tatooed curse? to refuse and to flee, to go on fleeing? Why didn't You turn away from me Your curse that burst out anew, and this time in that dark madness, that all this is my sacrifice of soul to save You, to repair Your weeping—that lunacy that only to You am I fleeing like that, that You are waiting for me, sanctifying me and my sacrifice, me, Your black bride ? . . .

Please, HaShem, why didn't You cast me from You then, punishing me for that delusion (and how could I hope, believe at all). Why didn't You reveal Your face even then, how after all You will reject me, despise my sacrifice so much, jealous and vengeful God? . . .

Now, after everything is over, after the weight of the Torah Curtain is removed, when everything is cut. To write now with hands and hours free of weaving, without the effort after hours of weaving, in the emptied room which has suddenly become spacious, broken open. From such a distance. How crazy everything looks. To write outside the net of webs that trapped me inside it—like a madman who peeps for a minute and sees honestly, with absolute sobriety, the sight of his ridiculous hop.

I fled to the street, to the heat that had become unbearably steamy during the commemoration. Everything was moving, turning dark around me in doughy waves. The mass of the dark sea, the neglect of the houses, the stubs of shutters. A turgid, damp covering, drained into heavy drops on my belly under the long cloth skirt. Through the blur, it seemed to me that the few people in the street were hurrying to scatter from the rising wave. A few tourists in colorful clothes fled from the torrential gray stream up the stone stairs of one of the hotels, huddling in exultation for some reason. In the distance on the boardwalk, a whore in high heels ran heavily, seeking shelter, and the black elastic waistline of her skirt stretched as she was pushed into the entrance of a building. Two cats leaped in front of me into the flow of the plague, passing through it with bristly tails. *They are the sign,* I raved, *they are the last sign that's needed to go on running despite the weakness, to get out, with all the strength that's left, to reach the ledge of the boardwalk fast. For there finally, facing the gigantic blue of the waves, Father raises his head and looks far away, and all the gray is opened and sparkling with slivers of salt and blue, opened and hot in the blue that is spread out . . .*

"Amalia, what happened to you? Tell me, what happened?" Isaiah ran after me with his hands held out. "Amalia! Wait, wait, Amalia!"

I made my way to an empty lot behind the boardwalk restaurants. I passed scraps of cartons, boards, broken fences. From below the smell of grilling singed the heavy salt-steeped wind.

"Amalia." He stretched his thin arm toward me. "Let's just sit down and eat something and you'll feel better." His fingers hovered over my arm for a moment, gushing coolness. I ran off, hurrying to climb over the iron fence of the lot, moving toward the empty boardwalk, crossing the construction site in the shadow of an iron hand of a silent crane toward the black wall of the sea. Here too the steam roiled, a pale light stooped from the restaurants, from their empty squares, stretched from the street-lamps to the rag of the moon. I moved forward in a frail delusion. Drawn to the memory of the warm, rough touch of the ledge of the boardwalk. The smooth touch of the painted iron pole, which was renewed in my hands.

And only the desire to hold the ledge there, and finish. Finish with everything . . . Just hold on with the wet touch under my hands to the stickiness of the paint, and let everything stop . . .

"Amalia." Isaiah ran after me. "Why don't you answer, Amalia!! I'm so moved, it's hard for me to find the words . . . But I really do under-stand how hard that was for you . . . I really do understand you, Amalia." Isaiah's excited words tapped out in the distance, outside the opaque cover that was sealed.

I clasped the iron ledge with both hands. Scales of wet paint. Only that for a moment in the dark. Like then. Firm dampness, smooth as a fish. Dense under the clasp . . . Behind us, the city pumped with heavy arms of heat and flow. And in front, the sea wall gurgled in the gloom. Some-where in the distance, thought still throbbed weakly. *I'll just get a little strength and I'll go back to them, to the hall, to the smell of cigarettes, to the turmoil, I didn't even tell Aunt Henia good-bye . . . I didn't say good-bye to her when I left . . . I'll just get a little strength, as soon as I can lift my hand from this mass of the wet iron . . .* The breath stopped, leaving one distant note. One note poured out. A slow, gray stone.

Behind me, Isaiah was still talking, with that same excitement. He kept pleading with me to go eat something, that the fast had ended long ago, that that would give me strength. I couldn't relate to him, to his worry. I couldn't even tell him to go, couldn't get rid of him before the rabbi gave us the blessing, before it would be too late. *How come he doesn't see, doesn't see? Let him run away . . .* I stood there, in awful shame, and only the weakness petrified, peeled off.

Suddenly the shadow of Isaiah's thin body jerked, and he called, embarrassed, confused, "How could I have forgotten, how could I have forgotten!" Pointing toward the dark screen of the sand and the waves. "How could I have forgotten! They're sanctifying the moon!"

Below, on the beach, not far from where we were leaning, a few men in black jackets and hats were swaying in prayer, their feet in the sand. They had probably come down to the open area from one of the synagogues in the nearby streets to get a better view of the moon.

"How could I have forgotten!" The words rushed from his profile, as if the blame were there. "They're sanctifying the moon, a special mitzvah at the end of Tisha b'Av . . . And I didn't even recite the Evening Prayer . . ." Isaiah stood there, with his thin body, and all the terror of the last days seemed to be drained into that amazement.

"Go, pray with them, Isaiah. I'll wait here," I said wearily, advancing stiffly toward the stairs I remembered leading to the sand.

The few worshippers hurried to finish the blessing. By the time we approached, some of them had begun taking off their prayer shawls, shaking the grains of sand out of them onto the beach. The others hastily gulped the end of the blessing, skipping bent over and waving their hands—*Just as I dance toward You but cannot touch You . . . Just as I dance toward You . . .* One tall man, whose broad hat jolted as he swayed, called out, "May it be Your will, HaShem, my God, to fill the flaw of the moon that there may be no diminution in it! That there may be no . . ." And spots of light and shadow raced over his hat.

Isaiah hurried down the steps, tramping in the sand toward the worshippers, and then stood still and bent over. I sat down in the alcove of the stairs, leaning on the corner, in the shadow of the wall. The dampness that rose from the rushing of the sea restored me a bit. Hunger had stopped oppressing me long ago, and the fluttering also grew dull, leaving some lucidity. For the first time in a long time. And great fatigue. A thin layer of sand climbed from the stairs onto my sandals, onto the edges of my toes, lapping their knuckles with a light cover of warmth.

Men who had completed their prayers passed by me, climbing the steps with the relief of someone who has finished, shaking the hems of their jackets to remove the Evil that was formed by the indictment of the flawed moon, not noticing me folded in the shadow of the stairs. They trod close to me, their clothes wafting anxiety, withdrawn. Someone, a tall man, was still murmuring: *"May this be a good sign and a good fortune for us . . . ,"* pulling behind him the elongated limbs of his shadow. The worshippers emerged onto the boardwalk and dropped off one by one with a brief farewell, hurrying to scatter among the streetlamps into the weekday night at the end of the fast.

The light waned. A screen of sand-soaked mist that evoked harsh smells quickly covered the strip of moon. Obscuring the praying figures with Isaiah swaying next to them, turning the beach dark, moving over the boardwalk toward the dark facades. The stormy haze increased all at once, swirling whirlpools of sand.

Confusion emerged among the men who were still standing on the shore for the Sanctification of the Moon. They stopped their prayer, examining the screen of cloud.

"The moon is covered!"

"Yes, covered." They discussed it, shaking their arms at the moon.

"Not clear enough to carry out the Commandment!"

"Stop, we've got to stop!"

And somebody concluded: "Strange, the cloud covered it all at once."

Now the air was completely murky. A black fog emerged, skittering quickly, casting a shadow on the expanse of sand, the stairs, on the road of the boardwalk, pressing toward the antennas in the mass of the dark city.

"Well, Feurstein, at least we are exempt from the Commandment."

"Bless God." The two were already climbing up the stairs when the prayer was stopped.

"If the sky is dark on the night after Tisha b'Av, who knows what awaits us in Elul . . ."

"Don't remind Satan!" They stood still, leaning on the iron railing of the boardwalk above the stairs where I was sitting, watching the bursts of the tempest.

"A sign, it's certainly a sign here, on the night of Tisha b'Av of all times," said the one called Feurstein in a raspy voice.

"The end of the world. Rain will fall on us in the middle of Av," answered the other man, bouncing his small hand over the ledge. "I saw in the book *Ne'ot HaDeshe* that the end of the period from the seventeenth of Tammuz to the ninth of Av is the beginning of the great repair. Sayings of the Rebbe of Sochoczow, an important book!"

Meanwhile, on the sand, the worshippers whose blessing had been cut short were packing up their belongings and starting to rise from the beach. The storm accelerated, wet gusts blew in the signs of the boardwalk, in the electric poles, shaking the cloth awnings of the restaurants, raising creaks of cracking and beating of iron chains.

"Well, Feurstein, let's go."

A salvo of grains was whipped up from the sand. I moved my arm to shield my eyes, and the sharp movement sprang forth from the shadow of the ledge. Only then did the two notice me leaning at their feet, eavesdropping on their conversation.

"Look, look!"

"Really, how they behave today. Where have we come . . . ," Feurstein grumbled in his complaining voice. And they were off, rolling their shadow above me.

At that time, the last of the worshippers were climbing the stairs, carefully going around the place where I was sitting, as if I myself were the accusing, barren moon, swelling up in vain every month, giving birth only to dust and darkness. The last one to totter up was Isaiah, telling them something, not noticing their reservations, trying to dissolve his panic. The worshippers avoided getting into conversation with him. Maybe they noticed that the moon was covered soon after that excited thin fellow with the meager beard joined their group, and now they were trying uncomfortably to shake him off.

"Amalia!" Isaiah hurried to me. "Amalia, as soon as I started, the moon was covered! I didn't even begin. It was covered the very moment I raised my eyes to sanctify the moon." He leaned over me with a choked voice. "I really don't understand. The worshippers said it's a sign that something bad will happen, God forbid. And in the month of Av of all times, in the month of our wedding. That's not good, Amalia, not . . ."

Isaiah didn't notice how, behind our backs, the worshippers were climbing into the gray vapor on the boardwalk, aiming accusing looks at us as they passed by, nor how they hurried to leave the empty beach, each one vanishing in the canyons of the streets. Nor did he pay attention to the storm increasing in the roar of wet grains. He just gripped my elbow hard and held on to the wounded words he cried out more to himself and the storm than to me: "That's what Rabbi Avuya Aseraf prophesied, that's what he shouted after us, isn't it? *He who doesn't build the Temple in his days it's as if he destroyed it.* And who knows if I built the Temple, who knows, God have mercy? Who knows?" he repeated to himself, trying to strengthen himself by repeating the same question over and over. "Who knows if I built it, who knows, who knows?" Isaiah, a lone string, stretched thin in terror against the black shore.

I stood up, sand pouring from the folds of my dress onto my feet, and Isaiah hovered wounded next to me, his thin hands hanging at his sides. For a moment we stood in silence, the last figures on the beach swept up in the tempestuous storm growing from the black pit of the sea.

Then Isaiah raised his face to me, inundated with pity. "Come, Amalia, let's go eat, you're so weak . . . Come, we've got to break the fast now." He held my hand in his thin fingers, and moved away (the last time he held my hand like that with his delicate fingers), leading me through the wall of the storm to the area of pale light flickering from the empty restaurants on the boardwalk. (Those last moments of walking from the sea emerge now in the silence at the end of the weaving, in the clarity now, filling the night gaping open with their presence. Isaiah leading me, attempting to console me and himself with his words, and I striding in silence at the end of his arm.)

"Amalia, if God wills, the Sanctification of the Moon can be done until the fifteenth of the month, until the day of the full moon . . . it can be done . . ."

At the entrance to the patio of the restaurant, he turned his face lighted with shyness again. "Let's go in, Amalia . . ." He very carefully passed the empty patio covered by a yellow awning that made an opaque canopy, moving a plastic chair from one of the tables toward me, sitting down across from me, leaning over. "Amalia . . . the blessing can be done, God willing, until . . . the day of our wedding. Don't worry, I'll get to bless that *it should renew itself as a crown of splendor for those born from the womb.* I'll intentionally make the repair," he said, raising his face to me, clutching my hand between his hands.

His breath passed over my cheek, my neck. The dampness of the

chair molded to my limbs. I couldn't take my eyes off the drops of wet-
ness on the table, and was amazed that I hadn't yet said anything to
Isaiah, hadn't told him that at least *he* would escape from the tempest rising in tongues of foam, racing into the demolished road, that only
Isaiah's fingers, the last living creature, still hovered on its broken stage.
His voice was swallowed up in the storm. His words didn't reach me. An
empty silence was smeared on the tempestuous space, separating me and
Isaiah. His thin hands moved in the distance, fluttering over my hand, like
a bird scared to land on a distant bank.

In the doorway of the restaurant stood two elderly waiters. One
moved toward us, holding the menu in front of him like a legal messen-
ger hurrying to wave an announcement in his hand. Isaiah distractedly
pointed to something. The waiter bowed and withdrew, with the other
one on his heels, disappearing into the restaurant in their sloppy suits.
Only then did I recognize the two waiters from Café Shoshana, whose
facade loomed over the square like a black cliff.

A yellowish glow danced on the drops on the damp table, and the
waiters already returned, dropping a few cold plates covered with a
lumpy dough and a pile of pitas on the table. Isaiah supported me as we
walked to the back of the patio for the ritual washing of hands. I recall
only the wet heaviness of the skirt slapping against my thighs.

Isaiah recited the blessing and broke the fast with a slow chewing.

"Eat, Amalia, eat." He held his hand out in a plea above the waves of
the spread, and he almost dipped his bread in my plate, feeding me like
a baby. "Have something to drink." Isaiah didn't take his eyes off my lips,
which slowly crushed the little bit of pale dough that immediately hardened in my gullet.

"Amalia," he repeated softly, letting his dark eyes linger on me. "I
really do understand what you're going through, all the suffering your
family had in the Shoah. But I believe with all my heart that we can . . .
together, God willing . . . You know . . . by the force of repentance we can
live in the light, Amalia. I'm already thinking about our home . . . How
we'll make the Sabbath." He laughed. "And also how, God willing . . ."
His words swelled in the damp yellowish tent.

And then a trail of light seemed to leap, passing over the plate with a
dull flare, and was extinguished. The two waiters appeared, stood at the

edge of the patio, watching a stampede that came whirling toward us through the stormy mist. The bloc of the guests at the commemoration burst forth from the darkness, approached with a kind of tight gyration. A dense bloc of many legs, advancing with erect necks hitched together to one shaft.

In the lead revolved Ludwig Stein, unsheathed like a sting in a scarlet blaze, and right behind him, the tilted skull of Dr. Halbersztam, whose arms were jerking like antennae on both sides. Pressed to them were the jacket of Sala's short suit, Hesiu Gut's drooping shoulders, next to the panic of Abek Honiger and Felicia, and the Baraks, who pecked with their heads as they walked quickly right in front of Helenka Weintraub, hanging on her husband's elbow, calling out something in a quick, sharp voice to Sala Mendel, leaving a small space for Aunt Henia, firmly clutching her white pocketbook. Father, as usual, walked unreconciled, tall and dark, and the part in his hair gleamed in the storm with a dark silver tone, and next to him with her energetic gait was Mala, as in the photograph from the Planty. Mother plodded along behind with an effort, accepting her place behind Mala's and Father's black backs, and her thin arms waved from the cloth dress, as if only the effort remained from all her walking.

The coil rushed along the dark sidewalk in a certain course, which it somehow had to complete. No one in the noisy trail paid any attention to the patio of the restaurant, to the two waiters observing them as from a riverbank of another time and place, or to me and Isaiah sitting at the table in the middle of the yellowish light. For a moment, they whirled in front of us, grating out fragments of conversations, passing in a tattered rustling, and went off into the stormy dark. Twitching in the distance. Gone.

The waiters returned from the front of the patio and stopped at the wall of the restaurant, with no obligation except to serve us, the only customers. Isaiah held my wrist, and his lips went on forming words, "You'll see, Amalia, I believe in it with all my heart . . ."

From the trampling that beat a little while ago on the boardwalk, only a gray rustle remained, and there, in the dark, somewhere beyond the patio yawned the deep furrow they sliced as they passed. Some dull body, lying supine. A stream of pain creeping on the ground, completely silent, advancing. And the offense, maybe even rage. If everything weren't so far away. And the knowledge that flickered once before. That there is no repair and no repentance. That I won't erect a name for them. And how could I have hoped at all? And that too was without pain now. Only a hushed, wretched understanding. And pity, endless. The shocking flash of awe in the congealed silence. And the knowledge, completely silent, that soon they will die. Like Father and like Mother. They and their memory. And the crushed pain. And their tramping with an effort, and the shouting. And me too, and Isaiah. And we won't ever give birth to a child. Everything will be erased. Like a buzzing mass of flies wiped out thoughtlessly by a rag. Silent knowledge that broke through as they passed, searing like a revelation of holiness. And helpless to get up or turn the head after them as they vanished in the distance, in the darkness. What for. And the dampness of the cold seat. And even though the words were not yet articulated, there was only the slow knowledge that I would be sacrificed. Like Catalina Terongi, like Garcia de Alarçon, who were burned at the stake, as Rabbi Israel told us—like Mala, with a razor blade, in the bathroom melted white. For nothing remained, nothing. Knowledge flickering through the black cover that was sealed. And everything beyond that flash of shine was so distant, alien. And the silence that finally descended. A solid, white paralysis of awe. Yes, with all that weakness then, there was a confidence of faith. A faith so precious, so beloved, now, when everything is unraveled.

Isaiah was still bending over me, resolutely holding my hand on the table, warmth flowing from his hands. And yet their warmth didn't blend with my hands. Only now, in memory, is the warmth of Isaiah's hands revived. From far away. Without really touching my collapsed sitting in the corner of the chair with my wrist held between his hands. By then I was very calm, as after a decision that has ripened far from the pain of growth, as after irrevocable knowledge. And also the voice that beat was splitting out of me as from a stranger's mouth: "Isaiah." A hollow voice, demolishing the silence.

"Isaiah. There won't be a wedding."

"I don't understand."

"No."

"Amalia . . ." Isaiah bent over emotionally. "It's really so hard . . . Rest, we'll talk afterward . . . Not now . . . This isn't a good time . . ."

". . . won't be a wedding, Isaiah."

"I don't understand, Amalia . . . What do you mean?" His face was gaping in a blanched gaze.

"No."

"But, Amalia . . ." His fingers were spread. ". . . you mean?"

"There won't be a wedding. It can't be."

"Why? Tell me why."

"I'm sorry, Isaiah."

The hovering of his fingers stopped.

We sat a little while longer without a word. The waiters came and gathered up the remains of food and the money with wide movements, as if they were hurrying to remove a blood-covered sheet. Without a word, they took my plate too, whose pale paste had practically not been touched. They heaped everything on a tray. Isaiah dropped my hand, but even if he had gone on holding it, I might not have noticed it in the striking silence. Even the heartbeats that pounded later in the skull, flooding the cheeks, and the breath, shook by themselves, like a throbbing system cut off from the silenced body of a machine.

The waiters disappeared inside the restaurant. Isaiah trembled silently, and his frightened face was open to the dark and the sea. Something seemed to die in me then, to die forever. If he had exploded, shaken my shoulders, yelled at me in pain—would something have burst out? Would we have been saved? Or would I have fled once again to the storm swelling from the sea?

Isaiah moved within himself, arguing at the dark. Nothing was in my hands anymore. I should fall at Isaiah's feet, plead with him to forgive me, pardon me for murdering, for killing with my own hands, I, the perverse creature. Even the wave of shame seemed no longer to touch the cold penetrating from the seat. Only the beatings struck, rushing, heavy, in the low horizon of the skull.

Yes, You accepted then in silence the sacrifice of my love for Isaiah, the sacrifice of his pure love, leaving us there, condemned, in that silence. You accepted the madness of my submission to You, imagining that that

is my martyrdom for me, for Mala, for Father, Mother . . . the sacrifice I
make to atone for the wound broken in You.

On the way back we didn't exchange a word. The last time we sat together. Pushed together on the seat of the bus making its way in the
night, with that temporary closeness of body against body. Only the
pain bleeding in the heaviness that grew harder as we climbed. The dark
tatters of the mountains crumbled mutely and re-emerged peak after
peak in the dark gliding upward, jolting us in a kind of deceptive lulling,
as a kind of solace. At the approaches to the mountain, the storm
stopped, and the starry sky was convex as far as the distant peaks gar-
landed with lights on the outskirts of Jerusalem.

We arrived late. By the time we got to the house, the dogs were barking into the night. Isaiah was silent at my side on the road going around
the mountain. At the last bend, where the gate could be seen, he tottered
a moment, his face crushed, and without a word, turned on his heel.
With a silent heart, I watched his taut back before I bent down to the gate.

After that I didn't see Isaiah for months. Not on the night of the fifteenth of Av, when the moon like grief hit between the torn windows all
night long, nor during the days of Elul or on Yom Kippur, not at the
striking of the willows to the dry branch at the end of Sukkoth. And not
afterward either, as autumn went on, and I began to weep at night for the
Shekhina, scooping up dirt on the threshold, sitting there until the East
turned pale, and the weariness collapsed me at sunrise onto the cold bed.
Even then, in the heart of paralysis, when I walked for days petrified with
awe, and only Isaiah's absence, always present, replaced Mala's rustle in
my breathing—not even then did he come. And by the time he came, an
iron wall had descended between me and him, and from the dirt of repair at night, I arose a new person.

He came in the dead of winter. He knocked in panic on the door, and
his beard was thick and strange. He rushed in, pulling me away from
work on the Torah Curtain, rushing me onto the path leading down between the tombstones, to the banned funeral of Rabbi Avuya Aseraf,
who died an unnatural death.

In the cemetery, among the wet slopes, Isaiah didn't enter the area that closed in on me anymore. I stood there in the chill, at the foot of the mountain, under the cypresses black with cold, in the pungent smell of dirt. And even Rabbi Avuya Aseraf's death didn't stir in me anything more than dizziness at the smell of mud that rose from the grave that was finally dug, as a compromise, at the edge of the cemetery. Isaiah stooped in a hasty prayer over the rabbi's shrouded body, and the chirps of the gravediggers' walkie-talkies shattered the cold wind, above their black rubber ponchos bent over the ditch. In the wet crevice two Arab children passed by on a donkey, striking the animal's belly, going with hatred past those who were hastily making a burial.

Forty-seven days of the Omer. Tomorrow evening Stein will come.

And suddenly everything seemed to stop. Maybe because of the Torah Curtain that was cut. The net that closed. And the effort that was burst with it. Like some drunkenness that vanished. Some tangled knot that was finally unraveled.

The Torah Curtain. Who would believe that someday it would reach its end, with the last flight of the shuttle? And then cutting short the cord dropping from the spindle. Who would believe that it would lie down like that, in heavy folds on the floor?

Speech is silenced. Why blaspheme? What difference does it make now if I go out into the night or if I scatter dirt on my hair and kneel alone, in the dark, whispering, *Lord of mercy, God of forgiveness* . . .

Reciting Your Name only out of habit, not out of salvation. Because of the custom of talking addressed so long to Your Name. A kind of partnership of fate because You joined the curves of the road, holding me like the rustle rising from the ridges into the night, like the echo of words opened between the skull and the fountain of dark, *Woe to the children on account of whose sins I destroyed My house and burnt My Temple and exiled them among the nations of the world.* Even the echo of the old words is already far away. Like years afterward. *Woe to the children, on account of whose sins I destroyed.*

———

And suddenly echoing in my head is the verse, *The dead praise not the Lord, neither any that go down into silence, but we will bless the Lord from this time forth and forevermore, halleluia.*

As if we, there, squeezed in the fluorescent-flooded hall of Café Shoshana, *that* is Your glory—the guests at the commemoration, standing in their crushed pride, I, escaping into the dark, grabbing the wet railing, and Isaiah rushing after me with all the tenderness of his limbs . . . As if *that*, after all, is Your glory . . . Only *that* is still living now, at the end of the night, facing the destruction lying here on the slopes in the dark.

It's hard now, beyond the distance, to talk about what was. Now, when the strings are cut off the beams and everything is stopped. And even the wrath that You rejected the sacrifice seemed to go away. Even the rage at the flaw sunk in You, judging us to eternal pain.

And only a kind of forgiveness, for You, for them, and for Father and for Mother and for us there.

And a yearning to stop, and to rest. To rest. Now. Without movement. Without a movement of the hand shifting the pen, the shuttle. Without a click of the tongue in speaking. Without any movement of thought. To end everything.

Suddenly after that long, convoluted night, the tension is relieved. After a night packed with words cut off from the fingers, calm like a soft blanket wraps the neck bent toward the window. The neck crushed with writing all night. From all the nights of writing.

eve of seven weeks

Friday. Eve of seven weeks of the Omer. Eve of Kingdom

of Kingdom. Tomorrow, when the Sabbath is over,

the holiday will begin, on the fiftieth day.

Almost afternoon. Seared light. White. Writing by day, for the first time, not in the circle of lamplight. Sitting now at the table instead of at the weaving stool. A milky luminescence is wiped from the window arch, turning the room dark. The loom is emptied. No longer hiding the bed, the closet, the dark rectangle of the opening to the corridor. The folded Torah Curtain laid at the feet of the loom. In the morning, strips of light lapped its edges.

A deep rustle of afternoon. Scent of fig tree. Hammers striking down the alley, and brief shouts. Apparently they're building there. The sounds that enter ever since the weaving stopped. The walls are also suddenly present. The layers of thick plaster in the arches. And the plaited wrought iron of the window lattice cuts the lighted haze. Traces of movements made here before me. Alien life that will continue to fill the room after I leave.

Last night Stein was here. He took all the material in the big cardboard boxes. They were at the bottom of the closet among the shoes. A smell of dry mud from the soles exploded when I took them out. At first, I didn't remember where I had pushed the boxes when I returned from wandering around the cemetery like a sleepwalker. For some reason, it seemed to me that they were behind the linens, and when I searched without finding them, he shouted from behind me (the only time he shouted), "Give me her photos, Amy!" Standing there with his face undone (and something in his scared look was like Mother when she raised her small hand to her forehead, helpless against a screaming customer).

And then he clasped the boxes, dropping into the wicker armchair, and his broad back trembled. And from the window came a dry night breeze, sounds of conversation from the alley. Clutching them on his lap and stroking them—the cardboard boxes with the photos from Hubert's darkroom . . . He also happened into our story—leaning his head on them, and his mouth speaks as if he weren't here: "I'm just for memory of her . . . for memory of Mala . . ."

"Yes." I nodded, my hands heavy on my kneecaps, as at moments when I rested from the effort of weaving. And from the windows the sound of chirping, and rock beats, and echoes of dogs barking far away.

"Yes . . ." I nodded at him and I seemed not to be here either. As back then, in his home, in Queens, the night before the trip, plodding along red brick buildings with the shadow of winter trees printed on them in the low sun, knowing that everything was simply an alien stage set that had to be crossed on the way to the encounter that would bind our lives together, inexorably. Just to ring the sharp bell, and his appearing, short, excited, at the door, and following him to the living room through the gloom smelling of liqueur and tobacco. Sitting across from him on the blue sofa in the cheap Indian skirt, as if I weren't there. And the words flowing from the globe of his head, on some vague winter morning. The whole plan, all the stops. And tea with sugar cubes in a silver bowl, as in my parents' house. And on the cabinet, the photos. Also the enlarged photo of her with the oval face from the heart-shaped locket. And other, white, faces from there. And in the corner, a small colored photo of the vegetable store, and in front of it, close together, Mother, Father, and me, four or five years old. Afterward, on the subway platform, not even thinking they could mug me, standing there with maybe three thousand dollars in cash, "for the trip," planted in the heavy coat, gazing at mice running on the gravel between the tracks, scampering almost mischievously, running around in the brief moment of silence until the train exploded into the station. Like Father and like Stein, like me, running for another moment past countries, cities, continents. Like the light of the low sun, flooding for a moment the old people pushing supermarket carts on the sidewalk on a winter morning in Queens.

Suddenly he sat up straight and shouted, "But how can I take boxes? How can I take them with me?"

"I'll bring you something," I said to give him heart, returning from the kitchen with a string bag. And for a moment we bent over, the two of us, Stein and I, stuffing the boxes into the woven sack together, until the corners of the boxes emerged from the loops of the net stretched to hold all that was stuffed into it.

Afterward we went out into the night. Waiting for the taxi that was supposed to return. Stein with the boxes of photos holding the handles of the bursting bag, and I next to him, taller, and the fabric of the skirt swelling on my legs. Standing and waiting, ostensibly for a taxi, on the side of the road suspended in the dark. Two nights before the holiday.

From the corner came the sound of a diesel engine. Stein pushed in, slammed the door of the taxi, which sped off, another short flicker of the yellow light of the distant traffic signal, and it disappeared, taking with it Stein and the boxes and the photos from Hubert's darkroom. A dull drumming of music was blown. And then my head bent as usual at the door, and the three steps of the entrance, in silence.

Whiteness of afternoon. In a few more hours the holiday will begin. Downtown, a few cars will resound among the bright dusty facades at sunset, and on the mountain, near the house of Rabbi Israel, knots of men and youths will make their way to the synagogues, their angular movements cutting the silence still illuminated on the slopes falling to the west. And tomorrow evening, when Rabbi Israel Gothelf returns from the Shavuoth Evening Prayer, he'll nod to the guest, the contributor Mr. Ludwig Stein, and on the cabinet, the candle flames will tremble. No, I have no complaint against Rabbi Israel, everything is dismissed, everything is dropped and expiated. And in the abandoned house of Rabbi Avuya Aseraf of blessed memory, on Shavuoth eve, the mist of excited bodies will not rise from the windows, and the rabbi wrapped in his long prayer shawl will not move shrouded in cigarette smoke. Only the dark of treetops will walk in the yard covered with wild bushes. And at the top of the hill, here, Fayge and Rabbi Levav will cross the yard, among the fruit trees flooded with light from their balcony. Two lovers in the waning of their days. And how should I have told them, what words should I have used to say good-bye, to say thanks?

As if something stopped. The space of Shavuoth, in another twenty-four hours, seems so far away. Only the approaching Sabbath is present now, with a new, penetrating clarity.

The ridge opposite is printed. Groups of black goats are stuck on the slope, under piles of junk. The slope there is so close to where I sit languidly, almost letting one hear the rolling steps of someone walking on the mountain path across the valley. As when I would bend over on my finger tips from the window of the living room, between the green curtains, to grab the branch of the tree that grew in the yard, not believing that the leaves of a real tree could exist there, at the edge of my bending. What right did I have to this grace? This closeness?

And on Mother's last Yom Kippur, when she sat all day in a corner of the women's section of the synagogue, with the stale odor of books and matrons, with an unfamiliar kerchief on her head, in the evening, after the fast, she prepared slices of honey cake on the pretty china with the amber glasses, and Father came back from the synagogue, and said in a soft voice, "A good year, a good year." And Mother's little hands tightly clasped each other next to the glass. And Father went on quietly, without raising his eyes, "It's hard. Very hard, Ruzia," and then he looked slowly with such warm eyes, and suddenly all the honey was poured out gold and soft, and my head grew warm from the pungency that I drank drop by drop. And I laughed so much at them, without fear, laughed and laughed. And Mother moved her head too with all the sparkling blue that was poured out, and scattering blue and light, poured in the room and sparkling. For in the end, when you go to the end of the street, at the end there's the sea, the sea's there, the sea . . .

And suddenly the words of the Talmud I learned from Rabbi Israel return, and now their meaning is so close . . .

Rab Judah said in the name of Rab, When Moses ascended on high he found the Holy One, blessed be He, engaged in affixing coronets to the letters. Said Moses: Lord of the Universe, who stays Thy hand?

He answered: There will arise a man, at the end of many generations, Akiba ben Joseph by name, who will expound upon each tittle heaps and heaps of laws.

Lord of the Universe, said Moses, permit me to see him.

He replied, Turn thee around.

Moses went and sat down behind eight rows. Not being able to follow their arguments he was ill at ease, but when they came to a certain subject and the disciples said to the master: Whence do you know it? and the latter replied: It is a law given unto Moses at Sinai, he was comforted.

Thereupon he returned to the Holy One, blessed be He, and said: Lord of the Universe, Thou hast such a man and Thou givest the Torah by me!

He replied, Silence, for such is My decree.

Then said Moses: Lord of the Universe, Thou hast shown me his Torah, show me his reward.

Turn thee around, said He; and Moses turned around and saw them weighing out his flesh at the market stalls. Lord of the Universe, cried Moses, such Torah, and such a reward!

He replied, Silence, for such is My decree.

When Rabbi Akiba was taken out for execution, it was the hour for the recital of the Sh'ma, and while they flayed his flesh with iron combs, he was accepting upon himself the kingship of heaven. His disciples said to him, Our teacher, even to this point? He said to them, All my days I have been troubled by this verse, with all my soul—*even if He takes my soul. I said, When shall I have the opportunity of fulfilling*

this? Now that I have the opportunity shall I not fulfill it? He pro-
longed the word Ehad—One—until he expired while saying it.

As if everything has a different meaning now. Completely different.

Afternoon. The light withdraws from the windowsills. Something rises
in the glow. Is opened. The valley is illuminated in the high sun. On the
slopes, the dirt blazes on the paths, on the village houses stuck to the rock.
Far away, the strip of road climbing up to the mountain covered with
tombstones. The bottom of the abyss is also illuminated, the black stain
of the orchards around the spring. And at the foot of the Old City walls
the ruins of the Temple sparkle in the sun standing in the height of the sky.

I stopped awhile. Now my eye falls on my hands covered with dust. The
traces stamped in them.

Another six hours until the Sabbath. To go out now? Immediately? Like
last year, at the dawn of Shavuoth, when I got up from the rim of the
wall, burning with a longing to go down, just go down, my body smit-
ten with walking. Running on the paths turning pale among the cliffs, the
warm wind rising toward me from the valley. Tramping on the trodden
path as I plunged, my steps beating on the rock, hairy hooves covered
with foam galloping . . .
　　And then, at the edge of the cliffs, revealed below, stuck on a terrace
in the rock wall, the little village with its five houses. The sun didn't
rise, and the gray sheaves of wheat piled in the yards in pale masses
stood out. On the flat roofs the couches were outlined and on them,
curled up with one another, like grapes in a bunch, were the sleeping families. Even now I don't know if I really saw that, or if in the sharpening
dawn a bend of a flickering gutter seemed like the folded leg of a young
woman, and the shoulder of a man soft with sleep, bound together under
one sheet. And maybe a bird that awoke in a bush made a rustling noise
and for a moment I imagined it was footsteps. Something dissolved then,
my breath seemed to be raw without my knowing exactly why; something stopped there, in the smell of donkey dung and the warmth of the
bodies of chickens wafting from the small village. And I didn't continue

on my way to the edge of the cliffs. I started back, and at my heels the piercing cackle of roosters, and the shrieks of dogs crazy with the dawn who scratched the gray space stretched in the East. I went through hedges, olive groves, climbing the terraces of the fields. Trying to take a shortcut. The sun struck with a hot surge as I went up toward the platform of the mountain, and the shadow of my walking tottered in front of me on the shining asphalt river. On the peak, the whole city was spread out before my eyes in one view, the domes, the turrets, the density of flickering stone buildings, spread out to the edges of the ridges.

Fatigue blended with dusty sweat. I went down the slope next to ruined concrete bunkers, going among tombstones, openings of caves in the rock. Going up from the valley on Shavuoth morning. And I reached the house, wearily moving aside the sign above the handle, the branch that Isaiah had left—as if I knew he'd come. And when I went inside, the light from the East still printed the shadow of the lattice flowers on the arms of the loom, on the bed.

Sometimes it seems as if nothing had ever happened, as if everything were only a vision going off, evaporating, in silence, swept away beyond the border of the end of the Counting, mixing us up together in a wind bellowing from the jaw of the shofar, confusing us in an impeccable unity. As if everything is already so far away from what will be done perhaps at the dawn of Shavuoth, movements of leaving that will suddenly hasten, binding the pages, lifting the Torah Curtain. Going . . .

(But now I can kneel and open the Torah Curtain once again, spread out the solid folds between my arms—three kinds of colors, white, red, and green, in the blue spread of the silk of the firmament, and the four forms, lion, bull, eagle, and man. And letters, and birds. Once again I can bury my face in the sweet smell of the threads, in the gold of the embroidered names, in everything buried there with all the humiliation, the acceptance of judgment.)

A cool cleanness wafts from the floor tiles. The whole house is purified. In the kitchen, a few simple dairy products for the last meal at the end of the Counting.

And maybe Isaiah will come at dawn, as last year. Will come so we can repent. *For example, a person engaged in illicit sexual relations with a woman. Afterward they meet in privacy, in the same country, while his love for her and his physical power still persist.* And maybe the whole thing was just to give us time, to give us more time, until the end of the Counting. (Dry is the sweat on his warm back, the tremor that will plow his curls with excitement. He'll bend over in the doorway, apologizing, the mountain turning pale behind him. "I came to see how you are . . ." His neck will tremble.

"Fine, well, happy holiday, Amalia . . ." He'll sway in the doorway, scared. "Well, I'll be going now . . ."

And something will stop him. Maybe my standing opposite him in the corridor now filling with light from the East, bursting from the flushed arches of the room, holding his head, surrounding us as he comes into the room behind me.)

Everything's spinning. The whole recounting, the whole Counting. And some forgotten joy shaking the spilling of the little bit of time that's left.

The glow through the lattice of the window on the pages, hovering on the paper. I rested my head on my hand. To stop a moment. It's hard now, after a calm, to imagine the waves of emotion that held me here. And far away, out of the fullness, the gurgle of words continues, *The whole world was created only for me, only for me.*

Have to stop. To complete the preparations. Preparation of the body and the washing. In a few more hours the expectation will stop. And finally perhaps I will find rest.

To finish, to put down the pen.

And still it seems as if time won't move anymore beyond the gliding of the slow day into the start of the Sabbath, to the Kingdom of Kingdom. As if everything is standing still at the meridian, in the last watch before the day declines. And there won't be any need to do anything anymore except to go on sitting like this with solid limbs, in the room that is emptied, at the table with a pile of bound sheets. A heavy mass, without movement, immersed in rest.

As I stood here night after night to say wholeheartedly, *For the sake of the sanctification of the Holy One, Blessed is He, and His Presence, in fear and love to unify the Name, yod-heh with vav-heh in perfect unity, in the name of all Israel. Behold I am prepared and ready to perform the commandment of counting the Omer, as is written in the Torah: And ye shall count unto you from the morrow after the Sabbath, from the day that ye brought the sheath of the wave offering; seven Sabbaths shall be complete: Even unto the morrow after the seventh Sabbath shall ye number fifty days; and ye shall offer a new meat offering unto the Lord. May the pleasantness of my Lord, our God, be upon us—may He establish our handiwork for us; our handiwork, may He establish.* Amen selah.

Just to go on sitting here, calmly, in the room filling with the Sabbath. As if the Counting were completed, as if the end of my work in the world had come.

I'll stop now. I'll put down the pen, so as not to disturb the pouring of the calm. And in that silence, I shall go wash. To be ready.

Last moments before the start of the Sabbath. The siren has

already sounded. Fast. A few more words before the sun

touches the West. Afterward, I'll bind the pages again.

White. Everything is white. A thread of blood drips from the navel of the city to the desert. On the mountain little white flowers have suddenly bloomed. I saw them as I sat outside on the slope waiting for the start of the Sabbath. And then I ran inside, to write something more before the end. Excitement unravels the breathing.

I didn't imagine I would open the bound pages again. I closed everything silently before I went into the shower, then went outside with wet hair to walk around the house one last time. At the top of the hill, I saw that they had cut down the ancient pine trees and fenced in a construction site. A bare light now floods the path where we walked. The folds of dying desire. And the pain, suddenly, like an empty path falling on the slope, and then immediately, death. From everything that happened, irrevocably . . . Men began gathering for afternoon prayer. I clung to the wall, hiding from them, and my heart was pounding.

The city drops out of the hold, changes. Everything that seemed close as breath has become foreign. And maybe never was really blended in my life. And how much I longed to be in You, and the taste of dirt fills my mouth with the flavor of Your kiss. And how I was to raise the weight of the Torah Curtain on my shoulders, to wrap myself in it with all my soul.

The candles are extinguished in the holders. Can't get up and recite the blessing. The light is coming to an end, and my hand is still reaching to write. And the storm has not yet vanished. As if something is still revealed, clarified for the first time.

As if a barrier was removed from the eye. The destruction exposed on the slopes, caustic, uncovered, as if this is the Covenant, and also the consolation. For there is no repair for the break. And there is no instant repentance. Only acceptance. What will be and what is and what was. Death here is consolation. The break hidden between us, King Who causes death and restores life.

As if everything that was was only to reveal to me, on the verge of the end of the Counting, the great tenderness hidden here between us in the destruction.

Everything is ready, I am purified, and I have laundered my dresses, and I have put on white. And yet, an abyss still seems to separate me from Shavuoth. Impossible to sink my fingers. And the more I advance, the more the appointed time only slips away from me.

Everything has stopped. In the pale light. Very silent and present. Poured with another peace in the breathing.

The photos will be printed in Stein's album. Will be placed among bound pages. Holding what remains of Mala Auerbach, Mala, Malinka. "The whole story." Blurry gray spots on the chrome flash, joining together into a hand held out to a keyboard, black hair pushed back while playing, a few figures at the streetcorner wrapped up in winter coats, her firm gait with the note case on the boulevard, and the milky, enlarged smile from the locket. Stein will gather the congregation for the publication of the album. In Café Shoshana or some other hall on the boardwalk, and all its windows will be kindled in the burning sunset. They'll mention me, maybe. They'll say I became more and more like her. Something in the movements of the head, the bend of the neck. They'll talk about the tall boy who came, an American, also a penitent. *Nice. They were supposed to get married right afterward.* They'll whisper across from the burnished copper face of the sea. They'll whisper there with their warm buzz, crowded in front of You, all flesh.

It's almost the Sabbath. And I'm still bent over here at the open window, savoring the new taste of calm. Putting the pen to the sheet of paper with a new ease. The gray pages, the whole pile. I'll open them in years to come, after everything. With wary fingers, I'll slowly open the binding of the sheets that were silent all those years. I'll lean on my thin arm and I'll read, slowly turning the pages, leaning over the writing with dull eyes. Then, at the end of a life of withdrawal, making my living by weaving holiness. Maybe still living here, between the same walls, which in time will become one piece with my limbs. Strict about prayer, out of piety, and at night still going out to the slope, for the Midnight Prayer, pouring dirt on my hair that has turned silver. I will slowly go through the pages, reading what is written with the transparent breathing of someone who has accepted and blessed everything. As it is said, *While the sun, or the light, or the moon, or the stars, be not darkened, nor the clouds return after the rain . . .*

The heart wants, but the legs are unwilling. Unmoving. *Do not throw me out in old age. Do not see that I am flesh, black.* Your Holy Spirit take from me, take me now. Take me. Peace is unraveled, inundating me.

On the verge of the Sabbath. The light grows deeper. Soon the red will turn pale, and still I am unable to move. Still writing. The pen doesn't leave the hand. And who are the Tablets and what is the writing? And what is the profanity? Only the body breathing in an expanding calm. And the dust of the broken Tablets blends with the breathing.

Suddenly the heart melts. What if all the preparations, the sanctifications, and the purification of the body were only so that Isaiah would come at the dawn of Shavuoth, would slip away on the path turning gray in the chill of the morning star? Is that why I came out of the house, to wait until the lighting of the candles on the sill, so that he would come early? Is that what is revealed now, melting my breathing?

Without a word, we'll sit down, like travelers resting from a long trip. Not having to say, to do anything. And only the time that is opened, opened, will echo from our heavy hands. All the warmth that will still flow into our room. And when Shavuoth morning rises, nothing will be as it was at first. And opposite, from the slopes molten in the sunrise, the call of the people will rise to us, done and heard.

The heart strikes. As if everything were once again speeded up. And the joy pours out uncontrollably.

I washed my clothes and placed the Torah Curtain next to the door. Along with the case for the pile of pages. To be ready. Even now I can hardly restrain myself until the night grows deep, and the dawn breaks out of the wind that will rise from the East when I leave here.

My life is still suspended, ahead. And the way back still seems to be opened, and the guards offer me food and drink in their huts going down to the desert. And here too, on the cliff, the gloom of the tempest is already awake, the resurrecting force that rises from the border of the Sabbath.

A short time. Last moments of twilight. On the blue ridge the light is held by the tops of the turrets, the treetops. Soon the mouth of the well will be closed. So, quickly, in the already flooding slowness of the Sabbath. To strum some more the chords of the story that is coming to an end, coming to a close.

The body is silent, wrapped in a distant dizziness. Like standing on the edge of a cliff. The paper and the fingers guiding the pen are slipping away. And now I don't know anymore if the Sabbath has started. The border is blurred. A whiteness is spreading now like a deep sleep behind the eyes. What a great blessing.

The time has come. Just to go on turning now, with no expectations anymore, for an answer . . . Just to go on turning to what is gaping there in the calm. Everything I shall give You. Everything. *Enter, O Bride.*

Just to go on turning, that's the prayer. Just to go on turning in the expanding space.

And the voice speaking between us is enough. Enough the words of the prayer muttered from my lips.

For that the blessing, *My Lord, open my lips.* For that. Just open more. You'll just go on muttering the voice from my throat, my tongue, my lips. Without any expectation anymore that You will accept, that You will hear.

And maybe that is the answer. Finally. That is the answer.

A calm. Suspended meanwhile, in the realm that is opening, with the exhalation of the breath in the turning.

Some calm in giving myself to what is opened, comes, to what is standing there. Even though I will never know if its appeal will be granted.

And past and present and future are mixed up. Without giving, without taking. For all is one.

Forever do I return to Your embrace. To the rising dryness of Your kiss. Nothing has changed. And Your taste now is like then, the first time, like the bitter rubber crumbs of the old ball under the big bed. Hiding fast when Father suddenly returned, as I was searching for the locket among the linens in the closet, blocking the shout with the filthy bitter rubber between my teeth so Father's playing won't stop, the black warmth of the violin pouring out, and the heart beating because the locket wasn't there,

I didn't find it! I searched and searched and it wasn't there! And the weeping cuts the throat choked with the sweetness of the playing, cuts it with a filthy dust of the old ball, shouting without a sound in the bitter crumbs, with the great offense that he had removed the locket, because nothing is left, little girl. And soon he'll leave too, along with the black warmth that was poured out, still poured out, soft. Already then, You were revealed to me in the rubber bitterness of the old ball melded with the softness pouring out.

And another long moment of silence. Even though the time has ended. Only deep waves mutely washing my body. Before the pen falls from my hand. Evening chill. Sonorous breathing.

This is my atonement to You in the world. With no more expectation, no supplication.

The light is fading. I took a long time to light the candles. I nearly crossed, Holy, Awesome, the border of the hour.

Only the relaxation. The rest from all work, without completion, without finishing. That's what the blessing is for. A relaxation of effort. Like lying on the ground, clinging to the warm dirt. In eternal rest. Open. The relaxation of holding. The calm that breaks out of the silent maw of the Sabbath.

To open the relaxation. To open. More. To let go. To forget. To open to the Sabbath flooding now. A taste of the World to Come. The submission to what is rising there, cloaked in darkness like an animal. Everything, everything I shall give to You. In one. *Ehad.*

My God and God of my fathers, *may You be pleased with my rest, may You be pleased with my rest.*

And the voice of the trumpet sounded long and waxed louder and louder. And the evening is quiet, so sweet in the dryness that is opened.

And in the morning, Shavuoth, the fiftieth day, at dawn, when I shall wear white, ready, the swallows will be shaken out of the Wailing Wall.

Slicing with their nimble bodies. Plunging. Casting shadows running over the heads of the packed audience, on the seared dust in the first light of sunrise. They will pass dizzily, inscribing quick lines in the stone.

The remnant of the light on the peak opposite is wiped out. Put down the pen.

The Lord gives and the Lord takes away; blessed be the Name of the Lord.

Sabbath.

1980–1992

Glossary

Amalia—(Heb., *Amal*) 1. work, labor; 2. trouble, evil. *Ia*—one of the names of God

Amidah—(lit., "standing") the silent prayer recited three times a day, also called The Eighteen Blessings

Counting of the Omer—(Heb., *Sefirat haOmer*) the injunction to count the forty-nine days from the second night of Passover until Shavuoth. The Kabbalists use the forty-nine days (seven times seven) to mark the ascent through the Sefirot from the impurity of the Egyptian bondage to the purity of the revelation at Sinai.

Ehad—(lit., "The One") the state of unification between the female and male attributes of God, a unity described as coupling (*Zivug*)

Elul—the last month of the Jewish calendar, during which time one prepares for the High Holy Days, which follow in the month of Tishrei

Fast of Monday and Thursday—the days traditionally ascribed for voluntary fasting and atonement after long festivals

HaShem—(lit., The Name) a euphemism for the name of God, so as not to take His Holy Name in vain

Havdalah—(lit., "differentiating") the ritual by which the Sabbath is ended and differentiated from the commencement of the week, involving the use of candle flame, spices, and wine

Idra—a section of the Zohar describing the death of Rabbi Simeon bar Yochai and his parting words.

kiddush—(lit., "sanctifying") a ritual held on the eve and on the day of the Sabbath, in which one says a blessing over a glass of wine, testifying to the completion of the creation of the world

Lag b' Omer—(lit., the thirty-third day of the Counting of the Omer)—the day the plague among Rabbi Akiva's students ceased, hence a day of festivities and bonfires. The bonfires are also held in celebration of the ascent to heaven of Rabbi Simeon Bar Yochai.

Melaveh Malkah—(lit., "escorting the Queen") the meal and festivities at the end of the Sabbath

Midnight Repair—(Heb., *Tikkun Khazot*) prayers recited at midnight in memory of the destruction of the Temple and for the restoration of the Land of Israel. Midnight was chosen because David arose at this hour to study and pray. In the Kabbalist tradition, two separate forms of service developed, Tikkun Rachel, at the first and darkest part of the night, and Tikkun Leah, toward dawn.

mikveh—(lit., "a collection [of water]") a pool or bath of clear water, immersion in which renders clean a person who has become ritually unclean. Immersion is also practiced as an aid to spirituality.

mitzvah—(lit., "a commandment") a religious good deed

muezzin—the one who calls Moslems to prayer

Passover—(Heb., *Pesach*) the spring holiday celebrating the Exodus from Egypt

Rashi—Rabbi Solomon Isaac (1041–1105 C.E.), leading commentator on the Bible and Talmud

Rosh Hashanah—(lit., "head of the year") the High Holy Day which occurs on the first day of the month of Tishrei and which celebrates the New Year

Rosh Hodesh—(lit., "head of the month") the first day of the beginning of the Jewish lunar month, when the moon is invisible

Sanctification of the Moon—(Heb., *Kiddush Levanah*)—prayer of thanksgiving recited outside at the monthly reappearance of the moon's crescent, which voices Israel's continuous hope for redemption

Scapegoat—(Heb., *Sa'ir l'Azazel*) part of the ancient ritual of Yom Kippur: a goat would be led from the Temple in Jerusalem to a cliff in the Judean Desert, from which it was thrown as an atonement for the sins of Israel

Sefirot—(Kabb. pl. literally, "spheres," "countings." Sin., Sefirah) the ten attributes of God: Supreme Crown (*Keter Elion*); Wisdom (*Hokhmah*); Intelligence (*Binah*); Love (*Hesed*); Power (*Gevurah*); Beauty (*Tiferet*); Eternity (*Nezah*); Majesty (*Hod*); Foundation (*Yesod*); Kingdom (*Malkhut*)

Seventeenth of Tammuz—a day of mourning and fasting to mark the beginning of the siege on Jerusalem that eventually led to the destruction of the Temple

Sh'ma—(lit., "hear") the essential expression of Jewish faith. "Hear O Israel, the Lord is God, the Lord is One"

Shavuoth—(lit., "weeks") the holiday celebrating the giving of the Torah and the covenant between God and the children of Israel. It marks the end of the forty-nine days of the Counting of the Omer. The Book of Ruth is read on Shavuoth.

Shekhina—the female Divine Presence.

Shells—(Heb., *kelipot*, Kabb.) shards of the Broken Vessels, in which sparks of the divine light still remain captured. Also referred to as the forces of evil or as sheer physical matter

Simeon bar Yochai (130–160 C.E.)—Tradition attributes to him the authorship of the Zohar and the role of leader of its mystical group of sages.

Sukkoth—(lit., "huts") the autumn Festival of the Tabernacles

Tanna—(from Aramaic, *teni* "study," "teach") a sage mentioned in the Mishnah or of Mishnaic times (first and second centuries C.E.)

Tikkun—(lit., "repair," "restoration," Kabb.) the slow repair of the cosmic catastrophe of The Breaking of the Vessels, by the restoration of the divine light captured by the *kelipot* (The Shells). Human activity can prepare the way for the Tikkun of the lower worlds, back to a state of *Ehad*.

Tish'a b'Av—the ninth day of the month of Av, a day of fasting and lamentation in memory of several significant events: the erection of the Golden Calf by the Children of Israel, who thus broke the Covenant with God; the shattering of the first tablets on which the Ten Commandments were inscribed by God; the destruction of the First and Second Temples

Tzitzit—(lit., fringe) fringed four-cornered garment worn by men throughout the day, as per Numbers (15:37) and Deuteronomy (22:12)

Vessels—(Heb., *kelim*, Kabb.) created in the process of the creation of the world, to contain the emanation of divine essence. The light being too strong, the Vessels and, among them, the seven lower Sefirot, broke. A cosmic catastrophe known as "The Breaking of the Vessels"

Yeshiva—school of traditional Jewish learning

Y-H-V-H—*Yod-Heh-Vav-Heh,* the Hebrew letters of the name of God, whose numerical value is 10,5,6,5

Yom Kippur—(lit., "The Day of Atonement") a day of fasting and atonement, one of the High Holy Days

Ze'ir Anpin—(lit., Aram., "miniature aspect" Kabb.) an anthropomorphic symbol of the lower divine configuration according to the Zohar, consisting of male and female aspects

Zohar—The Book of Splendor, the central work of the literature of the Kabbalah. Biblical commentary written as the story of a group of sages who engaged in mystical practice

About the Author

Michal Govrin is a writer, poet, and award-winning director of experimental Jewish theater. She received her Ph.D. from the University of Paris and currently teaches at the School of Visual Theater in Jerusalem. *The Name*, her first novel to be translated into English, won the 1997 Kugel Literary Prize. She was recently awarded the 1998 Israeli Prime Minister's Prize for Writers. Born in Tel Aviv, Govrin currently lives in Jerusalem.

About the Translator

Barbara Harshav translates fiction, poetry, and drama from Hebrew, French, German, and Yiddish. Her previous translations of Israeli literature include works by Yehudah Amichai, Yehudit Katzir, and Meir Shalev. She divides her time between Connecticut and Tel Aviv.